FILTHY GODS

FLIRTING
WITH
DISASTER

USA TODAY BESTSELLING AUTHOR
MICHELLE HERCULES

FLIRTING WITH DISASTER

FILTHY GODS BOOK ONE

MICHELLE HERCULES

INFINITE SKY PUBLISHING

Paperback ISBN: 978-1-950991-94-5

PLAYLIST

YOUNG GODS - Halsey
MAKE ME A MONSTER - World's First Cinema
BORN AGAIN - Black Veil Brides
THIS FEELING - The Chainsmokers & Kelsea Ballerina
I FEEL LIKE I'M DROWNING - Two Feet
LOVE IT WHEN YOU HATE ME - Avril Lavigne & blackbear
I DID SOMETHING BAD - Taylor Swift
I'M GONNA SHOW YOU CRAZY - Bebe Rexha
PRISONER - Miley Cyrus & Dua Lipa
KILLER INSIDE OF ME - Willyecho
GODZILLA - Eminem & Juice WRLD
DANCE, DANCE - Fall Out Boy
UNDISCLOSED DESIRES - Muse
NEW GRAVITY - MIYAVI
INSTEAD - Boxelder

ALEXIS

A YEAR AGO

I shove Carmen away from me, but all she does is laugh harder.

"Shut up. I do *not* have a thing for Tobey's Spider-Man. I'm a Tom Holland girl all the way."

She steps closer to me again, and throws her arm over my shoulder. "Liar. I saw your doodles. That Spidey looked exactly like Tobey Maguire."

"It did not!" I reply, shoving her to the side playfully.

"Fine. You're a bad artist, then."

"That was a caricature. Besides, I don't know how you could say it looked like Tobey Maguire. My drawing was cute as hell, something Tobey Maguire definitely wasn't, even at the peak of his career."

"Obviously not. But if I could pick a hottie from the early

2000s, I'd choose Jake Gyllenhaal. He was so dreamy in *Prince of Persia*."

"No way, Jose. I pick Heath Ledger."

Carmen sighs. "Ah, Heath. He was gorgeous too. What's his best version though? Heath in *10 Things I Hate About You* or *A Knight's Tale*?"

"Hmm, that's a tough one."

Carmen gets a dreamy look on her face. "Oh, I got it. Heath in *Brokeback Mountain*."

"Oh my God. Not *that* version. He cheats on his wife!"

"Yeah, but with Jake Gyllenhaal!" Carmen throws her hands up in the air in an overdramatic fashion, earning curious glances from the other pedestrians sharing the sidewalk with us.

"Is it weird that we have crushes on guys who are either dead or are old enough now to be our dads?" I ask.

She snorts. "Bitch, please. Of course not. Young women all around the world will still have crushes on Brad Pitt in *Legends of the Fall* even when the dude is a hundred years old."

"And let's not forget him in *Troy*," I add enthusiastically.

"Oh, Brad Pitt in *Troy* still gives me wet dreams." A lady in her fifties chuckles next to us.

"Magda!" The man with her pretends to be offended.

Carmen and I burst out laughing and hurry away from the tourists. That's what we get for loudly talking about hot celebrities in public.

Since neither of us has a car and we didn't feel like taking the bus, we decided to walk from her house to the diner. I owed Carmen a free meal after she rescued me from a bad date with Buck Thomas last semester, but we both forgot about it until this morning when there was nothing to eat at her place. It figures her stomach would do her brain's job.

Triton Cove is still as busy as ever with tourists, and Dad

won't like that Carmen is tagging along right now since the diner will be busy as hell. But a promise is a promise.

The sound of a fast-approaching vehicle draws our attention to the street. A shiny silver Porsche is racing down the road, coming in fast, way above the speed limit.

"Ah hell. Summer is definitely over when those rich assholes return to town," Carmen says in disgust.

Our coastal town is divided into two distinct sections. The golden side where the wealthiest families have their sprawling mansions facing the ocean, and the rusty side where the rest of us live. Triton Cove relies heavily on tourism, so most of the businesses are restaurants, hotels, and little shops. There isn't much in terms of white-collar jobs that pay well. Not that there aren't accountants, lawyers, or doctors, but the majority of the working class is blue-collar.

The sports car barely slows down as it turns right at the next intersection. The maniac behind the wheel is driving like he has a death wish. A few seconds later, there's the sound of car tires screeching and then a loud crash.

"What the hell!" I blurt out.

Carmen and I take off at a run to see what happened. It's obvious that the motherfucker driving the Porsche crashed into something. My heart is racing when we round the corner and I see the sports car half buried in Mr. Dane's convenience store.

"Oh no," Carmen mutters next to me.

A small crowd has already formed around the accident's perimeter. We keep going, but now I fear what I'm going to see as we get near the crash site. What if he hit someone and there's a mangled body there? What if he killed a person I know?

The car door opens and out comes the driver, staggering. He seems out of it, probably in shock. From where we stand, we have a clear view of his face. He's young, probably sixteen or seventeen like us. There's a gash on his forehead that's bleeding profusely, but he doesn't seem to notice. He's staring into the partially destroyed store. A woman's cry comes from inside. She's asking for help. Some folks attempt to enter the store through the gaping hole while another man approaches the young driver and asks if he's okay. He doesn't react, just keeps staring into the store with his ghostlike complexion. He must have hit someone and is now staring at what he's done.

Does he now regret driving his stupid car as if he were on a racetrack?

The ambulance and the police arrive, and soon we're asked to leave the area. Most of the people do, but Carmen and I remain close. I want to see who that rich boy hurt. When a paramedic tries to help him, he shrugs him off.

Some time passes before the other paramedics manage to exit the store with the guy's victim. It's Peter Danes, Mr. Danes's grandson. He's only ten.

"Oh no," Carmen gasps next to me.

Seeing the kid on that gurney, passed out and with a brace around his tiny neck, seems to snap the jackass out of his stupor.

"How is he? Is he going to be okay?" he asks the paramedic closest to him.

"We don't know yet. You need to get that gash taken care of," the man replies, his tone harsh.

I don't blame him one bit.

Peter's mother, who was following the paramedics closely, throws a hateful glance at the douche. "Look at him. Look at what you've done, you little piece of shit!"

"I'm so sorry. I didn't mean for this to happen," he replies feebly.

The cops pull him aside and begin to ask him questions. Had he been drinking? Was he high? He denies it all, and when he's asked to breathe into a breathalyzer, he doesn't refuse.

So, he's not drunk, but even if he were, it wouldn't matter. He's the son of someone important, and we all know nothing ever happens to the young gods who rule this town.

2

ALEXIS

PRESENT DAY

*I*t's the last week of summer break, and Triton Cove is bursting at the seams with tourists not yet ready to leave our idyllic coastal town and the wealthy locals who have returned from their extravagant trips abroad. That means my father's diner is as busy as ever, and I haven't had a moment to catch my breath.

Speed walking to the back of the counter, I almost collide with Tina, who's holding a tray of milkshakes and sodas.

"Slow down, Lexi. We can't afford accidents," she tells me.

"Sorry. It's crazy today."

I slide my orders over the kitchen counter. "Three house-special burgers, Kevin."

Our short-order cook—and Dad's second-in-command—wipes the sweat from his forehead with the back of his arm. "Will you please slow down, kid?"

"Can't. People are hungry."

I turn around too fast, and this time, I do collide with someone. My father.

"Lexi, take it easy. People can wait an extra two minutes for their orders. What I can't have is you breaking a limb."

"There's a line, Dad." I point outside the diner, where I can see a long line of customers waiting for their turn.

"Yeah, yeah. If they don't want to wait for the best burgers in town, they can head to the golden arches."

"Trust me, a lot of them are," I reply.

Dad twists his face into a grimace while he clutches his left arm. He seems to be in pain.

"What's wrong?"

"It's nothing, honey. Just a muscle spasm." He looks over my shoulder. "A booth just vacated. Let's clean that up so we can stop losing customers to the enemy."

He returns to his spot behind the cash register and rings up a customer waiting to pay for his pickup order. I stare at Dad for a while longer, worried he downplayed his discomfort for my benefit. He's been working harder in the past month, and even when the diner is closed, he burns the midnight oil in his office at home. Something is stressing him out, but he won't share it with me.

"Hey, waitress. We'd like a booth, please." An annoyed male voice draws my attention away from Dad.

A tall and muscular guy wearing a baseball cap, a distressed T-shirt, and jeans that probably cost more than I make in a month working at the diner is staring at me with his jaw clenched tight. He has sunglasses on, but I'm sure he's glowering.

Oh goody. One of the rich assholes from the golden side of town is my next customer, and he brought friends. Another guy and two girls.

"It will be ready in a minute."

9

I grab an empty tray to clear off the vacant table and walk slowly toward it. I could move faster, but the guy's tone annoyed me. I don't recognize him, so that means he's either a vacationer or he goes to Maverick Prep, a private school that caters to the wealthy population of Triton Cove.

Tina joins me at the booth and then takes the tray from my hand. "Let me help you before Richie Rich over there has an aneurysm."

"He can wait another minute like everyone else," I reply under my breath.

"He might be a good tipper, Lexi."

I glance over my shoulder and find the guy still has his sourpuss expression on. "Yeah, I doubt that."

Tina takes the tray away, which leaves me free to wipe the table clean. From the corner of my eye, I spot a customer's raised hand two booths down the row.

"I'll be with you in a second."

I turn around, and for the second time today, I bump into someone. This time, it's the annoying dude who apparently couldn't wait for me to finish setting up the table for him.

I jump back. "Sorry, I didn't see you there."

"Clearly," he retorts before sliding into the booth seat.

One of the girls in the group follows him, giving me the stink eye. When she's snuggled against him, she says loud enough for me to hear, "I don't know why you wanted to come here, Finn. The service is appalling."

I bite my tongue to keep from telling her to go somewhere else if she's not happy.

The guy glances at me briefly, still wearing his shades. He must think he's someone famous to wear sunglasses inside. *Dumbass.* I hope my face doesn't show how pissed off I am right now. I refuse to give those assholes the satisfaction of knowing they got to me.

"I was in the mood for their house-special burger. It's the

best in town."

His compliment surprises me, and despite my irritation with him, the corners of my lips twitch upward.

He catches my reaction and rewards me with a smirk of his own. *Damn it.* I really wish he kept the jerkface attitude going, because now I can see how gorgeous he is.

My face becomes warm, which means I'm blushing like a virginal idiot.

"I'll be back with the menus," I say hastily and whirl around, hoping to hide that stupid reaction from him.

When I return to their booth, they're engaged in deep conversation. I hear the word Maverick, which confirms they're locals. The question is, are their families from Triton Cove, or do they board at Maverick Prep?

Why do you care, Alexis?

They barely acknowledge my presence when I hand them the menus.

"I'm telling you, Finn. There's no way Aquaman would lose to Michael Phelps in a freestyle relay," the dark-haired guy says.

Oh jeez. That's what has them talking so passionately?

"I can't believe you're still discussing this. One is a fictional superhero. Of course Aquaman would win," the girl sitting next to the dark-haired guy replies. "Especially if we're talking about Jason Momoa's version."

Both guys groan in frustration, and that's my cue to interrupt. I don't have all day. "What can I get you to drink?"

The blonde sitting next to sunglasses guy glances at the menu and then snorts. "I can't believe you don't have calories listed under the items. How am I supposed to know what to order?"

"Come on, Tiffany. You're at a diner. Go nuts," the dark-haired boy says.

She throws him a glower. "Bite me, Cameron. What do you have here that has no calories?" she asks me.

"Water or coffee if you take it black," I reply.

Everyone at the table laughs save for the stupid blonde. It wasn't meant to be a joke, but whatever.

"You don't have salad?"

"Sure, but even salad has calories. You asked for no calories."

She narrows her eyes. "Are you making fun of me?"

Her date removes his hat and sunglasses, revealing chin-length curly dark-blond hair that looks so soft, he could play an angel on a TV show. But when his sky-blue eyes turn to me, my blood runs cold.

Yes, he could be an angel.

Lucifer.

"Get out," I say, my voice tight and cold.

"Excuse me?" the blow-up doll asks in a high-pitched tone.

"You heard me. Get out. All of you."

Fury is coursing through my veins like wildfire, making me shake from head to toe.

"Wait, are you kicking us out? For real?" the guy named Cameron asks, but I'm not looking at him. My eyes are glued to his friend, the one who last year crashed into Mr. Danes's store and put Peter Danes in a wheelchair.

I can't believe he had the audacity to show his face in this part of town after what he did. But why would he care when he received no real punishment, just some lousy community service?

"Yes, I am," I grit out.

Finn Novak—yeah, I learned his name after the accident—glares at me with so much anger that it turns his eyes darker. "I wouldn't do that if I were you."

I laugh without humor. "Oh yeah? What are you going to do about it? Hit me with your car and cripple me as well?"

His eyes widen at the same time the blood seems to drain from his face. I expect him to become angrier, but instead he looks guilty as hell.

"Where's the manager?" The blonde chick stretches her neck, searching.

"I'm the manager," I lie. "Get the hell out before I call the cops."

Like that would scare them. But for whatever reason, my threat seems to work. It doesn't matter that I'm not really the manager. I'm just a high school kid, after all, and Dad would never put that much responsibility on my shoulders. I could manage the place though; I practically grew up here, and one day when Dad retires, I'll take over.

I know my outburst will earn me a tongue-lashing from Dad, even if my motives are valid. I'm causing a scene, and not everyone here knows why I'm kicking out Finn Novak and his friends.

Cameron begins to slide out of the booth when the sound of glasses breaking followed by a scream has me turning around. Dad is on the floor, clutching at his chest.

I forget Finn and his friends, caring about nothing but my father passed out on the floor.

"Dad!" I run to him, skidding to a halt as I drop to my knees next to him. "Someone call an ambulance!"

His face is contorted in pain, and his eyes are closed. My vision becomes blurry as tears fill them. There's a lot of noise in the background, but I can't discern the sounds over the loud drumming of my pulse in my ears.

"Daddy, please. Talk to me." I touch his shoulder gently, afraid to cause him more pain.

His expression relaxes suddenly, as does his hold on his chest. It takes me a moment to understand what just happened, and then desperation hits me. There's a loud scream that sounds more like a wail, and I realize it came from me. I throw myself over my father's still body as ugly sobs wreak havoc through my body. There's no reaction, no rise and fall of his chest.

He's gone.

3

FINN

J'm still reeling from the altercation with the waitress when she bolts. I didn't think I'd be recognized after a year, and my hair is longer now, but she did. And the hate I saw shining in her righteous brown eyes cut me deeper than a knife. But the commotion among the other patrons pushes my turmoil to the back of my mind. Something tragic just happened.

Tiffany slides off the booth with her phone already in hand. Cameron and Jackie follow her example, but I'm more interested in watching what's happening firsthand than capturing it on camera.

The waitress is on her knees, crying as she stares at the man lying on the floor. There's a couple in front of me, but I'm a head taller than them, and I can see the scene clearly. The man is clutching at his chest. He must be having a heart attack. My uncle had one a few years back during a family function, and he looked exactly like that. He didn't make it.

Out in the distance, the sound of sirens approaching can be heard. It brings back the awful memories of the day I lost control of my car and crashed into a store. I hadn't been drinking, and I wasn't high, but a person can lose their minds without consuming anything. I want to leave, run as far away as I can so I won't hear the sirens anymore, but I can't. The cry of despair coming from the waitress is keeping me here, rooted to the spot. It's not the satisfaction of seeing her in that desperate state that has me frozen. To be honest, I don't know what it is.

She throws herself at the man and wails like the world is about to end. The woman in front of me gasps, covering her mouth with her hand. Her husband throws his arm over her shoulders and pulls her closer.

A sudden hush descends over the room, and all we can hear now are the sirens from the ambulance just outside the diner and the loud crying of the redheaded girl.

"Holy shit. Did he die?" Cameron asks loudly next to me.

His voice carries in the silence of the room, earning him discontented glances. I normally wouldn't care about the stares, but in this moment, it's smothering.

"Shut up, man," I snap.

Cameron throws me a glare, which I ignore. I can't take my eyes off the waitress. One of the diner's employees has to pry her away from the man so the paramedics can have access to him. They check his pulse and then confirm what everyone here already knew. It's too late for him. I expect the waitress's distress to renew, but she keeps crying quietly in the arms of her coworker.

I'm not unfamiliar with heartbreak, but I learned a long time ago to disconnect from the blows I've been dealt. I had one relapse last year, let my emotions take control, and ended up wrecking someone's life.

Feelings make you weak. Caring for others makes you weak. But as I watch the waitress crumble in front of the crowd, something stirs in my chest. It's not necessarily an ache, or sadness. It's a heaviness that is out of place.

"God, this is fucking morbid. I'll never be able to order a burger from now on without thinking about corpses," Tiffany chimes in.

"When have you ever ordered a burger in your life?" Cameron retorts.

I could tell her to shut up too, but I don't trust my voice to have any bite. There's a lump in my throat now.

The waitress follows the paramedics out, leaning on her friend for support. She doesn't glance in my direction. I wish I could have captured her gaze for just a second, though I don't know why. *So she could crush me with her hate once more?*

She's a stranger to me, and I'll probably never see her again. This scene won't prevent me from eating at another diner, but I know I'll never come back here.

"Well, that was eventful," Cameron pipes up no sooner than the crowd begins to dissipate. "I doubt any other outing for food will top this one."

"Don't be so sure. Luke will try to come up with something." Jackie laughs.

"Let's get out of here," I say, not making eye contact with any of them.

I should have come alone. Now their presence and their comments are grating on my nerves.

"Can we go to the beach club now?" Tiffany suggests. "The atmosphere is much more pleasant there than in this dive, and that was before the whole drama."

"A man just fucking died," I bark. "Try to show some shred of human decency." I open the diner door brusquely, almost tearing it off its hinges, and walk out.

My new Porsche is parked on the other side of the road. The

ambulance is still in front of the diner, blocking traffic. One of the paramedics is talking to the waitress, but she doesn't appear to be listening. I stop and stare like a fucking creep. I should keep going instead of prying into someone else's nightmare, but I can't make my legs take another step.

Finally, her stare meets mine, but her brown eyes seem to go straight through me. I don't see a shred of the hate she laid on me earlier. Her fire is gone.

"I thought you wanted to leave." Tiffany tugs my arm.

"Yes, but nowhere with you." I pull free from her hold and cross the street.

"You're such a jerk, Finn," she calls me out.

Tell me something I haven't heard before, sweetheart.

With the push of a button, my car comes to life. I rev the engine, letting the sound drown out my thoughts. Then I get out of there without a destination in mind. I just want to get rid of this foreign feeling swirling in my chest. I know guilt and remorse. I've felt those plenty in the last year. What's bothering me now isn't either. That girl just lost her father, and I feel *sorry* for her. I don't get it. It's not like I can relate to what she's going through. I wouldn't shed a tear if it had been my own father lying lifeless on that greasy floor. As a matter of fact, there isn't a single member of my family who I'd mourn. They're all assholes.

That's not true. I'd be crushed if Jason died. But even missing him terribly, I'm happy he got the fuck out of Triton Cove.

Not a minute into my drive, Luke calls. Out of my closest friends, he's the one I've known the longest. He was my best friend in kindergarten, then my mortal enemy through first and second grades, all thanks to his schizophrenic mother telling him I was possessed by a demon. Her family locked her up after an incident involving Luke that, to this day, I don't know the details about.

He's the craziest motherfucker I know, that's for sure. Not

the kind of crazy that earns you a one-way ticket to Shutter Island but the type that will cost your family thousands of dollars to smooth things over with law enforcement and any other person wanting to sue.

"What?" I answer.

"Oh, hello to you too, mate. Is that how you greet your best friend?"

"What's with the fake British accent?"

"What can I say? One week hanging out with William and Kate and I'm talking like them."

"Like you'd ever be allowed within ten feet of any member of the royal family."

"Bro, you wound me," he replies in his normal Californian accent. "Anyway, what's going on?"

"Are you saying you don't know?"

"Don't know what? I just landed a minute ago. Is there something to know?" he asks eagerly.

I let out a heavy sigh. It's best if Luke hears it from me.

"We went out to grab something to eat at Dennis's Diner, and the owner had a heart attack."

"Okaaay?"

"He died, dude. Right in front of us."

"Oh, bummer. He probably shouldn't have been eating all the junk he serves. Bad publicity for the joint, anyway."

I don't reply right away, annoyed with Luke's response. Or maybe I'm annoyed that his lack of empathy annoyed me.

Fuck. I need to do something drastic to get my mind out of this funk.

"Where are you right now?"

"I'm still on the tarmac. The driver is late."

"I'll pick you up." I signal to take the next right and head in the opposite direction I was going.

"Aww, you *did* miss me. Bro, I'm touched." He laughs.

18

"Yeah, whatever. I asked Cameron to tag along today, and the dumbass brought Jackie and Tiffany with him."

"Ew. Is he still fucking those two bimbos?"

"Probably. Although Tiffany was all over me today."

"She's annoying as fuck, but she gives good head."

"So do the strippers at Blue Lagoon, but with the advantage that we don't have to suffer the inane talk before and after."

Luke laughs. "I can't wait to hang out with your grumpy ass today. Hey, we could go to Blue Lagoon. I miss American pussy."

Sex wasn't on my mind, but maybe it's exactly what I need to get that waitress out of my head.

4

ALEXIS

*T*he past three days went by in a blur. I was too numb to notice anything. When my grandparents came to the hospital to pick me up, I didn't fight them even though I hadn't seen or spoken to them in five years. I let them make all the arrangements while I stayed curled up in their guest room bed.

I still can't wrap my mind around the fact that Dad is gone, that I will never hear his bad jokes or laughter again. He won't come see me play softball anymore and cheer me on even though I have more strikeouts than home runs.

A lonely tear escapes the corner of my eye when I'm swept under by an unbearable wave of sadness. I have every intention of spending another day in bed when Grandma storms into the room and proceeds to open all the heavy curtains. Sunlight invades my fortress of misery, hurting my eyes. I bury my face under the many pillows stacked up on the bed and try to ignore her.

"Alexis, I know you're hurting, but you can't waste away in that bed."

"Yes, I can."

"You need to get into the shower. The maid said you haven't left this bed in three days!"

"Leave me alone."

She yanks my comforter and sheet away and then steals my pillows too. "Get up. I won't tolerate that kind of attitude from you. You're a Montgomery. You're stronger than that."

I sit up, shaking suddenly with anger. "I'm not a Montgomery. I'm a Walker."

Grandma's steely gray eyes narrow. "Your father, for all his faults, wasn't a quitter. Whether you consider yourself a Montgomery or a Walker, your behavior is unacceptable. Get ready. We'll leave in an hour."

"Don't tell me what to do. You're not my fucking mother!"

Through the haze of tears, I catch her wince. My mother— her daughter—died seven years ago in a ski accident while on a trip with my grandparents. Dad and I didn't go. It wasn't our thing. Besides, my grandparents never approved of Mom marrying Dad. They believed him to be beneath their station. They belong to the glittering side of Triton Cove.

"No, I'm not your mother, nor your father, but you *are* my responsibility now. We're leaving for your father's funeral in an hour. Unless you want to spend the rest of your life regretting not attending the service, I'd suggest you do as I say."

The fury leaves my body in a loud whoosh like a balloon being deflated. An uncontrollable sob bubbles up my throat, and I hate that I'm crumbling in front of Grandma.

"I've bought a dress for you. It's in the closet, all pressed and ready to go."

I wipe off my wet cheeks. "Thank you."

21

Her expression softens, which surprises me. I expected her to gloat at my defeat.

"I know it seems like the end of the world now, but I promise you, Lexi, things will get better."

She walks out of the room, leaving me alone with my pain.

No, it won't, Grandma. Things will never get better.

I feel light-headed and out of breath as I trudge to the bathroom. The numbness is giving way to something much worse. A tsunami of emotions is rushing in my direction, ready to tear me apart. My breathing comes out in bursts as I clutch the sink so hard it turns my knuckles white. My throat constricts with the urge to yell as loud as I can until all the raw agony leaves my body. But I can't let it out or it will consume me whole. It will send me into a void where there's no way out. The only way to push it back, to stop it from consuming me, is to counterattack with a different kind of pain, something I can control.

I bring my forearm to my lips and sink my teeth into the soft flesh until blood fills my mouth and the sharp pain makes my head go quiet.

FINN

I THOUGHT I had managed to forget the diner waitress. She hadn't crossed my mind at all in the past three days. Luke, Cameron, and Reid kept me distracted. It's our last week before we have to return to our prison at Maverick Prep, and we're committed to milking every second of it.

I'm up before eight—a rare occurrence for me during summer break—because there are waves coming.

Unfortunately, that means I have to deal with Dad before he heads to his office. He walks into the dining room in his pristine, sharp suit and tie, and then he sits at the head of the table without so much as a "Good morning."

While he sets the napkin on his lap, he says, "I'm surprised to see you up this early, Finn."

"I have places to be." I reach for a piece of toast and add it to my plate of scrambled eggs and bacon.

The maid enters the room, carrying a tray with a small pot of freshly brewed coffee and fills Dad's cup. He ignores her, too busy staring at me as if he's trying to crack my skull open. It's a technique he uses with his employees, business partners, or anyone he wants to intimidate. That look used to work on me when I was a kid. Not anymore.

After the maid leaves, Dad reaches for a portion of the paper that has already been arranged for him next to his plate. He only reads the business and finance sections.

A stretch of silence follows, but I'm not a fool to believe that's the end of our little morning catch-up. Not a minute later, he opens his mouth again. "Where are you going?"

"Surfing with the guys."

Dad snorts, keeping his eyes glued to the paper. "Enjoy your days of leisure while they last. You'll be interning for me when school restarts next week."

Fuck. And just like that my mood turns sour. "I never agreed to that."

"While you live under my roof and I pay your bills, you'll do as I say."

"It's my senior year, or have you forgotten? My schoolwork will be doubled, plus I have swimming practice."

Dad sets his paper aside and turns his glowering up to eleven. "Do you think I give a damn about that ridiculous hobby of yours? You *will* come to the office twice a week, and that's final."

My blood is boiling, but save for carving up Dad with the butter knife as if he were a Thanksgiving turkey, the only thing I can do is swallow my anger and get out of here as fast as I can. I push my chair back and stand up, tossing my napkin on the plate of uneaten food.

"Where do you think you're going?" he asks.

"Like I said, I have plans."

On my way to the front door, I catch sight of the unwanted sections of Dad's newspaper lying on one of the consoles in the hallway. The maid must have forgotten to get rid of them. If Dad sees them, she's as good as gone. Personnel issues were never my concern, but today, I don't want anyone else to feel the sting of my father's wrath.

I grab the papers and walk out the door. Once in my car, I don't drive off right away, needing to get my emotions in check first. I'm still reeling from the conversation with him. I thought I was safe from being roped into his world while I was still in high school. He must have felt he was losing control over me after my accident last year, so demanding I go to his office twice a week is a way to tighten the leash. *Asshole.*

He wasn't happy when I became the captain of the swimming team. He probably didn't think I deserved it after he had to pay a hefty settlement to the Danes family. After that, any conversation about me making a career out of swimming was severely discouraged. Novaks don't compete in sports, unless it's for charity. That's what he said, but I know he's sabotaging swimming as punishment.

I still have the damn newspaper in my hand, now partially wrinkled from me holding it too tight. I toss it to the side, ready to finally get the hell out of here when a headline catches my eye: "Triton Cove mourns the loss of Dennis Walker, beloved owner of Dennis's Diner." There's a picture of the man standing in front of the diner, and next to him, a smiling redheaded girl.

Despite her young age in the picture, I recognize her right away. It's the waitress.

Unable to stop myself, I pick up the paper again and read the article. *Hell.* The funeral is today.

It shouldn't matter to me. I list a thousand reasons why I ought to forget the girl and keep the plans I had. But when I peel out of the garage, I know I won't be going to the beach.

ALEXIS

I WAS SHOCKED to see so many of Dad's friends at the service. I honestly thought I'd only see people my grandparents knew there. But save for a few old friends of my mother from before she met my father, every single person in that church was someone who knew Dad in some capacity. Grandma must have asked Kevin to help her with the list.

I've returned to a state of numbness, which is better than the alternative. It's the only way I can cope and go through the motions. My arm still throbs from the bite, and it'll take a few days for it to heal completely. It will most likely leave a mark, but as long as I don't wear anything without sleeves, it'll be okay.

I refused to speak during the service, and I know someday I'll regret my decision. But if I had gone up to the podium and tried to speak about Dad, I'd have lost it. I'm barely hanging on as it is.

The moment we leave the church and head to the cemetery, I feel I can breathe again. I didn't realize how stifling the atmosphere had been indoors.

We're burying Dad next to Mom in the Montgomery

family's plot. I never asked what Dad wanted for his funeral. He was young, and I thought I had decades before I had to worry about that. I was an idiot. Like death cares about age. It didn't when it took Mom away from me.

I don't think he'd mind that his final resting place is next to the love of his life though. I suppose I should thank my grandparents for doing that. I know they didn't make that decision lightly.

Not everyone at the church comes to the cemetery. Maybe they weren't invited. Fewer people is better, I guess.

The priest says his final prayer, and then Dad's coffin is lowered into the ground. Silent tears roll down my cheeks when I approach the hole to toss a single white rose over his casket.

It seems that this final act solidifies in my mind that it's finally over. I'm now an orphan, and I've never felt more alone in my entire life.

I can't bear to stay here for another second surrounded by familiar strangers. When I walk away from Dad's final resting place, I don't stop moving until I reach the road. The dark storm inside my mind is approaching again. I usually don't have episodes so close together, but it seems I've gone over the edge.

I see something that doesn't belong there: a red Porsche parked not far from all the other cars. I stop in my tracks. A tall figure stands next to it, and when our gazes meet, I let out a gasp. It's Finn Novak. The noise in my head, driving me to a precipice, recedes.

What is he doing here?

I'm so stunned that I don't move from my spot until he gets back into his car and drives away. If he had waited longer, I would have walked up to him and demanded to know how he dared show up here. Now I'll be forever curious about his motives. I doubt our paths will cross again.

"There you are, Lexi," Grandma says. "Ready to go home?"

"Home? Do you mean my dad's house?"

A shiver runs down my spine. I'm not prepared to go back there yet with all those memories ready to smother me.

"Oh no, dear. Our house, naturally. You'll be staying with us now."

"What?" My voice rises to a pitch.

I hadn't stopped to consider the practical side of things.

"Must I live with you?" I blurt out. "I'm almost eighteen. I can live on my own."

My grandparents share a meaningful glance, which implies they're hiding something from me.

"What is it?" I ask.

"We don't need to talk about that now, honey."

I know I should push for answers—this is about my life, after all—but I don't have it in me to argue in the middle of the cemetery when I just said my final goodbye to Dad. So I let them steer me back to their car, saving my energy to fight another day.

During the drive back to their mansion, my mind wanders back to Finn Novak. Knowing why he came to the cemetery isn't important in the grand scheme of things, but right now, it's the distraction I need.

5

ALEXIS

TWO DAYS LATER

*T*he hole in my chest is still bleeding, but two days after my dad's funeral, I'm finally able to get out of bed on my own without Grandma or her maid having to kick me into gear. Or worse, me having to resort to more drastic measures.

It's already Thursday, which means I only have a few days to get things in order and figure out how I'm going to keep the diner running. Oh my God, I probably need to hire someone as a manager. Kevin can't cook *and* handle the day-to-day operations.

I'm already hyperventilating when there's a knock on the door.

"Come in," I say, glad for the interruption.

"Hello, Miss Alexis. Your grandmother would like to know if you will be joining her for breakfast this morning."

I glance down at my pajamas. "Yes, I'll be down in a few minutes."

As soon as the maid closes the door, I get out of bed and go in search of something to wear. I'm surprised to see most of my clothes, if not everything I own, hanging in the walk-in closet. My shirts and underwear are all in drawers, neatly folded. I know I dressed myself in the past five days, but I have no recollection of noticing my clothes were here. My grandparents clearly believe I'm going to live with them during my senior year of high school. I have to set them straight.

I pick a pair of jeans and my favorite T-shirt to wear, needing to be in familiar and comfortable clothes to make my case with them.

I find both of them sitting at the large dining room table facing each other with four chairs on each side separating them. How they even talk with so much distance is beyond me. Though maybe they don't.

A huge spread of breads, pastries, muffins, and fruit is laid out on the table, enough for several people.

"Good morning," I say, pulling up a chair.

Grandpa sets his newspaper down and smiles at me. It's not a broad smile, but it reaches his eyes at least.

"Good morning, dear. I'm glad you're feeling better to join us," he says.

"What would you like to drink, Lexi? Orange juice, tea, milk perhaps?" Grandma asks.

"Coffee if you have it." I set the napkin on my lap to keep my hands busy and avoid making eye contact. "What's up with all this food? Are you expecting someone?"

"Oh no, dear. We didn't know what you like to eat for breakfast, so we got everything." Grandma smiles.

I notice the glaring absence of diner food. I don't know if they did it on purpose to spare me the pain or not. Either way, I'm glad there aren't any pancakes or bacon in sight.

"Wow, you shouldn't have. I'm easy to please." I reach for a chocolate croissant, which I haven't had in years.

A different maid than the one who usually comes to my room fills my cup with coffee. I say thanks and then take a bite of the flaky pastry. *God, it's delicious.*

"Oh, there's creamer for your coffee, but if you prefer milk, Anna will bring you some."

"Creamer is fine," I reply with my mouth still half-full.

Grandma's forehead crinkles a little, but she doesn't comment on my lack of manners. I'm sure she's giving me a pass because it's the first time I've ventured out of my room. As nice as all this luxury is, I'd feel like I lived in a gilded cage if I stayed here.

"Now that you're feeling a little more like yourself again, your grandfather and I would like to talk about practical matters."

I'm glad they broached the subject themselves. The lack of familiarity with them is unnerving. They're my grandparents, but I know nothing about them save for they're wealthy beyond my wildest imagination and they didn't like my dad.

"Yeah, we really need to talk about that. It just occurred to me that I have to speak with the diner's staff and ensure everything is running smoothly."

"The diner has been closed since Dennis... well, since that tragic day," Grandpa replies.

"What? The diner has been closed for five days? Why?"

"Because we have to make a decision about what to do with it."

I shake my head. "I don't understand. What is there to decide? I'm going to hire a manager and keep working there part time until I graduate from high school."

Grandpa turns his attention to Grandma, clenching his jaw. There it is again, that loaded glance shared between them.

"What's going on? You've been keeping something from me since Dad's funeral," I say.

"Do you want to tell her or should I, dear?" he asks Grandma.

"You'd better tell her, Richard. This is business. You know more about it."

Suddenly, the piece of croissant I ate feels like a rock in my stomach.

"Very well." Grandpa glances at me, looking all serious. "Your father was in dire financial trouble, Lexi. He'd been operating the diner in the red for over six months. He even took a second mortgage on the house to try to generate some cash flow."

A new heaviness sets in my chest, and my belly begins to ache. "What does that mean?"

"It means your father left you with nothing but an enormous amount of debt. We have to sell the diner, the house, everything he owned, and even so, that might not be enough to pay all his bills."

"No." My voice comes out strangled. "We can't sell the diner. That's all I have left of him."

And it will be like losing him all over again. I don't say that part out loud though.

"He didn't even have life insurance," Grandpa continues as if I hadn't spoken. "It boggles my mind how a father, a businessman, wouldn't acquire life insurance. It's irresponsible."

"Can you please stop criticizing him? He's dead. Saying how reckless he was won't change anything."

Grandpa's annoyed expression softens. "I'm so sorry, my dear. It angers me that he left you in this horrible financial situation. But fret not. Your grandmother and I will take care of everything. You won't want for anything."

I wipe off the tears that have rolled down my cheeks. It

seems all I do these days is cry and cry. But I have to be strong now. My future depends on it.

"Is there any way you can save the diner, Grandpa?"

"You mean keep that sinking business?" His bushy eyebrows shoot up.

"Yes, for me. I know it can be profitable. It was before."

He turns to Grandma, who I find watching me intensely. "What would you do with that diner if your grandfather paid all your father's debts?"

"I'd work there full time as soon as I graduate from high school."

Immediately, I sense I've said the wrong thing. Grandma's eyes flash with contempt while her lips flatten.

"Absolutely not. That's out of the question." Grandpa raises his voice, getting flustered again. "You're a Montgomery. You're going to college and getting a proper education. Then, if you feel like wasting away in that greasy diner, it's your decision."

"You can't force me to go to college."

"Are you saying you don't want to go?" Grandma asks, sounding genuinely surprised.

"I assumed I'd go, but it's not a big deal to me if I don't. The diner is more important."

"That diner was the thing that killed your father. I'm surprised you want to keep it as a reminder," Grandpa retorts.

"Don't you dare say that. The diner was what kept Dad and me going after Mom died." My voice quivers.

"No, that diner sucked away his life. You're still a kid. You have no idea the stress involved in owning a restaurant, living from month to month, barely skating by. That's it, I'm getting rid of that damn thing." Grandpa hits his fist on the table, rattling the china.

"If you do that, then this will be the last time you see me," I seethe.

"What do you mean, Lexi?" Grandma asks.

"If you sell the diner out of spite, I'll pack up my bags and leave. You'll never see me again."

"And where exactly would you go? You have no money, no skills that will get you a job that pays a livable wage," Grandpa retorts, making me even angrier. He's totally calling my bluff.

I push my chair back so hard it almost topples down. Standing up, I say, "I don't know, but I'll manage."

"Sit back down. You're not going anywhere," Grandma tells me. "Your grandfather is letting his emotions get away from him."

"I'm only speaking the truth. The fact that she's that stubborn just proves she's too young and immature to make any sensible decision."

"I'm not immature," I speak through clenched teeth, even though I *am* acting like a spoiled brat without brains.

I have no idea where I'd go. I could maybe crash at Carmen's for a week, but eventually I'd have to find a cheap place to rent. Only there's no such thing as cheap rentals in Triton Cove unless I'm willing to live in a dumpster with ten more people. I'm all bark and no bite.

"What if we said we could save the diner, hire a manager to turn that place around, and make it profitable on the condition that you have to graduate from high school and get a bachelor's degree in something sensible, like business administration perhaps?" Grandma offers calmly.

That sounds reasonable, but there must be a catch. I look at Grandpa, who is no longer paying attention to me. He's staring hard at Grandma, almost as if he's trying to communicate with her telepathically. I'm feeling quite exposed standing there between them, so I sit down again and ask for a better explanation of the terms.

"And all I have to do in return is graduate from high school and go to college?"

"Well, you wouldn't be returning to that pitiful public high school, naturally." Grandma waves her hand dismissively.

Aha. I knew there was more. "Classes start next Monday. Where am I supposed to go? Besides, all my friends go there."

"You'd attend the only appropriate school for someone of your status," Grandpa replies.

"I didn't know they had high schools that catered to bankrupt kids."

Grandma gives me a droll look. "Don't play sassy with us. We're speaking of your status as a Montgomery. And before you say anything, I know you don't see yourself as one of us, but you *are* our granddaughter, and it wouldn't be right to deprive you of the best education money can buy."

My stomach clenches tightly. There's only one place my grandparents could send me in Triton Cove, but I still ask, "Where am I supposed to go, then?"

"Maverick Prep, my dear."

"I've heard getting into that school is harder than getting into Harvard."

It's a lie. I've never heard such a thing. I'm sure their selection process is based on how much the parents have in their Swiss bank accounts.

"Oh please, they'd never say no to a Montgomery." Grandma snorts. "As long as you're not a moron, you'll be fine. You're not a moron, are you, Lexi?"

"No," I reply, offended. "I'm an honor student."

"We know, dear," Grandpa replies. "I've already spoken with the headmaster, and you're all set to start next Monday."

"What? You enrolled me before I agreed to go?"

"We didn't think you'd make such a fuss, Lexi. Frankly, I'm shocked that you're putting up a fight. I guarantee any kid in your old high school would give up a limb to attend Maverick Prep."

Not likely. We know the type of assholes who attend that school.

"I won't know anyone there," I argue.

"Oh, I'm sure you'll make new friends in no time," Grandma replies cheerfully.

I don't know why I'm still fighting this. Maybe it's my rebellious side that won't accept the battle is lost. They agreed to let me keep the diner, which is what matters in the end. Spending a year at Maverick sounds like a small price to pay.

6

FINN

THREE DAYS LATER

I was out of the house before the break of dawn. I wanted to get an hour in the Olympic-size pool at Maverick before anyone else arrived. As the captain of the Maverick Sharks, I have access even if the school isn't open to students yet. Not that any of us care about permission to use the school premises after hours. There's always someone with a spare key, no matter how many times the administration changes the locks and the security codes.

I had the displeasure of seeing Dad last night. He insisted on having a family dinner, which he used as an opportunity to criticize my life choices and list in excruciating detail how he was going to turn me into a responsible man in this coming year. God forbid I follow in my cousin's footsteps and smear the Novak name some more. Jason's rebellion against his shackles turned him into an anathema in our family. After what he and

36

his girlfriend went through, I don't judge him for his decision to get the fuck out of here. Sometimes, I'm envious he got away.

My father has always believed I'm irresponsible, even before the accident last year, because I refuse to follow the life plan he has for me. I'm not a sheep like my older sister, who follows the script of the perfect, dutiful daughter to a *T*. She was top of her class at Maverick, the fucking valedictorian, and now she's taking Yale by storm. And when she graduates with honors, she'll marry a man from a good family who my father no doubt has already selected.

Pathetic.

The swimming pool is the only place where I can forget my problems, where I can't hear my father's voice. Time doesn't matter, only each stroke of my arms and kick of my legs. I like to push myself to the limit, staying underwater until my lungs are on the verge of bursting, swimming until my limbs feel like they're about to fall off.

I've lost count of the number of laps I swam already when I come up for air and see a girl watching me from the other side of the glass. Her presence here is disturbing. She reminds me that there's a world outside that's always demanding, always ready to deliver a punch until I'm molded into conformity.

If she's here, it means I've run out of time. Classes will probably start soon. Bracing my hands on the edge, I push myself out of the pool and only then remove my goggles. I had every intention of ignoring the girl until I recognize her. It's the diner waitress dressed in a Maverick's school uniform.

Impossible. I must be seeing things.

I blink a couple of times, forcing my mind to see what's truly in front of me. But when that doesn't work, then I can only conclude the universe is conspiring against me.

Sure, let's bring the girl I've been obsessing over for the past week into my world.

I move closer to the glass separating us, keenly aware that

I'm not wearing much. I expect her gaze to drop to my naked chest and abs or even down to my crotch, but her brown eyes remain locked on mine. That irritates me more than if she had been ogling my body like all the other airheads in this school do.

"What are you staring at?" I bark.

She shakes her head, but her expression remains unfazed despite my harsh tone.

"I don't fucking know," she replies and then walks away.

I'm left fuming, shaken by her lack of emotion. She had plenty at the diner when she glared at me, probably wishing she could kill me with her stare. Today, I went out of my way to rattle her and ended up rattling myself.

CAMERON DROPS in the chair next to mine and leans closer. "You're not going to believe who I saw entering the headmaster's office."

His tone is conspiratorial and amused. He's the biggest gossiper in our group, and now he thinks he has the latest scoop. My mood hasn't improved since earlier, so I'm more than happy to burst his bubble.

"The waitress from the diner," I reply without making eye contact.

"What the hell?" He leans back. "How did you know?"

"I caught her spying on me while I was in the pool this morning."

"Is that so?" He curls his lips into a devious grin while his eyes shine with mischief.

"Whatever crazy idea you have brewing in your head, forget it."

"Cameron doesn't have crazy ideas. He has stupid ideas."

Luke takes his usual seat in front of me. "You want crazy, come to me."

"Fuck off, Halle," Cameron bites back.

Tiffany and Jackie walk into the classroom, claiming the seats closest to us. I groan internally. I was hoping we wouldn't be in any classes together. They're such pains in the ass. It doesn't help that I hooked up with Tiffany a few too many times last year and she thinks she has a claim on me now.

"Did you guys hear the latest news?" Jackie asks, smiling slyly.

"Yeah, darling. We all know about the waitress," Cameron replies bitterly, playing with his phone.

"What waitress?" Tiffany asks, looking at her friend with a frown.

Jackie shrugs. "No clue, but that's not the news I have, Cam. I'm surprised you of all people don't know."

He turns around, giving her his undivided attention. "All right. You got me. What do you know that I don't?"

"Halsey is back."

It's impossible not to notice how Cameron's spine becomes rigid. We all know not to speak her name in his presence.

"Are you sure?" he asks in a voice that's cold and tight.

It's clear that Jackie is taking great satisfaction from Cameron's reaction. She's such a bitch. I don't know why Cameron hangs out with her.

"Oh yeah, I bumped into her on the front steps earlier. We only spent a few minutes chatting, but she's back at Maverick for her senior year. You must be thrilled, Cam. You finally get your BFF back."

Cameron jumps off his chair so suddenly that it screeches against the floor. He runs off, forgetting to take his backpack with him. On the way out the door, he collides with Reid, who looks surprised when Cameron doesn't acknowledge him.

"What was that all about?" Tiffany asks.

I glower in Jackie's direction. "You had to rub in his face that Halsey was back, didn't you?"

She widens her eyes innocently. "How was I supposed to know he'd react like that? It's been years."

"What's up with Cam?" Reid drops into the chair Cameron just vacated, looking like he simply rolled out of bed and came to school. His uniform is rumpled, his long blond hair is as shaggy as ever, and there are dark circles under his eyes that not even his perpetual tan can hide.

"Halsey is back," Luke replies.

"Oh shit. That explains a lot."

More students come into the room, and when Julie Diamond and Emily Frost walk in together, both Reid and Luke curse under their breaths.

"Are you fucking kidding me?" Luke blurts loud enough for the newcomers to hear it.

Emily rewards him with a glacial glance that makes me shiver, even though her cold stare wasn't aimed at me. She still hasn't forgiven Luke for last year's stunt.

The deal between Reid and Julie is different though. Their families are enemies. The feud goes back generations, and both have been poisoned against one another.

No matter the circumstance, the fact that Emily and Julie are here will turn this class nuclear.

It could have been worse. Diner girl could be here too.

No sooner does the thought cross my mind than the redhead appears in the door. Her eyes sweep the room, no doubt searching for a vacant chair. When she catches me staring, the fingers clutching her backpack strap tighten.

"Oh, that's who Cameron thought you were talking about, Jackie," Tiffany says, then calls out to the redhead. "Hey, diner rat. Are you lost?"

As annoying as Tiffany is, I don't tell her to shut her trap this time. Instead, I lean back in my chair, linking my fingers behind my head to enjoy diner girl's humiliation better. My lips curl into a grin.

She narrows her eyes and then walks into the room, aiming for the seat next to the window. My smirk drops when she doesn't seem embarrassed by Tiffany's remark. Hell. I thought she was going to simply ignore Tiffany, but halfway, she stops and faces her.

"Better to be a rat than trash hiding underneath designer clothes."

Luke whistles, amused, and then says to Tiffany, "She knows your secret, Tiff."

Tiffany's eyes are bulging out of her skull, and her face is so red, I can't believe there isn't smoke coming out of her ears. Flattening her palms on the desk, she begins to stand, but Mr. Jonas, our English and Lit Studies teacher, enters the room, putting Tiffany's retaliation on hold.

7

ALEXIS

I try to ignore that Finn Novak is in the room. This school is huge, and I could have wound up in any advanced classes, so why am I in his? And not only his. The two stupid girls he brought to the diner are also here.

Carmen warned me that I'd be pushed around in my first week. The students here would try to break me, and if I took their insults meekly and didn't fight back, they'd think I was easy prey and torture me all year round. I didn't expect the games to start in first period.

I know I made an enemy when I called that obnoxious blonde trash. I don't care. I'm actually looking forward to her retaliation. The anticipation of a bloody battlefield is better than the enormous hole in my chest. It keeps the darkness inside me occupied.

"Good morning, class," the teacher says in an overly cheerful tone. "I hope you had a great summer."

"Probably better than yours," the freckled guy sitting in front of me mutters under his breath, and his neighbor laughs.

Assholes.

"Yes, Felix. I'm sure your month-long traveling through Europe was much better than me handling three kids under the age of five while attempting to build a tent in an overcrowded camping site in Florida," the teacher replies, earning chuckles from some of the students.

I'd laugh too if I didn't have a dark cloud of gloom hanging over my head. I'm not sure I'll ever be able to find joy again.

"Well, it seems we have a couple of new students joining us this year. My name is Mr. John Jonas, but you can call me Jon-Jon."

I wince. There's no way in hell I'm calling him by that ridiculous nickname.

The classroom door bangs open, and in comes the other new student. My jaw drops of its own accord. Eric Danes, Mr. Danes's oldest grandson, is standing there wearing the same uniform as me, looking like he'd rather be anywhere but here.

Mr. Jonas clears his throat. "Mr. Eric Danes, you're late. But I'll give you a pass since it's your first day."

He stares at the teacher in contempt, but when his gaze fixates on Finn, it turns murderous. Eric's younger brother is the one Finn hurt last year. What I don't understand is what Eric is doing here. The last I heard, he had joined a military school. He wasn't even around when the accident happened.

I look at Finn, curious about his reaction. His entire posture is tense, and his face is paler now. Suddenly, I don't feel so alone anymore. I don't know Eric at all, but he's someone from my world, and that has to count for something.

His gaze sweeps the room, and I try to make eye contact with him. There's a vacant seat next to mine, but Eric aims for the one in the far back. He doesn't even acknowledge me, which deflates my hopes. I'm sure he recognized me. There aren't a lot of redheads in town, and he's been to the diner once or twice. Maybe he thinks my presence here means I've switched sides.

I'm still mulling it over when the teacher turns to me. "Ms. Alexis Montgomery, why don't you tell us a little bit about yourself?"

I bristle in an instant. Fucking *A*. I can't believe my grandparents enrolled me in this stupid school as a Montgomery.

"The name is Alexis Walker," I reply through clenched teeth.

Mr. Jonas's smile wilts a fraction as his eyebrows furrow. "My mistake. The list I received said your last name was Montgomery. I'll have them fix it. But go on, tell us about yourself."

I let out a heavy sigh. The last thing I want is to give these people CliffsNotes about my life. "There's nothing to tell. I'm just a new student, boring as hell. You can go on with your lecture."

The teacher looks at me as if I'm an alien. I'm sure he's not used to a student who doesn't enjoy the limelight.

"I'm certain you're not boring," he presses.

"She doesn't want to talk about herself. Stop harassing her and start with the lesson already," a girl with white-blonde hair pulled back in a severe ponytail comes to my defense.

I almost snap and tell her I don't need anyone speaking for me, but she's not looking in my direction. She's busy having a staring contest with the teacher. Maybe I shouldn't antagonize her too. I can't declare war on every single student at Maverick just because I wish I wasn't here.

Mr. Jonas glances at the back of the room. "Mr. Eric Danes? Would you like to say a few words?"

I expect him to refuse an introduction like I did, but he stands up instead.

"Sure. You already know my name. I was born and raised in Triton Cove. My grandfather owns a small convenience store downtown where last year, Finn Novak crashed his Porsche through the window, putting my little brother in a wheelchair for life. I'm here because his father wanted to make sure Finn never forgets what he did or how much it cost his old man."

Eric sits back down nonchalantly as if he didn't just drop a nuclear bomb in the room. Everyone in Triton Cove knows what happened last year. I'm sure it's old news here at Maverick Prep, but even so, all the students are staring at either Eric or Finn in stunned silence.

I glance at Finn, who instead of throwing daggers in Eric's direction with his eyes, is looking down with shoulders hunched forward. He seems defeated, broken, nothing like the arrogant god who emerged from the school's swimming pool an hour ago. The sight should make me happy, but it does the opposite. It makes me unbearably sad for him and for Eric's family.

It's a dangerous thing to sympathize with the enemy, Alexis.

FINN

I'VE ALWAYS ENJOYED English and Lit Studies class, but if anyone asked me what Mr. Jonas talked about, I couldn't say. I spent the hour-long lecture reeling from Eric's declaration. I had no idea my father planned to give a scholarship to Peter Danes's brother. He's cruel beyond limits, but this is a new low even for him. He knows how wrecked I've been since the accident. Guilt carved a hole in my chest and is constantly threatening to swallow me whole.

I wanted to serve time for what I did, but that's not how Novaks fix their mistakes. We bribe, extort, and lie.

Glutton for punishment that I am, I glanced way too many times in Alexis's direction, seeking her loathing stare. But the few times I caught her looking back, I didn't see hate in her eyes. She felt sorry for me, and that's worse than hate.

I have to change that.

When the class ends, Luke leans closer and whispers, "Do you want to teach that motherfucker a lesson?"

"What?"

"Say the word, man, and we put Eric Danes in his place."

My initial thought is to say no. I've done enough damage to his family. But he did challenge me, and I can't let that slide. Show weakness in front of the sharks and they all think they can take a bite.

"Don't worry. I'll handle him," I say.

From the corner of my eye, I watch Eric walk past Alexis's desk. She looks up, but he doesn't see or simply chooses to ignore her. She frowns at his retreating back, and it occurs to me that maybe she was hoping he'd be her ally at Maverick. Did they know each other well before coming here? I feel a small annoyance at the possibility.

She packs her things absentmindedly, perhaps having already forgotten her argument with Tiffany. If she did, it's one sided. I know Tiffany didn't forget, and I expect her revenge will come sooner rather than later. Right now, I don't fucking care about their imminent clash. I'm too busy dealing with my own shit.

Cameron returns to the room then, distracting me from my inner thoughts.

"Cameron Godwin, you missed class," Mr. Jonas says.

"Yeah, yeah. And I'm sure it was quite a thrilling one," he says dismissively.

Mr. Jonas narrows his eyes but knows better than to push. Cameron's eyes are dark, filled with bad intentions. Everyone knows—even the faculty—not to mess with him when he's like that. I wonder if he talked to Halsey.

"Everything all right, man?" I ask.

He runs his fingers through his dark-brown hair in a shaken motion. "Everything is fucking perfect."

Alexis walks past us, heading for the door, and my eyes follow her. Cameron notices my interest and glances over his shoulder. "So, diner girl is in this class too, huh? That's going to be interesting."

Luke chuckles. "Bro, you don't know the half of it."

"Don't get your hopes up, Cam. She's not going to last long enough at Maverick to entertain you," Tiffany declares in an ominous way as she stands up.

Luke's lips break into a lazy smile. "Oh yeah? And what are you going to do to make her run away with her tail between her legs?"

Tiffany grins mischievously. "You'll have to wait and see."

I roll my eyes, already bored with the conversation, but refrain from making a comment. I don't want anyone to know about my obsession with Alexis. It's stirring something nasty in my chest, a putrid secret that has the power to destroy me if it ever sees the light of day.

Tiffany and Jackie walk out of the room, laughing about something. I must have checked out for a second and missed what they said. It doesn't matter. I'm relieved they didn't linger. I hope this is the only class I have to deal with them.

"How come no one told me diner girl was hot?" Luke asks.

"Because she isn't," I grumble.

"Sure, that's why you couldn't tear your eyes away from her during class." Reid laughs.

"Oh, like you couldn't stop staring at your archnemesis?" I fire back, even though I wasn't paying attention to what he was doing.

But my guess hits the mark. Reid's green eyes darken as his

face twists into a scowl. "If I was staring at Julie Diamond, it was because I was plotting how to make her suffer this semester."

"Wait a second. Julie Diamond is in this class?" Cameron shakes his head. "Does school administration want blood spilled on their property?"

"You didn't see her sitting right in the front row when you came in?" I ask.

"No, I was a bit distracted."

"So I guess you missed Emily Frost's presence too," Luke chimes in, his expression growing darker.

Cameron doesn't blink or speak for a few seconds. Then he tosses his head back and laughs from deep in his belly. And he doesn't even know that Eric Danes is in this class or what he said.

"What the fuck is wrong with him?" Reid asks.

"Dunno. It must be the Halsey effect." Luke shrugs.

At the mention of Cameron's former friend, he stops laughing and stares hard at all of us. "I'm just going to say this once. I don't fucking want to hear her name in my presence. She's dead to me."

Luke glances at me with both eyebrows arched. Yeah, I'm not buying this whole deal of Halsey is dead to Cameron either. But he's our friend. If he doesn't want to talk about the girl who obliterated his heart and smashed it in a million pieces, we won't.

Then I glance at the time on my phone and realize I'm going to be late for the meeting with my counselor. I hastily collect my stuff, sensing my friends staring at me as if I'm nuts.

"Where are you going in such a hurry, Finn?" Reid asks. "We have a free period now."

We're the only students left in the classroom. Even Mr. Jonas is gone.

"I have a meeting with Mr. Phillips to discuss my future."

"I thought your future had already been mapped out by your asshole father," Luke replies, dead serious.

He's my closest friend, the one I come to when I need to vent about my shitty family life. He knows almost everything save for the one secret I'll take to the grave.

"That's what he thinks," I reply.

"Bro, are you finally ready to follow in Jason's footsteps and let your rebellious side shine?" Cameron asks, grinning like a deranged idiot.

His question doesn't merit a response though. Or maybe I can't really answer that. There's a reason why I haven't told my father to go to hell yet. It's not fear that he'll cut me off financially. It's the ugly secret that keeps me from fighting his control.

8

ALEXIS

I stop in the middle of the hallway when I realize I'm going in the wrong direction. The numbers of the classrooms are getting higher instead of lower. I turn around suddenly and end up bumping into another student.

"Oops, I'm sorry," I say, stepping back

"It's okay. I wasn't paying attention either."

A pretty girl is smiling kindly at me, but her aquamarine eyes are super sad. They're a bit red too, as if she's been crying.

"Are you okay?" I ask.

She flattens her lips and nods. "Yeah. Of course. I'm Halsey, by the way."

"Nice to meet you. My name is Alexis. I'm new here."

"Me too. Where were you heading to?"

"Art class with Miss LaFleur."

"Oh, I know where that is. I can take you there."

I wonder how she knows if she's new here, but it's possible that she's already memorized the layout of the building.

"What about your class? Aren't you going to be late?"

"I have a free period now."

"Oh, I don't think I have any free periods."

She frowns. "How come?"

"My grandparents worked out my schedule with the headmaster."

Understanding dawns on her face. "Oh, you're *that* Alexis."

Immediately, I bristle. "What's that supposed to mean?"

A blush spreads through Halsey's tanned face. "I'm sorry. That came out wrong. What I mean to say was you're Richard and Lillian Montgomery's granddaughter. My parents are friends with them. They mentioned you to me, but I hadn't connected the dots until now. I'm prone to blurt out things without thinking."

"It's okay. I'm a bit on edge."

"I know what you mean. This school is intimidating even to me, and I know most of the students here."

"Are you a freshman?"

"Oh no. This is my senior year. I'm from Triton Cove, but I spent my first three years of high school at a boarding school in Switzerland."

"Why did you decide to come back?"

Halsey's expression darkens, and I have a feeling I stumbled upon a subject she's not keen on discussing with a stranger.

"I missed my parents," she says, and I sense the lie. "Come on. Miss LaFleur's studio is on the other side of the building."

"I only have five minutes. I'll never make it there in time."

"I know a shortcut. Come on." She veers toward the emergency exit door. It leads to a set of stairs that are currently devoid of students.

Halsey dashes up the steps, only stopping once we reach the top. We're now two stories up, and I'm pretty sure Miss

LaFleur's classroom was in the same level we were before. The heavy metal door is locked by a code padlock. Halsey knows the combination though. It opens to a long hallway, completely deserted.

"Where are we?" I ask.

"An unused part of the school. The plan is to expand, but we don't know when that's going to happen."

"How come you know the combination to the lock?"

"My father's company is responsible for the security in this place. Getting the combination was easy."

No wonder she knows her way around the building. One mystery solved.

We dash down the empty corridor and then down the opposite flight of stairs. When we return to the main hallway, most students have already gone into their classrooms.

"Miss LaFleur's studio is through that door." Halsey points to a door that's still open not far from us.

"Thanks for your help."

"My pleasure."

Loud male voices carry toward us in the now empty corridor, and a second later, Finn and his friends turn the corner. Finn's gaze zeroes in on me, and it's clear by the way his body tenses that he's surprised to see me there.

Cameron, Finn's dark-haired friend, glares in our direction, but I'm not sure if his glower is meant for me or Halsey.

"Oh, what a fortuitous encounter," the tallest of Finn's friends pipes up, smiling from ear to ear in a deranged manner.

"Shut up, Luke," Cameron snaps.

"I'd better go," Halsey says. "Good luck, Lexi."

I never told Halsey she could call me Lexi, but maybe that's how my grandparents referred to me when they were telling her parents about me. I don't mind the nickname. It's what all my friends call me.

Cameron's gaze narrows. "I see you're making new friends,

Halsey. Careful, diner girl. Halsey might look innocent, but she'll backstab you without a second thought."

"You know what? Fuck you, Cameron. And stay away from me."

She strides off in the opposite direction, and I take that as my cue to walk into the classroom. But a woman appears at the threshold, wearing an apron covered in dried paint. She must be Miss LaFleur.

"What's all this ruckus outside my studio?" she asks. I'd answer, but she's not paying attention to me. Her gaze is trained on the guys. "Finn, I didn't realize you'd be in my class this semester."

"I'm not," he replies in a clipped voice.

"Oh, that's too bad."

Cameron rolls his eyes, and I don't know why his reaction catches my attention.

"And you, young lady? Are you in my class?" Miss LaFleur asks me.

"Yes, ma'am."

"What are you waiting for, then? A formal invitation?" She steps aside, allowing me to walk into the studio.

It's double the size of my first-period classroom, and the tall windows allow as much natural light to flow in as possible. Each student gets their own easel, which have been arranged in a circle. There's only one left available, which means I'm the last student to arrive. Great.

I quickly look over the room, and the only familiar face I see is Eric Danes. But after he pretended he didn't know me in first period, I'm not inclined to approach him again. If he wants to fly solo here at Maverick, so be it. I'm not that starved for friendship.

He doesn't look up from his canvas when I cross the room. To be fair, only a couple students do, and even so, their attention only lasts a few seconds. I already love this class.

I set my backpack on the floor next to the available easel and glance briefly at my neighbors. The guy to my left has headphones on and seems completely oblivious to the world as he sketches on his white canvas. It looks like an action scene from a comic book.

The girl to my right, a raven-haired beauty, is staring at the rough drawing on her large sketchbook. It's a portrait of a guy, smoking a cigarette. I gasp out loud when I realize it's Eric Danes. My stupid audible reaction makes her look at me. Noticing where my focus is, she rips the page off and turns it into a ball.

"Why did you do that? It was pretty good," I say.

She averts my gaze when she answers, "It was just a doodle, and not today's assignment."

"And what's today's assignment?"

She doesn't answer and then proceeds to ignore me.

Fine, be an aloof bitch. I don't care.

Miss LaFleur is already back in the room, but she doesn't say a word as she sits behind her desk. *Shit.* I must have missed her instructions. I stretch my neck and see that every single student is concentrating on their pieces, even Eric Danes.

I begin to stand so I can ask her what I'm supposed to be doing when the guy on my left grabs my arm, startling me.

"Whatever you want from Miss LaFleur, don't bother," he tells me.

"Why?"

"She only has time for her male students, the good-looking ones."

"Are you serious?"

"Like a heart attack. Each semester, she picks one of the pretty boys as her favorite. Last year it was Finn Novak. This year I'm betting Eric Danes will be warming up her bed."

The girl next to me gasps loudly, making me turn to her to

see what got her attention. She's actually looking at us, wide eyed.

"Hey, Sage. Didn't your mother ever teach you it's rude to eavesdrop on other people's conversation?" my neighbor says.

Her face turns all shades of red before she looks away.

My jaw is still hanging loose while I process the information. I picture Finn and Miss LaFleur together, and the visual makes me sick.

"Are you saying she's sleeping with her students?" I whisper.

"Oh yeah. Big time."

"That's disgusting. Does the headmaster know?"

He snorts. "Like any of her students will ever confess that they're banging the teacher."

"Well, she's getting paid to teach everyone, not only her fuckboys," I retort angrily.

"What's there to teach? This is art class. We all work on our projects without having to worry about assignments and grades. Don't make a fuss and you'll get your *A*."

I glance at Miss LaFleur, who's getting paid to do nothing but sit on her ass and fuck her students. Anger bubbles up my throat.

I should leave things alone. I don't know if what this guy just told me is true or not.

But I find myself getting up from my chair and striding to her desk. She glances at me with an irritated air, as if I'm interrupting something important.

"May I help you?" she asks.

"I'd like to know when you plan to start the lecture."

"Excuse me?"

"Or did I miss your instructions?"

"Just do whatever you like. This class is all about self-expression."

"But you do have an actual plan, right?"

"You're the new student, I see. My approach is different than you might be used to. I don't believe in structured lessons. I find them to inhibit true art."

"If we're just expected to do whatever we like, then what exactly is your role here?"

Suddenly, I sense the entire classroom is staring at me. I'm creating a fuss, just like my neighbor told me to not do.

Miss LaFleur smiles tightly, but her green eyes flash with annoyance. "My role is to guide you in your journey if you need it. Most of my students are quite independent, but if you feel you require extra help, you can always come to me, Miss Walker. Loss can stifle the creative process sometimes."

I wince at the reminder that I just recently lost my father. Her words might sound kind to everyone else, but to me, they were wrapped in barbed wire and meant to inflict pain. There's a glint of victory in her eyes when she sees her blow hit the mark.

"I'll be fine, thanks."

I return to my easel, angrier than I was before.

No sooner do I sit down than my gossipy neighbor leans closer. "I told you to leave things alone. You just made an enemy."

"What's new? She can join the club."

9

FINN

$\mathcal{I}$ hurry to the meeting with my counselor only to find his door locked. I check my phone for any missed message or call, but I have nothing. Retracing my steps, I catch up with the guys just as they're heading to the quad.

"Done with your meeting already?" Luke asks me.

"Mr. Philips wasn't there. It's not like him to not show up."

"Why are you still frowning at your phone? Now you can hang out with us," Cameron pipes up.

"He didn't send me an email either," I reply.

Luke throws his arm over my shoulders. "Will you forget about your damn meeting? I'd much rather talk about the first bash of the semester. It has to top last year's party."

"You can forget hosting it at my parents' property again. My father threatened to send me to military school after you set fire to the barn," Reid chimes in, dead serious.

"It was an accident," Luke replies innocently.

"Yeah, like destroying Emily's prom decorations was also an accident?" I ask.

Luke shoves me off, annoyed now. "She got in the way of revenge. She deserved what happened."

"Bro, you really need to stop playing with fire." Cameron laughs.

"Never." To make a point, Luke flips his lighter on and runs his finger over the flame.

We round the corner and then stop in our tracks. Alexis and Halsey are standing in front of Miss LaFleur's studio, talking. Their conversation stops abruptly when they see us. The air becomes thick with tension. Cameron's body is as rigid as mine, and I don't need to look at his face to know he's glowering at Halsey.

"Oh, what a fortuitous encounter," Luke says, amused.

He does love to see things go up in flames, both literally and metaphorically.

"Shut up, Luke," Cameron retorts.

Halsey turns to Alexis. "I'd better go. Good luck, Lexi."

Lexi? Are they friends now?

If Cameron didn't already have a problem with Alexis for kicking us out of her father's diner, now that she's friends with Halsey, his animosity will only grow. I shouldn't care, but I do. Eric Danes's words messed with my head, but I haven't developed a knight-in-shining-armor complex yet. I don't want anyone to give her hell but me. She's mine to torment because I want her undivided hatred.

I'm a fucking basket case.

"I see you're making new friends, Halsey," Cameron says in a dangerously low tone. "Careful, diner girl. Halsey might look innocent, but she'll backstab you without a second thought."

Halsey's expression turns murderous in a flash. I've never seen her eyes spark with so much fury before. It's damn scary, if I'm being honest.

"You know what? Fuck you, Cameron. And stay away from me." She whirls around and heads in the opposite direction.

"What's all this ruckus outside my studio?" Miss LaFleur walks out of her classroom none too happy. But when her eyes land on me, her expression softens, and desire shines in her eyes. "Finn, I didn't realize you'd be in my class this semester."

Shit. I do not want to go there again with her. Like an idiot, I let her rope me into her seduction games last year. I was vulnerable, still reeling from the accident, and easily fell into her web. Fucking her was fun in the beginning, I won't deny it. The whole illicit aspect of our relationship was thrilling, but after a while, I got tired of it. But I quickly learned that Miss LaFleur doesn't accept her students leaving her. I had to drop out of her class to escape her viper clutches.

"I'm not," I reply in a curt tone.

"Oh, that's too bad," she replies disappointedly, then switches her attention to Alexis. "And you, young lady? Are you in my class?"

"Yes, ma'am."

"What are you waiting for, then? A formal invitation?"

Alexis quickly disappears through the door, and my gaze follows her. Unfortunately, Miss LaFleur caught me staring, and judging by the slash that is her lips now, she's not happy about my interest in Alexis.

"Fuck, I need to get out of here," Cameron declares, already moving toward the exit.

I follow him, ignoring the loaded glance Miss LaFleur spares me right before she returns to her class. She'd better not try to start things again. I don't have time for psychotic cougars.

"It seems Miss LaFleur still has a thing for you, Finn," Luke says, clasping my back.

"Fuck, don't even joke about that."

"I thought you liked fucking the teacher." He laughs.

"Yeah, until she turned into a nutjob." A shiver runs down my spine. "That woman is a menace."

"You can always report her," Reid chimes in.

"Dude, can you please pretend for a second that your dad is not the town's sheriff?" Cameron retorts, obviously irritated.

"Fuck off, Cam. It's because of my connections that we get away with the stuff we do."

Cameron snorts. "Sure. Whatever you say."

"If you're going to act like a dick because you can't handle being in the same school as Halsey, find another punching bag, asshole," Reid retorts.

"Hey! Cut it out. Both of you." I step between them before things escalate.

Out in the quad, there are a few students mingling. They turn to gawk at us, reminding me that we're still the kings of this school. *Whatever.* Luke heads for a bench under the biggest tree, and the students hanging there quickly scramble. He doesn't even have to tell them to get lost. No one wants to piss off the biggest pyromaniac in town. The only person outside our group who doesn't fear him is Emily Frost, much to Luke's chagrin.

Already with a cigarette between his lips, he takes a deep drag and then looks pointedly at me. "All right, Finn. Moment of truth. What's your deal with that redheaded chick?"

I bristle in an instant. "I have no deal with her."

"Bullshit. She kicked us out of that dumpster of a diner, and instead of vowing to destroy her, you keep giving her lovesick puppy eyes. It's disturbing." Cameron twists his face in disgust.

"Why is it disturbing?" Reid asks. "She's cute, and her family is loaded."

Cameron glares at him. "Her dad owned Dennis's Diner. How is she loaded?"

"What rock have you been living under?" Luke gives

Cameron an exasperated glance. "Her grandparents are the Montgomerys."

The look of surprise on Cameron's face would have been comical if they weren't talking about Alexis. I can't let my friends know how much she's gotten under my skin. They'll never leave me alone.

A little commotion at the edge of the courtyard catches my attention. "Hey, Reid. What's your father doing here?"

He looks over his shoulder and frowns. "Hell if I know."

We haven't done anything yet to warrant Will Bennett's visit to Maverick. He's not looking for Reid though. He glances briefly in our direction, then heads straight to the entrance of the school. The headmaster meets him at the front of the building, and by their tense postures, I know something bad happened.

"What do you think that's about?" Luke asks.

"No clue." He shifts his gaze back to the street, where the sheriff's car is parked. "But I know how we can find out."

We follow him, and when we're only a few paces from his dad's vehicle, Marina Garcia steps out of the car. She's a new addition to the sheriff's precinct, green and gullible. She also has a major crush on Reid, which he exploits to the max but has no intention of following through, and not because Marina is unfuckable. Reid knows if he messes with any of his father's employees, the punishment will be harsh.

"Hey, Marina. How's it going?"

"Hi, Reid." The petite brunette blushes like a schoolgirl.

Jesus, what's the matter with all the grown women in this town? Aren't they getting any dick from guys their age?

"Do you know what brought Daddy Dearest to my school?"

"Uh, I don't think I'm supposed to disclose that information."

"Ah, come on, Marina. Whatever happens in this town never stays a secret for too long. I just want to make sure my friends and I aren't in trouble." His face splits into a radiant smile, designed to make women throw their panties at him.

She shakes her head. "Oh no. It has nothing to do with you."

"It has to do with someone in this school. Otherwise Sheriff Bennett wouldn't be here," I say.

Maybe I shouldn't have opened my piehole, because she looks even more tight lipped than before.

"Come on, Marina." Reid nudges her shoulder with his. "Did a student at Maverick misbehave? I just want to know so I can avoid the troublemaker."

She glances at us, then at the front of the school before turning her attention back to Reid. "Piper Phillips has gone missing."

"Mr. Phillips's daughter?" I ask.

"Yes. He filed a report last night when she didn't come home from soccer practice."

"Damn it. How long has she been gone?" Reid asks, all signs of levity gone from his face.

"Seventeen hours."

"That's not that long. Maybe she's with a boyfriend or something," Cameron pipes up.

Marina shakes her head. "If she has a boyfriend, her parents and closest friends know nothing about it."

I rub my face, understanding now why Mr. Phillips missed our meeting and didn't call to cancel. The guy must be a fucking mess.

"Do you have any idea what might have happened to her?" I butt in again.

"No, this is an ongoing investigation, but if you know anything that can help locate Piper, please let us know."

From not wanting to say anything to asking for our help. Damn, this chick is helpless. If that's the level of professionals working for Sheriff Bennett, they'll never find Mr. Phillips's daughter.

10

ALEXIS

I didn't see Finn or his friends throughout the rest of the day. No one paid any attention to me after I left Miss LaFleur's class. The entire student body was buzzing about Sheriff Bennett's visit to the premises. I quickly learned through the gossip in the hallways that a Maverick student went missing, a freshman, daughter of a faculty member.

One comment about the missing student stayed with me. They were certain Piper Phillips had run away with her boyfriend and that looking for her was a waste of resources. From bits of conversation that I picked up, the picture I painted about the girl was that she was wild and reckless.

I hoped it was just a case of a rebellious teen, sick of her parents, and not an actual abduction. Triton Cove is relatively safe if you don't cross into the East Side, which is ruled by the Triads, a notorious motorcycle gang. They usually don't create trouble for the rest of us. Rumors say that's all part of a deal the leader of the Triads struck with the big shots in town. The Triads supply the rich with their drugs of choice, and in exchange, Sheriff Bennett looks the other way.

Grandma is expecting me, but I promised to meet Carmen after school. She's waiting for me just across from the diner, which is still closed, much to my annoyance.

Carmen lifts her gaze from her phone when she spots my brand-new car. It's a convertible, too flashy for my taste. I could have asked for a different car, but I foresee many battles in my future, and I have to choose them wisely. At the end of the day, it's just a car, and it gets me from *A* to *B*.

"My, my. Look at you. One week living with your grandparents and you already look like you're one of them."

I want to believe she's just teasing me, but I detect a hint of reproach in her tone. I choose to ignore it. The last thing I want is to argue with my best friend. My world is already in the dumpster; I can't handle losing another person I love.

"Shut up. I do not look like those stuck-up assholes." I park the car in front of her and wait until she gets in.

"You look good in that uniform," she says. "I'm sure if Dimitri saw you wearing that, he'd be having wet dreams for weeks."

Dimitri is the star quarterback at my old high school, and my crush during junior year. I hadn't thought about him at all since my life turned upside down. The only guy filling my headspace now is Finn Novak for reasons I can't begin to understand. I loathe what he did, what he represents. So why the hell can't I get him out of my mind?

"I couldn't care less about his reaction."

My reply has more bite than I intended, but I'm too busy glowering at the Closed sign on the diner's door to apologize for my rude remark.

"Sorry. I was just trying to lighten the mood."

"I know." I give her a tight smile.

"So, do you want to take this baby for a spin?" She pats the car's dashboard.

"I want to go home," I blurt out, not knowing until that moment that's what I wanted to do.

My grandparents have been to the house to pack my stuff, but I told them I'd like to go through Dad's things myself. They're getting ready to put the house on the market, but they haven't yet told me when that's going to happen. I think they're giving me time to sort through my shit.

"Are you sure?" Carmen asks softly.

I keep staring ahead when I answer through a choke, "Yeah. I'm sure."

Emotional numbness spreads through me during the drive to my former childhood home. I feel detached from my body as I take in the familiar streets. Carmen remains silent by my side, knowing inane chatter won't help me now.

When I finally pull into the driveway, the numbness has turned my body into stone. I can't move as I stare at the modest house with its faded yellow paint and shutters that have seen better days. It hasn't rained in over a week, and our little garden is as good as dead.

"We don't need to do this today, Lexi," Carmen breaks the silence after a while.

"Yes, we do." I open the door and get out of the car.

Dried leaves and dust have collected on the front porch, plus the pile of old newspapers. I guess my grandparents didn't take care of everything after all. I kick them aside in order to open the screen door. Carmen holds it for me while I unlock the dead bolt.

Inside, the smell of staleness hits me hard. It's been scorching hot in the past week, and it's clear that no one has been here recently. I bet when Grandma came to pack my clothes, she brought help and didn't stay long. She didn't even bother opening the windows to let fresh air in. She did cover some of the furniture with sheets though, making the place look like a haunted house.

I open the fridge, expecting to find food rotting inside, but it's completely empty. Checking the cabinets, I notice all the food is gone, but our plates and glasses are still there.

"What do you want to do first?" Carmen asks.

"Sort out Dad's room."

Each step I take down the corridor toward the master bedroom feels like a milestone. My heart is beating loud and fast, but also constricted. The door is closed, which only serves to work against my nerves more.

Inside, I find the room immaculate, spanking clean. My father was never a tidy person, and we couldn't afford a cleaning lady. If the room is organized like this, then it means my grandmother hired someone to straighten everything up.

I head for the closet, afraid she's already packed his clothes even though I asked her not to. But everything is there, untouched. The faint smell of my father's cologne still clings to everything. I didn't brace for it, and it hits me like a cannonball. A huge sob bubbles up my throat, and I have to bite the inside of my cheek to distract myself from the hollow pain in my chest.

"Lexi, are you okay?"

I nod. "Yeah. I just need a minute."

"Maybe we should start packing his office."

"No. I can do this. There should be large plastic bags under the kitchen sink. Do you mind grabbing them for me?"

"What do you need them for?"

"For the clothes. I'm donating everything."

"Are you sure?"

I look over my shoulder. "What am I supposed to do with all this? I can't wear any of these clothes. Besides, it's what Dad would have wanted."

"Maybe some of the guys at the diner want to keep something."

Shit. I hadn't thought about that.

"They can go through the bags. I just want everything packed away."

"Okay."

WITH CARMEN'S HELP, we emptied out my father's closet and dresser in less than two hours. When it came to knickknacks and mementos, I didn't allow my eyes to linger on anything for too long. Carmen collected the picture frames and photo albums without being prompted, and I'll be forever grateful for that.

We're now working through his office, which requires more of my attention. Some of the documents pertaining to his personal finances and the diner.

"What do you want to do with the papers in the filing cabinet?" Carmen asks.

"We should probably put them in boxes and bring them with us. I'll sort through them later."

She looks around, probably searching for the boxes.

"I believe there are some in the garage. I'll go get them."

Like everyone in this neighborhood, our garage was mostly used as a storage space. Anything we didn't need in the house, such as old furniture and seasonal decorations, is crammed in here. And now with Dad's old truck parked inside, it's almost impossible to get to anything. For a fleeting moment, I consider using his truck instead of the convertible my grandparents gave me, but I scratch that idea fast. If I can't handle staring too long at his personal belongings, how am I going to drive his truck? No, it's best if I sell it. The only thing I want from him is the diner. Even this house can go. It's just a glaring reminder of what I've lost.

I locate the empty boxes I need, but they're stuck behind

large plastic bins that are filled to the brim, judging by the difficulty I have pushing them out of the way. I lift the one on top of the stack, but the side handle breaks, and down it goes. Its lid pops open, and all the junk inside spills out: a collection of old broken toys, drawings I did eons ago, and a stack of letters held together by a thick elastic band.

They're odd among my childhood mementos, which is why I pick them up first. They're all addressed to Mom from Damian Walker. I don't know who he is, but judging by the last name, he must be a relative.

My heart begins to beat faster as a myriad of questions bounces around my head like a racquetball. *Who is he exactly? Why did he write to Mom and not Dad?*

But what makes me ignore the mess at my feet and forget what I came here for is something else. The address these letters came from is what's making me nervous. They're from Encina State Prison.

Carmen suddenly opens the garage door, startling me.

"Lexi, did you find the boxes?"

I tuck the stack of letters under my skirt's waistband, keeping them hidden underneath my jacket. "Yeah."

"What's the matter? You look like you've seen a ghost."

She has no idea how close to the truth that statement is.

"Nothing, nothing at all," I lie.

11

FINN

I barely see where I'm going as I drive from Maverick to my house. My body knows what to do, when to brake or shift gears. My mind is far away though, trapped in an endless loop of aggravation and obsession. And Alexis fucking Walker is in the middle of it all. I don't know how to extract her from my mind, and this whole deal is doing my head in.

After classes were over, I had swimming practice, but I couldn't find peace there either. My father hasn't been able to take that away from me yet, only the possibility of me competing professionally. The endless chatter about Piper Phillips's disappearance followed me into the pool area. After listening to the gossip for hours after Sheriff Bennett showed up, I was sick of it. It'd take a day or two until people found juicier news though.

My mood is shit, but when I see whose car is parked in front of my parents' house, my ill disposition takes a nosedive into a dumpster. Grandpa is here. *Fucking fantastic.* That means there's no chance I can escape into my room and avoid dinner with the family.

I walk on my tiptoes, trying to go upstairs without anyone seeing me, but my father and his old man are in the sitting room, having their predinner drinks, and spot me right away.

"Finn, where the hell have you been?" my father asks.

"Where do you think?" I point at my school uniform.

His lips curl into a sneer. "You'd better not be wasting your time in that pool, boy."

"I'm still on the swim team."

"Leave the boy alone, Florian." Grandpa stands and walks over.

My entire body goes rigid as repulsion takes control of it. One would think that after a year, I'd learn how to better rein in my reaction when I'm around him.

He claps me on the shoulder, smiling from ear to ear. "You're filling out nicely, Finn. Have you been working out?"

"No more than usual."

Grandpa flexes his arm, showing off his muscles. "Not bad for an old fart, huh?"

A year ago, I'd have rolled my eyes and laughed with him. He was my favorite person in the family. The blindfold has been removed though, and with it came the realization that this family is rotten to the very core, and I'm not immune to the disease that runs through my veins.

"Sure."

"Finn, darling. You're home," Mom says from the other side of the wide entry foyer.

She has a martini glass in her hand, and judging by her unfocused eyes, that's not her first one. There's a smile on her face, but now that I know the truth, I can catch the uneasiness in it. I'm surprised all she does to mask her pain is drink herself into a stupor. She's hidden it well all these years though. I never suspected a thing, but again, when did I ever pay any attention to anyone besides me?

"Hi, Mom. Sorry I'm late."

She waves her hand dismissively. "You arrived just in time. Dinner is served."

"It's not even six o'clock yet," Dad retorts, earning an annoyed glance from Mom.

"I'm hungry now," she snaps. "You're more than welcome to eat later."

She turns on her heels and strides toward the dining room. I'm surprised she doesn't lose her balance. I follow her closely, wondering if I can sneak a drink in me as well. I glance at the bar cart that only has the ingredients to make what she's drinking, nothing else. The vodka bottle is already below the half mark, and I bet anything she just opened it today.

Dad and Grandpa shuffle into the room, killing my chances of sneaking into the kitchen to procure booze for myself. Last year, my father would let me drink without batting an eyelash. The accident changed everything, even though I had been stone-cold sober when it happened.

Our private chef walks in and announces what's on the menu. I doubt anyone is listening. A server I don't recognize pours the drinks—water only for me. He brought Mom another martini, which prompts my father to glower disapprovingly. He doesn't make a comment to her though, which means he's going to take his frustration out on me.

No sooner does the server return to his corner in the room than Dad turns to me. "You're coming to the office tomorrow after school."

"I got your assistant's email."

"What is it exactly you'll have Finn do at the office, son?" Grandpa asks.

"Teach him how to be a man."

Grandpa rolls his eyes. "So fucking dramatic. He's a senior in high school. He should be enjoying his time, not being trapped in a stuffy office. There'll be plenty of time for him to become a man."

"It's because he was enjoying his time a little too much that I had to pay the Danes family six million dollars to keep Finn out of jail."

"I never asked you to do that," I retort.

Dad's eyes flash with anger. "Oh yeah, I forgot. You wanted to do time in prison. Bold words for a kid who knows nothing of the world. But don't worry, Finn. You'll get your punishment since you're so eager to suffer."

I clench my jaw so hard that my teeth grind together. No punishment will ever be enough to lessen the guilt I carry with me. Peter Danes will never walk again. I've ruined his life forever.

"For fuck's sake. Stop being such a stingy fuck. Six million dollars is pocket change for us." Grandpa gulps down the rest of his whiskey and then signals the server for a new one.

"So getting Eric Danes a scholarship at Maverick Prep is part of my sentence, then?"

Dad's eyes narrow. "Who the fuck is Eric Danes?"

Florian Novak is a manipulative prick, but if he was responsible for Eric's presence at Maverick, he'd be gloating about it. That means Eric lied. It didn't even occur to me that he could now afford to attend Maverick thanks to the settlement money.

Hell. I can't believe how easily I let him get under my skin. If he only knew he didn't have to bother with the deception. Just looking at his face does enough damage.

Two servers come into the room with the starters, giving us a small reprieve from this painful conversation. From the corner of my eye, I catch Mom getting a new drink. That's the third she's downed in my presence. Who knows what her total tally is?

I stare at the fancy salad plate in front of me but make no motion to touch it. My appetite has left the building.

"How was your first day back at school, honey?" Mom asks, pulling me back from my thoughts.

"Darker than most days."

"What kind of nonsense is that?" Grandpa asks. "Are you turning into one of those emo kids now, Finn?"

I glower at him. "No. I misspoke. I said darker when I should really have described the day as more fucked up than most days."

"Watch your tone, Finn," Dad reproaches in a tone meant to put the fear of God in me.

"Why was it a bad day, dear?" Mom chimes in again.

"We found out a student has gone missing. Piper Phillips."

Mom frowns. "Isn't that Paul Phillips's daughter?"

I'm taken aback that she knows who my counselor is. It isn't like she takes an interest in my academic development; all her questions about school are superficial.

"Yes."

"Any reason to suspect her disappearance was foul play?" Grandpa asks.

His expression is now blank, devoid of any mirth.

"We don't know yet. Wild rumors were circulating in the hallways today. The most popular one was that Piper ran away with her boyfriend."

"She was such a responsible kid. I find that highly unlikely," Mom replies.

"How the hell do you know so much about the girl, Marissa?" Dad asks, echoing the same question that crossed my mind.

A glint of guilt shines in her eyes, but soon the drunken haze returns to her blue eyes. "Piper has volunteered at many of my charity events. I hope Sheriff Bennett isn't really listening to those bullshit rumors. If she's gone missing, it wasn't by choice."

"It's sweet that you worry, Marissa, but kids nowadays hide more dark secrets in their closets than you can possibly imagine," Grandpa replies, his tone somber now.

Once upon a time, I'd believe his change in demeanor was because he cared. Now his serious expression points to a much more sinister motive.

"I'm sure the girl is fine. She'll probably turn up in a couple of days when her money runs out," Dad retorts dismissively. "I heard Richard Montgomery's granddaughter has enrolled at Maverick. Now *that's* a more interesting topic."

Fuck. He had to go and mention Alexis.

"Why?" I ask.

Dad wipes his mouth and then calmly places his napkin on his lap again. "Do you know her?"

"She's in one of my classes."

"I want you to get closer to her, Finn." He gives me a loaded glance, and for the life of me, I can't decipher what it means.

"She hates my guts."

Dad flattens his lips in response. "I suggest you change that fast."

"Why do you care if I'm friends with Alexis? She's nothing, just the daughter of a lowly diner owner."

I know she's more than that, but I can't help but antagonize my father.

"I don't give a rat's ass about the girl or who her father was. If you had shown any interest in the family business, you'd know associating with the Montgomerys is a smart move."

"So you want me to become friends with her to get close to her grandfather? Is that it?"

His eyes gleam with predatorial calculation. "Sure, let's start with friendship. That's your first assignment working for me, Finn. Whatever you did to that girl to make her hate you, you'd better fix it quickly."

12

ALEXIS

"*H*ow was your first day of school?" Grandma asks me the moment I step foot inside the house.

Standing at the top of the stairs, I suspect she was on the lookout, waiting for me to come home. Maybe she suspected I'd make a dash to my bedroom and she wouldn't be able to grill me until dinnertime. She guessed correctly.

"Fine."

"Did you make any new friends?" She descends the final steps.

"No."

Technically, not a lie. Just because one student showed me a secret shortcut doesn't mean we're friends.

"No? How is that possible?" She looks genuinely surprised.

"I don't know, Grandma. Everyone seemed more interested in hanging out with their old friends or focusing on academics. It's fine. I wasn't in the mood to be social anyway."

"Well, you certainly took your time coming home. I know classes finished hours ago. Where did you go? I texted you."

Irritation makes me see red, and I blurt out the first thing that crosses my mind. "Is this what living with you will be like?"

She steps back, frowning as if my question doesn't make sense. "I beg your pardon?"

"Are you going to be constantly monitoring the time I come home, how often I speak on the phone?"

"Of course not. But I expect you to let me know if you'll be late so I don't worry. Is a little bit of consideration too much to ask? I heard about what happened to Piper Philips."

I didn't even contemplate the possibility that she would know about the missing student. Does it make me a horrible person that Piper's disappearance was nothing but a blip on my radar today?

Guilt vanquishes my anger. I don't even know why I snapped at Grandma like that.

I drop my defiant chin a fraction. "No, it's not too much to ask. I went by the house today and went through Dad's things. I'm sorry I didn't tell you I wasn't coming straight home. I'm not used to having anyone check on me like that."

"Yes, your father was a little bit too carefree about your upbringing. Well, at least you didn't turn into a deranged kid or get knocked up."

Blush creeps up to my cheeks. "Grandma!"

"You're blushing. Does speaking about intercourse make you embarrassed?"

"If you keep calling sex intercourse, yeah."

Oh my god. I can't believe I'm having this conversation with Grandma in the middle of her entry foyer. What a one-eighty in topic.

She's watching me through slits now. "Do we need to have a conversation about the birds and the bees?"

My jaw drops to the floor. "No, we do not."

"Are you being careful?"

I shake my head as I walk around her. "I'm not talking about this with you."

"Where do you think you're going? Dinner will be served in half an hour."

"I want to change. I'll be down soon."

Mercifully, she doesn't follow me. Of all the things Grandma could surprise me with, Sex Ed wasn't what I imagined. Little does she know she has nothing to fear. My V-card is still intact, and I have no desire to change that anytime soon. All the boys I dated in high school weren't special enough to make me want to have sex with them. Well, save for Dimitri, but he never even glanced my way.

I could have just done it to get it over with like Carmen suggested, but I was never one to do things just because everyone else was.

Immediately, the image of Finn stepping out of the pool in all his glistening glory comes to the forefront of my mind. Heat spreads through my cheeks and other parts of my body, making me mortified even though there's no one around to witness my reaction.

I lied to him when he asked why I was staring at him. Of course I knew the reason. He looked like Triton himself coming out of the ocean, all wet and wearing nothing but a Speedo. I shouldn't notice anything about him besides his arrogance, but the problem is Finn seems to be more than a spoiled rich guy. I still don't know what he was doing at the cemetery on the day of Dad's funeral, for instance.

Before he entered my mind, I had every intention of taking my time, but now I can't be alone with my thoughts. I pull the stack of letters from my purse and stare at them until Damian Walker's address is imprinted on my retinas. What secrets will be revealed inside these envelopes? A quick online search will tell me his link to Dad and why he's in prison, but I'm too chicken to do that right before I have to pretend to be fine in front of my grandparents. I hide the letters in one of my dresser drawers, then quickly change out of my school uniform.

Once downstairs, I find Grandpa and Grandma having a cocktail in one of their many lavish rooms.

"Ah, Lexi. There you are," Grandpa greets me with a smile. "Lillian told me you went by your dad's house and packed his things. I have to say, I'm proud of you for doing that so soon."

I shrug. "Avoiding it wouldn't make the task any easier. I shoved everything into garbage bags and asked Carmen to deal with the donations. Maybe some of the guys from the diner want something."

"And Carmen is?"

"My best friend."

"Oh, then we should invite her to come over soon," he says cheerfully, making me suspect I've walked into a trap.

"Would you like something to drink, Lexi?" Grandma asks me. "Water, juice, soda perhaps?"

"No, thanks." I narrow my eyes. "What's going on here? Why are you being so nice?"

Grandpa turns to his wife. "You tell her, dear."

"Oh fine. It just occurred to me that your eighteenth birthday is approaching. With the whirlwind of recent events, I didn't realize it was so close."

God. My eighteenth birthday. Even I forgot it's coming in two weeks. That's a date I've been looking forward to for years, but now I couldn't give a rat's ass about it.

"It happens." I shrug.

"Turning eighteen is a big deal, Lexi. We can't let the date go by without a celebration."

"I don't want a party, Grandma."

Her smile wilts. "Honey, I understand your hesitance in celebrating your birthday considering what you've lost, but I think Dennis wouldn't have wanted you to stay blue for the rest of your life."

I know he wouldn't. Hell, if his ghost could manifest in front of me right now, he'd be telling me to party like a rock star. He always used to say, "Live each day as if it were your last, because tomorrow is not guaranteed." If only I had known how little time I'd have with him, maybe I'd have appreciated him more.

"What do you have in mind?" I ask.

"A black-tie party sounds appropriate. We need to get you a dress as soon as possible. I'll call Mirella LaRusso. She dresses all the top celebrities in LA."

"Wow, a black-tie event. I don't think I've ever been to one. Are you sure it isn't too much?"

"You're our only granddaughter, Alexis. Of course it isn't too much."

"Can I invite all my friends from my old high school?"

Grandma frowns. "Well, if that's what you want. But sometimes our world can be a little intimidating for people outside our circle. Think about that. However, we're definitely inviting all your classmates from Maverick Prep."

My stomach tightens. Most of those people don't even know I exist, and those who do want to see me gone. I'm not sure why I'm not opposing this idea on the spot. The original plan I had for my birthday was far less sophisticated. Maybe it's because Grandma is genuinely excited about planning the party.

Or maybe I'm looking forward to seeing a certain arrogant person outside of school.

I don't know why I can't get him out of my head. Nothing has changed. He's still the guy who crashed into a store and hurt a kid. He's still the one who walks as if he's the king of the world. Just because he seems to have more facets to his persona doesn't warrant my unhealthy obsession.

Am I that desperate for a distraction from the darkness swirling in my chest? Is Finn my new coping mechanism?

"Can I veto the list of who gets invited?" I ask.

"Well, it depends, dear. Is there anyone you wouldn't want to invite?" Grandma asks.

"There are two girls in my class who have been horrible to me. I don't know their last names, though. I don't want them at my birthday party."

"Consider it done. If they've been horrible to you, they're not on the list," Grandpa replies, resolute.

"Absolutely," Grandma agrees. "Please find out their last names so I don't invite them by accident."

"Will do."

I smile, thinking about Tiffany's and Jackie's reaction when they're the only ones not invited. Is it petty? Sure. And the old me would rather wipe off their arrogant smirks with my fists. But I live in a different world now, whether I like it or not. And on the golden side of Triton Cove, being blacklisted from a Montgomery party is a much better retaliation.

13

FINN

*L*uke finds me just as I'm about to enter the chemistry lab. As is his usual greeting, he invades my personal space by throwing his arm over my shoulder.

"Good morning, Finn," he says overenthusiastically.

"You're awfully chipper. How many cups of coffee have you had already?"

"Eh, no clue."

I push him off me. "Well, pipe down a little. Some of us are still not fully awake yet."

He sticks his tongue out. "Damn it, Finn. You're really taking this brooding business to the next level."

I pinch the bridge of my nose. "My grandfather came to dinner last night."

Luke gives me a droll look, reminding me he doesn't know why that asshole's visit would put me in a funk.

"Is he also giving you a hard time about being an irresponsible son of a bitch? I thought he was the fun one."

"Yeah, Grandpa is still the same goofball as always, getting on my father's nerves. Since he can't argue with his old man, I end up paying for it."

The half lie feels bitter on my tongue. I enter the classroom, avoiding eye contact with my best friend. I freeze when I see Alexis is also in this class. She's sitting alone at a table far back, distracted as she gazes out the window.

"What are you looking at?" He follows my eyes. "Ah, diner girl. What's your deal with her anyway?"

"Fuck if I know."

She glances in our direction, and her body tenses. I look away first and head to a random table in the middle of the room. Luke takes the seat next to mine and immediately begins bouncing his legs up and down in fidgety motions.

"Dude, will you quit? You're making *me* anxious."

"I can't stop it."

I look at him closely. "This isn't only caused by caffeine, is it?"

He clenches his jaw tight and keeps looking ahead. "I'm fine, Finn. Stop looking for things that aren't there."

I snort, shaking my head. "You're lying." Luke shoots up from his chair, startling me. "Where the hell are you going?"

"I'm not in the mood to be called a liar by someone who's been lying to me for over a year."

He heads to the back of the class and, to my dismay, takes the empty seat next to Alexis. She seems as surprised about this new development as I am. She then looks around, no doubt trying to find another empty chair. But the class has filled out, and the only chair available is the one Luke just vacated. I try not to feel anything when she comes to that realization and her shoulders sag forward. She'd rather sit next to Luke than me.

The last student comes running through the door just as the

teacher was getting set up to start the lecture. *Hell and damn*. It's Halsey.

Her face falls when she sees that the only seat available is next to mine. Yippee. It seems I'm the stinky kid who no one wants as a neighbor. It's not like I want to sit next to her either.

She slides into the chair, ignoring me. She hasn't done anything to me personally, but she hurt Cameron so badly, he doesn't allow us to speak her name out loud in front of him.

"Good morning, everyone," the teacher says. "Welcome to the chemistry lab. My name is Mr. Kaufman."

He proceeds to bore us with his background—he's new to the school—and what we can expect to learn this semester. It's easy to let my mind wander far away from here. Well, perhaps not that far away when the girl occupying my thoughts is just a few desks behind me. I only snap back to the here and now when I hear Halsey curse softly under her breath.

"What?" I ask, forgetting for a moment I was supposed to pretend she doesn't exist.

"Are you deaf? You're my lab partner," she grits out.

"Bullshit," I say out loud.

"Excuse me?" The teacher's eyebrows furrow.

"Why is Halsey my partner? Isn't it supposed to be our choice?"

"Not in my class. Your partner is the one you're sitting next to."

"Can we change partners?" Halsey asks.

Mr. Kaufman removes his thick-rimmed glasses in an overdramatic fashion that I'm sure he's practiced in front of the mirror to get the effect just right.

"If I allow one person to change partners, then everyone would want that, and it'd be chaos. I'm sure you and Mr. Finn Novak will work out just fine."

Seething, I glance over my shoulder. Luke is smiling smugly, and when he sees me glowering, his grin becomes wider.

Motherfucker. He knows Cameron is going to blow when he finds out I have to work with Halsey. But the truth is that's not why I'm pissed at him at the moment. He'll be working closely with Alexis, and I want to be in his place.

***

ALEXIS

"You've got to be kidding me," I blurt out, not caring if the blondie next to me hears it.

"Ah, darling. Are you upset you're stuck with me for the rest of the semester?" he asks through his laughter.

I turn to him. "Listen, I take schoolwork seriously."

"And are you saying I don't?" He arches his eyebrows.

I almost reply that I don't think he does, but I don't know him well enough to make that statement.

"That's not what I'm saying at all. I'm just letting you know how I view academics."

He leans forward, getting so close that I can detect the cigarette smell under his minty breath. "I have the highest GPA in school. Ask around if you don't believe me."

I doubt he's lying about that. It'd be too easy to find out the truth. I'm glad now that I didn't make an ass out of myself by slinging assumptions his way.

"That's great. I guess I lucked out, then."

"Be straight with me, Alexis. You got your panties twisted in a bunch because Finn is my best friend, and for whatever reason, you have an issue with him."

I narrow my eyes, debating whether I should tell him why I don't like his bestie. But in the end, I decide to keep my mouth shut. I don't owe anyone here an explanation.

"My panties are fine, thanks." I face forward, purposely trying to not look in Finn's direction.

"If it makes you feel any better, Finn is more upset about this turn of events than you."

Clenching my jaw, I try my best to not take his bait, but hell, I'm too curious for my own good.

"Fine, I'll bite. Why is that?"

"For two reasons. One, he's stuck with Halsey, which means he'll have to deal with Cameron's wrath. And two, he hates me now that I'll get to know you better than he ever will."

"Whoa. Hold your horses there, bucko. We're lab partners. There will be no getting to know each other better."

"We'll see. A lot can be learned by pure observation only." He smiles wickedly, getting on my nerves.

"Whatever."

"What's the matter, sugar? Are you afraid I'll discover all your dark secrets?"

My spine goes rigid, which I'm sure blondie notices. "I have nothing to hide."

"Darling, in this town, everyone has something to hide, even a Miss Perfect like yourself."

I snort to hide my discomfort. "I don't know where you get the notion that I'm perfect. In case you forgot, I'm diner girl."

"So what? You didn't grow up surrounded by riches, but that doesn't make you less perfect. I've heard about you, always slaving away in that diner, helping Daddy Dearest."

I curl my fingers tighter around my pencil. "Shut up. You know nothing about me. *Nothing*."

The teacher clears his throat and looks pointedly at us. Finn turns to glare at us as well, and this time I hold his stare. I almost ask him what he's looking at, but that would only draw more unnecessary attention to me. It's already bad enough that I'm saddled with blondie here, who looks like he just won the jackpot. I'll have to watch my back around him.

14

ALEXIS

*A*s soon as the chemistry lab is over, I jump out of my chair and head out. Luke—that's blondie's name—proved to be as annoying as I expected. Plus, the guy couldn't stop bouncing his legs up and down, and it became distracting. At least he didn't lie about being a good student. He knows his stuff, which will make our partnership more bearable.

I'm already in the hallway when Halsey calls my name. "Alexis, wait."

"Hey."

"Where are you going in such a hurry?"

"I couldn't take another minute next to my lab partner. He's insufferable."

"Do you want to trade?"

"Why? You don't like Finn either?"

"I don't have any issues with him. He's the one who has a problem with me."

"Why?"

Her expression darkens. "It's a long story. I'll tell you one day."

Shit. Are they exes? Somehow, the idea gives me a flash of retroactive jealousy.

I must be going insane. That's the only explanation. I do not have a crush on him, no matter how attractive I find him. He put Eric's little brother in a wheelchair. I have to keep reminding myself of that.

"Did you date?" The question rolls off my tongue before I can stop myself.

"Me and Finn? Oh God no." I stare at her for a moment too long, and she notices it. "Why do you ask? Are you interested in him?"

Blush spreads through my cheeks, forcing me to look away to hide my reaction. "Hell no."

"Hmm. He's nice to look at, but my advice is to stay away from him and all his friends."

"Because they're all assholes?"

"I don't think they're worse than the rest of the people who go here. But they're poison."

"Poison? If you don't want me to believe they're bad to the bone, then that's the wrong choice of word."

She shakes her head. "What did I say yesterday? Word vomit is my disease. What I meant to say was disaster follows them everywhere, and usually the people near them tend to get hit by the debris."

"I'll keep that in mind, but I don't think I'm in any danger of getting close to them, unless I have to for school."

"What class do you have next?"

"Spanish. I need to switch my books. That's my locker over there." I point ahead.

The icy blonde who told the English teacher to leave me alone yesterday is coming toward us. She doesn't stop or say hello, but when she walks past me, she says, "I'd be careful when you open your locker."

"Why?" I turn to look over my shoulder since she keeps on walking.

I get no answer from her, which pisses me off. Where does she get off saying shit like that without giving more information? Unless it wasn't advice.

"That was odd," Halsey says.

"Yeah, for real. Do you know that girl?"

"Not really. She didn't hang out in my circle before I moved to Europe."

"Well, I still need to switch my books. Let's find out what kind of nasty surprise awaits me."

A foul stench reaches my nose as I stand near my locker. Someone definitely messed with it.

"What's that god-awful smell?" Halsey asks.

Bracing myself for the worst, I open the locker. Rotten garbage spills out, and the stench is so awful, it almost makes me gag. All my books are ruined.

People either laugh or make disgusted sounds. The humiliation makes me see red, and my eyes sting.

"Who's trash now?" Tiffany asks, and then she laughs with her friends, including the other bitch who came to the diner.

I curl my hands into fists as my entire body prepares to wipe the amusement off her face. I make a motion in her direction, but Halsey blocks my way, holding my arms.

"Don't do it, Lexi. The school has zero tolerance for violence. If you punch Tiffany, you'll be expelled, and that's what she wants."

My head is buzzing with violent thoughts. I'm shaking with anger unleashed, which feeds the monster. I sense the darkness forming, growing larger and out of control. But I can't let that happen, not here. I dig my nails into my palms until they break skin. The little bit of pain is enough this time to make me regain some of my control.

"I'm okay. I won't kill the bitch right this second. You can let go of me."

Halsey stares at me for a couple of beats before releasing me.

"What are you going to do?"

"Right now? I'm going to Spanish class." I lift my chin and stare at Tiffany with a promise of retaliation.

When I turn, I find Finn and Luke in the crowd. Luke is amused by the spectacle, but Finn looks as angry as me as he stares in Tiffany's direction.

Fine. He isn't a total asshole, but that means nothing. Maybe he just dislikes his friend's bullying methods.

I keep going without looking back, but to say I'm calmer would be a lie. I'm still shaking thanks to the suppressed aggression.

I'm glad Halsey stopped me from making a mistake. If I get expelled from Maverick, there's no chance I'd keep the diner. I have to remember that the next time the urge to maim that bitch hits me again. If her game is to get rid of me, she won't stop at locker vandalism.

The Spanish classroom is still empty, so I get my choice of seat. I head to the back to avoid the stares. Since there's no one here, I text Carmen, telling her what Tiffany did. Maverick has a strict policy of no cell phones in class, but that's not the case at my old high school. Carmen replies quickly, telling me in detail what she plans to do to Tiffany if she ever crosses her path. The visual brings a smile to my face.

"You seem awfully happy for someone who just had her locker trashed," Finn says from the desk next to mine.

"What are you doing here?" I ask, startled.

Hell, how did I not hear when he came in?

"It seems we have Spanish class together too. Fate must have plans for us," he says with a stony face, leaving me floundering to decipher if he's being sarcastic or not.

"Right. Was it fate that sent you to my father's funeral?"

He clenches his jaw but doesn't look away. "In a way, yes."

"What is that supposed to mean?"

He avoids my gaze and stares at the front of the class. More students have come into the room, and they're now paying close attention to us. If I'm not careful, soon there will be rumors flying around that there's something going on between Finn and me. I don't want to have any association with him, even if it's made up by gossipy tongues.

"Nothing. Forget I said anything," he replies.

Jackie enters the room, and immediately her dark gaze settles on us. With a perverse smile on her red-tinted lips, she makes a beeline in our direction. A Louis Vuitton handbag is draped over her arm, and her school jacket is adorned with expensive-looking brooches. If Maverick Prep were a person, she'd be it.

"Finn, what are you doing sitting next to her? I thought your community service days were over."

"Oh, I'm done with that, but apparently I like doing charity work, which is the reason I've tolerated your presence until now."

Her fake smile disappears in the blink of an eye. "Excuse me?"

"I realize now it was wasted," he continues as if she hadn't spoken. "Run along, Jackie. I'm sick of looking at your plastic face."

Her mouth makes a perfect O, giving her a comical look of outrage. I smirk even though it was Finn who delivered the punch.

"You're taking her side after she tried to kick us out of her disgusting diner?" Her voice rises.

Finn leans back in his chair, lacing his fingers behind his

head. "Taking her side?" He snorts. "Oh no, honey. I don't give a shit about either of you, but you're the one who's standing there thinking you're a queen, when in fact you're nothing but a pawn."

His remark about me pisses me off, and even if I try to justify that I'm angry because he put me in the same boat with Jackie, the sting goes beyond that. I shouldn't care that he doesn't give a shit about me, but my ego does.

"Hola, buenos días, clase. Soy Guzmán Redondo, su profesor de español."

Jackie's nostrils flare as she attempts to rein in her rage. I know the look well. I've stared at it in the mirror more times than I care to count.

"Señorita Wen, tome asiento, por favor," the teacher continues.

"This isn't over, Finn."

Jackie whirls around and takes a seat as far away from us as possible. Finn seems unfazed by her last comment. I'm sure threats like those are slung around in this school too many times for anyone to care.

But maybe he *should* worry. I know the glint of crazy in someone's eyes when I see it, and Jackie Wen definitely had that.

15

FINN

*A*lexis stays in her bubble for part of the class, and I stay in mine. I've already said too many things I shouldn't, so it's in my best interest to keep my cakehole shut. All changes when *el profesor* decides to pair us up for an assignment.

She raises her hand to draw his attention.

"Tienes una pregunta, Señorita Walker?"

"Sí, me gustaría cambiar de socios."

I turn to her. "Really? I'm beginning to think I've done something to you personally."

"You exist. That's plenty," she replies without making eye contact.

She truly hates me, which should be enough to make me forget about my little obsession if I wasn't a sick fuck. The more she tries to push me away or throw insults at me, the more I want to get closer to her. My father's request is at the back of my mind too. Going against him this time seems foolish when the assignment is so appealing to me.

"Lo siento, pero no cambios. Estoy seguro de que una vez que conozca mejor al Señor Novak, verá que no lo encontrará tan mal."

"What did he say?" a student two desks ahead asks his friend.

"He said I'm not that bad once you get to know me," I reply and then flash Alexis a deranged smile designed to get on her nerves.

She narrows her eyes, and I can almost hear all the insults she's thinking but can't say out loud.

"Quit looking so smug," she grits out.

"Are you coming here, or should I come to you?"

She stands and pushes her desk closer to mine as loudly as possible. The teacher frowns in our direction but doesn't say a word.

"I guess that answers that."

"Please don't talk to me outside the scope of this project." She opens a new Word document on her laptop and titles it "Una entrevista con un gilipollas."

I whistle. "Wow, you're really taking this grudge thing to extremes. One would think you're using your hate to mask other feelings."

She whips her face to mine, glowering. "You're delusional if you think I have any other feelings for you besides contempt."

"I could hate you too, you know. You humiliated me in front of strangers, reminded me that I'm a piece of shit who doesn't deserve to be breathing."

I had no intention of speaking the truth like that. I prefer the guilt I carry to be an invisible cross. My remark doesn't fall on deaf ears though. Alexis seems surprised by my outburst, losing a bit of her prickly edges.

She deletes the "asshole" from her title and types my name instead.

"Let's just try to go through this assignment as quickly as possible. There's no reason we can't get it done before this class is over."

My phone vibrates in my pocket, and since it's connected to my laptop, the message I just received also flashes on my screen. It's an invitation from Luke to the semester bash at his house this weekend. The bastard went ahead and planned the whole thing without telling anyone. That means he's up to no good. I notice Alexis quickly closing the message window from her laptop too.

"Let me guess. You also got an invitation to Luke's party?"

"Were you snooping?"

"God, are you always cagey like that?"

She lets out a frustrated sigh. "Yeah, I was invited. I don't know how he got my number, though. I didn't give it to him."

"There's no personal information that Luke can't get his hands on."

Her forehead crinkles. "Why? Is he a hacker?"

I shrug. "Sorry, honey. We aren't friends, and that question is beyond the scope of the project."

"Is it? We're supposed to interview each other and dive deep. I think you being best friends with a criminal would give great insight about your character."

I smirk, catching on to where she's going with that. "I thought we had already established that I'm the scum of the earth."

"Do you want to know the truth?" She's watching me intensely now, and I feel exposed as if she can see through the mask.

"Sure."

"I do think you're scum, but I also believe there's more to you than that. The question is, when I peel off the first layer, will I find something worse?"

My stomach clenches painfully, and it's a chore to keep my

body relaxed. If she gets too close, she may very well discover the monster I hide is far worse than her most wicked nightmares. Yet I do want her to try to unveil all my darkest secrets. Maybe I want her to peer into my soul and run away in fear.

"I don't know, sugar," I reply in a voice that's a little too tight for comfort. "But if you want to know the real me, it will take more than asking me a few questions in class."

She swallows hard, and it's audible. "Are you daring me, Finn Novak?"

A mischievous smile appears on my face. "Take it as you like, Alexis Walker. If you want to know the real me, come to Luke's party this weekend."

"If I come, will you tell me what you were doing at the cemetery that day?"

I narrow my eyes. "Why are you so keen to know that?"

She drops her eyes to the desk and doesn't answer for a couple of beats. Then she lifts her gaze and looks at me from under her eyelashes. That's a sexy move girls like to pull when they want to get railed by me, but I don't think that's what Alexis is doing.

It works though. Suddenly, my cock is very much awake, and I want nothing more than to slam my lips over hers and claim her mouth.

"If you do your assignment right, maybe you'll get the answer to that too," she replies.

ALEXIS

FOR THE SECOND TIME TODAY, I booked it out of a classroom like the devil was after me. In this instance, it wasn't because my companion was an annoying ass. I was flirting with Finn big time. I don't know when our barbs exchange became charged with electricity, but by the end of the lecture, it felt like I was running a fever with the way my face was in flames and my body sensitive to the touch.

I run to the bathroom, needing to splash my cheeks with cold water before I combust. In my hurry, I bump into Icy Barbie.

"Watch it," she snaps at me, already moving to get out of the bathroom.

But I clasp her arm, stopping her from leaving. "Wait. How did you know to warn me about my locker?"

"I could smell the stench as I walked by it."

"Did you see who did it?"

She snorts. "No. But even if I had, I wouldn't tell. Snitches get stitches. Can I go now?"

I release her arm and step back. "Thanks for the heads-up, anyway. And for yesterday in English class."

She cocks her head to the side and watches me through slitted eyes. "Somehow, I don't think you need anyone to help you fight your battles."

"You're right about that. But I'm not myself lately, and... well, thank you. I owe you one."

"Do you really mean that?"

"Yeah. Why? Do you need a favor?"

"Actually, I do. You were invited to Luke Halle's party, right?"

"Yep. Weren't you?"

She chortles. "Oh, that prick wouldn't invite me. We don't get along, but I want to go anyway. You can bring a plus-one."

I barely looked at the invitation, and if there's a guest list, I'd probably ask Carmen to come with me. But Icy Barbie did help me twice.

"You want to crash his party? Why?"

"Reasons. So, can I be your date?"

"How well do you know Finn Novak and his circle of friends?"

"Unfortunately, too well. So, is that a yes?"

I could use more friends here. Especially ones who don't like the school kings. But hell, I'm not going to trust someone blindly like that.

"I don't even know your name," I say.

"It's Emily Frost."

Appropriate.

"All right, Emily Frost. You can be my plus-one. But I might not stay long."

"Oh, don't worry. I don't plan on lingering there either. Just long enough." She smiles devilishly, making me suspect she has ulterior motives.

"Long enough for what?"

"It's best if you don't know."

She walks out of the restroom, leaving me with the feeling that I just made a huge mistake.

16

FINN

I can't figure Alexis Walker out. One moment she glares at me as if she wishes she could kill me with a single glance. In the next, she acts like she wants me to push her against the wall and fuck her until she can't remember her own name. The words leaving her mouth are dipped in honey and covered in shards of glass. With her, I feel way out of my depth, and that's driving me crazy. I've been playing this game for a long time now, and I can't believe I'm losing the match to a rookie.

I never thought I'd be glad to be heading to my father's office today. It's a chore I had been dreading all week, but now that it's here, it's a welcome distraction from the thoughts ping-ponging in my head. I must find a way to get the upper hand with Alexis or I'll lose the war before I can begin to figure her out.

Dad's office takes up the entire top floor of the most luxurious business complex in Triton Cove. The construction company my grandfather started more than fifty years ago is responsible for most of the buildings in this town. The asshole likes to say he's the founder of Triton Cove; before him, there was nothing here but wild vegetation and sand.

The receptionist glances up from her computer screen and smiles. "Hello, Finn. Welcome to Novak Construction."

"I know where I am…." I narrow my eyes to read her name tag. "Harper."

Her smile tightens. "Of course. Your father is in a meeting, but he said you can take any open desk and get settled."

"Okay."

I walk past her desk and through the glass door into the office area. Dad has adapted to the open-floor trend, and save for his top guys and himself, no one gets an office with a door, not even managers or directors.

On purpose, I didn't tie my long hair in a ponytail, which I know will annoy him, and I'm still in my school uniform because I didn't see the point of changing into another set of stuffy clothes. I spot a vacant desk and drop my backpack there. I'm thirsty though, and I also need to use the restroom, so I continue down the corridor, passing the common restrooms, knowing there's a private one near the VP's office. Any other employee would catch shit if they used it. Dad would tell me I need to earn the perk, but he's not here, and right now, I'm pulling the one-day-this-will-be-mine card.

On the way out, threads of conversation reach me. I recognize my father's voice. He's in the VP of finance's office, and the door didn't shut all the way. On my tiptoes, I come closer and eavesdrop on their meeting.

"Florian, I told you we shouldn't have bought those lands near the reserve. It was a risk with those jackasses from Green Earth trying to make the entire area protected."

"The bill won't pass."

"I know it won't. But now construction is delayed. We can't

MICHELLE HERCULES

get our permits. If we don't break ground soon, we'll need more capital to remain afloat."

"Damn it. I had Mayor Wen in my pocket, but that cunt decided to wait until after the election to take care of things. She doesn't want to lose the support of the earth-loving hippies."

"Something has to give. Either we get her to change her mind and fast or we find new money soon."

I decide I've heard enough and return to my desk. Now my father's motives become crystal clear. Richard Montgomery is a venture capitalist, but he's smart as hell, and he wouldn't just put his money in any business. I'm sure Dad already tried to get money from him and failed. However, if I were to become more than friends with Alexis, then Richard could be compelled to invest.

Son of a bitch.

While I wait, I text Luke and tell him what Daddy Dearest wants from me. His response is several eggplant emojis, followed by droplets of water. I snort, shaking my head. Of course he'd think this is a laughing matter.

I reply swiftly.

ME: You're a dick.

LUKE: And you're a whiny pussy. Alexis is a hot piece of ass, and you're already drooling over her.

Asshole. He's not wrong, and that's the fucking problem. I don't want my father's shady dealings to get in the middle of my personal life.

Ten minutes later, Dad walks over to my desk and asks me to follow him into his office.

"Close the door, please," he tells me as he takes a seat behind his desk.

I drop into the chair facing him and blurt out, "I know the company is in trouble and why you want me to get close to Alexis."

He leans back in his chair and watches me in silence for a couple of beats. "You heard my conversation with Derek."

"Just enough to get the big picture."

He leans forward, resting his forearms on the desk. "Then you know that pissing off the mayor's daughter was a stupid move, Finn."

"How the hell do you know what I told Jackie today?"

"I got a call from the mayor. Her precious daughter came into her office in tears to complain about you."

I snort. "Crocodile tears. Jackie is a two-faced bitch. I simply put her in her place."

Dad hits the desk hard with a closed fist. "I don't care if Jackie Wen is a cunt like her mother. You will do whatever it takes to get back in her good graces again."

Flaring my nostrils, I ask, "Do you want me to fuck Jackie too?"

"You've been sticking your dick inside any pussy that opens up for you, what's one more? Do what you must to fix this. I can't risk losing the mayor's support now."

"Great. So now I'm your whore."

"Don't be so dramatic. Neither girl is unappealing. You'd fuck them for sport. All I'm asking is to do it for business."

There's no chance in hell I'm going to let my father control my dick too. But I can't be an idiot about it. If he wants me to grow up, think like a businessman, so be it.

"I can't have my cake and eat it too. Jackie hates Alexis and vice versa. If I hook up with Jackie, you bet that Alexis will find out and I'll lose any chance with her. Getting Jackie's favor is pointless anyway. You know her mother won't make a decision before the election. Her margins are too narrow. She needs the green vote."

Dad scrutinizes me for a moment. "Go on."

"You need an in with Richard Montgomery more. You want

me to date his granddaughter? Done. But I want something in return."

"Isn't saving your family from ruin enough?"

I laugh without humor. "Spare me the guilt trip. A bad business deal won't ruin us. I'm aware we have offshore accounts."

He narrows his eyes. "Let me guess, my father told you about them?"

I nod. "I want you to stop boycotting swimming."

A vein in his forehead throbs. It must be killing him that he doesn't have the upper hand.

"You're still on the team, aren't you?"

"I want you to stop prohibiting me from competing professionally."

His expression morphs into one of disgust. "Fine. I won't get in the way. But you have to deliver Richard Montgomery to me on a silver platter."

The corners of my lips twitch upward. "You have a deal."

17

ALEXIS

*T*oday there's no Grandma ambush when I come home. I'd go straight to my room, but I'm starving, so I make a pit stop in the kitchen first. My grandparents have a private chef and a maid, but no one is around. I doubt Grandma steps foot in the kitchen save for to give orders.

I find everything I need in the fridge to make a sandwich, and once that's done, I grab a bottle of water and head to the stairs. In the hallway, I hear Grandma's voice. She's in one of the rooms, speaking on the phone. I'd continue toward the stairs, but a name makes me stop in my tracks.

Damian Walker.

Grandma is talking about him, and judging by her agitated tone, she's not happy about the topic. I tiptoe toward the den, glad the hardwood floors are covered by expensive rugs and my footsteps are muffled.

The door isn't completely shut, so from outside, I can hear the conversation clearly.

"I don't care that he's out due to good behavior. We must keep him away from Lexi, Richard."

A pause, and then she continues. "Can't we get a restraining order?"

Whoa. Why would they want to do that? How dangerous is he?

"I don't care that he's her... uncle. What if he decides to talk? The truth will shatter her."

Her words hit me like a sucker punch. I stagger backward, afraid if I keep listening, I might not be able to keep from bursting into the room and demanding to know everything. It's what I should do, but self-preservation takes control. I'm already hanging by a thread; I don't want to spiral into a dark void unprepared.

I hurry back to my bedroom, locking the door for good measure. I set the sandwich and water bottle on my desk, no longer interested in them. I can't eat or drink when there's a huge knot in my belly now.

Shaking, I retrieve the stack of letters I found in Dad's garage and bring them to my bed. When I free them from the elastic band, an old photograph slips from between two envelopes. With shaking hands, I pick it up. It's my mother standing between Dad and a young man. They look so happy. I flip the picture around, and read the note scribbled in Mom's handwriting: "Dennis, Evelyn, and Damian, Olympus Bay, 2002."

I open the one on top. The postmark says it was mailed fourteen years ago.

Dear Evelyn,

. . .

I'M sorry it took so long to reply to your letter. I sat down many times and stared at a blank page, but the words simply wouldn't come. How can I put on paper what I can barely grasp or understand? There hasn't been a day I haven't thought about you, Dennis, and Alexis. I want you to know one thing though. I don't regret what I've done.

Life in prison is as bad as they say, but I don't want you to worry about me. Whenever I'm having a rough day, thinking about you, remembering the twinkle in your eyes when you smiled, makes my penance a little less impossible.

I shouldn't be writing you this. I promised Dennis I wouldn't. You're married to him now, my brother, my best friend. I may have seen you first, loved you first, but deep down I know you only ever saw him, loved him. And that's okay with me. I'll forever cherish our memories. I won't seek you out when I get out of prison. It's for the best. Maybe we'll have a chance in another lifetime.

I want you to be happy, Evelyn.

LOVE,

Damian

I SET THE LETTER DOWN, stunned. My pulse is drumming loudly in my ears, and I'm dizzy.

Damian Walker, my uncle, was in love with my mother. Maybe even had an affair with her before she got together with Dad. I wish I knew what she wrote him. Had she known before he went to jail that he was still in love with her?

I'm not sure if I can stomach reading the other letters now. What if his feelings weren't one sided? What if Mom was in love with him too? God, the idea makes me sick to my stomach. Dad loved her with all his heart.

Suddenly, I get angry. How dare Damian write a love letter to my mother? What kind of piece of shit does that to his own brother?

I jump out of bed and get my laptop out of my bag. I need to know what Damian did to send him to Encina Island.

The search yields several links. I don't need to click on any of them; the headlines of the articles are enough. Damian Walker was sent to prison for manslaughter.

I rest my head in my hands. No wonder Dad never talked about him.

I get now why Grandma was freaking out. I would be too if I were in her shoes. But why would Damian come looking for me?

The penny finally drops.

Dad is gone, and I'm the only family he has left.

Shit.

Pulling my hair back, I begin to pace. My heart is beating dangerously fast now, and it's getting harder to breathe. I'm on the verge of a panic attack, which means the darkness is surging, gaining force. My arm hasn't healed from the last time that happened, but if I don't do it, who knows where my mind will take me, what I'll do?

I'm about to rush to the bathroom when a ping from my phone gets my attention. I stop, glancing at my purse and debating what to do. In the end, I opt for the phone. Maybe it's Carmen with gossip so juicy, it'll distract me.

But it's not a message from her. It's from Finn.

Jesus Christ. Maybe fate *is* playing with us. How would he know to send me a picture of him wearing nothing but his Speedo when I so desperately needed a good distraction? I don't care about his motives, nor do I care that he's done something awful in the past. The monster inside me is craving the strange game Finn and I are playing. The hate, the longing, the push and pull.

The text accompanying his picture says it's for our Spanish project.

I smile at the half-baked excuse. He probably expects me to freak out.

Oh sweet Finn, you don't know what kind of creature you're flirting with.

I get comfortable in bed, shoving the damn letters aside. I don't want to think about them, about how my uncle is a killer. All I want to do is beat Finn at this game.

Biting my lip, I type my reply.

ME: Thanks. Full disclosure: I plan on getting off looking at that.

I press Send before I chicken out.

The three dots that appear on my screen have me holding my breath.

FINN: I call bull. You wouldn't.

ME: Are you daring me?

It takes him a while to reply. He's probably mulling over the perfect response.

FINN: Yeah, I am.

ME: Are you hard thinking about me touching myself?

FINN: What do you think?

ME: I think you're already touching yourself, wishing it was my mouth wrapped around you.

FINN: You got me. Are you doing the same?

That makes me pause. *What the hell am I doing? Sexting Finn, the guy who I'm supposed to hate with all my guts?*

The darkness has grown quiet, but I'm not safe from losing control.

Shit.

I toss my phone aside and bring my legs up, hugging my knees.

I overplayed my hand, and Finn has called my bluff. I have no choice but to let him win this round.

18

ALEXIS

TWO DAYS LATER

I don't know what I was thinking when I started sexting Finn. Like an idiot, I thought I'd rattle him. Fucking kill me. I'm a virgin with no game.

By some miracle, I managed to avoid him for the next two days. Maybe I put him off by not following through with the texts. Who tells a guy time and time again they don't like them only to turn around and try to sex them up? He must think I'm a basket case.

He wouldn't be wrong.

After the locker incident, the headmaster assigned me a new one—the trashed locker had to be completely replaced because the stench didn't go away even after being cleaned with bleach. I couldn't even bask in the idea that Tiffany had to get her hands dirty to execute her prank, because Halsey pointed out that she must have forced someone else to do the deed.

I wish I could say I'm being extra vigilant, knowing she'll try again to get me expelled, but I have other things to worry about, such as the big secret I discovered. Damian Walker, my uncle, was in love with my mother. I could only stomach reading the one letter, which was enough to make my head spin. Was she in love with him too? What about Dad? When she died, he almost did too from grief. Even the suspicion that she might have been unfaithful to him is too much to bear.

Emily finds me in the hallway while I'm lost in my head.

"What's wrong with you?" she asks.

"Dealing with some family issues."

The reply rolls out of my mouth unbidden. I don't know why I went with the truth. I don't know her.

"Ah, those. I have them to spare. We're still on for tonight, right?"

Shit. I completely forgot about the party, that's how out of it I've been the past few days. Part of me wants to bail, but if I don't go, everyone here will think it's because of what Tiffany did. Hell if I'm going to let them think I'm afraid of that bitch.

Besides, there's the Spanish assignment. Finn promised to show me the real Finn Novak there. I have to swallow my mortification and face him eventually. Plus, it would be a nice distraction from the problems whirling in my head.

"Yeah. Totally," I reply.

"Good."

Before she heads off in the opposite direction, I ask her, "What are you planning to do at the party, Emily?"

"I told you before. It's best if you don't know. Don't worry, it won't touch you."

I'm done with classes for the day, so I head out. Halfway toward the parking lot, my phone rings. It could be Grandma, and since I'm trying my best to stay on her good side, I fish the device out. It's not her, it's Carmen.

"Hey, what's up?" I say, forcing cheer into my tone.

She already knows about the letters. I couldn't keep that secret to myself. It's too big, and I needed someone to talk to.

"You sound much better today. Are you heading home now?"

"Yeah, I just got out of school. Why?"

"I have plans for us tonight, chica. You've been moping around about those letters, so I figured a good night out with the crew would cheer you up."

Crap. I never mentioned to Carmen that I was going to Luke's party because it'd be awkward to not invite her. I never planned to tell her about it, to be honest.

"That's sounds great, but I can't tonight," I say, feeling guilty as hell.

"Why not?"

"Someone from Maverick is throwing a party."

"You can't be serious. You're really going to ditch your actual friends to hang out with those phony assholes?"

"Trust me. I don't want to go, but Finn Novak is holding our Spanish assignment over my head. He wants to finish the interview at the party."

"Riiight. And you gladly agreed to that. Just tell me the truth, Lexi. You have a thing for that son of a bitch."

"I don't have a thing for him," I grit out.

"Who don't you have a thing for?" Finn whispers in my ear, making me jump out of my skin.

"What the hell! Boundaries, have you ever heard of those?" I press the phone to my chest.

He chuckles, making the corners of his blue eyes crinkle. "Sorry, Alexis. Didn't mean to startle you."

"Hello, Lexi. Are you there?" Carmen asks on the phone.

Still giving Finn the stink eye, I reply, "Yeah, I'm here. I have to go. I'll talk to you later, okay?"

"Whatever."

She ends the call, leaving me with a bad taste in my mouth. Carmen is pissed, and I have no one to blame but myself. I should have told her about Luke's party before she made plans with our old crew. Now she must think I'm switching sides and forgetting where I come from.

"Is everything okay?" Finn asks.

I shake my head. "It's fine. What did you want?"

"You've been avoiding me."

"No, I haven't. Why would you think that?"

"You've made a point of vanishing whenever we crossed paths in the hallways for the past two days."

"You think too much of yourself."

"Do I now?" He moves closer, turning up the Greek god act to the max. Even fully dressed, there's no denying that underneath all those clothes, he was built to conquer and obliterate girls' hearts.

Finn Novak is a walking wet dream, and right now I so wish that he was as ugly as I believed his heart to be.

What if he isn't though? What if when I peel off the layers, I don't find a monster?

"What do you think you're doing?" I step back, afraid of the proximity.

I'm surprised when he stops moving. He pulls back suddenly, almost as if he became aware of something.

"I just wanted to see if all those texts you sent me were the truth or simply part of a game. I have my answer now."

"If it was a game, you started it."

"True. I did send you that picture. My fault. You don't need to be afraid of me, Alexis. I'm not going to keep playing a game you're not really into."

I should be glad that he's backing down, but I'm fucking mad. I want him to push. I need him to be bad, not only to make it easier for me to keep hating him but also to keep my own darkness distracted.

"Hey, Finn. Are you coming or not?" Reid Bennett calls out from across the street.

I look in his direction, but something else catches my attention. Dad's truck parked not far from where Reid is.

What the hell?

I suck in a sharp breath, and Finn notices it.

"What's wrong?"

I don't answer because I can't find my voice. My entire body is on lockdown as I stare at the familiar truck. Then a tall figure gets out, sending my pulse skyrocketing. I've never met him before, but I memorized his face from my online search.

"Alexis, what's the fucking matter? You look as white as a ghost."

"I... I have to go."

I hurry down the rest of the steps until I'm standing a yard away from my uncle. My grandparents want to keep him away from me, as they should. He's a killer.

I could have done more research. I could have read all the letters. I didn't do any of those things because I was afraid of what it could trigger. But seeing him in the flesh is giving me courage instead of feeding the fear.

I have so many questions running through my head. *How did he get a hold of my dad's truck? What is he doing here?*

But the first thing that comes out of my mouth is, "Did you have an affair with my mother?"

FINN

I STAY ROOTED to the ground as I watch Alexis run down the steps toward the man standing in front of an old truck. He's older, probably in his late thirties. I've never seen him before in my life, but judging by the vehicle, he doesn't run in the same circles I do. It doesn't matter though. He came for Alexis, and that's stirring feelings that I shouldn't entertain.

"Yo, what the hell, man?" Reid walks over. "Why are you standing there like a fucking statue?"

"Do you recognize that man speaking to Alexis?" I nod in their direction.

Reid follows my line of sight. "I'll be damned. I do. I can't believe he showed up here."

"Who is he?"

"That's her uncle, Damian Walker."

It's ridiculous how relieved I become after hearing that. Damn everything to hell, I was jealous.

"I didn't know she had an uncle."

Why would I know that though? She only recently came into my world. But Reid seems oblivious to my slipup.

He shrugs. "Not many people know. Her grandparents made sure his name was forgotten. He's been in Encina for the last fourteen years."

I whip my face to him, shocked. "He's been in prison? What for?"

Reid's eyes grow darker. "Manslaughter."

I pass a hand over my face. "Son of a bitch. Do you think she knows that?"

He shrugs. "I don't know, bro. But why do you care?"

"What if he's dangerous?"

I look in their direction again and see Alexis is getting into her car.

"Do you think he'd do something to his own niece?" Reid asks.

"Who did he kill?"

"A lowlife who deserved killing. Dad's tight lipped about the whole thing. All I know is the Montgomerys are freaking out and don't want Damian Walker near Alexis."

She drives away, and her uncle follows her. I'm not sure if they agreed to go somewhere together or not.

"Shit. I gotta go."

"Wait. Are you still coming to the beach?"

"No, man. I can't."

I have to go after Alexis and make sure she's safe.

19

ALEXIS

*D*amian's face turned as white as a sheet when I asked him if he was having an affair with my mother. He said we shouldn't be talking out in public, but he agreed to answer my questions at a place where no one would call security on him.

It occurred to me that he knows my grandparents don't want him to come near me. They must have alerted the school. I don't know what will happen if the administration calls the cops on him. Would he be sent back to Encina?

Automatically, I think about taking him to the diner, but then I remember I can't. My eyes fill with tears because it's like I'm losing Dad all over again. I bite the inside of my cheek hard enough to draw blood. I usually don't resort to that, but I'm driving, and I need the shot of physical pain to forget the other kind, the one that leaves me hollow.

In the end, I opt to take Damian to La Reina, a Mexican

restaurant by the water where Carmen works. If she made plans to go out tonight, she might not have a shift this afternoon. Either way, I know most of the crew, and I'll feel safer there than anywhere else.

Cristiano, Carmen's cousin, is the one who walks over when Damian and I enter the place. He begins to smile, but when he notices my companion, his brows furrow.

"Hey, Lexi. I didn't expect to see you here today. Carmen is off."

"I figured. Can you get us a table outside?"

"Yeah, no problem."

He grabs a couple of menus and then leads us across the restaurant that, at this hour, is practically empty. Out on the patio, there's only one table occupied but by no one I recognize. Probably out-of-towners. Perfect. I'm not completely alone with my uncle, but I won't get stared at out here.

Once we're seated, Cristiano asks, "Can I get you something to drink?"

"Water for me," I say.

"Same," Damian replies.

Cristiano gives him a long glance before he says he'll be right back.

I pretend to be interested in the menu in front of me, but I see nothing. A stretch of uncomfortable silence follows. After my outburst, it seems I lost my bravado.

"I did not have an affair with your mother," he says, answering my earlier question.

I lift my gaze to his, finding an ocean of sadness in his blue eyes. I realize they're the same color as Dad's. But his facial features are different. More rugged. Dangerous.

"But you loved her," I reply.

He nods. "I did. With all my heart. She only had eyes for Dennis though."

"Did my father know about your feelings for her?"

His face blanches. He grows silent, but he doesn't take his eyes away from mine.

Finally, he nods. "Yes."

Anger surges through me. I curl my hands into fists, trying to fight the ugliness that's bubbling up my throat.

"He's always known," Damian continues.

"Are you saying he went after Mom even knowing you had feelings for her?"

He drops his gaze to the table. "It's complicated."

"You said you'd answer all my questions."

"Some memories are better off staying in the past."

My heart is racing. I'm torn between the desire to know everything, and the need to protect myself. In the end, I choose self-preservation. It doesn't matter anymore what happened between him and Mom. My parents are dead and he can't come between them anymore.

"Tell me about the man you killed. Do you regret it?"

He looks at me with a new intensity in his gaze, a steely energy that sends chills down my spine. "No. I didn't intend to kill him, but I'd do it again if I had to. The bastard deserved to die, Lexi."

His admission should terrify me, but oddly, his honesty brings me a sense of calmness. Never mind that I was feeling a lot of animosity toward him a minute ago.

"Why?"

"What do you know about the case?"

"Not much. I didn't even know you existed until I found the letters you wrote to Mom from prison."

His eyes widen. "I can't believe she kept them."

"I read one of them. That's why I asked if you and she... you know."

"Her folks don't want me coming near you. I'll keep my distance if that's what you want as well."

I drop my eyes to the table. "I don't know what I want. I

haven't been able to process the fact that I have an uncle, or that he spent fourteen years in prison for killing someone."

"I might not stay in Triton Cove anyway."

I look up. "You're leaving?"

He glances at the water. "It's probably better for you if I go. I had to do things in Encina that might come back to haunt me. I don't want you to pay for my sins."

"What do you mean? Are you in danger?"

He smiles tightly. "I—"

"Hi, Lexi. Sorry I'm late," Finn fucking Novak appears suddenly next to our table.

Damian seems taken aback by his presence as well, but surely not for the same reasons as me.

I'm stunned into silence, which is why I don't say anything before Finn pulls up the chair next to mine and sits down. He leans closer and kisses me on the cheek, sending an electric spark through my body.

"What are you doing here?" I ask.

"Uh, you texted me asking me to come, remember?" He shakes his head and looks at Damian. "Hi, I'm Finn Novak, Lexi's boyfriend. Nice to meet you."

Boyfriend? What?

Damian looks from Finn to me. "You're dating a *Novak?*"

He not only sounds surprised but also incredulous. And why did he put so much emphasis on Finn's last name?

"Uh…," I start.

"It's new," Finn cuts in. "But you wouldn't know, would you? Weren't you just released from prison?"

"Finn, what the hell?" I glower at him.

I don't know what game he's playing now. I could end this farce though, tell Damian that Finn is nothing to me. But like a psycho, I follow along, if only to see how far he'll go.

"No, I wouldn't," Damian replies, then stands up. "I'd better go, Lexi. It was nice catching up with you."

Shit. Shit. I don't want him to leave yet. "Wait." I jump out of my chair. "What if I do want to keep in touch? How do I reach you?"

"I got a temp job at Saul's Garage. You can call them, and if I'm not around, I'll get the message later."

"What about my father's truck? Are you just going to keep it?"

Damian's lips curl into a crooked grin. "Yeah. That's my truck, after all. Dennis was only keeping it for me."

He looks over my shoulder at Finn. "You'd better take care of Lexi. You don't want to get on my bad side."

I watch Damian walk away until he disappears inside the restaurant. Cristiano comes out soon after with the water we ordered. *Jeez. He sure took his time.* When he sees Finn at my table, his expression becomes murderous. Thankfully, he doesn't address Finn, only glares at him.

Fucking fantastic. He's going to tell Carmen, and she'll get even madder at me.

I pull out the chair Damian vacated. There's no chance in hell I'm sitting next to Finn again.

"What the hell was that, Finn? Why did you follow me here?"

"I saw you leave, and that guy followed you. He's a killer, Alexis. I wanted to make sure you're okay."

My eyebrows shoot to the heavens. "You thought my uncle would hurt me?"

He leans back in his chair and crosses his arms. "He's your uncle only on paper. Do you even remember him from before he killed someone with his bare hands?"

I wince at Finn's description of the crime. I purposely avoided looking up the gruesome details.

His eyes become sharp. "You didn't even know how he did it, did you?"

"I didn't care to know."

My reply seems to surprise him. "How could you be so careless as to agree to go with him anywhere like that?"

I glower, not liking Finn's reproachable tone one bit. *Who the fuck does he think he is?*

"I don't see how any of that is your business. We're nothing, Finn, not even friends."

His eyes narrow, flashing with annoyance. "You're right. I don't know what I was thinking." Before I can reply, he gets up. "I'll see you tonight."

20

ALEXIS

I should have asked Emily what to wear to Luke's party. My go-to person to ask for fashion advice is Carmen, but since she's not answering any of my messages or returning my calls, I have to figure it out on my own.

Emily texts me to let me know she's pulling into my grandparents' driveway. I told Grandma I was going to the party with a friend, and after much insistence, I revealed it was Emily Frost, which prompted Grandma to insist she come in to say hello.

Emily is from one of the oldest and most traditional families in Triton Cove, which means my grandparents know her parents well.

I run down the stairs wearing a pair of skinny jeans, high-heeled sandals, and a cute beaded top. Emily is wearing a tailored suit and tie, and her hair is pulled back in a severe bun. Her lips are bright red though, and she's wearing stiletto heels with bottoms that match her lipstick. She looks like a badass businesswoman, but also, she makes me look underdressed.

She's engaged in polite conversation with my grandparents right at the bottom of the stairs. When they turn my way, I can tell Grandma disapproves of my choice of clothes.

"Hi, Emily. Sorry to keep you waiting," I say.

"No worries." She gives me an elevator glance. "You have nothing better to wear?"

Jesus, I knew she was cold, but I didn't realize she was blunt too.

"Alexis, I bought you so many gorgeous dresses. Surely you can find one that you'd rather wear," Grandma says.

"I think she looks fine, Lillian," Grandpa pipes up, surprising me.

"What's wrong with my clothes?" I glance down. "My top has sparkling beading."

"Do you want people to keep calling you 'diner rat' forever?" Emily raises an eyebrow.

Grandma twists her face into a scowl. "Diner rat? What's that all about? Alexis is a Montgomery. Who is calling her that?"

"No one, Grandma." I grab Emily's hand. "Come on. Help me pick a dress."

I hurry up the stairs, still clutching the girl's hand. When we reach the landing, she says, "You can let go now."

"Why did you have to make that comment in front of my grandparents? They'll probably call the headmaster."

"Sorry, I wasn't aware they didn't know."

I give her a droll look, noticing the smirk she's sporting. She totally did that on purpose, though why, I don't know.

"Whatever. I have no idea what Maverick students wear to parties. I thought it was an informal get-together."

"Sure it is, but everyone there will be wearing clothes that cost thousands of dollars, even if they're ripped jeans. And I know the pair you're wearing is not a designer brand."

"I don't care about labels."

"I don't either, but in this world, appearances mean more than anything. Showing off money is more powerful than a sucker punch. Right now, Tiffany is winning by a landslide in this feud of yours."

"She's the one who started it by calling me diner rat."

Emily cocks her head to the side. "I heard you kicked her out of your dad's diner."

I clamp my jaw shut, not wanting to talk about that day. However, I have to say something or Emily will keep staring at me as if she can read my mind.

"My problem was with Finn. But I don't want to talk about that now."

"Regardless, you need to put that bitch in her place. Wear something that'll make every guy at the party wish they were getting into your pants."

"I don't want them thinking that," I say, exasperated.

"Okay. Make *Finn* want to get into your pants. That should do it. Tiffany has a major crush on him."

Hell. I'm not surprised about that. She was all over him when they came into the diner, but so far, I haven't seen Finn with her in school.

I point at my walk-in closet. "Go on, find me something to wear that will make Tiffany green with envy."

"Do you think I'm an expert in fashion?" She arches an eyebrow.

"Clearly you're better than me."

She shakes her head. "You have no idea. Appearances can be so deceiving."

I'm left wondering what she meant by that as she goes into my closet to search through my clothes.

"I think I found something." She pulls out a simple silk black dress from the hanger.

"You want me to wear that? Isn't it a bit plain?"

"Trust me. This one is a classic. You can't go wrong with a basic black dress, especially if it's from Chanel."

Emily pulls the tag off and tosses it at me. I glance at the price and almost gag. "Ten thousand dollars for a dress? What is it made of, diamonds?"

She smiles. "You're so cute. It's almost too easy to forget you're a Montgomery."

"I'm a Walker."

Emily rolls her eyes. "Get dressed. I don't want to be the last one to arrive."

"All right. Can I keep the sandals though?"

She drops her gaze to my feet. "Are those knockoffs?"

I shrug. "I don't know. I got them at Steven Madden. They're comfy."

With a sigh, she pinches the bridge of her nose. "You really need a crash course on how to survive at Maverick Prep. Let me see if I can find something."

She ventures back into my closet, and a moment later, she returns carrying a pair of black sandals that sparkle when the lights hit the rhinestones. "Here, wear these."

"Jesus, those heels are high as fuck. I'll probably fall and break my neck."

"As long as you fall into Finn's arms, you'll be fine." She smirks.

"Why do you keep bringing him up?"

"You seriously don't know?"

"Nope." I try to keep my face neutral, completely Switzerland, but I'm not sure if I'm fooling Emily.

To my frustration, she simply laughs and shakes her head. "Okay, then."

"You're not going to tell me?"

She heads for the door. "I'll wait for you downstairs. Don't take too long."

FINN

I'VE BEEN HIDING from the crowd since I got to Luke's sprawling mansion. The basement is our secret haven, filled to the brim with games and a fully stocked bar. It's off-limits to anyone outside our inner circle, and that includes Jackie and Tiffany. I made sure to warn Cameron that if he wants to keep fucking those two, he'd better find somewhere else to do it, far away from me.

The motherfucker is now sulking in a chair, drinking top-shelf whiskey and smoking a joint. I can't touch drugs, especially now that competitive swimming is back in my life. But I also don't plan to drink anything. I want to be stone sober for when Alexis arrives, which means I'm on edge.

I'm not sure yet how to handle her. There's a fine line between hate and desire, and I'm toying with it. I want to hurt her for making me obsess about her, for having the audacity to pity me. I need her to watch me with condemning eyes and lacerate me with cruel words. At the same time, I can't push her too far or she might break. The deal I struck with my father is hanging over my head.

I've already fucked up this afternoon by following her like a dumbass. It's all about control, and no matter what I do, I can't let her have any.

Luke drops next to me on the couch, already half-drunk. "Dude, turn that frown upside down. This is a party."

"Fuck off," I retort, annoyed.

"Are you still thinking about Alexis and her uncle?" Reid asks from the side of the pool table.

"No," I lie.

Cameron snorts. "I can't believe you followed her. That was pathetic, Finn."

"I had my reasons. But you should know, right? You can't even hear the name Halsey without getting bent out of shape."

"Fuck you." He jumps from the chair and disappears up the stairs.

"Why do you keep pushing him like that?" Reid asks.

I glower. "So it's okay for him to get all over my grill, but I can't say shit about Halsey?"

"You've got to be kidding me." Luke sits straighter, glancing at his phone.

"What now?" I try to see what got him so tense all of a sudden.

"Your girl Alexis arrived, and she brought Emily fucking Frost with her."

It's an effort to appear like I don't give a damn that Alexis is here. I want to head back to the party and seek her out immediately. But after I played the stalker game this afternoon, looking for her right away will reek of desperation.

Reid laughs. "That's a plot twist I didn't see coming. Emily never goes anywhere, and when she decides to step out of her cage, it's to crash your party."

Luke jumps from the couch, still staring at his phone. "If she's here, she's up to something."

I snort. "Like what? Do you think she came to sabotage your party?"

He gives me a deranged look. "That's exactly what I think she's doing here."

I trade a worried glance with Reid. Luke is unpredictable on most days, but when he's been drinking, he turns explosive. When he heads back to the party, we both follow him.

The number of people has doubled since we disappeared into the basement. Loud music is pouring through the speakers.

Luke hired a famous DJ to entertain his guests; he's stationed outside by the swimming pool, where a group of people is already dancing like they're at a rave, careless of who's watching.

I don't make eye contact with anyone I pass by, and most know to just stare without trying to engage me in shit. I do pinpoint Tiffany and Jackie hanging out with a few guys from the lacrosse team. My eyes linger on them long enough to catch their murderous stares.

My lips quirk into a grin. *They want to wage war against me? Bring it on.*

Before Luke can find his target, another person who shouldn't be here crosses our path. Eric Danes. *Fucking hell.* Luke glances briefly in his direction without slowing down. That tells me all I need to know. If he's not surprised by Eric's presence here, it means he invited the jackass.

"Is he for real?" Reid asks.

I'm not sure who he's referring to, Eric for showing up or Luke for inviting him. It doesn't matter anyway.

"You go after Luke. I'll deal with Danes."

Reid's eyes shine with a knowing glint as he nods, and then he follows Luke. I change course, keenly aware that everyone in the vicinity will be watching my interaction with Eric like a hawk.

"What are you doing here?" I ask, stopping close enough to invade his personal space.

I'm taller than him, and I use that advantage to the fullest. But he doesn't seem intimidated by my stance. He lifts his chin arrogantly, watching me with so much hatred, I feel it deep in my bones.

"What is it now, Finn? Can't deal with seeing me on your turf?"

"I don't know what games you think you're playing, but I won't let you mess with my life."

He lifts an eyebrow. "And how exactly are you going to stop me? Run me over with your new Porsche?"

I'd flinch if I hadn't already heard that insult before from Alexis. Instead, I smirk. Seeing Eric's eyes shine with renewed anger is exactly what I was aiming to achieve.

"I don't need to resort to physical aggression. There are plenty of ways to make someone's life miserable."

He narrows his eyes a fraction. "Is this the part where you tell me to drop out or I'll regret it?"

"I don't give a damn that you're a student at Maverick. As far as I'm concerned, you can blow the money you got from my father however you like. Just don't get too comfortable. The likes of you never hold on to cash for too long. You'll be back to counting pennies within the year."

Grinning, he shakes his head. "Really? Is that all you got? Cheap insults and empty threats?"

I conceal my irritation, keeping the arrogant mask in place. "Enjoy life on the golden side while you can. Cross me again and you'll know why we're called gods."

Disgust at myself spreads like a disease through me. And when I turn around to walk away from Eric, and my gaze connects with Alexis's loathing stare, it makes me feel worse by a million. She's standing close enough and must have heard every word I exchanged with Danes.

Without missing a beat, I stride in her direction.

"Ready to work on our assignment?" I ask casually.

Her expression twists into a scowl. "Don't bother. I got everything I need."

She whirls around and strides away before I can offer a reply. I force myself to stay where I am and not follow her, even if I'm dying to inflict as much pain as I'm sure to receive.

21

ALEXIS

I. Am. An. Idiot.
I should have known Finn has no redeeming qualities. Whatever I saw during our first class together must have been a figment of my imagination. He's a selfish, entitled prick who doesn't feel an ounce of remorse for what he did to Eric's brother.

And to think I felt sorry for him.

My vision is tinted red as I stride away from him, elbowing whoever gets in my way. The sandals Emily picked for me pinch my toes, and the pain only serves to aggravate me more. I can't believe I ditched hanging out with my friends to come here. Maybe it's not too late and I can meet Carmen.

Emily disappeared as soon as we got inside Luke's mansion. She said she wouldn't stay long. I wonder if she's ready to go. I regret not driving to the party.

I stretch my neck, trying to find her in the crowded room.

Her white-blonde hair shouldn't be hard to pinpoint. My stomach sinks when I don't see her anywhere.

Maybe she's outside.

I turn around and almost collide with Luke. I step back, swallowing the automatic apology that bubbles up my throat. He was the one who crashed into me, after all.

"What the hell?" I say instead.

"Where is she?" he yells in my face, his blue eyes sparkling with fury.

"Lower your voice, jackass. I'm not in the mood for more assholery antics."

He grabs my arms, digging his fingers into my exposed skin. "Cut the crap, diner girl. Where the fuck is Emily?"

I shove him off me. "What's your fucking problem? I don't know where Emily is."

He doesn't try to grab me again, but he's still crowding me. "What did she say to you?"

"Nothing. Why are you losing your shit because I brought Emily to your party?"

He threads his fingers through his long bangs and then yanks them back hard. "She stole something from me."

"Why would she steal from you?"

His eyes narrow, turning ice cold. "Tell your friend that if she doesn't return my property in one piece, she's as good as dead."

A shiver runs down my spine as Luke's threat pierces my chest. I've heard people vow to kill in the heat of an argument before, but I've never once believed they'd go through with it until now. My heart is racing and doesn't slow down even when Luke walks away.

I glance at my surroundings, but no one seems to care that the party's host just threatened to murder someone in cold blood. My hands are shaking when I fish my phone out of my purse. I call Emily. It only rings once before it goes to voice mail.

Son of a bitch. Did she just ignore my call?

What did you expect, Alexis? They're all assholes.

That's it. I'm out of here.

I don't find more roadblocks—a.k.a. deranged egomaniacs—on the way to the front door. Now I have to try to get an Uber to pick me up. Unlike most of the wealthy population of Triton Cove, Luke doesn't live in a beachfront mansion. We're in the middle of nowhere, and to get to the main road, it's a long walk. I curse the sandals I'm wearing. Not only do they hurt like a mother, but it's hard to walk fast in them.

My heart sinks when the Uber app shows no cars are available in my area. *Are you serious?*

I'm about to call Carmen when I hear footsteps behind me. Without slowing down, I look over my shoulder. *Fuck.* It's Tiffany, Jackie, and a few people I haven't had the displeasure of meeting yet.

"Hey, diner rat. Leaving so soon?" Tiffany asks.

I don't fall for her goading. For starters, she came with an entourage. I'm not dumb enough to respond when I'm seriously outnumbered.

"Hey, bitch. I'm talking to you," she continues.

I dig my nails into my palms. I should have known I wouldn't get rid of them so easily.

"I heard you. I'm simply choosing to ignore you."

Someone grabs my arm and yanks me back.

"Hey!"

It's not Tiffany manhandling me but one of her guy friends.

"Let go of me, asshole." I try to pull my arm free, but he simply holds me tighter.

"Oh, she's feisty." The jackass laughs.

Busy trying to pry his fingers from my arm, I don't notice the second jerk approach from my other side. He grabs my free arm, and now I'm trapped between two guys who are much stronger than me. My pulse races, thundering in my ears. We're too far from the house and concealed by shadows. Tiffany and her friends can do anything they want to me, and no one will come to the rescue. Even if I screamed, I doubt I'd be heard.

"Let go of me," I demand.

Tiffany moves closer, smiling in a chilling way.

Hell, I thought Luke looked like a psycho before. He has nothing on this bitch.

"We can't. You see, the party is about to get wicked good, and we don't want you to miss it."

"Whatever you're planning, it won't work. I'm not going to drop out of Maverick."

"Who says I want you to drop out? On the contrary. After I'm done with you tonight, I want you to stay." She looks over her shoulder, extending her hand. "Jackie."

Smirking, Tiffany's minion pulls something small from her purse. I can't see what it is until Tiffany has it in her hands.

Clippers.

What the actual fuck?

"What do you think you're doing with those?" I keep my eyes on the little appliance.

"You're too cocky for a diner rat. It's time to put you back in your place." She turns on the clippers and moves them closer to my head.

I thrash against the assholes holding me, angling my head back and away from the clippers' sharp blades.

"Hold her still, dumbasses," Tiffany barks at the guys. "I want to shave her head, not cut her throat."

"I think she'd look good with a nasty scar on her cheek." Jackie snickers.

Cunt.

Tiffany cocks her head to the side, pretending to mull it over. "True. But first her hair."

"Grab a fistful of it, Trevor, so she can't jerk her head away," a third guy in the group suggests.

My scalp burns when the asshole follows his friend's advice. I yelp, making my audience laugh. *Motherfuckers.*

Underneath the fear, I sense my darkness building, growing at alarming speed. Not even the pain inflicted by Trevor is working against it. I don't want to lose control in front of these people. I never know what happens in those episodes because blackouts follow. Tears gather in my eyes as the feeling of impotence overwhelms me.

"What are you doing?" a female voice asks from the darkness.

Tiffany turns around. "Run along, Halsey. This doesn't concern you."

"Were you planning on shaving her head? Are you insane?" she asks, coming closer.

"Ugh, she's going to ruin the fun," Jackie complains.

The third guy in the group sneaks up behind Halsey and traps her in his beefy arms. "No, she won't. Let's shave her head too."

"Get your hands off me, jackass!" She tries to elbow his stomach, but he's holding her in a boa constrictor vise.

"Excellent idea." Tiffany smiles like a psycho.

Halsey struggles more, but she's no match for the baboon holding her. She tried to help me, and now they're going to make her pay. I begin to shake from head to toe, but it isn't from fear anymore. I'm on the verge of snapping.

Suddenly, the guy restraining Halsey is yanked back. She staggers forward, almost dropping to her knees. The next thing I see is Cameron delivering a knockout punch to the guy's chin. His face snaps back right before he trips over his own feet and drops to the ground. Immediately, Trevor and his friend release me and step back.

Cameron glances at Halsey briefly, and then his irate glare

lands on Tiffany and Jackie. "What the fuck do you think you're doing?"

"Teaching the diner rat a lesson." Tiffany shrugs. "Halsey was collateral damage."

"Do you think I care about Halsey?" Cameron retorts angrily.

"If you didn't care, why did you stop the fun?" Jackie raises an eyebrow.

I'm still reeling from being manhandled. Cameron's interruption stopped me from losing control, but I'm not out of the woods yet. The darkness is still swirling, ready to overwhelm my senses. I need to get out of here before Cameron decides to join forces with his fuck buddies.

I walk over to Halsey. "Are you okay?" I ask.

"Yes."

Cameron glances at us, and judging by his glower, I suspect he's one second from commanding Tiffany and Jackie to resume their hazing.

Approaching headlights draw our attention to the road. I squeeze my eyes to protect them from the sudden glare. The car stops closer to Halsey and me, and when the window lowers, I see Emily behind the wheel.

"Ready to go?" she asks.

"Fuck yeah," I say.

I don't bother circling around to the passenger side. Halsey and I take the back seat, and no sooner does the door shut than Emily makes a U-turn and heads to the main road. My heart is still beating as if it's about to burst out of my chest even though the worst is over.

"Where the hell did you go?" I ask, not hiding my annoyance. "I thought you ditched me."

"I did. I had to leave the party in a hurry."

"Because you stole something from Luke."

"Yep."

"What did you take?" Halsey asks.

"Something he cherishes beyond reason," Emily replies enigmatically.

"He wants to kill you," I say.

"I know."

"Why did you come back?" I lean forward, trying to see the reflection of her eyes in the rearview mirror.

"To be honest, I don't know. I guess I felt guilty for leaving you alone in shark-infested waters."

"So you risked Luke's wrath to rescue Lexi?" Halsey asks.

"I'm not afraid of him. Trust me, there's nothing he can do to me that I haven't experienced before, or worse."

Hell. That's a loaded statement.

I put a pin in it. Now is not the time to try to unpack that with Emily.

"Thanks for coming back," I say.

"What kind of fuckfest did I interrupt?"

"Tiffany thought shaving my head was a good idea. Halsey tried to help and ended up getting a ticket for a buzz cut too."

"That bitch brought clippers to a party?" She snorts. "It makes me wonder what else she was packing in that tiny designer bag of hers."

"I'm sure shaving my head wasn't a spur-of-the-moment idea. They came prepared."

"And Cameron? Was he a part of it, or did he just want to watch?"

"He defended me, sort of," Halsey replies in a small voice. "But he clearly regretted doing it."

"Why does he hate you so much?" I turn to Halsey.

She looks out the window and sighs loudly. "Because I broke his heart."

22

FINN

*I*t's been at least twenty minutes since I lost Alexis in the crowd. I've been wandering aimlessly, already on my third drink. Now that she bailed on me, there's no need for my sobriety. There's no sign of Luke, Cameron, or Reid anywhere. I call Reid to make sure Luke didn't do something stupid. Nothing's been set on fire yet; I take that as a good sign.

Reid's phone rings until it goes to voice mail. *Fucking hell.* I toss the rest of my drink back and then call Cameron. He doesn't answer either.

I decide to go see if Luke is in his bedroom when I catch sight of Reid coming out of a powder room to my right. He's acting cagey, glancing in both directions before moving along. His hair is disheveled, and he's fixing his pants. Dumbass. If he's trying to hide what he'd been up to, he's doing a piss-poor job.

I step closer to him, clasping his shoulder. "Where's Luke?"

A shadow of guilt crosses his eyes. "Uh, I don't know."

I nudge him back, irritated. "You were supposed to keep an eye on him while I dealt with Danes."

His remorseful expression turns into a glower. Straightening his jacket, he retorts, "I'm not his fucking babysitter."

"Be thankful that nothing went up in flames while you were fucking some airhead."

He pushes his messy hair back. "Whatever. Don't be a hater because you didn't get any. Where's Alexis?"

"Don't fucking know. Probably gone."

His shrewd gaze locks on my face. "Struck out already with diner girl? Hell, Finn, you must be losing your touch."

I open my mouth to retort, almost falling for Reid's trap, but then wise up. Shaking my head, I say, "Let's find that pyromaniac before he finds Emily Frost."

As if summoned, Luke comes rushing down the stairs, looking like a deranged fuck.

I shoot my arm out, stopping him from blasting past us. "Where are you going?"

"After that fucking bitch."

I step in front of him. "You're not going after anyone in this state. How much have you drunk? You smell flammable."

He pushes me away. "Fuck off, Finn. You're not my father."

Reid and I trade a glance and a silent message. It'll take the two of us to restrain Luke until he's no longer on the verge of killing someone.

Jesus fucking Christ. What did Emily do to him? I've never seen him this hell-bent on revenge.

We rush after Luke, boxing him in from both sides and securing his arms.

"You're coming with us, jackass, whether you like it or not," I grit out.

His murderous gaze sets on me, so intense, I might have balked at it if I hadn't known Luke for so long. I can take his wrath.

"What the fuck is going on now?" Cameron asks as he appears in front of us.

His green eyes are a storm of bad emotions. This party must have been cursed, because so far only Reid seems immune to the crazy.

"Prissy boys one and two got it into their heads that I need to calm down," Luke replies. "Pretty soon they'll be singing Taylor fucking Swift."

"Shut up, asshole. I just don't want to see you wind up at Encina Island because of some stupid vendetta against Emily Frost," I say.

Cameron snorts. "Emily already left."

"I know she did. I saw her car pass through the front gate fifteen minutes ago."

"Fifteen?" Cameron's brows shoot up. "More like five. I guess she came back to rescue her new buddies—diner girl and traitor bitch."

"Wait. Halsey was here too?" Reid asks, then bursts out laughing a second later.

"Shut up, Bennett," Cameron growls.

"Can you two goons let go of me already?" Luke strains against our hold.

"Not until you give up your idiotic idea. If you need to make Emily pay, it can wait until tomorrow," I say.

"I don't subscribe to the notion that revenge is a dish best served cold. I believe in immediate retaliation."

"We know you do," Reid chimes in. "But you aren't leaving this house alone."

"Fine. Come with me, then. I don't care."

I give Reid an exasperated glance. He had to give Luke the idea of a group trip.

He replies with a what-was-I-supposed-to-say shrug.

"Awesome. I'm sick of this party already," Cameron grumbles. "Let's go."

"Where exactly are we going?" I butt in. "We don't know where Emily went."

"I can find out easily," Reid says, releasing Luke.

Now that he's not a flight risk, I drop my hand from his arm too and search for the nearest booze station. I'm not drunk enough for this shit. Reid can drive since he's done nothing but screw some random chick in the bathroom.

"Oh yeah? How? Stalking Emily on social media?" Cameron snorts. "Good luck with that."

Reid gives Cameron a droll look. "Not Emily, dumbass. Halsey."

The blood seems to vanish from his face, and in the next second, his expression contorts into rage. "You're following her?"

"Don't look so shocked, bruh. Everyone does. She has a massive following," Luke pipes up.

Cameron whips his face to mine. "Do you follow her too?"

I shrug. "I don't know. Maybe. You know I don't give a shit about social media."

Still looking like he's about to have an aneurysm, Cameron rests his hands on his hips. "Fucking traitors."

"Yeah, whatever. Let's see if the one who shall not be named checked in anywhere." Reid looks at his phone.

While Reid searches, Luke lights up a cigarette, and Cameron continues to glower into space. I finally catch sight of someone holding a bottle of Patrón as he dances to the beat of the song. I stride toward the guy and pull the bottle from his hand.

"Hey!" He glares, but when he sees I'm the one who confiscated his drink, he grins. "Finn! Dance with us, man."

"Nah, the tequila will suffice."

I whirl around with the bottle's rim already pressed against my lips. The strong liquid warms my throat and chest as it spreads through my body.

By the time I return to my friends, Reid is sporting a victorious grin.

"Found her?" I ask.

"Yep. You're not going to believe where Halsey, Emily, and Alexis are."

"Judging by your maniacal expression, the last place on Triton Cove we would think of," I say.

"La Salamandra?" Cameron says, frowning as he stares at Reid's phone.

He shoves him away. "Hey, quit snooping. Wanna see pictures of Halsey, follow her yourself."

Cameron steps back. "Ain't gonna happen."

"What are we waiting for? Let's bounce," Luke says before he walks away from his own party.

ALEXIS

AFTER HALSEY'S DECLARATION, silence falls inside the car, which is disturbed a minute later by the sound of my phone pinging with an incoming text. I'm shocked when I read Carmen's name on the screen.

"Finally," I mumble to myself.

Halsey glances at me. "Who texted you?"

"My best friend."

CARMEN: Thought I should send you proof of what you're missing.

The text came with the attached image of Carmen surrounded by my old crew: Vinny, Cristiano, Taluah and—gasp —Dimitri.

Shit. He had never hung out with us before. Damn. She's really rubbing it in.

ME: Where are you?

CARMEN: La Salamandra.

My jaw drops. La Salamandra is the most infamous club on our side of Triton Cove. It's notorious for wild parties, and it's also kind of dangerous thanks to its location. It's right at the edge of the Triads' territory.

ME: Can you get me in?

CARMEN: What about your fancy party?

ME: Left it already. I'll tell you about it when I see you.

CARMEN: Fine. I'll get you in, but you have to pay our tab.

I roll my eyes. She's quickly learned to take advantage of my new financial situation. I don't mind though. I'm happy to pay for my friends.

ME: Deal.

"I'm not ready to go home yet," I tell Halsey and Emily. "Do you wanna hang out?"

"And do what exactly?" Emily asks.

"My friends are at La Salamandra. They can get us in."

"I've never heard of it. Is it new?" Halsey asks.

"No."

Emily looks at me through the rearview mirror. "Where is this place exactly?"

"My side of town. Next to the old railroad."

Halsey sighs. "I don't know. I think I've had enough excitement for one evening."

"Are you upset because of what happened with Tiffany or is it Cameron?" I ask.

"Both, but mostly Cameron."

I'm surprised by her honest answer. I thought everyone at Maverick kept their weakness close to their chests.

"All those boys are rotten, even the sheriff's son," Emily says with venom.

My heart squeezes tight when the scene with Finn and Eric comes to the forefront of my mind. Finn acted despicably, and I was only shocked because I'm a moron.

"You know what?" I exclaim. "We're not going to let those fuckboys ruin our evening."

"Hmm. I don't know," Emily says.

"Lexi is right," Halsey chimes in. "I'm done being upset because a jackass thinks he's entitled to punish me forever."

"You should get revenge like I did."

She shakes her head. "The best revenge is to live life to the fullest and let the haters eat their hearts out."

Wow. That was deep. I wish I could take the high road in most situations, but I'm too short tempered for that.

"Come on, Emily. When was the last time you had fun?" I ask.

"What makes you think I don't? I had plenty tonight."

"Whatever you wanted to accomplish at Luke's party, you succeeded. He was raving mad. We should celebrate, and maybe you can fill us in about your feud with blondie," I press.

I'm not sure why I want Emily to come so badly. It's definitely not because she's our ride. I could easily ask her to drop us off downtown, and from there I'm sure we could find an Uber.

After a moment of silence, she replies, "What the hell? Why not?"

Halsey's mouth gapes as if she was expecting a resounding no.

"Huzzah!" I throw my fist in the air.

"Huzzah?" Emily asks as Halsey snickers.

"What? Too retro?" I laugh.

"Don't say that word in front of people unless you want another lynching."

Her comment knocks my good mood down a peg.

"I wasn't lynched."

"And that's thanks to this biatch here. I hope people on your side of Triton Cove are nicer than the assholes who attend Maverick."

"For sure. A hundo p," I reply with vehemence, but as the words leave my mouth, I begin to worry about Carmen's reaction when she sees I brought Emily and Halsey with me.

Ah hell. Too late now.

23

ALEXIS

"*A*re you sure this is the place?" Emily leans over the steering wheel as her car moves forward at a crawl over the loose gravel on the road.

"Yep." I pull my phone out and text Carmen that we're here.

"I don't see any sign," Halsey pipes up.

I lift my gaze and point at the building. "How about that huge salamander painting on the front wall?"

"Oh."

Emily parks in the first available spot she finds.

"My car better be in one piece by the time we get back."

I open my mouth to reassure her, but I stop in time. I can't make that promise. The area *is* sketchy.

"Don't worry, Emily. It'll be fine," Halsey replies optimistically before she opens the door and gets out.

"Is it me, or did her mood do a one-eighty faster than a demon-induced head spin?" Emily asks.

"Don't know, but good for her," I reply. "I can't move on from bad things that quickly."

"Me neither."

My phone pings. It must be a text from Carmen.

CARMEN: I'm out. Where are you?

ME: Walking from the car. Be there in a sec.

"Come on. My friend is waiting for us."

I get out and wait for Emily to follow me. We join Halsey, who's standing in front of the car and typing something on her phone.

"Let's take a selfie with La Salamandra behind us," she says.

"Ugh. Must we?" Emily groans.

"Yep. I want everyone to know we're having a great time."

Emily's stride is less poised than before as she joins Halsey. It must not be easy to walk in those stiletto heels over uneven ground. We get as close as we can to Halsey while she raises her arm with phone in hand.

"Now say bite meeeee."

I force a smile, hoping it doesn't come across fake as fuck. Halsey takes several pictures and then shows us.

"I think the second one is the best. What do you think?" she asks.

"I don't care. Can we go now?" Emily replies grumpily.

"The second one is good," I say.

Halsey smiles as she types the caption to the picture and then posts it to her Instagram account. I glance at her number of followers and balk.

"You have over a million followers?"

"Yeah." She grins and then puts her phone away.

On the way to the front of La Salamandra, we cross paths with some people who stare at us as if we're lost. Considering what we're wearing, I don't blame them. They don't make a comment though. But when Carmen sees my approach with Emily and Halsey in tow, she scowls.

"You didn't tell me you were bringing an entourage." She crosses her arms over her chest.

"They were with me when you texted. Don't worry, they aren't like the rest of them."

"Hi, I'm Halsey." She waves at Carmen, smiling from ear to ear.

She narrows her eyes. "You look familiar. Aren't you an influencer or something?"

Ah, of course Carmen would recognize Halsey. She spends way too much time on social media.

Halsey shrugs. "I guess."

"This is Emily. She drove here," I add.

Carmen glances over at her and raises an eyebrow. "Did you just come from a board meeting?"

She scoffs and then turns to me. "You said your friends were nicer than the fuckers from Maverick."

Before Carmen can say something bitchy, I reply, "They are. Carmen must be hungry, right, Carmen?" I look pointedly at her.

She tones down her animosity a fraction. "Yeah, starving. Come on."

"So what exactly is this place?" Emily asks. "A restaurant? A club?"

"It's everything and more," Carmen says and then turns to the mean-looking bouncer. "These are my friends. Lazaro okayed them to come in with me."

The guy looks at us suspiciously, takes note of our fancy threads, and then calls someone on his earpiece.

I lean closer to Carmen and ask, "Who's Lazaro?"

"A friend of Cristiano. Speaking of which, who was the guy who came with you to the restaurant today?"

I knew the big mouth would tell Carmen. I'm a little upset that she didn't call me immediately to ask about him.

"My uncle."

Her eyes widen, but before she can say a word, the bouncer signals us to go in.

Immediately, the loud music from the live band fills my ears. The place is dark, save for the lights coming from the stage and the bar. I can't make out most of the people here. I follow Carmen closely, afraid to lose her in the crowd. She heads to an area with a few tables. This part of the club has better illumination, but it's still on the dim side.

My friends are sitting around a large booth, drinking beer. They're all underage, but I don't think it matters here. I wouldn't be surprised if the Triads own the place.

"Look who I found," Carmen announces.

"Hey! Lexi is here," Vinny says with extra cheer.

"And she brought friends." Cristiano smiles slyly as he appreciates the girls.

"This is Halsey and Emily." I make the introductions and then notice a guy I don't recognize. He must be Cristiano's friend.

"That's Lazaro," Carmen tells me.

He ignores the introduction, seeming more interested in drinking his beer. He's hot in a broody way with dark hair and a sharp jawline. I'm surprised Carmen didn't say anything about him. He's totally her type. When he finally glances in our direction, a shiver runs down my spine, and not the good kind. His piercing blue eyes are ice cold.

Someone touches my arm, and when I turn, I see Dimitri there, smiling.

"Hi, Lexi. I didn't think you'd come."

"Hey, Dimitri."

I should say something else, but it seems I forgot how to string sentences together. Here's the guy who I had a crush on last year actually acknowledging my existence, and my mind is blank. My tongue is tied, and not because I'm nervous. He's still gorgeous, but I feel nothing.

"How is life on the golden side?" he asks.

"Not much different than my old life," I lie.

He grows serious. "I'm sorry about your dad. He had the best burgers in town."

The constant ache in my chest flares up, making my throat tight.

"Thanks."

A stretch of silence follows, and not even the music in the background can make it less awkward.

"Do you wanna dance?" he blurts out.

"Uh…."

"Lexi would love to dance," Carmen answers for me, giving me an encouraging smile.

Shit. I wish she didn't open her big mouth.

I glance at Halsey and Emily, hoping they can save me from the situation. Emily's attention is diverted, her gaze trained on the band on the stage, and the grin on Halsey's face tells me she's not going to help.

"Go on, Lexi. I need to use the restroom anyway," she tells me.

Emily's attention switches to her fast, tensing. "I'm coming with you."

Fucking great. There go my two excuses. I could pull the restroom card too, but something tells me I should save that one for later.

Forcing a smile to my lips, I turn to Dimitri. "All right. Let's see what you got, QB."

Gag me. Did I really call him that? Ugh.

He places his hand on my lower back as he guides me to the dance floor. Thanks to his size, he can carve a path through the throng of people easily. It doesn't occur to me until we're at the edge of the dance floor that no one gave him a stink eye or complained. He's popular in town thanks to being the star of the football team, but the crowd is mixed here, and I bet some of the people don't give a rat's ass about who he is.

It's sheer bad luck that the band switches to a sexy tune that begs for close proximity. Dimitri's hands find my hips and pull me to him as if it's his God-given right to command my body. I tense, immediately grabbing his arm to offer a little resistance.

"Relax, Lexi. I won't bite." He grins.

My heart is racing, but I force a smile through the uneasiness. "Who says I'm nervous?"

"Good. I don't want you to be."

Taking a deep breath, I attempt to let go of the tension. I spent many hours last year daydreaming about Dimitri, and now that something is finally happening, I'm acting like he has a disease.

What's wrong with me?

He begins to grind his pelvis against mine, and it doesn't take long for me to feel his enthusiasm. My heart seems to hammer louder in my chest. I bring forth all the memories of when I drooled over him, when I pictured him kissing me and doing other things. It's not working. Maybe the surroundings aren't helping.

I close my eyes and focus on his touch. He must have taken that as a sign, because his lips find my neck. Goose bumps break out on my skin, and I shiver.

But everything goes to hell when the scene of Finn stepping out of the pool invades my mind. I jerk back from Dimitri, letting out a gasp. His brows furrow, emphasizing the glint of confusion in his eyes. My face becomes hot, and like a coward, I look away only to find Finn standing mere feet away from me, his hard gaze locked on me.

24

FINN

"*J*esus fucking Christ, what is this place?" Cameron asks as we stride toward the front of La Salamandra, a dive bar by the looks of it.

The building's paint is faded, and the crowd hanging out in front of it looks like they just came out of Encina Island. I bet coming here was Alexis's idea. Who else would hang out in such a hellhole?

"Who cares?" Luke grumbles.

"Shit, this is almost on top of Triad territory," Reid pipes up.

"That shouldn't be a problem for you." Cameron smirks. "Doesn't your dad have an agreement with them?"

Reid rolls his eyes. "Allegedly."

"Let's get this shit show over with already," I reply, annoyed that I was roped into coming here.

I don't want Alexis to think for a second that I came after her.

We ignore the line to get in and head straight for the door. People bitch about it, but it's like white noise in the background. The bouncer levels us with a bored look.

"The line starts all the way back there," he deadpans.

"We're VIPs." Luke extends his hand for a hundred-dollar bill handshake.

The money disappears in the blink of an eye, and a second later, we're entering the dark and loud third-rate club. There's a live band playing some bullshit song I don't recognize, but people seem into it. They're grinding against one another in sync with it. They could be extras in the *Dirty Dancing* movie.

"Hell, how are we supposed to find anyone here?" Reid asks.

"Let's check the dance floor," I say, simply because it's the most illuminated area in the club. Doubt Emily would be there though.

I turn around and realize to my dismay that Cameron and Luke have already disappeared. *Son of a bitch.*

"Where the fuck did they go?" I ask.

"Cameron must have gone to the bar. Luke is another story."

I shake my head. "Whatever. I'm done trying to avoid a disaster. If Emily did something to piss off Luke, that's her problem."

"I thought the whole point of tagging along was to prevent Luke from going overboard with his retaliation."

I groan loudly. "Fine. Let's split and try to find the idiot or Emily."

"I'll check out back," he replies.

I push my way through the sea of people, and with each passing second inside this dump, my annoyance grows. I swear I'm going to make Luke pay for this.

After a minute of fighting against a wall of sweaty and drunk patrons, I finally reach the edge of the dance floor. Then I stop in my tracks, surprised by the sight in front of me. Alexis is dancing with some prick in a way that can only be described as foreplay. I shouldn't care, but the vision sets my teeth on edge. Hell, I didn't realize what I wanted from her until this moment. I need to claim her, make her want no one else but me. Then I can crush her for making me crave her like this.

When the guy kisses her neck, it sends a rush of rage through me. I clench my jaw hard, fighting to remain rooted to the spot. She steps back, almost as if the contact wasn't wanted. Bullshit. She was grinding him a second ago. So is she a tease too?

Sensing my stare, she looks my way. Her eyes widen.

A smirk blossoms on my lips. *It's showtime.*

I walk over and pull her away from the dumbass she's with.

"Hey. What the fuck do you think you're doing?" he asks, already taking on an aggressive stance.

Judging by his size and physique, he must be a jock. Like I give a shit.

"Fuck off, buddy. I'm taking over," I tell him.

"What are you doing, Finn?" she asks but doesn't try to break free from my hold.

Interesting.

"You know this asshole?" the guy asks.

"Yeah, he goes to Maverick."

The look of disgust on his face is priceless. It makes me smile harder.

"Now that introductions have been made, run along," I tell him.

"The hell I will. I don't care who you are. Let go of Lexi or—"

"Or what?" I raise an eyebrow. "You'll pummel me to the ground?"

Alexis turns to him. "It's fine, Dimitri. I need to speak to Finn anyway. I'll look for you later."

The dude's face twists into a scowl. He must not be used to being ditched like that. I want to laugh but keep my amusement contained to an arrogant smirk.

"Whatever." He strides off, pushing whoever is in front of him out of the way.

"Nice fella," I say.

Alexis finally pulls free from me. "What do you want, Finn? Did you follow me here?"

I snort. "Aren't you delusional? I came with Luke. He's looking for your friend."

Her face blanches. "Luke is here?"

"Yep. Judging by your expression, you already know of his reputation."

She rubs her forearms. "I've experienced it firsthand."

I watch her through slitted eyes. "What's that supposed to mean?"

She shakes her head. "Never mind. We need to find Emily before he does."

"We?" I arch my eyebrows.

With a heavy sigh, she puts her hands on her hips and tries to stare me down. It's actually cute that she thinks she could intimidate me.

"You came with him. You must care about what he does or you wouldn't have bothered."

"Touché. Where is Emily, then?"

"The last time I saw her, she was going to the restroom."

I step into Alexis's space, making her tense. But underneath the nervousness, I also detect something else. Maybe yearning.

I clasp her hand and then venture into a darker part of the club. She lets me steer her without a fight. I should be disappointed that she didn't complain, but I'm enjoying this situation too much to care. I finally see the sign for the restroom, but before we get any closer, we bump into a tearstained Halsey.

Alexis yanks her hand from mine then.

"What happened?" she asks.

Halsey glances at me first, but it's fleeting. "Nothing."

Bullshit. I bet a limb that Cameron found her already. Since I have no desire to stick my finger in that hornet's nest, I ask, "Where's Emily?"

"I don't know. I lost her on the way to the restroom. I'm quite ready to go home."

"Let's go back to the table," Alexis suggests. "Maybe she's there."

I don't try to take Alexis's hand again. Now that there's a witness, I doubt she'd let me. It's okay. I don't need an audience for the games we'll be playing.

After another minute, we cross into an area where there are a few tables scattered. Alexis stops in front of one where a couple is currently sucking face.

"Hey, Vinny," she calls.

The guy leans back and looks at her. "What's up, Lexi?"

"Where is everyone?"

"Dunno. Carmen left with some douche from your new school, and Cristiano disappeared somewhere with Lazaro."

"Wait. Carmen left with a random guy?" Alexis asks.

"Yep," the girl replies. "He's pretty hot, so I don't blame her."

"Uh, rude much?" Vinny complains. "You can't be making comments about some other dude's hotness in front of me."

"Whatever."

"What did he look like?" I ask.

Alexis's friends turn to me, but it's the guy who speaks. "Who are you?"

"Never mind him," Alexis grits out.

"It was Cameron," Halsey mumbles. "She left with Cameron."

Duh. I should have known. I don't know why I didn't connect the dots sooner. Hooking up with a random girl to torture Halsey fits his MO. He's such a dumbass.

"I'm sorry, Halsey," Alexis says.

She shakes her head. "Don't worry about me. We need to find Emily."

"Maybe she's outside," the girl at the table says. "There's a second bar in the back."

"Let's go check," I say.

I press my hand to Alexis's lower back, spreading my fingers to touch part of her sweet ass. She tenses again and tries to move faster, but it's crowded, and she can't escape me that easily. As she moves, I purposely slide my hand lower until it's firmly where I want. She bats it away, looking over her shoulder to glower at me. I grin in response.

Instead of finding fresh air outside, we're greeted by a cloud of smoke. This is the place where I'd find Luke for sure if he'd come here to party. I scan the open area, trying to find one of the blond heads. I don't see either of them, but I do pinpoint a familiar face. Alexis's uncle. He's in a far corner, a little removed from the crowd, speaking to a shady character in a leather jacket. Judging by his body language and interaction with the other man, I'd say it's not a friendly conversation.

It's best if Alexis doesn't see him. I begin to steer her in the opposite direction when she resists.

Shit. She's seen her uncle too.

"Hold on," she says.

I step in front of her, blocking her path. "I don't think now is a good idea to say hello to Uncle Dearest."

She glares at me. "I fail to see how you have any say in what I do."

"I thought you wanted to find your friend."

"I think I see her," Halsey chimes in.

We both follow her line of vision, but if Emily was somewhere nearby, she vanished in the blink of an eye.

"Where?" Alexis asks.

"I swear I saw her rush toward the exit."

A loud pop sounds in the air, reminding me of the Fourth of July. Only it wasn't fireworks but the noise of a shot fired. Pandemonium ensues with people screaming and running for the exit. I grab Alexis and Halsey by their arms and make a run for the side gate leading to the parking lot. It's either that or be trampled by the mob trying to escape. I don't stop running until I get back to Reid's car.

"Oh my God. What was that?" Halsey asks.

"Someone decided to pull a *Sons of Anarchy* move," I say.

"We need to go back. Emily might still be there," Alexis says.

"I'm not," the girl in question replies from behind us.

I turn and immediately notice one of her jacket sleeves has been ripped off the seams. She's missing a couple of buttons on her white shirt too, and there's a noticeable swelling on her left cheek.

Fuck. Did Luke do that to her? As much as he craves chaos, I don't believe he'd ever beat a girl.

"What happened to you?" Alexis asks.

"Nothing." Her expression is closed off.

"Emily, did Lu—" Halsey starts.

"I said it was nothing," she replies through clenched teeth. "Let's get the hell out of here."

25

ALEXIS

I tried to get Emily to talk on the drive back from La Salamandra, but she threatened to make Halsey and me walk home if we didn't shut up.

Monday morning comes, and I'm still none the wiser about what happened to her. Someone ripped her clothes and struck her face, that I know. And the only person who had a vendetta against her that evening was Luke.

What happened on Friday night consumed my thoughts throughout the weekend. So many things happened that I'm still processing. What was my uncle doing there? Who fired the gun? Did Carmen really hook up with Cameron? To boot, she decided to blow me off again. She ignored all my calls and text messages, and only replied when I said I was going to the police if she didn't respond. But all she said was that she was fine.

Maybe I pissed her off again by bringing Emily and Halsey

to La Salamandra, but hell, that's no reason to give me the silent treatment. I'd rather she yelled at me.

To make matters worse, even my new friends ignored me. Neither Halsey nor Emily replied to my messages. I didn't insist with them, considering we don't have that kind of relationship yet. But I checked Halsey's social media profiles, and she didn't post anything new after Friday.

I'm on pins and needles as I tread through the hallways of Maverick. If feels like I'm walking through a minefield wearing a blindfold. I don't know where I stand with anyone, including Finn. He acted like a real jerk at the club, but then he also got Halsey and me to safety. And I saw the consternated look on his face when he took stock of Emily's condition. He must have also concluded that Luke roughed Emily up, and maybe that bothered him.

I shouldn't entertain thoughts that Finn has any redeemable qualities. I already fell for that bullshit once. I still don't know why I let him rescue me from Dimitri. It's pure insanity that I considered Finn Novak to be a better option than my former crush.

The first people I see on my way to first period are Satan's spawns, a.k.a. Tiffany and Jackie. I brace for the worst. I haven't forgotten their prank last Friday either, but I also haven't thought of a way to retaliate.

Jesus, one week in this place and I'm thinking like everyone. "Hate and Retribution" should be the motto of this school.

"Good morning, Lexi," Tiffany greets me in a sugary tone. "I love what you did to your hair."

I force a bright smile to my face. "Oh, I didn't do anything. Some people are just born with glorious locks."

To emphasize my words, I toss my hair back. I know I'm playing with fire by flaunting my asset like that when they were so close to shaving my head, but I'm not going to let them know I'm afraid of them.

"It would be such a shame if something were to happen to it," Jackie replies maliciously.

I shrug. "Not really. My hair grows like a weed. I've shaved it all off before, you know, to donate it to charity. I looked super cute with a buzz cut. I guess I have the bone structure to pull it off."

Tiffany twists her face into a scowl. "I seriously doubt that."

"I don't care what you think."

I leave before they can get a reply in, feeling victorious for a whole minute. Then I enter the classroom and see Finn and two of his friends are already inside. Not Luke though. Reid's head is down on this desk. He must be napping. Cameron is distracted by his phone and doesn't even look up when I walk past his desk. Finn follows my movements and keeps staring until I sit down at the desk across the aisle. He's the one who switched seats; I'm not going to move and give him the satisfaction. But his attention annoys me.

"What?" I snap.

His lips curl into a grin, and I realize my reaction is exactly what he wanted to achieve.

"Good morning to you too, Lexi," he says in a seductive voice, one I haven't heard before.

I wish I could say it does nothing to me, but my toes curl inside my shoes. *Stupid-ass hormones.*

"Whatever."

I look away, pulling my laptop out of my bag. I keep my eyes glued to the screen, even when Tiffany's and Jackie's annoying voices announce their arrival. A moment later, someone's backpack bumps into my arm, getting my attention.

"Sorry," Eric mumbles without looking at me.

"I guess it's asshole day today," I say loud enough for him to hear.

He stops in his tracks and turns around. "Excuse me?"

"You heard me." I hold his stare, not one bit intimidated by his glare.

He shakes his head and then continues down the aisle to his seat in the last row.

Finn leans sideways, getting closer to my desk. "Not a fan of Eric Danes either, huh?"

"I don't like rude people in general."

"Nah, I don't think that's the reason."

I should know better than to fall for his baiting, but I glance at him and immediately become trapped by his sky-blue eyes. God, I hate how pretty he is.

"Please enlighten me, Finn Novak. What *is* the reason?"

"I think you're pissed that Danes didn't acknowledge your presence. You thought he'd be an ally because you come from the same world."

I clench my jaw hard, hating that Finn figured me out so easily.

"You're wrong," I say.

"I'm not and you know it. Face it, Alexis. You and I aren't that different. You didn't grow up surrounded by luxury, but you're one of the young gods of this town whether you like it or not."

"Why? Because my grandparents are wealthy?"

"No, because you're filthy just like the rest of us." He returns to his side of the aisle, leaving my jaw hanging loose.

He called me filthy, and I have no rebuff for that.

Mr. Jonas walks in, greeting everyone with a cheery "Good morning," and I lose my chance to offer a retort.

Maybe I couldn't come up with an immediate reply because deep down, I know Finn might be right. How else would I explain the darkness swirling in my chest, or the feeling of suppressed rage that I fear will erupt and wreak havoc on my world?

The next hour is torturous. I'm too conscious of Finn sitting on the other side of the aisle with his godlike looks and infuriatingly smug attitude. When the class ends, I can't wait to get out of the room.

It's only when I'm in the hallway that I realize Emily never showed up. I text her again, but I doubt she'll reply.

On my way to Miss LaFleur's class, I keep my eyes peeled for Halsey, but if she's in school today, I miss her too. The hallways are buzzing though, more so than normal. That usually means juicy gossip. I make an effort to listen to bits of conversation until I hear the name Piper Phillips. That was the student who went missing last week.

I stop next to a couple of girls and ask, "What's going on?"

"Piper Phillips is back," one of them says.

"So she wasn't missing?"

"Apparently not. I bet she did run away with a guy, and he probably got sick of the idiot after a week and dumped her." The second girl snickers.

I step away from the duo, afraid I'll choke on their toxicity. Whether she ran away with a guy or not is irrelevant to me. I'm glad she wasn't kidnapped, or worse, killed.

It takes me five minutes to reach the other side of the building, but before I enter Miss LaFleur's classroom, I take a couple of steadying breaths.

There are two assholes in this class, the pedophile teacher and Eric Danes. I wonder who's going to piss me off the most today.

FINN

"What's your deal with diner girl, Finn?" Cameron asks me as soon as we step foot in the hallway.

"Just having some fun."

"Anyone heard from Luke? I haven't seen him since Friday," Reid changes the subject, and I'm grateful he has the attention span of a gnat.

After the girls left with Emily last Friday, Luke eventually found me. He had a busted lip, and his clothes were also worse for the wear. He denied laying a hand on Emily, but he also didn't elaborate on what happened to them. I've known him long enough to not pry. I'm also not surprised he didn't show up today.

"He's probably still recovering from a massive hangover," Cameron replies.

"Since we don't have to accommodate his disgusting smoking habit, where do you want to hang out during our free period?" Reid asks.

"I could eat," I say. "I had an early morning session at the pool."

We begin to move toward the cafeteria. If we leave campus in search of food, we won't come back. Cameron and Reid might not care to skip classes, but I can't afford to ditch them now that I'm allowed to compete again. A bad attendance record means I can't be on the team.

For the first time since school started, I'm feeling like myself. That doesn't mean I forgot all my demons, but the little game I started with Alexis is distracting me from them. She's going to retaliate soon, and I can't wait for it.

I hear the name Piper Phillips whispered among the students, and that makes me pause. I stop a freshman passing by and ask for the deets.

"Oh, Piper showed up for class this morning like nothing happened. I guess she wasn't kidnapped after all."

Relief washes over me. I can't say that her disappearance

occupied much of my thoughts in the past week, but I'm glad she's okay. Her father must be relieved. I do wonder for a fleeting moment where she's been all this time, but it's soon forgotten when Julie Diamond crosses our path. She ignores us, saving all her loathing for Reid.

"Man, Julie is looking good today," Cameron pipes up as he turns his head to check out her ass.

Reid's face becomes a cold mask, but a muscle in his jaw tics from him clenching it so hard. He doesn't offer Cameron a retort though.

"I don't know why you don't tap that. Hate sex is the best," Cameron continues.

"Oh yeah? Why don't you fuck Halsey, then?" Reid replies.

In the blink of an eye, Cameron has him up against a locker, holding him in place by his neck.

"What the fuck, Cameron? Are you insane?" Reid croaks.

"Don't ever say anything like that again. Do you understand me?" he grits out.

Reid's face is getting red, but he's not going to bow down to Cameron's demand. He's too fucking stubborn.

I yank Cameron off Reid by the back of his jacket. He jerks free of my hold and turns with a fist pulled back already.

"What? Are you going to punch me?"

It's more of a dare than a question.

People are staring and pointing their cameras at us. Fucking great. Within the next minute, everyone at Maverick will know about this.

Reid fixes his jacket while keeping his glower trained on Cameron. "You're a crazy motherfucker, Cameron. Get your shit straight or stay the fuck away from me."

Cameron's still breathing hard, but he doesn't say a word to Reid, who whirls around and strides away.

I glance at the small crowd that gathered around us and bark, "Show's over, assholes. Run along."

Only when Cameron and I are alone do I open my mouth again.

"That was bullshit."

"Reid has a big mouth."

"Yeah. So? He didn't say anything that warranted you going berserk on his ass."

"You heard what the asshole said."

"Maybe you *should* fuck her and get this shit over with. We're all tired of you masking your obsession with Halsey with hate. You're not fooling anyone, Cam, only yourself."

A myriad of emotions flashes in his green eyes in the span of seconds, but anger is the one that prevails.

"Fuck you, Finn."

I don't move from where I stand as I watch him leave.

Hell, I should have known the day would turn to shit sooner rather than later.

26

ALEXIS

I survived Miss LaFleur's class. Besides giving me a scathing glance when I walked in, she ignored me during the hour-long do-what-you-want lecture. And Eric Danes didn't show. Two for two. I doubt my luck will hold out the rest of the day, though.

Once I'm out in the hallway, I check my phone for messages again. Nothing from Carmen, Halsey, or Emily, but there's a message from Grandma asking me what day is good this week to meet with the party planner. God, I forgot about my birthday bash. I make a mental note to give Grandma the list of people who should be banned. The three assholes who helped Tiffany and Jackie must be included. I have to find out their names.

I head into the locker room to change into my PE uniform. Unfortunately, those two bitches are also in the same class. They're not in the locker room yet, so I change as quickly as I can. Half-empty locker rooms are the best places for an ambush. It occurs to me that it might not be safe to shower after class. I wouldn't put it past them to switch my shampoo for Nair. My hair does grow fast, but I don't want to lose it.

I'm surprised to see Halsey in the gym already. She's sitting on the bleachers, looking lost in thought.

"Hey," I say as I drop next to her.

"Oh, hi, Lexi."

"You missed first period."

"Yeah."

"Everything okay?"

She nods. "Just had to deal with some personal stuff."

It's obvious she's in evasion mode. I'm curious, but I'm not a pest, so I don't push.

"Have you heard from Emily at all?" I ask instead.

"No. I'm worried about her. We should check on her after school."

"I don't know where she lives. Do you?"

A pretty brunette with shoulder-length hair and sun-kissed skin walks over. I think she's in my English class, but I didn't see her there today.

"Hi, do you mind if I join you?" she asks with a smile.

"Hey, Julie. Yeah, of course," Halsey replies. "I don't remember seeing you here last week."

"I made changes to my schedule." She sits down next to Halsey and then leans forward to look at me. "God, I'm so rude. I'm Julie Diamond, by the way."

"Nice to meet you, Julie. I'm—"

"Alexis Walker. I know."

Halsey nudges my arm. "You're famous already. Pretty soon you'll have more social media followers than me."

"Ha! I don't think so. Why am I famous, though?"

"Hmm, let's see. You're the lost granddaughter of the

Montgomerys, you have a hot and dangerous uncle who has just been released from prison, and you're on Finn Novak's radar," Julie replies.

I'm taken aback by her list.

"Wow, that's a lot to unpack. Although, I'm not my grandparents' lost granddaughter."

"Fine, but you *do* have a hot uncle, and you *have* caught Finn's attention." She smirks.

I grumble and look away. I suppose my uncle is attractive. And only a blind person would have missed how Finn has gone out of his way to get into my head.

"Why did you change your schedule?" Halsey asks.

"I couldn't suffer English with Reid. He's the worst."

"Not worse than Cameron." Halsey snorts.

"Being an asshole must be a requirement to join their little mean boys' club," I pipe up. "But honestly, Luke is the vilest of them all."

"He's the craziest, but I don't think he's the vilest. Considering the shitty family life he has, I'm surprised he can function in society," Julie replies.

I open my mouth to ask for more intel, but the PE teacher is already here, and the gym has filled up with other students, including my nemeses, who glance in my direction but decide to leave me in peace for now.

The reason, I soon discover, is that they've spotted someone weaker to mess with. A younger student, probably a freshman. They make a mean remark, which turns the girl's face beet red.

Jerks.

"Who is that?" I ask.

"Oh, that's Piper Phillips," Halsey replies.

"Why is she in our PE class?" I stand up when the teacher signals us to join her in the middle of the court.

"Because she's wicked good at volleyball. The best spiker in the entire school, and Coach Meyer wants her best students training with seniors," Julie replies.

We join the rest of the class, and soon the PE teacher divides us into four teams of six. We're playing volleyball today. I'm glad I ended up on a team with Halsey and Julie. Piper is also with us, and the two heinous bitches are on the opposing team.

"How good are you, Lexi?" Halsey asks.

I smirk. "I can hold my own."

The PE teacher turns to Piper. "You need to get your hair out of the way, Miss Phillips."

"I don't have a hair band."

The older woman sighs, clearly annoyed, and then pulls an elastic band from her fanny pack. "Here. Use this."

Piper's face falls. I don't understand what the big deal is. Why would she want her hair to get in the way?

When she lifts her mane to make a ponytail, I see what she was trying to hide: a tattoo of an intricate mask. The skin is still a little red, so I assume she got inked recently. It's illegal in California to get one before you're eighteen, but nothing seems to deter these rich kids.

The game starts, and soon I forget Piper and her new tat. Tiffany and Jackie are determined to win this match, playing aggressively like they want to obliterate me in particular with the ball. Their intention is to hurt, but the PE teacher seems unbothered by it. I receive one serve from Jackie that leaves a burning mark on my arms. I'll have bruises all over.

Fucking bitch.

The teacher only whistles when Tiffany hits Piper in the face with the ball. The girl cries out, dropping to her knees. Laughing, Jackie high-fives her friend.

"You did that on purpose!" I take a step forward, but Halsey holds me back.

Tiffany places a hand over her chest, twisting her face into a mocking expression. "How dare you? I'd never."

"Bullshit. I saw you," Julie retorts.

"Hey, hey, hey!" The teacher steps onto the court, keeping us apart. "Enough with this."

She turns to Piper and asks, "Are you okay, Miss Phillips?"

"I think so."

The teacher helps her get back on her feet and inspects her face. "You're a little red. If it swells up, go to the nurse's office."

"My head is already pounding. May I go now?"

"Of course."

"It seems you're down a player." Jackie snickers.

"Thanks for pointing that out, Miss Wen." The teacher glowers. "Miss Duran, you can sit your ass on the bench for now."

"What? That's unfair," Tiffany whines.

The teacher shrugs. "You took one of their players out. That's more than fair in my book."

I watch the idiot trudge to the bleachers, but I'm far from satisfied with the outcome. How am I supposed to dole out payback if she's not playing?

WITHOUT OUR BEST PLAYER, we didn't win. I'm usually not a sore loser, but today, I'm sulking. At least Jackie's team didn't win by her merit. All their fuckups were thanks to her. We got to enjoy her getting chewed out by her teammates. Silver linings and all.

Once PE is over, Julie runs off to her private fencing class, skipping a shower in the locker room. I'm still leery of Tiffany and Jackie, but I can't simply not shower. I'm busy checking that my shampoo and conditioner haven't been tampered with when Halsey announces she needs to go.

"Aren't you going to shower first?" I ask in a slightly panicked voice.

Crap.

"I can't. I have to go home." She shoves her phone in her bag and bangs the locker door shut.

"Shit," I curse under my breath.

"What's wrong?"

"Don't judge me, but I'm not really keen on getting naked while Tiffany and Jackie are around."

"Oh, I see." She bites her lower lip, seeming to ponder for a second, then says, "I have an idea. Grab your things and come with me."

I don't question her, glad that she might have a solution. This is not ideal—I can't hide from those bitches every time—but until I come up with a way to neutralize them for good, I'll take whatever I can get.

"Where are we going?" I ask, trying to keep up with Halsey's fast pace.

"You know how the school has an entire new floor not being used? Well, they were also building new locker room facilities for the male swim team. Construction is done, but it's not in use yet."

"Let me guess, you have the key."

"Yeah, well, not a key, the passcode."

Halsey leads me past the pool area, which is currently empty. I see the sign for the old locker room, but we walk farther down the hallway until she stops in front of a wide door. There's a keypad next to it.

"The passcode is 3-3-4-9," she tells me as she types it in.

"And you're sure it's okay to use it?"

"I never said it was okay, so don't get caught."

"I'll be sure to be superfast. Thank you."

"No problem."

I push the door open and am immediately hit by the smell of fresh paint. Despite that, the room is sparkling clean and a million times nicer than our locker room. *Damn, why can't we get upgraded facilities too?*

I set my duffel bag on a bench and then test the shower first before I undress. Powerful jets rain down on my hand. *Nice.* I remove my sweaty clothes, grab my products and towel, and head to the shower area. It's a little unnerving to be naked in this empty room when I'm not supposed to be here, but better than showering next to Tiffany and Jackie.

I hang my towel on the peg nearest to me and then get under the jets. Humming, I open the shampoo bottle but then freeze. *Hell, what if those hellhounds did tamper with it?* I sniff it again. It doesn't smell different, but I can't be a hundred-percent sure.

Fuck it. I'll wash my hair properly at home. I'll just lather my body with soap and call it a day.

I'm all foamy when I hear the door bang against the wall.

Shit. Someone is here.

I turn around too fast and slip on the wet tiles, almost losing my balance. It takes serious contortionist moves to remain upright.

"My, my. What a delightful surprise," Finn purrs.

Instinctively, I cover myself to the best of my ability, but in hindsight, I should have reached for the towel. Now I'll have to flash my boobs to grab it.

"What the hell are you doing here?" I ask, fighting the erratic beating of my heart.

Crossing his arms, he leans against the wall where my towel is hanging.

Fuck.

"I came here to check out the facilities."

"How did you get the code?"

God, woman. Why are you asking all these stupid questions? You need to get the hell out of here.

"From Coach. And I'm guessing you got it from Halsey?" He grins.

"Yeah. Now stop ogling me and hand me my towel."

He shakes his head. "I'm afraid I can't do that. You see, you're trespassing. This area is for members of the male swim team."

"Finn, I swear to God, if you don't get out of here, I'll scream bloody murder."

He raises an arrogant eyebrow. "And who's going to hear you?"

I know he'll stop me from getting the towel myself. I *cannot* let him put his hands on me while I'm in my birthday suit.

"You want something. Name your terms."

"You learn fast, Lexi. I told you you're just like the rest of us."

"Don't call me that. You haven't earned the right. It's Alexis to you."

He smirks. "Is that so? Fine. Alexis, then. This is what's going to happen. I'm going to sit here, keeping your towel warm in my hands, while you finish getting clean."

"You want to watch me shower?" My voice rises to a pitch.

"Yes, and I won't be satisfied until every inch of your body is properly lathered and rinsed, including the places that are hard to reach." His hungry gaze drops to my crotch area.

"You're a perv."

He chuckles. "No, I'm just concerned about your current state. After all, you are so… *filthy.*"

My heart is thundering in my chest. Finn is really going to make me do this. I could try to wrestle the towel from him, but there's zero chance I'd succeed. It would only be more humiliating.

Glowering, I drop my arms to my sides. There's no point covering my intimate parts now. I don't move for a moment, taking perverted satisfaction in watching Finn's gaze widen and his Adam's apple bob up and down.

"Take your fill, asshole. This is the first and last time you'll see me naked."

He narrows his eyes. "You're not doing what I told you."

Keeping my gaze locked with his, I reach for the liquid soap. My pulse is racing, but for a different reason now. A strange exhilaration is taking over me. It's depraved and twisted; it feeds my inner darkness. This situation should have made me spiral, but oddly, I'm in control.

I take my time lathering my entire body, spending extra seconds around my breasts, making my nipples turn hard. Slowly, I glide my fingers down my stomach, skipping my sex for now to continue down my legs. Finn's smoldering stare feels like an angry lover's caress. My clit is throbbing, begging to be teased.

Shit. I'm turned on. If I touch myself now, I run the serious risk of climaxing. I can't let my body betray me like that.

"You missed a spot," he says, his voice thick with need.

I give props to him. The boy has some serious self-control. He doesn't even twitch in his seat, but I can see the bulge in his pants. He's hurting just like I am.

I finally glide my fingers between my legs. A zing of pleasure shoots down my thighs when I press against my sensitive spot. God, I want to keep playing with myself until the ache goes away, but if Finn can resist the urge to seek release, so can I.

Reluctantly, I pull my hand away and let the hot shower jets rinse all the soap away. Closing my eyes, I tilt my head up and give my back to him. When I face him again, he's standing with my towel in hand.

Nervousness makes an appearance again. *What the hell is going to happen now?* I turn off the shower and amble toward him, noticing he's no longer watching me with desire. Loathing is all I see in his eyes.

He throws the towel at me.

"If I ever catch you here again, I'll do more than watch you play with yourself."

"Oh yeah? What are you going to do? Force yourself on me?"

He scoffs. "I'll fuck you soon enough, darling. You're going to beg for it."

I let out a derisive laugh to mask the ugly truth that he isn't wrong.

"What *are* you going to do, then?"

"I'll have my phone in hand."

27

FINN

I wanted peace and quiet after the altercation between Reid and Cameron. I didn't expect to find a naked Alexis using the brand-new showers assigned to my team. It seemed like a sign from the gods or a gift. There she was, the object of my obsession, vulnerable and alone. It was almost too easy. Only it turned out she's made of stronger stuff than most sheep who attend Maverick.

It was torture to simply watch her touch herself and not move a muscle. My cock was straining so hard against my pants, I was afraid any sudden movement would make me jizz in them. I knew she was beautiful, but I couldn't have imagined she was breathtaking.

I had to leave the locker room in a hurry before I made a wrong move. She wasn't ready to be claimed yet, but she will be soon.

I wasn't planning on ditching any classes today, but I'm still sporting a raging boner minutes after my interaction with her. I sprint to the old locker room and change into my Speedo. I'd jerk off if my demented mind didn't think it'd be admitting defeat. A few laps in the pool ought to take care of my problem.

The moment I'm underwater, I regain my strength. Maybe I *am* a descendant of Triton himself. I've never felt more at home than I do when submerged. As I predicted, my erection goes away after a couple of strokes. I don't leave the pool though, swimming until I notice I'm no longer alone. When I come up for air, I don't investigate who came into the pool area until I reach the ladder.

"I should have known it was you," Coach Kramer says. "Aren't you supposed to be in class?"

Breathing hard, I remove my goggles.

"I had a free period. I lost track of time."

Coach watches me through slitted eyes. "I'll pretend I believe you. Get out and make sure there isn't a repeat. I'd hate to suspend you from the team because you're forgetting your academics."

"Yes, sir."

He heads to his office and I go to the showers. By the time I'm back in my uniform and in the hallway, people are already milling about, either going to grab lunch at the cafeteria or sit outside. I spot Alexis at the end of the corridor, taking something from her locker. Her hair is still damp. I grin.

"What are you smiling about?" Reid asks, stepping next to me.

"Where did you go?" I deflect. "I thought you left campus."

"Nah, I went to the library."

I wrinkle my nose, smelling sex all over him. "That a new code for a hookup?"

He laughs. "Nope. I said I went to the library. I didn't say it was for reading."

I roll my eyes. "I take it you're over your fight with Cam?"

Reid furrows his brows. "Fuck no. If Cameron wants to get back in my good graces, he has to grovel. I'm not one of his doormat bitches."

"Just leave me out of it."

"Count on it. But back to my earlier question. Why were you smiling like you just had the best fuck of your life?"

I glower. "Dude, don't insult me."

Reid glances at Alexis, who is now walking away from us.

"Your hair is wet. Her hair is wet. Bruh, you just railed diner girl, didn't you?" He claps my shoulder.

"Not yet. Soon, though."

"And then what? Wham, bam, thank you, ma'am?"

I give him a droll look. "What do you think?"

"I don't know, man. You've been acting hella strange since that chick came into our lives."

I've been acting differently for a year, but I'm not going to point that out. One of the reasons I like Reid is because he's as observant as a spoon. Sometimes I need easy, and Luke and Cameron are the opposite of that.

"I gotta go. Coach Kramer already chewed me out for ditching class."

"All right. See you later."

MY DAY IS FAR from over when I leave Maverick. I'm halfway to my father's office when the asshole calls me.

"I'm on my way," I say before he decides to yell at me for something.

"Turn around and go home. Your mother is having one of her episodes, and I don't have the patience to deal with that shit today."

Saying Mom is having an episode doesn't really narrow things down for me. Is she drunk? High on her prescription drugs? But Dad already hung up, so I can't grill him for more details. Not that he'd give me any. He probably doesn't know jack.

I take the next exit and head home. I should be feeling great that I got a free pass, but dealing with Mom is no picnic either. I hope she's just drunk; when she mixes drugs and alcohol, it's a real headache.

Ten minutes later, I'm pulling up in front of the house and immediately know what sent Mom into a fit: Grandpa's car is parked in front of the guesthouse, and servants are unpacking his trunk.

"What fresh hell is this?" I mumble to myself.

I get out of the car, annoyed as fuck already, and stride into the house.

"Mom?" I call out.

"Finn, my boy," Grandpa greets me from the receiving room with a broad smile on his face.

"Uh, what are you doing here? And what's up with all that luggage?"

"Oh, I'm doing a bit of renovation."

"You have a guesthouse."

"Eh, it will be a mess outside, and I hate all the noise and strangers on my property. What's the matter, Finn? Not happy to spend some weeks with this old man?" He clasps my shoulder and chuckles.

No. I'm fucking livid. No wonder my mother is freaking out.

"I'm going to check on Mom."

"Oh, I think she's taking a nap. Women's woes, migraine or something."

I ignore his sexist remark and head for the stairs, going up two steps at a time. My parents haven't slept in the same bed since I was little. They don't just have separate bedrooms—they live on opposite wings in the mansion. Like most couples in their stratosphere, their marriage is one of convenience, a merger of assets, if you will. That's a future that's also expected of my sister and me. Hell, Dad is already pimping me out to further his agenda.

Letting out a heavy breath, I knock on Mom's door and call her. She doesn't reply, so I head in. The living area is a mess with clothes scattered everywhere, an empty vodka bottle on the table, and a tray with lunch that wasn't touched.

The double door to her bedroom is open, and from where I stand, I can see Mom sound asleep, snoring up a storm. I walk over to double-check she didn't vomit. Anger swells in me when I see her smeared makeup and tear-streaked face. I curl my hands into fists, fighting the urge to destroy things.

There's nothing I can do now, but one day, I'll make them all pay.

28

ALEXIS

J had to do a lot of pretending the rest of the school day. I couldn't let anyone see I was rattled. Finn got under my skin, and I'm raving mad that I allowed him to do it. I thought for a moment that I had some control over him, but he was only letting the rope loose so I could hang myself with it.

I'm too much on edge to go home. Sitting behind the steering wheel, I call Carmen again. She doesn't answer. Fuck it. Forget sending a message. I'm going over to her house. She's not working today because the restaurant is closed on Mondays, so she should be home.

On the drive there, I run through what I want to say to her. It's not fair for her to get mad at me for making friends at Maverick. Does she want me to be a pariah at that stupid prep school forever?

Carmen's house is only a few blocks away from my former

home. Not wanting to be assaulted by memories that will chafe the wound that's not healed, I take a different, longer route.

My phone rings, and for a second, I think it's her calling me back. But when I see Grandma's name flash on the screen, I send it to voice mail. She'll be furious, but I don't want her to derail my thoughts.

After another minute, I'm parking in front of Carmen's place. Her cousin's car is in the driveway, so there's hope she's home. She doesn't own her own vehicle, and Cristiano lets her borrow his vintage Camaro.

My stomach is coiled tight as I walk to the front door. This nervousness is a foreign feeling when associated with my best friend. I ring the bell once, which immediately sends Carmen's chihuahua into a barking frenzy. An annoyed female voice tells Fenrir to shush. It could either be Carmen's mother or her aunt. Their voices are almost identical.

When the door opens, it's her mom who's standing on the other side.

"Lexi, *cariño*. What are you doing here?"

"I came to see Carmen. Is she home?"

Her mouth makes a perfect O. "Oh no. Carmen is at one of her friends'."

Disappointment washes over me. "Who? Taluah?"

"No. She told me it's a new girl. I can't remember the name now. Why don't you give her a call?"

I nod, unable to tell Mrs. Concepción that Carmen is avoiding them.

"Yeah, I'll do that. Thank you."

Before, I was on edge; now I'm just depressed. My mood swings are giving me whiplash, and I'm not even a broody vampire. I should just go home and forget Carmen for now. But instead of taking the exit that would lead me to my grandparents' place, I keep going and head to Triton Cove's industrial district—more specifically, to Saul's Garage. I don't want to think about Finn, and I can't fix my situation with Carmen. But I can get to know my uncle, or at least try.

I hadn't looked for him before because I was so damn scared, not of him but of the past. But enough is enough. I'm not a coward.

The parking lot in front of the garage is full, though probably most of the cars are here to be fixed. Someone pulls out from right in front of the office door, and I snag it. Once I'm inside, an older man with a mop of white hair glances at me from behind the counter.

"Can I help you, miss?"

"I'm looking for Damian Walker."

A spark of recognition hits the man's eyes. "Oh my. I can't believe I didn't recognize you right away. You're Alexis, Dennis Walker's little girl."

I grin through the pang of sadness. "Not that little anymore."

He chuckles. "Well, anyone your age is a kid to me. I'm Saul, by the way. Damian is in the shop. You can go around the building. You should find him under one of the cars.

"Okay. Thanks."

I receive curious glances from the mechanics in the garage as I follow Saul's instructions. One of them asks me if they can be of assistance, but he's way less friendly than his boss. He also eyes my school uniform with disdain.

"I'm looking for Damian Walker."

One of the guys laughs. "Jesus Christ, Walker. Are you sniffing around the kindergarten now?"

Heat rushes to my cheeks. "He's my uncle!"

The big-mouth douche looks at me apologetically. "Sorry, girlie."

Damian slides from under the car to my right and stares at me, frowning.

"Is everything okay, Lexi?"

"Uh, yeah."

Shit. I didn't expect to have an audience. It's bad enough that I don't know what to say or how to act around him.

He jumps to his feet and says, "I'm due a break. Let's head inside."

"Okay."

He turns to his coworkers. "Stay clear of the break room."

"You're not the boss of me," the first mean dude grumbles.

My uncle levels the guy with a glower that promises there will be severe repercussions if his order isn't followed. The idiot's aggression level lowers considerably as he drops his gaze to the ground.

All right. My uncle is a badass. Pride fills my chest, never mind that the man spent more than a decade in prison for killing someone.

I follow him to the break room, which is a small kitchen with a round table in the middle. There's no stove, just a microwave, a coffee machine, and a fridge. From inside the room, we can see the shop through the window. I peer outside, expecting to find his coworkers peeking at us, but they've made themselves scares already.

"Would you like a soda or a snack?" He points at the two vending machines in the corner.

"No, I'm good. Thanks."

"Do you want to sit down?"

"Sure."

God, this is awkward.

"I'm glad you came by," he says after a moment. "I wasn't sure you would."

"Me neither. It was a spur-of-the-moment thing."

"Right. How is your boyfriend?"

"Boyfriend?" I frown.

"Finn Novak."

Hell, I forgot that asshole lied to my uncle. I'm about to tell him the truth, but then I also remember how surprised he seemed to be that I was dating a Novak.

"He's good. Do you have a problem with his family?"

He tenses visibly, but he doesn't look away. "I'd prefer it if you weren't involved with the boy."

"Why?"

I see conflict shining in his eyes. He's keeping something from me.

"Hey, you can't go in there!" someone shouts from the garage.

My uncle jumps to his feet and looks through the window. Then he curses and turns to me.

"I need you to get in there." He points at the restroom door.

"What's going on?"

He grabs my arm and pulls me up from the chair. "Just do it, please."

I rush to the restroom, propelled by the urgency in his tone. Whoever is coming to see my uncle has rattled him. My heart is hammering loudly in my chest as I stare at the closed door. I don't lock it because it will show from the outside that it's occupied.

"What the hell are you doing here? I said I'd come to you," my uncle tells someone.

"Careful now, Damian. You're forgetting your place. We don't take orders from pawns like you."

He laughs. "If I'm the pawn, then what are you? Gordon's fetch dog?"

There's a scuffle and the noise of a chair tumbling down. I stop breathing for a second.

"You have a smart mouth for someone with a death sentence hanging over your head. The only reason you're still breathing is because you're useful to us."

"Let go of me," my uncle grits out.

"Consider this your only warning. If you don't deliver your

end of the bargain, you can say goodbye to your freedom. It'll be back to Encina Island for you."

"I earned my parole fair and square."

"Sure, but it'd be so easy to mess that up, wouldn't it?"

The door to the break room opens and shuts again, but I don't dare move from my hiding spot. I wait a couple minutes, then slowly push the door forward and peek outside. Damian is standing in front of the window with his arms crossed over his chest.

"Is he gone?" I ask.

"Yes."

"Who was that man?"

He looks over his shoulder. "No one you should worry about. It's late. Your grandmother must be worried."

"Stop evading me. I'm not a child!"

His steely gray eyes narrow. "You *are* a child, Lexi. The less you know about my life, the better."

"Why did he say you have a death sentence hanging over your head? Who did you piss off in prison?"

"I'm not having this conversation with you. Go home." He strides out of the room before I can offer a retort.

I follow him, but in the shop, there are too many witnesses. He resumes his work under the car, effectively cutting off any possibility of a conversation.

Fuming, I march out of the garage. My father was such a sweet man. How could he be related to that pigheaded jerk?

I don't try to rein in my anger. It's keeping me from obsessing about what I learned today. I've watched too many cop shows to know no one survives prison without striking deals with bad people. He's indebted to someone dangerous, though.

It's not too far of a leap to assume the Triads are involved somehow. The question is, are they the ones who my uncle owes a favor, or are they the ones who want to kill him?

29

ALEXIS

I'm such a hot mess during the drive back home that I barely notice my surroundings. I also don't give much thought when I see the fancy sports car parked in front of my grandparents' house. So when I walk in and hear Finn's distinct voice, the shock feels like a bucket of ice-cold water was poured over my head.

Still in denial, I head to the living room. Nope. I didn't imagine it. There he is, talking with Grandma as if they're old friends. I have to pick up my jaw from the floor and try to keep my heart from leaping to my throat.

Finn turns to me, sporting a smug grin on his devilishly handsome face.

"What are you doing here?" I blurt out.

Grandma furrows her brows, staring at me disapprovingly. No surprise. She probably thinks Finn is a saint. Plus, I ignored her call earlier.

"Our Spanish assignment is due tomorrow, and we never got together to work on it."

Damn everything to hell. I completely forgot about the stupid assignment. The last thing I want is to work on a school project with Finn, especially after what he made me do in the shower. Never mind that I'm still reeling from my visit to Saul's Garage. My heart is beating a staccato rhythm now, and my palms are sweaty.

"You could have called," I tell him.

"I did. It went straight to voice mail."

Keeping my glare locked on his face, I pull my phone out of my purse. The screen is black. I must have run out of battery.

"We could have worked on it via a conference call," I retort.

Grandma glares at me. "Alexis, you're being extremely rude. I think it's lovely that Finn came over. Dinner will be served in ten minutes. Go wash up."

"I'm not really hungry." I cross my arms. "I don't think Finn wants to stay for dinner anyway."

"Nonsense. It's always best to work on a full stomach." She turns to Finn. "Unless your family is expecting you for supper."

He laughs. "Oh no. We don't follow a proper meal schedule in my house. I usually make do with a sandwich for dinner."

"Oh, that's terrible. I insist you stay for dinner, then."

"I don't want to impose, Mrs. Montgomery."

She smiles at him. "You're not imposing at all. We love hosting."

"Do I have time to shower, at least?" I ask, then immediately berate myself for the stupid question.

Finn's eyes light up with mischief, making my face burn like lava. Now he's thinking about my earlier shower session.

You're an idiot, Alexis.

Grandma opens her mouth to reply, but the front door opens and in comes Grandpa. He stops short when he notices Finn.

"Oh, hello there," he says.

Finn strides toward Grandpa and extends his hand. "Good afternoon, Mr. Montgomery."

"Good afternoon, young man. I didn't realize we were expecting your visit today." He looks at Grandma as if this was planned and she simply forgot to let him know.

"Alexis and I need to finish a project due tomorrow," Finn replies.

Grandpa's frown vanishes in a flash. "Oh, marvelous. So you're staying for dinner, I assume."

"Mrs. Montgomery was kind enough to invite me."

I watch the exchange while seething inside. Finn is going out of his way to be super polite, and it's grating on my nerves. Everyone is ignoring the fact that he came here on a whim and at an inappropriate time. I wonder what my grandparents would think if they knew what Finn made me do today.

Grandma's maid comes into the room and announces dinner will be served in ten minutes.

"Excellent. I'll have time for a predinner cocktail. Care to join me, Finn?"

"He's eighteen, Grandpa," I retort.

Grandpa's bushy eyebrows furrow while Finn looks at me, amused.

"I wasn't suggesting he drink an alcoholic beverage, Alexis. Good grief."

"I'd love a drink, Mr. Montgomery," Finn replies.

Grandpa heads into the room across the entry hall, and Finn follows him. No sooner are they out of earshot than Grandma corners me.

"You didn't tell me Finn was your partner in school."

"Only for one project. Hardly a big deal."

"It *is* a big deal, Lexi. He's from a good family, and he's so well mannered. You need friends like him."

"I *do not* need friends like Finn," I grit out. "Besides, I already have friends."

The words feel bitter on my tongue. I don't know if that's true anymore. Carmen won't call me back, and I'm afraid that if I reach out to Vinny or Taluah, they'll blow me off too. We weren't as close friends as Carmen and me.

Grandma waves a dismissive hand and then heads to the kitchen. At least she forgot to yell at me for sending her call to voice mail.

Grumbling, I go to the powder room to wash my hands but stop short when I hear Finn's baritone laughter.

Great. He's already won over Grandpa too.

FINN

I DIDN'T PLAN on coming to the Montgomerys after I left the house. I simply couldn't stay, knowing Grandpa was in the vicinity. I had every intention to go check on Luke when the calendar app on my phone reminded me of the Spanish assignment. That gave me a better option to cope with my turbulent feelings. I knew I'd piss off Alexis even more if I showed up at her grandparents' place out of the blue. Besides getting her rattled, it would also help further my agenda. Dad wants a deal with Richard Montgomery badly, and if I don't show results soon, I can kiss swimming goodbye. He'd probably yank me off the team just to spite me.

I thought sucking up to the Montgomerys would be hard—I hate that kind of shit. But seeing Alexis's growing irritation throughout dinner more than made up for it.

When Mrs. Montgomery offers dessert, I decline. I've played

with my feisty little mouse for too long; it's time to actually do some work.

Alexis stands up and says she'll be right back. I walk out of the dining room a second later and pretend to use the restroom, but the moment she vanishes up the stairs, I follow her. It simply won't do to come here and not get a peek of her bedroom. It takes me a couple of tries before I open the right door. Like the rookie she is, she didn't lock it. She's not in the main area, so I assume she's using the bathroom. I let myself in, and then I do lock the door. I don't want to be interrupted.

I give the room a cursory glance, but nothing catches my attention. I walk over to a large dresser and open the first drawer. As I suspected, it's where she keeps her lingerie. If what I see can be called that. I pull out a pair of cotton panties and immediately come to a realization. My lips curl upward.

I put the panties back, then feel something strange hidden under the layers of soft fabric. I push the undies aside and find a stack of old letters, bound together by an elastic band. *Curiouser and curiouser.* I pick them up and flip them over to read the return address.

Shit. It's from Encina State Prison. Why was Alexis's uncle sending letters to his sister-in-law and not his brother?

"What the hell!" Alexis screeches.

I jump, startled. The discovery distracted me. Like a moron, I drop the stack of letters back in the drawer, trying to hide that I was snooping. Like she hadn't caught me red-handed.

She reaches me in three long strides and pushes me back.

"I can't believe you came into my room uninvited and invaded my privacy like that."

"Relax, it's not like I haven't seen all of you anyway."

"You're an asshole!" She shoves me again, and this time I fall on her bed.

I can only allow one hit at me, not two. I grab her arms and toss her on the mattress, using the momentum to roll on top of her and pin her down.

"Let go of me!" she growls.

"Or what? You'll scream for help? You know it'll be your word against mine. Who do you think your grandparents will believe?"

"Me. They'll believe me."

She squirms under me. It only serves to turn me on. I wonder if she realizes that.

"I wouldn't bet on it. I have them eating out of the palm of my hand already. I'm the golden boy from a perfect family. They don't want to see the monster. They'd make any excuse to believe my pretty lies."

"So you admit it, then? That you're a monster?"

"I don't remember ever trying to hide that from you, darling."

"Just let go of me already. I thought you wanted to work on the Spanish assignment." Her argument is feeble. She knows she won't break free until I allow it.

"Oh we are. If I remember correctly, the instructions said we should get to know each other. I have a nagging suspicion about you, but I can only be certain one way."

I bring her arms up and pin them above her head using one hand. Then I slowly skim my free hand down the side of her body. She changed from her school uniform into an oversized T-shirt and sweatpants—the most unsexy combination she could have thought of. Not that it would work. I have a picture of her naked body imprinted on my brain.

"I thought sexual assault wasn't your game."

I lean forward, bringing my lips to her ear. "It isn't assault when both parties want it."

"I asked you to let go," she repeats, but it has way less bite than before.

My fingers trace the skin above the waistband of her sweats, and her breathing hitches. I look into her eyes, reading defiance there but not fear. Keeping our gazes locked, I slide my hand into her pants, finding another pair of simple cotton underwear. She goes very still save for the rapid rising and falling of her chest.

"What are you doing?" she whispers.

"Tell me the truth, Lexi. Did you like touching yourself while I watched?"

"No."

I cup her pussy, finding her panties already soaking wet. "You're such a little liar, aren't you?"

"I can't help how my body reacts. It's biology."

"Then maybe I should do what nature demands."

"W-What?" Her eyes widen.

I slide her panties to the side and insert a finger into her. Tight, so tight. She buckles and hisses.

"Please—"

"Please what?"

She shakes her head, but the word "no" never leaves her lips. I pull my finger back and then shove two in. There's resistance there, so I don't push. It'd be a shame to take her V-card with my fingers instead of my cock.

"You don't want me to stop, do you? You enjoy being defiled by me, the monster you loathe."

"You're wrong."

I press my thumb against her clit, eliciting a moan from her. Flush spreads through her cheeks, and then she turns her head to the side.

"Look at me, Alexis. I want to feel your hate when I make you come."

She snaps her gaze back to mine. "If that's your intention, you don't need to go through all this trouble. I already hate you."

I increase the pace of my hand, and Alexis's body reacts accordingly. She becomes even tighter around my fingers.

Defiance begins to share space with desire. Her full lips part slightly, making me crave her mouth as much as I do her body. But kissing her would be surrendering to her. That isn't what this is about.

Her face becomes redder as the first wave of release comes through. She clenches her jaw tight, determined to not make a sound, to not let me know the extent of her pleasure. I move my fingers faster, gliding them in and out with ease when her body begins to shake.

Fuck. I'm dangerously close to jizzing in my pants. My balls are tight to the point of aching. I'm getting double punishment for doing this to her.

Only when she stops trembling do I stop fingering her. I fix her panties and then roll off her. She closes her eyes and doesn't move a muscle, but her hands are curled into fists now, her nails digging into the soft flesh of her palms. The tension hasn't left her face either.

I throw my legs to the side of the bed and get up. I'm tempted to lick my fingers, find out what she tastes like, but that could be a fatal error on my part.

"Leave. Now," she tells me, her voice hard and cold.

She sits up then, holding my stare. There's something different about her gaze now. The hate is there, but it's different than before. It has no warmth, no fire. It's almost like I'm looking at a complete stranger, someone who doesn't have a soul.

A chill runs down my spine. I might have pushed her too far.

"What about our assignment?"

Her lips curl in a chilling way. "I have plenty of material."

I don't know what that's supposed to mean, but I'd better leave while my balls are still attached to my body. I think she's on the verge of ripping them off.

"I'll see you tomorrow, Lexi."

30

ALEXIS

I blink my eyes open and don't know where I am for a second. My head is pounding though, almost as if I had a hangover. I massage my temples, trying to clear the sleepy fog. Suddenly, yesterday's memories come tumbling down. Finn came over, we had dinner with my grandparents, and then....

Hell. I let him touch me in a way no other guy has ever done before. I didn't even put up a fight. No, I enjoyed every second of it. But after he got me off, I don't remember a thing. My mind is blank.

My heart squeezes tightly in my chest. I get up at once, almost as if I've been electrocuted. Dark spots in my memory are never a good thing. What happened between Finn and me during the time I can't remember? I pull my hair back, yanking at the strands. I should have stopped him. Letting him play with me must have triggered the darkness, and I was too fucking distracted to try to control it.

I turn my head and glance at the clock on my nightstand. Shit, it's already seven. I need to hurry or I'll be late for class.

I search for a fresh pair of panties in my drawer. All my undergarments are in disarray. Fucking Finn. He did this when he went snooping. I begin to sort them, and then something crucial comes to my attention.

"The letters," I mumble. "Where the hell are the letters?"

I take everything out in a frenzy, and in less than a minute, bras and panties are scattered around my feet. But no stack of letters.

Son of a bitch.

"I can't believe this. He took them."

A new kind of panic begins to rise up my throat. I can't imagine what Finn will do with the information he gains from those letters. And the worst of all is that I don't fucking know what they contain. I've been too chicken to read them.

In a blur, I get dressed. Once downstairs, I rush past my grandparents, who are already at the table to have breakfast. I tell them I'm late for school and walk out the door.

My mind is whirling as I drive over the speed limit. I'm lucky I don't get pulled over. I make it to school with five minutes to spare. Even so, I run to the front steps, aware that I must look like a veritable deranged person. I have no idea what I'll do when I see Finn, but I'm mad enough to know I might go psycho on his ass.

It's my luck—or my downfall—that I spot him at his locker alone for a change. He's distracted, so I slam my palm against the locker next to his. He jerks back, but his surprised expression quickly morphs into a sensual grin.

"Good morning, Alexis."

"Cut the crap, Finn. Where are they?"

His eyebrows furrow. "Where are what?"

I step into his personal space, poking him in the chest.

"Don't fucking play games with me. Where are the letters you took from my drawer?"

"I didn't take them," he replies exasperatedly.

"Bullshit!"

He keeps staring at me as if I'm crazy. Meanwhile, we've gathered quite a few onlookers. Then he shakes his head. "You saw when I left. How could I have taken anything from your room without you noticing?"

Cold dread licks the back of my neck, sending shivers down my spine. My stomach clenches painfully as another possibility for the missing letters comes to my mind.

Nervously, I glance at the crowd. They're listening to every single word exchanged between us. I can't ask what I need to while we have an audience.

The bell rings, which means I've run out of time.

Finn hitches his backpack over one shoulder and shuts his locker. "I'm heading to class."

I follow him in silence, ignoring the side-glances he gives me. He must think I'm a lunatic. He can join the club. I already think I'm one.

I head for the same seat as last time, but Finn decides to sit closer to me. Why, though? I'm acting like a psycho. Maybe he's into that.

I spare the thought only a second before my mind begins to whirl. I'm stressing about what could have happened to those letters too much to worry about Finn.

When I flip my laptop open, I'm prompted to insert my password. Odd. I usually shut it off overnight. A Word document appears on the screen—my Spanish assignment. The one I have no recollection of writing. My pulse accelerates as I read the report. It's good, but it doesn't sound like I wrote it. It's passive-aggressive, as if whoever penned it had a grievance against Finn but couldn't make up their mind if they hated him or simply didn't give a shit about him.

I turn to Finn with a question on the tip of my tongue. Did he use my laptop last night?

Sensing my stare, he looks at me.

"What now?"

I lose my bravado—or better yet, recover my cognitive functions. Finn wouldn't write about himself like that.

God, I'm losing my mind.

"Nothing." I look at my laptop again.

We were supposed to upload the assignment to the student portal last night. I wonder if it was done. Logging into the portal, I search for the document. Yep, it was. The time stamp shows two in the morning.

"Finn, what time did you leave last night?" I ask without looking at him.

Someone drops into the seat next to mine, scaring the crap out of me.

"I knew it wouldn't take long for you guys to hook up," Luke says.

I open my mouth to deny it, but I can't. Does letting Finn finger me into oblivion count?

"We didn't," he replies nonchalantly. "Where have you been?"

Luke shrugs. "Nowhere. Everywhere."

Now that Finn got Luke's attention, I have time to really look at him. His lower lip was busted recently, and he has a bruise under his left eye.

"Did Emily do that to you?" I blurt out.

Luke gives me a quizzical glance. "Do you really think a girl could do this to my face?"

I narrow my eyes to slits. "If she was motivated enough. What did you do to her last Friday?"

He glowers. "I didn't do jack to your friend, all right?"

"Then who tore her jacket?"

Immediately, his eyes grow darker. "Why don't you ask her?"

The chemistry lab teacher enters the room, effectively cutting off any reply I might have.

Finn glances at the empty seat next to his.

Wait, where's Halsey?

While the teacher is busy setting up his laptop, I shoot her a quick message.

ME: Are you coming to school today?

HALSEY: No.

I wait for her to elaborate, but there are no more messages from her.

"She's not coming, is she?" Finn asks.

I whip my face to his. "Did you just read my text?"

He snorts. "No, but I could guess you were texting Halsey."

It would be pretty hard for him to see what I wrote from across the aisle.

"No, she's not coming."

"Great," Finn mumbles under his breath, then raises his hand. "Mr. Kaufman, Halsey isn't coming. I'm gonna work with Luke and his partner today."

Wait, what? He wants to work with us?

And hell, I don't even get a name, just Luke's partner? Jackass.

In true Finn fashion, he doesn't wait for the teacher's reply before he slides his desk and chair closer to ours. I glance at Mr. Kaufman, who looks annoyed at the lack of respect but doesn't open his mouth to put Finn in his place. I suspect all teachers at Maverick are afraid to stand up to their students. It's no wonder these assholes are all entitled.

"What's the matter, Alexis? Don't want me to work with you?" Finn asks through a grin.

"I don't remember telling you it was okay."

"Aw, but we had so much fun working on our Spanish assignment yesterday." He laughs.

"For fuck's sake. Do you want me to leave?" Luke retorts.

"Why would you say that?" I ask.

"I'm clearly the third wheel here."

"Quit being so dramatic," Finn replies.

Grumbling, Luke flips his book open. "You'd better pray we're working with fire today."

"I think we'd better pray that we aren't," I say, earning a chuckle from Finn.

I wasn't trying to be funny, yet my body goes all warm and fuzzy because he thought I was amusing.

Hell, I can't allow myself the distraction when Damian's letters are gone and I have missing hours from my memory.

FINN

ALEXIS IS ACTING weird as shit today, and I don't think it has anything to do with what I did to her. Her accusation came out of left field. She kicked me out of her room; how could I have possibly taken her letters? And then she wanted to know what time I left.

She has basket case written all over her, and if I were any smarter, I'd quit while I'm ahead. Too bad I'm not sane myself, and now I'm damn curious to see where this story will lead. She's either messing with my head or she has some serious issues. Neither scenario is appealing, but it's clear I'm a glutton for punishment when it comes to her.

She speed walks out of the classroom as soon as the bell rings. I hurry after her, even knowing I'm going to hear crap from Luke later. Before she can disappear into the crowd, I grab her by the arm.

"Hey! What the hell?" she snaps.

"You owe me answers."

I steer her in the opposite direction we were supposed to go. We might be late for Spanish class, but I don't give a flying fuck about that now. I open the door to the janitor's storage room and push Alexis in before following. She whirls around as the door shuts again, fuming.

"What the hell do you think you're doing?"

I press forward, forcing her to step back until she has nowhere to go. Only when I'm invading her space do I say, "You accused me of something that I couldn't possibly have done. I want to know why."

She raises her chin to keep her gaze locked with mine. But despite her bravado, her lips quiver.

"Because my letters are gone, and you were the only one who knew about them."

"How can you be so sure? Are you saying your grandmother doesn't snoop around?"

The widening of her eyes tells me she hadn't considered that scenario. Interesting.

"Why did you want to know what time I left?" I ask.

"I can't remember."

"Liar." I grab her by the hips and pull her flush to my body.

She lets out a little gasp that makes it hard to focus on the task at hand. Sexing Alexis up wasn't the plan. But it seems whenever I'm near her, I can't resist the urge to touch her. It was that damn shower.

"You don't remember me leaving at all, do you?" I ask, going with my hunch.

Now her eyes are as round as saucers, and her breathing turns shallow. It seems I struck a nerve.

Before I can get the truth from her, she does something I didn't expect. She curls her hands around the lapels of my jacket and pulls me toward her, crashing her mouth into mine with the urgency of someone desperate for air.

Her soft lips short-circuit my brain, and even knowing

kissing her back is a terrible idea, I can't stop myself from taking possession of her mouth and branding her with my tongue. I press my entire frame against hers, opening her legs with mine. The friction of my pants against her core makes her moan like a kitten, reminding me all too well of how wet she gets when she's horny.

God, I want to fuck her with my fingers again.

The door behind us opens suddenly, and the noise of the busy hallway invades our little bubble. I break the kiss to tell whoever is standing at the threshold to get lost.

"I don't think so. You two better come with me."

My entire body goes taut.

Damn everything to hell.

It's Miss LaFleur.

31

FINN

*A*lexis won't look at me as we sit across from Mr. Cain, the school's headmaster. Miss LaFleur is standing in the corner of the room, staring daggers at Alexis. Mr. Cain tries to appear severe, but he simply looks annoyed. No one gives a shit if students are fucking on the premises, even if it's against the school's code of conduct. Hence no teacher would make a big deal about it—besides Miss LaFleur, and she only did it because I stopped fucking her.

"I can't tell you how disappointed I am in the two of you, especially you, Miss Montgomery," the headmaster says.

"My last name is Walker," she grits out. "And why are you singling me out? It takes two to tango, and Finn was the one who dragged me into that storage room."

"To talk. You were the one who attacked my mouth," I point out.

Alexis whips her face to mine, glaring as if she wished she could kill me with her gaze.

"So unbecoming of a young woman," Miss LaFleur pipes up.

"You're one to talk," Alexis barks, surprising me.

Shit. Does she already know?

Jesus, Finn. Of course she does. It wasn't like you tried to keep your illicit affair a secret.

"Miss Mont—I mean Walker," the headmaster starts. "I was willing to give you a free pass this time, but I won't tolerate this kind of disrespect toward a member of the faculty. I'm afraid I must give you a week of detention and call your grandparents."

She crosses her arms and nods toward me. "Is he getting detention too?"

"Well...."

"I don't see why Mr. Novak should be punished when he already stated Miss Walker was the one who initiated the kiss," Miss LaFleur chimes in.

Alexis's face goes beet red. I can see she's about to explode and dig an even deeper hole for herself. By all means, I should let her do it, but I'm annoyed as fuck with Miss LaFleur, so I'd rather piss her off than let Alexis get into more trouble.

"We were both wrong. I'll take the same punishment as Alexis. It's only fair," I say.

I fight the grin as I take in Miss LaFleur's reaction. She's livid, and I'm here for it.

"Sounds good to me," Mr. Cain replies, clearly keen on getting rid of us. "You may return to class now."

I let Alexis walk out of his office first, counting in my head the seconds until she'll make a remark.

"I can't believe you slept with that woman," she blurts out as soon as we step into the hallway.

"Allegedly. And you sound jealous."

She snorts. "Please. Just because I kissed you? Don't let that go to your head. I think Miss Pedo there is the one dying with envy."

"Yeah, yeah." I loop my arm around Alexis's waist and push her against a locker.

"What are you doing? Trying to get us longer detention?"

"Hmm." I nuzzle her neck. "Maybe I just like to see you flustered."

I lick below her ear, tasting vanilla and orange. She shivers, melting into me. Regrettably, I step back, schooling my expression into a mask of cold boredom.

"See you in Spanish."

I walk away without a glance back. My lips twitch upward. She took me by surprise with that kiss, but I'm back pulling the strings once again.

ALEXIS

WHEN I ARRIVE HOME, both my grandparents are waiting for me in the living room. That doesn't bode well. I try to head straight for the stairs, but it was a ridiculous attempt to escape.

"Alexis, get in here, young lady," Grandma commands.

I take a deep breath and turn around.

"Yes, Grandma?"

"The headmaster called. You got detention?" Her voice rises to a pitch, making me wince.

"And for kissing a boy in a broom closet," Grandpa adds, exasperated.

My face and ears burn. This is so mortifying, and I have no one to blame but myself. I came on to Finn, but only so he would stop asking questions. He was getting too close to finding out about my blackouts.

"It was just kissing. No big deal. I'm almost eighteen."

I wonder if they would be this angry if they knew I was kissing Finn. They didn't mention his name, so it's possible the headmaster didn't disclose that information.

"It doesn't matter. The rules are the rules. It took a great deal of persuasion and the promise of a sizable donation at this week's school charity event to convince Mr. Cain to not put that detention on your permanent record," Grandpa replies.

"What charity event?" I ask. This is the first time I'm hearing about it.

Grandma makes an aghast face. "Maverick's annual charity event. It's held at the school. We used to attend when your mother went there. Surely you've seen posters in the hallways."

Have I? I don't know. But I can't count on my memory anyway, which reminds me of my current problem.

"I've been too focused on catching up with academics to pay attention to the school's social calendar."

Grandpa snorts. "I'd believe that if you weren't busy kissing boys."

I open my mouth to blame Finn but decide it's better if they don't know all the details. If they suspected there's something going on between us, they'd start planning our wedding.

"Don't worry. It won't happen again. Did you come home early just to yell at me?"

His bushy eyebrows shoot up. "Don't be absurd. I could have yelled at you later. I have a meeting at your father's greasy diner, and I thought it would be more appropriate if I changed clothes first."

My heart lurches forward at the mention of Dad's diner. "You're going there now? Can I come? Who are you meeting?"

"Whoa. Slow down, Lexi. Yes, I'm leaving soon. If you want to tag along, you'd better change."

I glance down at my school uniform. "Why do I need to change?"

"Because of all the dust, dear," Grandma replies.

"What dust? From being closed for so long?"

"No. From the renovation," she says.

"What renovation?"

I can't hide the surprise from my tone or ignore the sudden pang in my chest. I didn't want anything to change, but it's pointless to complain now.

My grandparents exchange a glance.

"Lillian, you didn't tell Lexi we would be doing upgrades to the diner before reopening?" Grandpa asks.

"You told me you were going to," she replies, arching her eyebrows.

"I never said such a thing."

I pinch the bridge of my nose. "That's okay. Now I know. I'll go change. Be right back."

WHEN MY GRANDPARENTS SAY RENOVATION, it's not a simple matter of a fresh coat of paint. It's a gut job. I've avoided driving past the diner in self-preservation, so I didn't know the extent of the damage. A huge container is standing in front of the diner, and it's already half-full.

"What the hell!" I shout in the car.

"Lexi! Language," Grandma chastises me.

"Will I find anything left inside?"

"Don't be so dramatic. We plan to keep the décor the same, only it will be brand new and not a health department fine waiting to happen," she replies.

I ball my hands into fists, taking deep breaths to control my temper. Throwing a tantrum won't change anything now. Plus, the sooner the renovation is done, the sooner we can reopen it, and that's all that matters.

Grandpa parks the car across the street, then calls whoever he's supposed to meet here. Neither of them makes a motion to get out of the car, so I go ahead and open the door. It's better if they're not around when I take in the devastation of the place I associated the most with Dad. God, I'm already getting choked up and I'm not even inside yet.

As Grandma warned me, there's dust everywhere. No surprise, considering the workers tore everything out and all that's left are the bones. There's only one guy working in the main area, cleaning up the space. He nods in acknowledgment of my presence but doesn't slow down.

The kitchen is only semi-gutted, and that's where I head. There's a small crew of three guys currently busy unplugging the cooking equipment. I can't get to my father's office at the back because the route is completely blocked off.

A fourth man comes from inside, covered in dust.

"Hey, chief. I found something," he tells what I assume is his supervisor.

"What is it?" the older man asks.

"A small portable safe. It was buried in the wall."

My eyes widen. "Can I see that?"

The supervisor glances at me, frowning. "You shouldn't be here, miss."

I ignore his remark and step closer. "The safe. Hand it over, please."

The man hesitates, so I press. "It belonged to my father. I'm his daughter."

Even after I identify myself, he doesn't comply.

What the actual fuck? Was he planning to keep it?

"Hand. It. Over." I extend my hand, glaring at the man now.

Reluctantly, he finally gives it to me. I grab it with both hands, instinctively assuming it's heavy. I wasn't wrong. It's made out of solid steel. For a moment, it occurs to me that this safe might not have belonged to my father at all. God knows how long it had been buried in the wall.

But then I notice the design of a flying eagle etched on the door of the safe. It's a copy of the tattoo Dad had on the back of his neck. This can't be a coincidence. This safe belonged to him.

The question is, why did he feel the need to hide it behind a wall?

32

ALEXIS

I don't like how the workers are looking at me now with an unveiled grievance. My sixth sense tells me they weren't planning to report what they found to the general contractor. There's no way that grumpy supervisor is leading this renovation.

With the safe in my hands, I walk out of the diner and find my grandparents speaking with a man I don't recognize.

"What in the world do you have there, Lexi?" Grandma asks, eyeing the dusty object with disgust.

"It's a safe. One of the guys found it buried in a wall in Dad's office."

"You don't say," Grandpa replies.

"It could have been put there before Mr. Walker bought the diner," the man pipes up. "Hi there, kiddo. I'm Stuart Macedo, the general contractor."

Kiddo? I'm annoyed instantly. I'm not a child.

"I had a hunch," I say coldly. "Where did you find those men working inside?"

He furrows his eyebrows. "Why do you ask?"

"They didn't seem happy to hand over the safe to me."

A shadow of concern flashes in the man's eyes. "I'll have a word with them."

"You do that, Stuart," Grandpa chimes in, then turns to me. "What do you plan to do with that, Lexi?"

"Find a way to open it. It belonged to my father."

"How do you know, honey?" Grandma asks. "You heard Stuart. It could have been put there before your father bought the place."

"The design on the front. It matches Dad's tattoo."

Grandpa leans closer to inspect the safe. "Ah, I see. Indeed, there's a carved design on it."

"Good luck trying to open that unless you know the combination," Stuart offers his unsolicited advice.

"I'll figure it out," I reply without looking at him. "When are you going to be done with your meeting, Grandpa?"

"Well, Stuart just got here. He was going to walk me through the progress."

"I'm going to wait in the car, if you don't mind," I tell him.

"Oh, then I'm going to check Janice's store," Grandma pipes up. "She's expecting new items from New York."

Grandpa resumes his conversation with Stuart while Grandma heads over to the antique store down the block. I'm surprised she even knows about it since this isn't her usual habitat. But Janice does sell unique things, and her shop is a hit with tourists, all thanks to the free press she gets from magazines.

I open the trunk of Grandpa's car and put the safe there, guessing he would kill me if I got his pristine leather interior dirty. It's better if I keep the safe away from prying eyes anyway. When I circle around the vehicle, I spot Cristiano walking out of a store not far from me and heading in the opposite direction.

Maybe he knows what's going on with Carmen. I hurry after him and call his name. He stops as if he'd been pulled back by a string, all tense. Then he slowly turns around and levels me with a glare.

"You have some nerve talking to me," he seethes.

I halt in my tracks, surprised to see the loathing in his gaze.

"What are you talking about?" I ask.

"Really, Alexis? You're going to play dumb with me? Save your theatrics for the assholes you hang out with now."

"Theatrics? You're not making any sense. None of you are, to be honest. Carmen totally ghosted me after Salamandra, and now you're acting like I have a contagious disease."

He twists his face into a scowl. "*You* are the disease. Carmen was right to shut you down. And after the stunt you pulled last night, you'd better stay away from us if you know what's good for you."

Dread drips down my spine, so cold it seeps into my skin, freezing my blood.

"What happened last night?" I ask in a low voice.

"Fuck you, Alexis!" He whirls around and crosses the street.

Dumbfounded, I watch him leave while I wrestle with the turmoil in my head. It's becoming clear that bad things happened during the hours of my evening I can't remember. So far I know I kicked Finn out of my bedroom, and my letters have gone missing. It's possible I moved them to a different hiding place, but now I can't remember where. It sucks, but it's a better alternative than someone having possession of them.

What happened between Carmen and me, though? It must have been awful or Cristiano wouldn't have acted like that.

I pull my phone out and call Taluah. It rings once before it goes to voice mail. *What the hell? Did she just ignore my call?* My fingers are shaking as I check social media.

"Son of a bitch," I mumble.

I can't see her profile or any of my old friends'. That means they've blocked me. Tears sting my eyes. I've become anathema to them, and I don't even know why.

"Lexi," Grandpa calls me.

Quickly, I wipe a tear that escaped my eye and turn around. He's standing next to his car with the driver's door open. I guess he's done with his meeting.

Shoving my sadness deep inside me, I return to the car. My breakdown will have to wait until when I'm alone; I can't lose my shit in front of them. Grandma is already in the car, which works for me. I'm not sure how long I can keep my emotions bottled inside.

During the drive, I try my best to tune my grandparents' chatter out, but it's impossible when Grandma's topic veers toward my birthday party celebration and the charity event this coming Friday.

"I think we need to go shopping for another dress for you, Lexi."

"Why? There are a bunch hanging in my closet with the tag still on."

"I guess you're right. I'm just so excited to have another girl to shop for."

I can hear the smile in her voice. Despite everything that's going on with me, I feel guilty that she never had the chance to spoil me after my mother died. Their relationship with my father was too strained for any connection to happen.

"What exactly happens during the charity event?" I ask.

"A lot of businesses donate items for a silent auction. It's a great opportunity for parents and faculty to mingle too."

"Oh fun."

I look out the window, already dreading the event but also oddly excited about it. I'm sure my grandparents will parade me around like a prized horse, thus giving more ammunition to those hateful people to use against me. But Finn will be there with his folks, and I'm curious to meet the people who turned him into the arrogant prick he is.

An arrogant prick you'd like to ride, Alexis.

I rub my legs together as I remember his fingers between them. Why did that memory have to spring in my head while I'm in my grandparents' car?

My phone pings in my purse, rescuing my mind from the gutter. Or maybe not. It's a text from the devil himself.

FINN: How is my filthy little virgin?

I gasp out loud, not prepared for that kind of question. *How the hell did he know I was thinking about him?*

Grandma twists in her seat to check on me. "What's wrong, Lexi?"

I drop the phone back into my purse, afraid she'll be able to read the message.

"Nothing."

"That didn't sound like nothing," Grandpa piles on.

"Uh, one of my old friends sent me a scary text message, that's all."

"That's just bizarre," Grandpa retorts, shaking his head. "I bet none of your new friends at Maverick would do that kind of thing."

No. They'd do something much worse, like try to shave my head, which reminds me. "I have the names of the people I don't want at my birthday party."

"Oh dear. I'm afraid it's too late. I've already sent out the invitations."

"What?"

"I assumed you had changed your mind since you never provided me the name of the students. I couldn't wait forever. It's already last minute as it is."

I pinch the bridge of my nose. "Did you invite *everyone?*"

"No, of course not everyone."

213

"Did you invite Tiffany Duran and Jackie Wen, by any chance?"

"Yes, why?"

My heart sinks. I can't have those two bitches at my birthday party.

"Those are the two who have been giving me a hard time."

"I'm afraid you'll just have to suck it up, Lexi," Grandpa says. "Jackie is the mayor's daughter, and I have business dealings with Tony Duran, Tiffany's father. I couldn't simply not invite them."

I bite the inside of my cheek to keep from screaming in frustration.

"Did you invite Emily Frost, Halsey Jameson, and Julie Diamond, at least?"

"Not Julie Diamond."

"Why not?"

"The Diamonds and the Bennets don't get along, and we thought inviting the sheriff's son was more appropriate."

"I barely exchanged a few words with the guy. Julie is my friend."

Not technically, but she seems nice. And she earns bonus points for not getting along with one of Finn's buddies.

"Oh all right. I'll send an invite to Julie, but I can't uninvite Reid Bennet."

"I don't care if he comes or not."

My phone pings again, but I fight the urge to check if it was another naughty message from Finn. I'm beginning to hate how he can play me like a violin instead of simply hating *him*.

33

FINN

"I just got a call from the school headmaster," my father tells me when I step into his office, not holding back the glower.

"I didn't think you took those calls." I drop onto the chair facing his oversized desk.

"I usually don't, but your mother decided to ignore her fucking duties."

Taking a deep breath, I bite my tongue. Allowing my father to rile me up will be a mistake. He's looking for a reason to punish me; I can see that in his eyes.

"I don't understand why you're annoyed. The reason I got detention was to further your agenda."

He leans back in his chair, frowning. "Is that so?"

"Did Mr. Cain tell you why he was calling?"

"Do you think I spoke to him? My assistant took the

message. You got in trouble for breaking the student code of conduct or something I don't give a shit to know."

"Then why are you on my case?"

"Because I don't pay a fortune in tuition to be bothered by this nonsense."

"I was making out with Alexis Walker. That's why I got in trouble. It's what you want, right?"

His eyes narrow to slits. "What I want is Richard Montgomery's money."

"I had dinner with them the other night. He loves me already."

My father nods. "Good. Is he going to be at the charity event this week?"

"I don't know."

"Well, find out. And try not to fuck things up with the girl before I have a deal. Understood?"

"Yes, sir," I grit out. "May I go now?" I begin to rise from my chair.

"You may return to your desk and read all the reports I sent you. We'll discuss them tomorrow."

I don't say another word as I walk out of his office, but when I see all the fucking attachments in the email he sent me, I wish I could keep walking out of the building and never come back. Needing a pick-me-up, I text Alexis, hoping she'll keep me entertained for the rest of the afternoon. She doesn't answer the text, though. Maybe she didn't like that I called her a filthy little virgin.

You overplayed your hand, dumbass.

More annoyed than before, I toss my phone aside and squint at the screen. I guess I have to do this without distractions, then. But if Alexis thinks she can ignore me without paying the price, she's mistaken. I know exactly what my next move will be, and that helps me finish the workday without slitting my wrists.

ALEXIS

AFTER I TRY the wrong combination for the thousandth time, I push away from my desk to fish out my phone from the bag. I need a distraction, and maybe reading a message from Finn will help. But it turns out the second message I received earlier wasn't from him but from a hair product company I subscribed to.

"Ugh! Stupid marketing spam." I toss my phone on the bed and then jump out of my skin when I hear a male chuckle from my bedroom door.

Finn is standing there, smiling like a fiend and hot enough to melt a popsicle in the freezer.

"What are you doing here?" I ask.

He enters my room and locks the door behind him. Invading my privacy is becoming a bad habit of his.

"You didn't answer my text."

"I didn't think it deserved a reply," I grind out.

He keeps walking, but I force myself to stay rooted to the floor. He's not going to coerce me in my own room.

"Were you mad that I guessed your secret?"

"You didn't guess anything."

He raises an eyebrow. "Are you saying you're not a virgin?"

"Mind your damn business. And get out of my room."

His blue eyes become darker, predatory. I swallow the lump in my throat, hating how my body is reacting to the danger emanating from him. He's a bad person. He hurt an innocent child. Why do I crave his touch? Why do I want him to taint me with his cruel hands?

Because you know you're as bad as he is.

Fuck, where did that thought come from?

"I'm not going anywhere, sweetheart, until you tell me what other secr—" His gaze moves to the safe on my desk. "What's that?"

Like an idiot, I step in front of it, which only serves to increase his curiosity.

"Nothing."

"It looks like a vintage safe. Were you trying to open it?"

"Why do you care?" I cross my arms.

His lips curl into a crooked grin. "You're absolutely the worst at hiding what's important to you."

I feel my face heat up. Once again, Finn reads me like an open book and uses that to his full advantage. I have to step up my game. I can't keep throwing myself at him when he comes too close to finding out the secrets I'm trying to hide.

"Unless you can guess the combination of the safe, you're of no use to me."

"How badly do you want to open that?" He steps closer.

"That's a trick question, isn't it?"

He shakes his head. "No tricks. What if I could help you? What would you give me in return?"

"I don't need your help. I just want you to leave."

"If I do leave, and then your safe disappears, are you going to accuse me of stealing it too?"

He had to go and remind me about those letters. I let out a tired sigh. "Just go away, Finn. I'm not in the mood for your stupid games."

Like the arrogant ass he is, he doesn't heed my words. Instead, he invades my space and cups my cheek. Electric sparks seem to crackle underneath his caress, and my heart races.

"Are you going to kiss me again to stop me from uncovering how fucked up you are, my filthy virgin?"

Anger erupts from the pit of my stomach. I shove him back with all the strength I have. "I'm not your anything!"

He reaches for my arm and yanks me toward him. I hit his body straight on, letting out a loud *humph*, which gets swallowed almost immediately by his mouth claiming mine. I'm too angry to surrender to his assault meekly. I pound against his chest with my fists, even though my lips open for his invasive tongue.

He pulls back, a vortex of heat, rage, and desire in his gaze. "Stop fighting me. I know you want this as much as I do."

"You know nothing about me."

"I know you want my fingers inside your pussy again. I know you fantasize about me pounding you into oblivion while your grandparents sip their aperitifs downstairs. You want me to defile you, Alexis. You need me to hurt you."

Tears gather in my eyes from hearing the truth from his odious mouth. How can he know my deepest, most shameful secrets?

"That's how you get off, then? By hurting people?"

"No. I just want to hurt *you*."

His vicious reply feels like a punch to my chest, caving it in. "Why?"

He seems to hesitate, but his gaze stays locked on mine as if searching for more secrets. Finally, he says, "Because you can hurt me just as bad."

What? I must have misheard him. He wouldn't admit his weakness to me, unless he's not really telling the truth and this is part of his twisted mind games.

A knock on the door interrupts us. "Lexi?"

Finn takes a step back, releasing me.

"Yes, Grandma?" I answer, keeping my eyes on him.

She tries the door. "Why is this door locked?"

He mouths, "You're in trouble," then smiles.

Fucking asshole.

"Privacy," I reply.

"You're late for dinner. Come down."

"I'll be there in a second."

Only when I hear her footsteps recede do I dare ask Finn, "My grandparents have no idea you're here, do they?"

His smile broadens, turning wolfish. "Nope. I came in through the kitchen. Aren't you glad I was stealthy?"

"Only if you can leave in the same manner."

"Fine, but on one condition."

"I'm not bargaining with you!"

He shrugs. "I don't care either way. If you don't want your grandparents to know I was here, be my date at the charity event this Friday."

My jaw drops. "Why?"

"Because I want you to."

"Let me guess. You get everything you want, right?"

"Always."

What an arrogant ass. If he thinks I'm going to simply bow down to his wishes, he's sorely mistaken.

"Not this time, asshole. Make your presence known. I don't care."

"Okay, then."

He releases his long hair from the man bun and runs his hand through his curls, successfully making a mess out of it. Then he untucks his shirt and makes sure it's wrinkled, as if he'd been fooling around with someone.

Son of a bitch.

"What are you doing?"

"Making sure they know what we've been up to in here." He winks at me before veering for the door.

I grab the back of his shirt before he can walk out. "I'm not going to let you set me up."

"You know how to stop me."

The desire to win this round with Finn is great, but I'm not sure if it's worth getting in trouble with my grandparents. They weren't happy about my detention. With the way my life is going, I need to keep all my allies, even if it's them.

"Fine. You win."

He grins from ear to ear. "I always do."

34

ALEXIS

*I*t's been two days since I found my father's safe, and I still haven't been able to crack the code. Grandpa asked me casually this morning about it and offered to pay for an expert to help. But that meant sending the safe out of town, which I refused.

While I was consumed with worry about all the shitty things that have happened to me recently, the last couple days passed in a blur at school. To be fair, nothing major happened save for Emily showing up for class and acting like she didn't know me. Whatever happened that evening at La Salamandra did something to her, but I don't have any bandwidth left to be concerned about her problems on top of my own.

Despite the bargain I struck with Finn to be his date at the charity event tonight, he didn't mention our arrangement at school or make plans to pick me up. So I'm riding with my grandparents, wearing a cocktail dress that makes me feel like an impostor. Designer dresses and shoes are not things I ever cared about, and maybe I'll never get used to them.

I'm a little bit anxious as I enter Maverick's with my grandparents for a myriad of reasons, but the most pressing one is not knowing what kind of trap Finn laid out for me. I don't believe for one second that he only wants an innocent date.

The entry hallway is busy already with parents and students mingling. My grandparents spot the headmaster and make a beeline for him. I can't believe they didn't drag me along. I keep walking so I'm not blocking the way while searching for Finn. I spot Emily ahead of me, standing next to an older man who looks even more glacial than her. Judging by their similar hair color, I guess that's her father.

She turns in my direction, but her gaze stays on me for only a few seconds before her attention diverts to someone else— Luke Halle. She doesn't stiffen upon seeing him or narrow her eyes. I'm not ashamed to admit that I'm watching them with rapt attention now. Not knowing what happened at La Salamandra is driving me insane.

A hand slides across my lower back, making me jump.

"What are you looking at?" Finn asks, following my line of sight.

His hand stays on me, warm and possessive. Like an idiot, I don't move away.

"Nothing," I reply.

"Hmm. You have to stop trying to lie, babe. You're terrible at it."

I glare at him. "What do you want?"

His eyes widen in a way that conveys surprised innocence. Paired with his golden curls, it makes him look like a guardian angel. Too bad he's bad to the bone and all he wants is to torment me. "I'm your date, remember?"

"I thought you forgot."

"I'd never forget our sweet arrangement, Alexis." He smiles

wickedly, right before he laces his fingers with mine. "Come on. I want you to meet my parents."

Oh crap. That's exactly what I was hoping to avoid.

"Why? We aren't dating for real."

He ignores my comment and steers me to the school's open atrium, where the items for the silent auction have been arranged elegantly on displays around the room. There are a few high tables in the center, and some parents have already flocked to them in order to set their drinks and canapés down. It's an informal setup to allow people to mingle.

Next to one of those tables, a tall man with broad shoulders and dark-blond hair is looking bored next to a beautiful woman while she chats with a member of the school staff.

"Dad, Mom, I'd like you to meet Alexis Walker, my girlfriend."

My stomach coils tightly. I did not sign up for being his fake girlfriend.

Finn squeezes my hand, sensing that I'm about to yank free from his grasp.

I expect his father to glower at me considering who my dad was, but surprisingly, the man beams.

Extending his hand, he says, "Nice to meet you, Alexis. I've heard so much about you."

"You have?"

He shakes my hand enthusiastically, and then it's Finn's mother's turn to do the same. I'm in a daze when the third person in the group turns to me.

"I don't think we've officially met. I'm Mr. Phillips."

"You're Piper's dad," I blurt out, regretting my outburst when a flash of anguish shows in his eyes.

"Yes. Do you know her?"

"We have PE together."

Finn's dad clears his throat. "I trust your grandparents are here. I'd love to say hello."

I glance around, suddenly very much looking forward to being rescued by them. When I finally locate them at the entrance of the atrium, an exhale of relief whooshes out of me.

"There they are," I say.

I wave to catch their attention. They see me, but before they cross the room, Finn's mother lets out a small gasp.

"What is it, Marissa?" his father snaps.

"What's Grandpa doing here?" Finn asks before his mother can reply.

I follow his eyes and see an older man with white hair talking to Piper. She smiles politely at something he said, but even from across the room, I notice her discomfort.

"There you are, Lexi," Grandma says, joining us. "We've been looking all over for you."

"I was kidnapped by Finn," I say without thinking.

Finn is still staring at his grandfather and doesn't offer a reply to my jab. His father scowls at him for a brief second before turning to my folks with a smile that has too many teeth.

"Richard, Lillian. Lovely to see you again."

"Indeed. I wasn't expecting to see you here, Florian," Grandpa says.

"My schedule usually conflicts with such events, but I made the effort to come this time. It's Finn's senior year, after all."

Mr. Phillips makes an excuse and walks away from our group. I don't blame him. I'd want to leave too. This forced conversation is already setting my teeth on edge.

"Yes, it's a very important year." Grandpa nods. "When Evelyn was a student here, we never missed an event. I believe the last time we were here was when that dreadful fire happened. Your nephew Jason performed, didn't he?"

Finn tenses slightly, making me curious.

"Yes, I believe so. I was not in attendance. The fire was a terrible incident. I'm glad no one got hurt," Florian replies. "I have to say, I'm thrilled that Finn and Alexis are dating."

Way to change the subject, dude.

"Is that so?" Grandma raises an eyebrow.

My face bursts into flames, and I don't know what to do with myself.

"I'll be right back," Finn says out of the blue and strides away.

Are you kidding me? I'm pissed, and I notice I'm not the only one. It looks like his father wants to drag him back by the collar of his shirt. He obviously can't act on it, so he opts for pasting a fake smile on his face and carrying on the conversation with my grandparents.

Finn's mother is too busy draining her drink to offer anything to the conversation, a fact I'm sure Grandma notices. I wait a minute until I come up with an excuse of my own and go after the jackass. He's surprised me twice already tonight. I have to know what he's plotting.

***

FINN

IT WASN'T my intention to leave Alexis alone with my parents, but I had to go check on Piper. She was visibly rattled after speaking to my grandfather, and I want to know why. I don't see the bastard once I exit the atrium, but I catch sight of Piper walking out of the restroom.

I hurry to catch up with her.

"Hey, Piper. How's it going?"

She stops abruptly and looks at me as if she can't believe I'm talking to her. I can't blame her. Under normal circumstances, she wouldn't have registered on my radar.

"I'm okay."

"I saw you talking to my grandfather. What did he want?"

Her eyes grow rounder, and her body tenses visibly. "No-Nothing."

I raise an eyebrow. "Nothing?"

She drops her gaze to the floor. "Uh, he just wanted to say he was glad I returned home safely."

"Did he now?"

Still keeping her head down, she nods.

"Where did you go when you ran away from home?"

As if jolted by an electric shock, she looks up. "I didn't run away. And why do you care?"

Whoa. From meek to cornered animal in the blink of an eye. *What are you trying to hide, Piper?*

"I like your father, and I'm just trying to look out for you. There are a lot of creeps in this town, and I'd hate if you fell in with the wrong crowd."

"I didn't," she seethes.

I don't believe that for a second. Piper is afraid of something. Seeing my grandfather talking to her is doing nothing to put my mind at ease. The man is a bastard.

"You don't need to be afraid. I can help."

She laughs without humor. "That's rich. I know your reputation, Finn. You don't care about anyone but yourself."

I wince, not expecting the backlash. For the first time in my life, I'm actually trying to help someone without ulterior motives, and this is what I get.

"The offer stands."

"I don't need your help." She stomps off and exits the building through a side door.

I rub my face as I attempt to deal with the turmoil that's now whirling inside my chest. My father will be furious that I left. And I'll probably lose all the progress I made with Alexis, but I can't go back to the event while I have all these dark theories swimming in my head. I don't think Piper is safe, but I have no fucking clue how to help her.

35

ALEXIS

I totally eavesdropped on Finn's conversation with Piper. I was jealous at first when I saw them talking. The thought that he had claimed to be my boyfriend only to sneak out and hook up with another girl crossed my mind. But he wasn't trying to seduce Piper. He wanted to help her.

My jaded brain obviously concluded that was part of his plan, but when she left in a huff, I caught a glimpse of his expression. He didn't smile wickedly as if he was playing a game. He was concerned.

When he veered toward the pool area, I waited a minute and followed him.

Now here I am, standing just outside the glass and watching Finn swim lap after lap. I'm beginning to suspect this is his coping mechanism. He's in his Speedo, making me wonder if he was wearing the damn thing underneath his clothes.

I should return to the party. My grandparents are probably

wondering why I'm taking so long, but I can't make myself move. I'm transfixed by the water god in front of me.

He switches styles and dives deeper in the pool as if he suspects I'm spying on him.

Minutes go by, and he doesn't come up for air. I move closer to the window, almost pressing my nose against it. I see Finn's shape at the bottom of the pool. Unmoving.

What the hell is he doing?

With my heart racing, I walk away from the window and barge into the pool area. I don't care if Finn sees me now. Bubbles of air rise to the surface, but he still won't move. I don't know how long he's been under, but it's probably more than five minutes.

He's a swimmer. He can probably hold his breath for a long time, but with every second that passes, my anxiety increases.

His shadow moves; he's coming up finally. His head doesn't break the surface, though. He's floating on his belly, face still submerged.

Shit. Did I just stand here and let him drown?

Without thinking, I toss my purse to the side and jump into the pool with my clothes and shoes on. Water splashes all around me, and then Finn's head jerks up.

"What the hell are you doing?" he asks.

My heart is still thundering, but for different reasons now. He's staring at me as if I'm a lunatic.

"I thought you drowned."

His eyebrows shoot to the heavens. "In case you forgot, I know how to swim."

"You didn't come up for air for minutes, and then you were just floating there."

The corners of his lips twitch upward. "Babe, you jumped into the pool with clothes on and everything to save me?"

I splash water on his face. "Yes, jackass. Don't know why you're so smug about it."

He swims forward and pulls me flush against his body before I have a chance to escape. Not that I could anyway. I'm in his domain. He's the shark, and I'm the dumb seal pup who thought helping the predator was a good idea.

"Let me go," I say, but my lack of any real attempt to push him off is telling.

"You care about me, Lexi. Confess."

"That's a giant leap. I don't need to care about someone to try to save their life."

"I already said you're a terrible liar. Why do you insist on trying?"

"The only liar here is you. Why did you introduce me to your parents as your girlfriend?"

He narrows his eyes slightly. "I thought it'd piss my dad off if he thought I was dating the diner rat."

The reminder of the horrible nickname Tiffany gave me should be my wake-up call. But for the first time since meeting Finn, I catch his deception.

"Your nose is growing, Pinocchio."

He reaches for the back of my head and grabs a fistful of hair, yanking it hard. The pain is just enough to make me more aroused than angry.

"That's not the only thing that's growing."

He pulls my face to his and slants his lips over mine roughly. His tongue invades my mouth in a hostile takeover. My only chance at survival is surrendering to him. God, I love the way he kisses me, as if he doesn't know if he should worship me or punish me. It's the same thing for me. I hate that I want his fiery touches, that he can get under my skin so easily. Most of all, I loathe myself for not despising him as hard as I should.

With his free hand, he brings my hips forward, making me feel every inch of his erection. Unlike me, he's wearing appropriate attire for the pool, and the flimsy spandex fabric offers no barrier. We float together until my back hits the tiled wall, and then every bit of Finn's body presses against mine. The kissing intensifies, our tongues moving frenetically, giving and taking without rhythm or thought.

I'm caught in a circle of fire not even the water can douse. When he cups my pussy, that should be my cue to stop this craziness. We're out in the open, and anyone can see us. If we're caught, I'd get more than detention. Yet I don't care. I want his fingers inside me. I want oblivion and for him to take me there.

I gasp against his mouth when he pushes my underwear aside and shoves his fingers into me.

"You love when I'm inside you, don't you, my filthy virgin?" His warm breath fans against my skin.

Not wanting to admit the truth, I grab his face between my hands and reclaim his mouth. He only lets me have my way for a few seconds before he pulls back.

"You're not pulling that crap again. Answer me, or I'll stop."

I shake my head. "I'm calling your bluff."

He grins and then pushes off me, leaving me cold and bereft, much to my surprise. My flushed skin misses his contact immediately.

"I never bluff."

"And I'll never admit to something that isn't true."

"Lie to me. I dare you."

"You said I shouldn't because I'm so terrible at it."

A victorious smile blossoms on his face. "Exactly."

I'm turned on as hell, but I'm not going to beg this horrible boy to finger me. I'm not that desperate.

"Sorry, honey, but you'll never hear the word 'love' from me when it comes to you."

I turn around and push myself out of the pool. My soaked dress weighs a ton, and I don't know how I'm going to explain my current state to my grandparents, but I grin nonetheless as I walk out of the pool area.

I just won my first round against Finn.

My amusement wanes quickly as the noise of the charity event reaches me in the hallway. I can't go back to the atrium looking like a drowned rat. I veer for the girls' locker room, hoping I can make myself less, I don't know, wet.

Shit. That's not going to work. My last resort is to call for help. Emily is out of the question, but maybe Halsey will come to the rescue.

I'm such an idiot. Why did I have to play the savior?

My mind replays the hot-as-hell scene in the pool as I burst into the locker room. I expected to find the place empty, not to walk into a couple hooking up against one of the lockers. They freeze, and then the guy looks over his shoulder.

It's Reid Bennet. He's angling his body in a way that I can't see who his partner is.

"Get out," he snaps.

"You get out. This is the girls' locker room, not a motel on the side of the road."

"I swear to God, diner rat, if you don't leave now, I'm going to make your existence a living hell."

"Get in line."

I veer for my locker, knowing I left a towel in there, and pretend the douche canoe isn't glowering at me.

"It's okay, Reid," a female voice I recognize says.

I turn around in time to see Julie step away from Reid's body shield. *Holy shit.* I didn't expect her to be his hookup. Even being new to this school, I know about the feud between their families.

"You two?" I blurt out.

"You'd better not say a word about us, diner rat." Reid takes a menacing step toward me, but it's less effective when his fly is open.

"If you want me to keep your secret, you'd better stop calling me that."

I have no intention of blabbing, especially considering Julie seems like a nice girl.

"She won't say a word," Julie pipes up. "Right, Alexis?"

"I won't, but your boyfriend needs to be nicer to me."

She winces while Reid's face twists into a scowl.

"She's not my girlfriend. This was nothing. A meaningless fuck."

What a jackass. Even if that's the case, he didn't need to broadcast it like that. Julie looks hurt by his outburst, but her expression quickly morphs into one of annoyance.

"Right. Totally meaningless," she says. "Run along now. You shouldn't be here."

Reid sneers in her direction, then strides toward the exit, finally closing his fly.

"God, what do you see in him?" I ask.

"Don't know. You're not going to tell anyone, right? My family would disown me if they found out."

"Your secret is safe with me."

"Thank you." She tilts her head to the side. "What happened to you?"

"I was trying to help someone who didn't need to be rescued."

She narrows her eyes. "You're talking about Finn."

I cross my arms. "Maybe."

"No need to get defensive. I know all about being attracted to the wrong guy. There's something about those boys…." She shakes her head. "Never mind. You can't go back to the party like that."

"I know. I came in here to try to salvage the situation."

"Do you have clothes in your locker?"

"No, just a towel."

"I have a spare PE uniform in mine. You can borrow it."

A wave of relief washes over me. "Really? Thank you."

She nods. "You scratch my back, I scratch yours. Besides, if you're entertaining the idea of having any kind of relationship with one of the filthy gods, you need a support system."

Denial is on the tip of my tongue, but I *am* in a twisted relationship with Finn whether I like it or not.

"Can you also sneak me out of here? I don't want to explain to my grandparents why my makeup is smeared and I had to change clothes."

"Sure. These parties are a borefest anyway. Why do you think I was screwing Reid in the locker room?"

I quirk an eyebrow. "You were screwing the enemy because you were bored?"

She shrugs. "What other reason would I have to get near that arrogant ass?"

"Uh, maybe you like him?"

The corners of her lips twitch upward. "Oh boy. You're a romantic, aren't you?"

"Hell no. I'm the opposite of romantic."

Julie watches me as if she doesn't believe me. "I hope so, for your own good. Guys like Reid and Finn are a good distraction in bed, but falling in love with one of them has disaster written all over it."

36

FINN

*A*lexis managed to corrupt my sanctuary with her Good Samaritan act, forcing me to return to the party prematurely. I'm far from a bad mood though. I didn't get her to confess what was obvious, but I learned something important: she's exactly where I want her to be. Now I just need her to start acting on her hate so I can bear my sins as if they weren't smothering.

I shower and change back into my fancy clothes. When I find my father, he looks like he's going to punch me in the face right here in front of all these people. *Fuck.* I must have screwed up things for him with Alexis's grandfather.

"Where the hell did you go?" he asks through clenched teeth.

"I went to check on Piper."

"Your hair is wet." Mom picks up one of my locks.

In a knee-jerk reaction, I lean away from her, glowering.

Then I notice her eyes are bloodshot. Hell, she's already wasted. No surprise considering who decided to crash this party.

"Where are the Montgomerys?" I ask.

"They left after they failed to find their granddaughter. You'd better not have anything to do with it, Finn."

"I did nothing to Alexis. She jumped in the pool on her own," I retort, regretting my outburst instantly.

"Who jumped in the pool?" Miss LaFleur asks, joining us at the high table.

My skin crawls at her proximity and the way she smiles at me seductively. Hell, I was indeed in a dark place last year to have fallen into her bed.

"No one," I grit out.

"It looks like you've been swimming, Finn."

A vein on my father's forehead throbs. He narrows his eyes, and I know I'm utterly fucked.

"Is that what you were doing instead of fulfilling your family duties?" he asks in a dangerously low tone.

My face burns as a mix of anger and shame spread through my veins. He's going to make a scene in front of everyone and humiliate me.

When I don't reply immediately, he hits the table with a closed fist, knocking over my mother's drink. "Answer me!"

"Florian," Mom whisper-shouts.

"What in the world is going on here?" My grandfather appears out of nowhere, clasping a firm hand over my shoulder.

My hands ball into fists, and I clench my jaw while I fight the urge to shove him off me.

"Stay out of it, Dad," my father retorts.

"I think I've had enough of social obligations for one evening. I'm going home. Finn, are you coming?" my mother asks.

"Yeah."

I step away from my grandfather with pleasure and leave the

damn atrium in step with Mom. I'm sure my father is scowling at my back. There's no doubt in my mind that this conversation will continue at home. Only I have no intention of making it easy for him. I'm dropping Mom off, and then I'll go somewhere else.

ALEXIS

IT'S BEEN hours since my grandparents came back home and yelled at me for ditching them at the charity event. I couldn't tell them the reason I had to bail earlier. The truth wouldn't help my case anyway. They wouldn't believe I thought Finn, the captain of the swim team, was drowning and I jumped in to save him.

During the time I spent locked in my room, I tried to open the damn safe. But it's clear I can't do this on my own and my curiosity is quickly turning into an obsession.

I think about Finn and his offer to help. There's a high chance he wasn't telling the truth, but I'm weak and pathetic when it comes to him, because I'm already going to my walk-in closet to change into sensible clothes that are perfect for sneaking out.

I'm wearing black from head to toe, and the high turtleneck sweater gives no illusion that I'm going to seek him out as a ploy to continue what we started in that damn pool. I grab the biggest bag I can find and shove my father's safe in it. You can still see the top of it, but it's definitely less conspicuous.

My grandparents didn't ground me, but it's obvious they won't allow me to leave the house at this hour. It's already past ten, and after the fiasco that was the charity event, I know I'm skating on thin ice.

Taking a deep breath, I call Finn. My heart races as I wait on pins and needles for him to answer the phone. The longer it rings, the more nervous I become. It'll go to voice mail soon. Though it's better than ringing once and then going to voice mail, a clear indication he rejected my call.

A beep sounds, and then Finn's voice tells me to leave a message. I press the red button quickly, knowing if I say anything, it'll sound ridiculous and desperate.

"What the hell am I doing?" I mutter out loud.

Great. Now I'm talking to myself.

I stare into nothing, keenly aware that my heart is still beating faster than normal. When my phone rings in my hand, it scares the shit out of me. It's Finn calling me back. My stomach tightens as suddenly as the shakes that take over my body.

"Hello?" I answer.

"Miss me already, my filthy virgin?" His voice is seductive and at odds with his mocking question.

I clench my jaw so hard it hurts my molars.

"Stop calling me that," I snap.

"I'll stop calling you that when I take your virginal status away."

Not even a minute in this conversation and he's already being hateful. Yet my body is more than on board with the idea of Finn being my first, the guy I'm supposed to hate with every fiber of my being. I'm so messed up in the head it's not even funny.

"This is not a booty call, so get that idea out of your head."

"Impossible. Let's put a pin in it for now. Why are you calling if not to beg me to fuck you into oblivion?"

Desire curls around the base of my spine, but I fight the urge to rub my legs together and alleviate the ache. I'm not *that* desperate.

"You said you could help me with the safe. Did you really mean it?"

"Yeah, I meant it."

He doesn't elaborate, no doubt waiting for me to go ahead and ask.

"Can you help me, then? Tonight."

"I can, but it's going to cost you."

I knew that already, but hearing him say it out loud sends a thrill of excitement down my back. What depraved favor will Finn ask in return?

"How much?"

He chuckles. "Oh no. I don't want money. You're cute for trying that route."

"I'm not having sex with you if that's what you have in mind," I reply through clenched teeth, but deep down I know I'm full of shit. If Finn tries to sex me up, there's a high probability I'll crumble like a sandcastle.

"I'm two minutes away from your house. See you soon, Alexis."

FINN

I DIDN'T KNOW what I planned to do when Alexis called. After I dropped Mom off at home, I drove aimlessly. I could have called one of my friends, but I wasn't in the mood to be surrounded by anyone. The ugly secret I've been trying to forget seems to be intent on coming to the surface. What if by keeping my mouth shut, I'm doing more harm than good? What if people need to know the evil that's roaming freely in Triton Cove?

I drove to the beach and stayed there for hours. Not even the pitch-black darkness that descended after sunset drove me away. It was only when my phone rang and I saw Alexis's name on the screen that I snapped out of my pity party. It was too windy at the beach, so I let the call go to voice mail and only called back when I was in the car. Making her wait was a bonus.

Now I'm driving to her grandparents' house, going over the speed limit because I can't fucking wait to see her again. This feeling is nothing I've ever felt before, and I can't put a name to it. Sure, I can come up with excuses, say it's just a game, but deep down, I know it's more than that.

Hell, I'm not going to analyze this shit now. I have a favor to gain.

I make it to Alexis's place in record time, but guessing she's in the doghouse with her grandparents, I park in front of the gated mansion and text her. Two minutes later, the smaller gate opens, and out comes Alexis, wearing an all-black ensemble that makes her look like a spy. If it weren't for her flaming-red hair, she'd blend in with the darkness.

After the beach, I put my car's top down, needing to feel the wind on my face. She veers for the back seat first and dumps the large bag she was carrying there. I glance over my shoulder and confirm it's her father's safe. Quickly, she takes the seat next to me and shuts the door hard, keeping her stare ahead.

"What's the matter, babe?"

"Can we please just go?" She looks at the house.

"Not without a proper greeting."

I lean across the gap between us, reaching for the back of her head with my hand. Before she can react or pull away, I claim her lips. Funny how I didn't want to cross that line with her, and now I can't help kissing her any chance I get.

She only lets me savor her for a few seconds before tensing. I pull back without a word and shift gears, then peel out of the parking spot.

After a minute, she says, "Thank you for picking me up."

"Don't thank me yet. I have ulterior motives, remember?"

She snorts. "I didn't forget. What is it that you want in return?"

"Nothing scandalous."

"I'm sure we have different views of what's scandalous."

"I want the same thing I asked at the pool. Your admission that you want me to fuck you."

I tear my eyes from the road for a second to see her reaction. Her jaw is clenched shut. I hit a nerve, as I guessed I would. She's too stubborn to accept she's falling for the devil.

"Fine. I'll say what you want to hear *when* you open my dad's safe."

My lips curl into a grin. "You have a deal."

"Where are we going? Your house?"

"No."

"Then where?"

"You'll see."

"I swear to God, Finn. If this is another one of your schemes to humiliate me, I'm going to fucking lose my mind. And trust me, you don't want that to happen."

Usually when people warn you like that, it means nothing. Too much barking and no biting. But somehow, I don't believe Alexis is bluffing. I remember her chilly expression when she kicked me out of her room. When she's angry at someone for real, you'd better hope it's not at you. And yet here I am, poking the angry bear with a short stick.

We don't speak for several minutes, but it's Alexis who breaks the silence first.

"Finn, I think we're being followed."

I glance at the rearview mirror and see headlights behind us. "Why do you think they're following us?"

"Because the same car has been on our tail since we left my grandparents' house."

"So? You're being paranoid."

She turns in her seat and looks behind us. "I'm not being paranoid."

"Fine, let's test it out. Hold tight."

I put the pedal to metal, pushing way past the speed limit. Immediately, the car behind us accelerates to keep pace with us.

Son of a bitch. They are *following us.*

I take a sharp right at the last second, hoping to lose them, but the asshole manages to keep up. I realize we're on the winding road that leads to Luke's house, which is deserted at this hour. Not the best path when you're being chased by God knows who.

My heart is racing at the speed my car is going. The last time I drove this fast, I wound up crashing into the Danes's store. An accident on this perilous road will most likely be fatal for both of us.

Alexis glances back again. "They're still there."

"I know."

A familiar sharp bend is coming up. I'll have to slow down to make it. And that's when the gunshots begin. Alexis screams, ducking forward and covering her head with her hands.

Jesus fucking Christ. Shit just got real.

The deadly distraction costs me. It's too late to press on the brakes to make the curve. I yank the hand brake instead, a reckless move I haven't pulled in forever. The tires screech loudly as the car spins out of control. The smell of burning rubber reaches my nose a second before the rear end crashes against a tree. The impact jolts my entire body, and the airbags do little to help.

My ears are ringing, and the world hasn't stopped spinning even though we're no longer moving. I turn to Alexis, reaching for her hand. She looks at me with round, frightened eyes. Her breaths are coming in bursts.

A car braking to a stop nearby snaps me into motion. We crashed, but the motherfuckers firing at us didn't.

"We need to get out of here. Can you run?"

"I-I think so."

I unbuckle my seat belt and jump out, not bothering with opening the door. From my periphery, I see Alexis reach for the bag with the safe.

Is she for real? That monstrosity will only slow her down.

"Leave the safe, Alexis," I hiss.

She ignores my command and hoists the heavy burden over her shoulder.

I hear a gun cocking and freeze.

"Listen to your boyfriend, sweetheart, and no one gets hurt."

Two men wearing ski masks are now standing in front of their car, but only one of them has a gun.

"What do you want with it? It's just an old safe. There probably isn't anything valuable in it," Alexis argues, clutching the bag protectively.

The guy with the gun stalks toward her. "I'm not going to ask again. Drop the bag, or I'll blow your head off."

"Let it go, Alexis," I urge.

She glances at me, scared at first, but then something changes in her gaze. Fuck. It's the soulless look again. I brace for things to go from bad to bloody any second now.

The thief uses her brief distraction to his advantage and reaches for the bag.

But she wasn't distracted. She jumps back while the jackass has his beefy hands on the bag strap, making him stagger forward. He still has the gun though, so I reach for it before he has the chance to aim at her again.

In the background, the second guy curses. He runs to assist while I struggle to pry the gun from his partner. I lose sight of Alexis in the confusion.

The gun goes off, and a burning pain grazes my shoulder. *Hell.* I don't let go of the weapon though. Anger erupts in the pit of my stomach. I push past the agony and headbutt the asshole who's still trying to pull the gun free from my hold. He lets go, holding his nose with both hands.

Before he can run or attack me again, Alexis swings the bag with the safe inside and hits the man on the head. A sickening crunch echoes in the night before he falls to the ground with a loud thud, unmoving. Blood quickly pours from the wound. Alexis just bashed his head in.

Behind her, I see the second assailant on the ground as well, either passed out or dead like his companion.

Nothing can be heard besides the noise of our labored breathing. I don't move, trying to process what the hell just happened.

Alexis drops the bag with the safe as if she can't hold on to it any longer. It looks heavy as fuck, which doesn't explain how she was able to swing that thing with such force. She looks at the man she just killed and then at me.

"Wh-What happened?"

The confused glint in her eyes tells me she might not really know.

Fuck.

37

ALEXIS

One man is definitely dead, the other at least unconscious, and I have no idea how that happened. Judging by the way Finn is looking at me, I'd say I'm responsible for it, only I don't have any memory of doing anything.

He rubs his face and then curses, "Son of a bitch."

I hug myself, feeling wretched and terrified. My eyes prickle, but I have to fight the tears. I can't lose my shit now.

Finn hisses and then touches his shoulder. It's then that I notice he's bleeding.

"You're hurt," I say.

"I think it's just a superficial wound."

I step closer, half expecting him to pull away, but he lets me approach and inspect the damage. "You were shot."

"Yeah, because someone decided to play Black Widow."

I flinch, pulling back as the guilt in my chest grows. "I'm sorry. I-I don't know what happened."

"You really can't remember a thing, can you?" He watches me through slitted eyes.

Unable to withstand his scrutinizing gaze, I look away. "Stressful situations trigger blank spots in my memory."

He steps closer and touches my arm. "Whoever you became was a badass, so don't feel too bad about it."

I whip my face to his. "How can you say that? I killed a man!"

"He would have killed us both. It was self-defense."

My jaw drops. I can't believe Finn is trying to make me feel better instead of running for the hills. I just gave him irrefutable proof that I'm a psycho who should be locked up.

Shaking my head, I drop my chin as I lose the battle against the tears that manage to roll down my cheeks. A loud sob escapes my lips, and then Finn is pulling me into his arms.

"It's going to be okay," he says.

"Why are you being nice to me? I could have gotten you killed."

"Fuck if I know."

He leans back and forces me to look into his eyes by pinching my chin between his forefinger and thumb. "Why were those men after your father's safe?"

"I have no idea." I glance at the bloody bag on the ground. "One more reason to try to open it."

"That'll have to wait. There's no way we can get out of here without calling the sheriff's department first."

The mention of cops sends me spiraling to panic town. They'll find out I'm a lunatic when I can't tell them what happened.

"This is a nightmare," I whisper to myself.

"Don't worry. The sheriff is an old family friend." Finn smiles, already pulling his cell phone out of his pocket.

"What are we going to tell them?"

He raises an eyebrow. "The truth, of course."

My stomach bottoms out. How am I going to tell the truth if I don't remember a thing?

I glance at the wreckage that's now Finn's car. The entire back side is caved in. We're lucky only the rear end got the brunt of the collision with the tree. I find a small boulder not too far from the wreck and sit down because my legs suddenly can't hold my weight.

Lost in my head, I don't hear a word Finn says on his phone call. He's already put the phone away when I finally snap out of my dark thoughts. I see him grab something from the glove compartment of his car, then walk toward the second assailant —the not dead one.

"What are you doing?"

"Making sure he doesn't give us trouble in case he wakes up." He drops into a crouch and then grunts.

His distress propels me into action. This mess is my doing, and he got hurt because of me. I stop next to him and take the resistance band from his hand. I don't even want to ask why he had one in his car.

"I'll do it. You shouldn't move your arm."

"I'm fine."

Revulsion takes hold of me as I tie the criminal's hands behind his back. My hands are shaking, and it takes too long to finish the task. Finn unfurls from his crouch first and then moves closer to the man's head.

"Let's see who's behind the mask." He bends over to pull the ski mask from the unconscious man.

"No!" I shout for no reason.

He freezes and glances at me as if I've lost my mind. "Why the hell not? Aren't you curious?"

I rise from my crouch and take several steps back. "Yes and no. I think we should wait for the sheriff."

"Fine." He pulls his hand back and then returns to his car.

"We should probably clean your wound," I say, hating how I just made everything worse.

Finn opens his mouth, but the sound of sirens approaching in the distance cuts off his reply.

"The cavalry is coming."

Tightness in my stomach almost makes me bend forward like a pretzel. I'm shaking from head to toe now, and the urge to hurl is immense. I'm not sure why the sirens are so triggering to me. I killed a man in self-defense. He had a gun, and he was going to shoot Finn. I have nothing to fear, so why am I losing my mind to crippling panic? I don't think self-harm will do me any good now. The darkness that usually precedes my blackouts isn't there. Maybe because it already manifested and had its fun —cue the dead guy on the road. I shiver at the thought.

When the headlights shine on the deserted road, I'm about to jump out of my skin. Three police cars and an ambulance stop near the wreckage. I'm getting light-headed and nauseated at the same time. I don't know which is worse. I focus on the flashing lights above the vehicles, hoping the intermittent change of colors will soothe me.

Sheriff Bennet gets out of his car, and to my surprise, his son, Reid, does too. *Why is he here?* I'm on his blacklist thanks to me catching him with Julie; therefore, his presence is far from comforting.

The sheriff stops next to the body first while his deputies head for the man who isn't dead. Finn, who was standing away from me, moves closer to my side. I appreciate his effort to show a united front. I wasn't expecting it.

After a moment, the sheriff and Reid head in our direction.

"Are you two all right?" the sheriff asks.

"I'm fine."

He glances at Finn. "You need to let the paramedics check that wound, son."

"Don't you want my statement first?"

"I can get it later. How about you, Miss Walker? Are you injured?"

"N-No."

"Do you know why those men tried to hurt you?"

I open my mouth to tell him that I believe they were after my father's safe, but Finn talks over me. "They wanted my car."

The sheriff's eyebrows fly up his forehead. "That's a lot of trouble to steal a car. It'd be easier to try to take it when the vehicle wasn't moving."

"I'm just telling you what happened."

Sheriff Bennet glances at me. "Is that true, Miss Walker?"

"Yeah. Why would he lie?"

"Because it's a little far-fetched," Reid chimes in.

I can't see Finn's expression, but I'm going to assume he's not happy with his friend right now.

"I don't think it's far-fetched," I say. "You don't know what motivates people or what kind of deranged thoughts go through their heads."

Sheriff Bennet's lips turn into a thin, flat line, but he doesn't make another comment about Finn's inaccurate description of the events. He simply jots it down in his notebook, then asks the dreaded question.

"Who killed the attacker?"

"I did," Finn says.

My jaw drops. It's one thing for him to lie about the reason we almost got killed, but quite another for him to take the blame for something I did. I turn to him, hoping to catch his gaze and learn his reasoning, but he keeps his eyes locked with the sheriff's.

I'm in utter shock by this turn of events. I don't know why Finn would do such a thing, and I can't help but wonder what that lie is going to cost me.

38

FINN

*C*lutching the edge of the desk, I wipe the blood from my busted lip. I shouldn't have talked back to my father when he's in this berserk mode, but after nearly dying at the end of a gun barrel, his fists and angry words don't scare me.

He was beside himself when Sheriff Bennet finally contacted him. And when he learned about my statement, it was a miracle he didn't strike me in the precinct in front of everyone. Thankfully Alexis had already left with her grandfather at that point.

"The only solace I can take from this mess is that you can't swim anymore," he seethes.

I touch the bandage on my shoulder. The bullet only grazed the skin, and according to the paramedics, it should heal in a couple weeks. I purposely keep that information to myself. Let the asshole believe my dreams of swimming professionally are over.

Dad turns around and pours another dose of whiskey—his fourth—and gulps it down in one go.

"Are you done?" Grandpa asks him.

The bastard insisted on being in the room and watched Dad punish me without lifting a finger to help. Dad glowers at him, but he doesn't dare snap at his old man. There are some lines he won't cross.

Grandpa takes Dad's silence as an answer. He stands up and turns to me. "Come on, Finn. I'd like to have a private word with you."

I rebel against the idea of going anywhere with the man, but if I don't, I'll be subjected to more abuse from Dad. My right eye is already swelling up from the punch I received the moment I stepped foot in his office.

I get up and follow Grandpa out. He doesn't say a word as he veers to the guesthouse. Once there, he makes a beeline for the bar in the living room and fills a glass with whiskey almost up to the top.

"Here. Drink this." He hands me the glass.

It's not an offer but an order. I don't see the point in refusing it when I so desperately need a drink. Throwing my head back, I swallow it in big gulps. It's smooth and doesn't burn my throat. Nothing but the best for the Novaks. I set the glass down on the counter with a loud thud and immediately begin to feel the effects of the spirits.

"Feeling better?" he asks.

This sounds like a trick question. If I say no, will he make me drink more? I don't want to get wasted while alone with him. To say I don't trust the bastard is an understatement.

"I'll live."

His shrewd gaze doesn't leave my face. "Yes, yes you will. Now I want you to tell me the truth about what happened tonight."

Sudden tension coils around my body. I knew Grandpa had ulterior motives for bringing me here.

"What makes you think the statement I gave Sheriff Bennet wasn't the truth?"

"I wasn't born yesterday, son. No one would dare lift a finger against a Novak unless they were desperate."

I can't help the scowl that appears on my face. "You think we're invincible, don't you?"

His eyes shine with malice as he smiles. "I don't think. I know, and the sooner you start believing that, the easier your life will be."

"What's that supposed to mean?"

"You've been moping around and letting your father bully you since the accident last year. Enough is enough, Finn."

My hands ball into fists at my sides. "You don't know anything about me."

Or the fact that he's the reason I got into that wreck. If it's up to me, he'll never find out I know the truth.

"That's where you're wrong, my boy. I know everything about you. You let your father use you as a whore because you feel guilty."

Hell, he's not wrong about that, and I hate him more than ever for having figured me out.

"Of course I feel guilty. I've condemned a kid to a wheelchair for the rest of his life."

With a roll of his eyes, he turns his attention to a wooden box sitting next to the bottle of whiskey. Its intricate pattern depicts a Venetian mask, which for some reason strikes me as odd among his things.

"Accidents happen," he replies as an afterthought, then takes a cigar from the box next to the peculiar one.

God, I want to sock him in the face. My father just used my own face as a punching bag, but he can't summon from me the same loathing I feel for the bastard standing in front of me.

"Are you done?" I ask through clenched teeth. "It's been a long night, and I'd like to rest."

His eyes narrow, and I can almost see the gears in his perverted mind at work. There's a high chance he won't let me go until I spill the beans, but my father already roughed me up, and I didn't confess. He knows he'll have to use other means to get me to talk.

He nods. "You go to bed, Finn. We can resume our conversation tomorrow. Nothing like time to make a fella wise up."

ALEXIS

I CRIED MYSELF TO SLEEP. Grandpa was furious about what happened, but he kept his feelings bottled up and didn't reprimand me for sneaking out of the house. I headed straight for my room as soon as we got back into the house, ignoring Grandma's worried gaze as she clutched her proverbial pearls.

I'm bleary eyed when I wake up, and I sense puffiness around them. Glancing at the clock, I see it's only seven. No wonder I'm bone tired, but I'm also too restless to fall back asleep. I jump out of bed and into the shower. There's somewhere I have to be.

I should take my time under the hot jets—God knows I need to relax—but I don't linger. I barely look at myself in the mirror. The quick glance tells me I look like death. My phone pings loudly somewhere in my room, making me jump out of my skin.

Thinking it's Finn, I hurry to it, but it's not his message that's flashing on my screen. It's a text from my uncle.

DAMIAN: Happy birthday.

Oh yeah. With everything that happened, I forgot the date.

ME: Thanks.

DAMIAN: I heard about what happened. Are you okay?

I need a moment to answer that. *Am I okay? No, I'm far from it.* I killed a man, and I don't remember a second of how it happened. The person who's supposed to be my enemy lied to cover for me, and I'm about to do something stupid.

ME: Yes. I just need time to process everything.

DAMIAN: What happened to the safe?

Chills roll down my spine.

ME: How do you know about the safe?

I wait on pins and needles for his reply, but it doesn't come. *Oh for fuck's sake. You're not going to leave me hanging.* I call him back, but it goes straight to voice mail. *What the hell?* I'm so angry that I end up biting the inside of my cheek, and not on purpose this time.

It's my eighteenth birthday, a date I've been looking forward to for like forever. I can't believe this is how it's going. I try not to think about my father, or how all my childhood friends have deserted me. My eyes prickle, but I refuse to surrender to this overwhelming sadness again. I had a plan before my uncle texted me, and I'm going to stick to it.

I walk out of my bedroom on my tiptoes. It's possible my grandparents are still in bed, but I don't want to risk getting caught by them as I try to sneak out. If I spend today under their judgmental gazes, I might snap again.

On my way out of the house, I cross paths with one of the maids. She opens her mouth to address me, but I put my finger to my lips and whisper, "You didn't see me."

I don't know if she'll keep my secret, but as long as she doesn't stop me from walking out, I'm fine with it. My car is parked where I left it after school in the guest space. I'm glad I didn't bother with the garage.

My mind is going a hundred miles an hour, running through everything I've been through in the last twenty-four hours. For that reason, I barely see the road, and when I arrive at my destination, I wonder how I got there in one piece.

Now parked in front of the humongous mansion, insecurity grips me. *What the hell am I doing?* I didn't think things through, that's for sure. Like most sprawling mansions in this area, the property is gated. How do I get in without announcing my presence? It was never my intention to broadcast my arrival to everyone in the house. I was hoping to pull a sneaky move like Finn did, but I obviously lack his skills.

The gate opens to allow a commercial van to exit the property, and I realize it's now or never. I jump out of my car and make a break for it, managing to slide through just before it closes again.

This is dumb, Alexis. They have security cameras everywhere.

Case in point, I don't make it past the fountain in front of the house before two beefy security guards block my path.

"This is private property. Turn around before we call the cops," one of them says.

"I'm a friend of Finn's."

"Right. Come on now, girl." He grabs my arm tightly and drags me back to the gate.

"Let go of me! I'm a Montgomery, damn it!"

I can't believe I used my grandparents' last name instead of my own. Shame takes over me. I just betrayed my father's memory to get out of trouble.

"Release the girl," a grumpy male voice orders.

Immediately, the security dude drops my arm. "Good morning, Mr. Novak."

An old man with a mop of white hair is standing in front of the guesthouse wearing a robe and holding a cup. His eyes are as blue as Finn's, icy and calculating. Even if I hadn't seen him at the school charity event, I would know he's Finn's grandfather. It doesn't make me feel good to be under his scrutiny, though.

I rub the sore spot from the security guard's iron grip and say, "I'm a friend of Finn's."

"I know who you are, young lady. Go on. The front door is probably unlocked."

Not knowing what else to say, I hurry toward it. I can't shake off the sensation that the old man is glaring at my back.

The door is indeed unlocked, but stepping into the foyer and away from his gaze doesn't calm my accelerated heartbeat.

In fact, now that I've crossed into Finn's territory, I'm more nervous than before.

39

FINN

I wake up with a grimace. My shoulder is burning. I must have moved wrong while asleep and pulled my stitches. It's not only that part of my body that's killing me—it's only the most acute pain. The skin underneath my eye is tender to the touch, and my head is pounding.

Groaning, I get up. Staying in bed all day won't make me feel better, it'll only make it easier for members of my family to corner me.

I look as bad as I feel when I check my reflection in the mirror. My cheek is yellowing out, and I have a line of dried blood on my lower lip. It's shower time and then the beach. I can't swim, but nothing will keep me away from the shore.

I'm down to my underwear when I hear my bedroom door open. *For fuck's sake. Already?* I make a motion to shut my bathroom door but stop when I see who invaded my privacy.

"Finn? Are you in here?"

To say I'm shocked is an understatement. It's probably why my heart is drumming faster in my chest. I step out of the bathroom, unbothered by my state of undress. She came in here uninvited, let her squirm in discomfort.

Her pretty brown eyes widen as she takes me in, but it's her lips, partially open, that have my full attention. I want to kiss her again so desperately that it feels like a compulsion.

"What are you doing here?"

"I came to thank you for last night. What happened to you?" She takes a step closer.

"This is nothing."

"Finn... did your father do that to you?"

"Do not feel pity for me," I grit out.

She recoils as if my words were a blow. "I have many feelings where you're concerned, and none of them are pity."

I smirk, shortening the distance between us. "Oh yeah? What feeling brought you here this morning, Lexi?"

She raises an eyebrow. "You're not going to call me 'filthy virgin' anymore?"

"Do you want me to?" I sneak my arm around her waist.

"No."

I chuckle. "Ah, again with the lies. You didn't answer my question. Why are you here?"

"I already answered that. To thank you, but also to ask you why?"

"Why what?" I lean forward, needing to take a whiff of her sweet scent. She shivers when I nuzzle her neck.

"Why did you lie to the sheriff?"

I lean back and look straight into her eyes. I don't know why I did it. Maybe I was trying to protect her from more scrutiny. Recurring blackouts aren't normal.

"Leverage," I lie. "I like having you under my thumb."

She tries to pull back, but I hold her tighter.

"You're a jerk. I shouldn't have come here."

She wants to flee, and that just sets me off. I'm done toying with my food. This shark needs to eat.

"I've enjoyed our little game, my filthy virgin, but I'm done playing." I grab a fistful of her soft hair, twisting it hard enough around my hand to cause pain.

She whimpers, and a hint of fear shines in her eyes. Her body melts against mine though, and when I slant my mouth over hers, she doesn't resist. I forgot my busted lip, but tasting her sweetness is worth the pain. I tilt her head to the side, deepening the kiss while I try to control how fast the fire is spreading through my veins.

"I'm going to fuck you," I whisper against her lips.

"You said you wouldn't touch me if I didn't confess."

"Words aren't necessary. You coming here is all the confession I need."

She gasps as I cut off her reply with my tongue. I don't even count what we're doing as kissing. It's too wild and savage. This is pure need, reckless and demanding, mixed with hate. Yes, I hate her for making me want her so bad, for driving me to do illogical things.

I ignore the burning in my shoulder as I push her back until she falls onto the bed. She's shaking as she stares at me with her innocent doe eyes. Only I know there's a side of her that's anything but sweet. It's dark and dangerous, and it calls to me even though it should send me running to the hills.

Her breathing is coming out in bursts, and the fast rise and fall of her chest only makes me want to peel off her clothes and ravish her breasts. She's terrified of what's happening, but she's also turned on. Maybe that's her kink.

"How's it going to be, my filthy virgin? Am I going to rip your clothes off, or are you going to undress on your own?"

She leans on her elbows, making the thin fabric of her T-shirt stretch over her luscious tits.

"What do *you* want?"

My eyebrows shoot up. "You're giving me the choice?"

"You've earned it. After all, you lied for me."

There she goes again, trying to wrestle the control away from me.

I narrow my eyes. "You shouldn't have done that."

ALEXIS

I REALIZE my mistake almost immediately. Finn's gaze darkens, allowing me to see several layers of his personality in a split second. But the one that prevails is the scariest. He grabs me by the hips and flips me over on the mattress. Then comes the sound of fabric being torn, and the cool air licking my now exposed skin.

My heart is racing, propelled by fear and exhilaration. Finn's fingers are suddenly between my legs, probing, invasive, and it takes great effort to not moan out loud. I'm so aroused, he can easily glide his fingers inside me, but he doesn't go that route this time. Instead, he pounces, pinning me against the mattress with his body.

His cock is hard as it presses against my ass.

"Any final words, my sweet filthy virgin, before I can no longer call you that?" he whispers in my ear.

"Yes, happy birthday to me."

He tenses for a second. I caught him by surprise again, and I know he doesn't like when that happens.

"It's your birthday today? For real?"

"Yep. Eighteen."

He bites my shoulder lightly, sending a ripple of pleasure down my back. "Well, then, happy birthday, babe."

That's the only warning I get before Finn's erection plunges into me. The pain is searing and nothing like I've ever felt before. It's like he's ripping me apart and completing me at the same time. I press my face against the mattress and cry out, muffling the sound. My agony doesn't deter him or make him go slower, though. On the contrary, he seems to thrive on it.

He digs his fingers in my hips and lifts them off the mattress so he can plunge in and out faster and harder. This new position forces me to rest on my forearms, and now there's no hiding the sounds coming out of me. The whimpers quickly become something else, moans of pleasure that make me ashamed of my actions. I'm debasing myself to him, the enemy, and no one forced me to. I've wanted this to happen since he made me shower in front of him. How can I crave someone so intensely as I hate him? It defies logic, it proves that I'm so fucked up in the head that Finn Novak has become my new punishment of choice.

When I don't think it's possible for this tainted pleasure to heighten further, Finn grabs my hair again and yanks it back hard. My neck stretches to the max, and I could alleviate the pain by standing straighter, but hell, this feels too good.

"You're too quiet, babe. I want to hear you cry some more."

"If you want to hear me scream, you have to work for it."

Maybe it's in my head, but Finn seems to grow larger inside me. He brings his lips near my ear and groans like a savage. Then he bites my shoulder, not a light nibble like before but an actual shark bite that does make me scream in pain and ecstasy.

The orgasm hits me like a devastating tsunami, sending me toward the depths of the ocean, tumbling and spinning out of control.

"Fuck," Finn growls, moving faster and faster until he explodes inside me.

His body shakes while he keeps screwing me relentlessly as if he's chasing a second orgasm. As for me, I'm spent from sensory overload. My arms turn into jelly, and I topple forward, dragging Finn with me. He crushes me with his entire body weight, cutting off my air supply.

"I can't breathe!"

He doesn't move for a couple beats, and I honestly think he's going to keep smothering me until I pass out. But he does finally pull out and roll off me. I turn my face into his side with my eyes closed because I can't bear to look at him yet.

We don't speak for several minutes, and the only sound in the room is our erratic breathing. The mattress moves underneath me, and then I open my eyes in time to see Finn walk to the bathroom in all his naked glory.

Damn, he has a fine ass.

He doesn't look over his shoulder before he shuts the door hard. I shouldn't let his coldness get to me; his behavior is nothing new, after all. Yet I *am* hurt. I'm an idiot. Finn is an asshole through and through.

I chose this. I'm not going to start second-guessing myself and suffer from buyer's remorse. But I can't stay here and wait for him to kick me out, so I jump off the bed and search for my pants. I see them lying on the floor, torn into two pieces.

Shit. How am I supposed to get out of here now?

I glance around his room and right away find something that might work. Moving fast, I grab the pair of sweatpants draped over a chair and put them on. Finn is much bigger than me, so I'm swimming in them.

From the other side of the bathroom door, I hear the shower turn on. I wish I could take one and clean up the mess Finn left behind. But that would mean sticking around, and fuck that.

I slip out of his room and pray I don't bump into anyone as I make my escape.

40

ALEXIS

I didn't see anybody on my exit out of the Novak mansion, not even creepy Grandpa. Thank God. Once again, I barely notice the drive, but this time, my thoughts are occupied with what just happened between Finn and me. I knew it was coming, and I naively believed that once I got that out of my system, I could go back to hating him without the craving. But as I replay the scene in my head, my body lights up again, ready for the second round. However, judging by the way Finn acted like I was a disposable blow-up doll, or worse, a hooker, I don't think that's in the cards.

We didn't use protection, which was stupid on so many levels, but he didn't seem to care if he knocked me up. I'm grateful that I've been on the pill for a while—one less thing to worry about. I won't let myself obsess about the other issues now. I don't have it in me.

As I approach my grandparents' mansion, I notice a familiar

car parked just outside. It's Cristiano's Camaro. Ah hell. I don't need another confrontation with him while I'm covered in Finn's jizz. I have every intention of blowing past the gates once they open and pretending I didn't recognize his car, but he accelerates as I approach and blocks my path.

I groan. "Are you fucking kidding me?"

Only it's not Cristiano who exits the vehicle but Carmen. A pang in my chest has me holding on to the steering wheel too tight. If she came here to yell at me for something I've done and don't remember, I don't know what I'll do.

I don't make a move to get out of my car, so she walks to my window and knocks on it.

"Fucking hell," I mutter as I lower the glass. "What are you doing here?"

She shoves her hands in her jeans pockets and dips her chin. "Cristiano told me he bumped into you."

"So you just came here to pile on?"

She raises her eyes to mine. "No. I came because... I figured I owed it to our friendship to hear you out."

My shields are still up, but Carmen looks sincere. And I have been miserable since my altercation with Cristiano.

"Okay. We can talk."

She nods, smiling ever so slightly, and then returns to her car to unblock my path. At this hour, I have no hope that my grandparents are still in their quarters, but at least with Carmen's presence, I can probably escape their inquisition.

I wait until she joins me in front of the house, and we walk in together. As I suspected, the moment I step foot inside, Grandma walks out of the living room.

"Lexi, what in—oh, I didn't realize you had company."

"Hello, Mrs. Montgomery," Carmen says.

"Lillian? Is that Alexis?" Grandpa calls from the den.

"Yes, Richard. She's with Carmen."

Grandpa joins us in the foyer, looking a little flustered. "Oh. Hello, Carmen. I didn't realize you were coming today."

"Yes, I had to congratulate the birthday girl in person." She smiles, and then I wonder if that's the real reason she came.

"Ah, yes. Naturally. Well, we haven't even done that yet since Alexis snuck out of the house before we were even up!"

"Sorry, Grandpa. I had to... be somewhere."

"What in the world are you wearing?" Grandma finally notices my attire. "Are those boy pants?"

Heat rushes to my cheeks, which means I must look like a tomato. How am I going to explain this to them?

"Oh, those are mine. I mean, they're Cristiano's. We met for coffee, and the klutzo here managed to spill the whole thing on her pants. Lucky for her it was iced coffee."

Warmth spreads over my chest. This is the Carmen I knew, my best friend who comes up with lies on the fly to save my skin.

I nod along. "Yep, stupid me. Cristiano left these in his car. I just borrowed them."

Grandma wrinkles her nose as if she smells something bad. "Well, go change. You look ridiculous. And come down once you're done so we can have a proper breakfast."

"Okay, Grandma." I turn to Carmen. "Let's go to my room."

It's hard not to sprint up the stairs, but I don't want to give my grandparents the impression that I'm running away from them.

"Thanks for saving my ass back there," I tell Carmen the moment she closes the door behind her.

"No problem." She shrugs. "Just like old times, huh?"

"Yeah. Listen, I don't know what I did to piss you off, but I'm truly sorry about it."

She tilts her head to the side, narrowing her eyes. "You don't know?"

I shake my head. "Cristiano mentioned I did something horrible to you, but I don't know what."

She furrows her eyebrows. "You mean like you were drunk and don't remember?"

Shit. I don't know what to say. I'd love nothing more than to confide in someone about my blackouts. Carmen is my best friend, and she would normally be my go-to person, but something holds me back. There's the fact that we haven't really spoken since I moved in with my grandparents, and then she had all our friends block me on social media.

"Yeah, like that," I lie.

She purses her lips, then gives me a *whatever* shrug. "Don't stress about it."

"Are you going to tell me what I did, at least?"

"Nah, it's not important." She flops on my bed and pulls a pillow over her lap. "Are you going to fess up about whose pants you're wearing?"

My face becomes hot again, doing my head in. This is my best friend. Why would I be embarrassed to tell her I let Finn fuck me?

Duh, because it's Finn, and you're supposed to hate him.

"No one important. I'm going to take a quick shower. Be right back."

I rush to the bathroom before she can get another word out. I still don't know where we stand, and I'm not ready for her to be all judgmental. Yes, Finn is the enemy. I hate him. But I also feel a connection to him that I can't explain.

I turn on the shower and peel off the borrowed pants. His release has dried out, but I shove the pants into the sink and soak the fabric through. I want to erase all evidence of what I did, even though the memory will be with me forever.

Only when I'm completely naked do I realize that I should have brought a change of clothes to the bathroom instead of getting dressed in front of Carmen. I never had any issues with being naked in front of her before, but things aren't as they were.

I put on my bathrobe and walk out, catching Carmen in the middle of a raid. She's deep into my chest of drawers, shoving clothes to the side, obviously looking for something. My heart constricts to the point that I can't breathe.

"What the hell?"

It's clear I caught her red-handed when she jumps at the sound of my voice.

"Lexi, it's not what you think."

"Oh yeah? Are you going to say you *weren't* going through my things?" I take a step forward, trying to control the shakes that are suddenly wreaking havoc on my body, but the rage is clawing its way up nonetheless, tingeing everything red.

"I wasn't. I swear."

Her eyes are widely innocent, but I know what I saw. She's lying through her teeth, and I want to know why.

"What were you hoping to find, Carmen? Money?"

Tears fill her brown eyes, and her lips quiver. I'd buy her bullshit if I didn't know her any better. She used to pull that shit with her mom all the time.

"You don't understand, okay?"

She bolts for the door, running like a coward instead of telling me the truth.

A myriad of feelings rush through me, but I'm too enraged to analyze each one now. I go after her, disregarding the fact that I'm very naked under my bathrobe. Even in high heels, she's superfast, all thanks to her position on the track team. But I'm fueled by anger and am able to grab the back of her jacket before she can get down the stairs.

"Let go of me!" She tries to shrug off my hold.

"Not until you tell me the real reason you showed up today."

Resentment shines in her eyes. "I'll never tell you. You don't deserve to know the truth."

Something snaps inside me as the sound of a thousand hornets seems to buzz in my ears. The world goes dark for a fleeting moment, but when I regain my sight, Carmen is lying at the foot of the stairs.

"Carmen!" I yell.

The maid, who must have come to the entry foyer to investigate the ruckus, is glowering at me. Then she helps Carmen get back on her feet. They exchange words in Spanish, too fast for me to understand what they're saying.

My grandparents join the scene, clearly astonished.

"What in the world happened here?" Grandpa asks, eyes narrowed at Carmen.

"Miss Alexis pushed her friend down the stairs," the maid answers.

"No, I didn—" I don't finish the sentence. I did black out for a second. What if in that moment, I pushed Carmen? "I didn't mean to."

"I'm sure it was just an accident," Grandma butts in. "Are you okay, dear?"

"I didn't break anything, if that's what you're worried about. I won't sue," Carmen retorts, not disguising her anger.

Why does she get to play the victim? This wouldn't have happened if she hadn't come here under false pretenses.

She turns around and strides out the front door without a glance back. If she was truly blameless, she'd make a scene, curse my name, vow to never speak to me again. But she simply left in a hurry, probably afraid I'd tell everyone I caught her going through my things. I'd never do that, though.

I pivot to return to my room, thinking it's better if I stay there until the day is over.

"Alexis, where do you think you're going?" Grandma asks. "You owe us an explanation."

"I know, Grandma, but I don't have one to give you."

She doesn't follow me into my room, but I lock the door for

good measure. I'm sure she has a spare key, but I do feel better for the extra barrier.

Suddenly I'm exhausted. I lean against the door and rest my head on the hard surface. In my periphery, I see the mess Carmen's searching left behind. I kept Damian's letters to my mother in the drawer before they went missing. But how would Carmen know about them? Why would she go through the trouble to come here and search for them?

I don't think that's what she was looking for, but then what else could it be?

41

FINN

*W*hen I'm done with the shower, Alexis is gone. I didn't expect her to linger after I simply disappeared into the bathroom without saying a word. I didn't trust myself in that moment. I knew I'd fuck her eventually. We'd been playing the cat-and-mouse game for weeks, but I didn't expect to catch feelings beyond lust. I wanted to cuddle her, ask if she was okay.

Her torn pants and underwear are in the same spot I left them. There's no way she walked out of here half-naked. A quick glance around my room tells me she took the sweatpants that were draped over the chair. The corners of my lips twitch up, but a scowl replaces my amusement when I realize I *like* the idea of her wearing my clothes.

I finish getting ready with every intention of keeping my plans to head to the beach when my phone rings. It's Luke. I haven't really talked to him in a while.

"Hey, isn't it too early for you to be awake?"

"I haven't been to bed." His voice is coarse, usually a sign he's been drinking and smoking nonstop.

"Please don't tell me I need to bail you out of jail," I joke, knowing very well he didn't spend the night there. I would have known about it by now.

"It's Cameron. Shit... you need to come over, man."

"What happened?"

Something crashes in the background, making Luke curse under his breath. "I can't explain it over the phone. Just come to my place ASAP."

The urgency in his voice propels me into action. I search for my car fob only to remember it's in the shop for repair after the crash. *Son of a bitch.* I guess I'll have to borrow one of the SUVs, then.

I duck out of my room, hoping I won't bump into my parents. Dad might want to use my face as a punching bag again, and Mom would most definitely make me feel guilty for leaving her alone with Grandpa around. I bet she's still passed out from all the bingeing she did yesterday.

In the garage, I notice the Maserati SUV my father prefers is gone. A breath of relief whooshes out of me. The asshole must have gone to the office already. Thank fuck.

I slide behind the steering wheel of a year-old Escalade and find the fob in the armrest compartment. The moment I pass through the gate, the tension in my shoulders lessens considerably. It's a fucking pain in the ass that I can't swim until my stitches are out. I'm due to spend some time in the pool—hopefully without interruptions next time. Although Alexis's disruption was more than welcome.

My pulse accelerates as euphoria courses through my veins. I don't know what's happening to me, but I can't let Alexis trigger these stupid-ass happy feelings in my chest. She was a distraction from my guilt, and then part of my father's twisted games.

I accelerate, going over the speed limit and forcing my mind to focus on the situation I'm about to face.

I knew Halsey coming back to Triton Cove would mess with Cameron's head, but I had no idea he was still so hung up on her. It's been three years since the event that made him curse her name and vow to hate her forever. How long does it take to get over a damn crush?

It's hard for me to put myself in his shoes. I've never felt anything like that for anyone before. That all-consuming feeling that makes you lose your mind.

Alexis's face pops into my head. I lied to the sheriff to cover for her. It wasn't part of a game; I just wanted to protect her for reasons I still don't understand. Does that mean I'm turning into Cameron and letting a girl derail my thoughts and control my life?

Hell to the fuck no.

I can't let that happen. I'd end things if I didn't have the deal with my father hanging over my head. But there are perks, I can't deny that. Fucking Alexis was good fun, and I can't wait for a repeat. I just have to stop caring about what happens to her. Easy peasy when it's been drilled into my brain since I was a toddler that feelings make you weak.

I don't realize I spaced out until the exit to Luke's house comes up. I have to press on the brakes hard because it's a sharp curve, and I almost don't make it. The rear wheels slide across the asphalt, burning rubber. I manage to regain control of the car, but it was a close one.

My heart is racing a hundred miles an hour. I pass a hand over my face. *Son of a bitch.* If I get into another wreck, my father will send me to a military school in the middle of nowhere. He's threatened that before.

I make sure to keep a light foot on the gas pedal. These winding roads are dangerous as fuck. After another ten minutes, I finally cross onto Luke's property. I see Reid is also here. Shit must have reached DEFCON 1 in order for Luke to call all of us. The last time we had a situation like that was with Jason two years ago.

Shoving all my problems to the side, I put my game face on and head into the mansion. As usual, I'm greeted by no one. The place is huge, and one can easily get lost in here.

"Luke?" My voice echoes against the walls and high ceiling.

I pull my cell phone out to call him, but hurried footsteps coming from the grand staircase draw my attention. I look up and see Sage, who's paler than usual.

"Hey, Sage. Where's your brother?"

Her eyebrows furrow. "I don't know. I haven't seen him today."

I sigh. "It's okay. I'll find him."

"Okay. Would you tell him I went to the beach?"

Now it's my turn to frown. "You're going to the beach?"

She straightens her spine. "Yes, do you have a problem with that?"

Touchy. Jesus, what's up with everyone today? I raise my hands, palms facing her. "Nope. Not at all. Have fun."

I turn around, my phone glued to my ear. It rings a couple times before Luke picks up.

"You'd better be here already," he says.

"Yeah. Where the hell are you guys?"

"By the pool."

He ends the call before I can get another word in. I'll find out what's going on with Cameron soon enough.

When I walk outside, I'm not prepared for the scene I walk into. I expected Cameron to be raging, breaking things. Instead, he's sitting in the shallow part of the pool, hugging his knees and crying. Reid is next to him, and he seems frustrated as hell.

"The fuck?" I blurt out.

Luke turns to me, and his brows shoot to the heavens. "What the hell happened to your face?"

Shit, I forgot about the bruising. "Daddy Dearest didn't appreciate that I got into another car wreck."

"Hmm. Well, let's unpack that later. As you can see, Cameron is in pieces."

Reid looks at us. "He's not making any sense. He keeps repeating that he should have been there. That it's his fault."

I stride toward the pool. "Let me talk to him."

Reid stands, and we trade places. Cameron barely acknowledges my presence.

"Cam, come on, man. You're freaking us out. What happened?" I ask softly.

He shakes his head. "I can't tell you."

"Why not?"

He turns to me then, his green eyes piercing me with his anguish. I've never seen him look like that, not even when Halsey left Triton Cove.

"Because I promised I wouldn't tell. And for once, I'm going to keep my word."

Suspicion takes hold of me. Squinting, I ask, "Does this have anything to do with Halsey?"

He flinches, and I have my answer. I'm not even surprised. Only she can mess with Cameron's head like this. I get angry, sick and tired of seeing my friend hit rock bottom because of that girl. I stand up and get out of the pool. I don't even care that my pants are now soaked.

"What are we going to do about him?" Reid asks.

Sparing another glance at Cameron, I run my fingers through my hair. "We can't let him go anywhere in this state."

"I hid his car keys already," Luke says. "I won't let him leave."

I nod. "That's for the best."

"Shouldn't we give him a Xanax or something?" Reid crosses his arms, his eyes still on Cameron.

"Yeah, something," Luke mutters.

I stay until we coax Cameron out of the pool and make him calm down. My chest is heavy when I finally slip out before the guys can corner me to ask about my face. I'm not in the mood for questions. But I do call Halsey on my way home. She doesn't answer, so I leave her a message.

"Halsey, this is Finn. I don't know what the fuck you did to Cameron, but if you mess with him again, you'll wish you never returned to Triton Cove."

42

ALEXIS

I wake up earlier than usual on Monday after avoiding my grandparents all day yesterday, and almost immediately, I feel a tightness in my chest that's out of place. It's almost as if I'm guilty of something. I shove the sheets aside and get up, noticing then that I'm not wearing pajamas.

What the fuck? I remember changing into them last night. Now I'm wearing a long-sleeve black T-shirt and black yoga pants. I look like a spy. I rub my eyes, flinching when my fingers brush against a tender spot. Quickly, I run into the bathroom and gasp when I see the scratch on my left cheek. My pulse skyrockets, and getting air into my lungs becomes difficult. Something happened last night, and if I can't remember, it means another blackout episode.

Wheezing, I brace my hands against the sink and let my head fall between my shoulders. The darkness has never taken over while I was asleep before. This is getting out of hand. I'm afraid to know what I did this time around.

A knock on the door startles me. I jump and go back into my room.

"Who is it?" I croak.

"Lexi, you're going to be late for school if you don't get moving," Grandma says.

"What? But it's still early."

"It's almost eight!"

No, that's not possible. I checked the time before getting out of bed. It wasn't even six.

I march to the window and yank the curtains open. The sun is already shining bright in the sky. That means I lost a couple hours I can't account for.

"You'd better get going, young lady," Grandma continues.

There's no time to freak out about how I'm quickly unraveling. I focus on getting ready for school in record time and rush out of my room knowing breakfast isn't an option. I'm not hungry anyway.

Before I walk out the front door, I notice there's a new maid in the house. Did the previous one get sacked because she accused me of pushing Carmen down the stairs, or did she quit? A sliver of remorse pierces my chest. I hope my grandparents didn't fire her because of me. What Carmen did wasn't right, but I would never hurt her on purpose. What kind of person do I become when these blackouts happen?

Someone capable of killing.

Chills run down my spine as I remember that horrible scene on the road: a man with his head smashed in, the other assailant unconscious. I don't know what's going to happen to Finn. Will he get in trouble for taking the blame? He already has a smear on his record thanks to the car accident last year. I can't believe he'd risk more problems for himself only to have me indebted to him. I don't think I'll ever understand his twisted mind games.

And now my father's safe is in police custody as evidence. It was used as a weapon, and nobody told me when I could get it back. This situation is horrible, but at least I know the safe will be secured. Those criminals went through a lot of trouble to try to steal it. Whatever is inside must be worth a lot.

I don't know what to expect at school this morning. I try to portray aloofness even though I'm screaming inside. I have so much shit going on in my life, but the prospect of seeing Finn again is what's twisting my stomach into knots right now. How is he going to act around me now that he got what he wanted? As crazy as our relationship is, I'm not ready to end it yet. I need his viciousness more than ever.

It's my luck that I see Finn as soon as I step foot in the hallway. My heart skips a beat, and the yearning that hits me is as potent as it is insane. Hell. Why does he still pull me in even after I tasted the forbidden fruit?

It's impossible to see him, even if from afar, and not remember his fiery kisses, the feel of his cock inside me. His hair is damp, which makes me think of him swimming in the pool—which he obviously can't do until his wound heals. It doesn't stop my brain from having dirty thoughts though. The image of Finn wearing his Speedo comes to the forefront of my mind, not helping me one bit.

Ignoring my accelerated pulse and how my body is shaking, I set my chin high and pretend I don't see him. Instead, I make a beeline for my locker. I don't need anything from it, only time to get my thoughts in order. My ears are buzzing thanks to the blood rushing to my face. I close my eyes and focus on my breathing. I can't have a panic attack now.

"Good morning, Lexi," Finn purrs near my ear, startling me.

I jump back, letting out a little gasp. My face becomes hotter, a fact he notices and—if his sexy smile is any indication—takes great pleasure in it. But then his eyes zero in on the scratch on my cheek.

"Quit sneaking up on people." I shut the door with a bang.

"I don't sneak up on anyone. You're the one who likes to do that." He touches my face just below the mark on my cheek. "What happened to you?"

I want to bask in his caress, but I lean back before I combust where I stand. "Nothing."

He squints. "Did someone hurt you?"

Ah shit. It didn't even occur to me that he'd make a big deal out of it.

"No. And getting back to your earlier statement about sneaking up on you, I was just returning the favor."

"You left without saying goodbye." He tucks a strand of my hair behind my ear, giving me goose bumps where his fingertips brush my skin. His voice is low, seductive, and it's quickly turning me into a pool of goo.

"I didn't think you wanted me to stick around," I grit out. "Or maybe you're just upset that you didn't have the opportunity to kick me out."

His eyebrows furrow. "You're insane if you thought for one second that I'd kick you out. I'm upset because I didn't have seconds."

I'm still processing his words when he kisses the corner of my mouth. Okay, I'm on fire now. I need a hose down.

Finn steps back, smiling like a fiend, and then takes my hand. "Come on. We don't want to be late for class."

I'm in too much of a state of shock to do anything besides let him steer me toward our next class. People turn to gawk at us, and then the gossip starts. Jackie and Tiffany are hanging out right in front of the classroom, and their eyes almost pop out of their sockets when they see our joined hands. But then they

look at our faces—Finn all bruised and me with the scratch—
and I can almost see the gears in their evil minds working to
come up with the perfect jab.

"It seems someone likes trash after all," Jackie remarks.

Wow, no comment about our appearances. I guess I expected
too much from her peanut-size brain. But I bristle nonetheless.

Finn's reaction is an amused chuckle. "Your insults are as
stale as your mother's political campaign. I wonder what's going
to happen when she loses the support of all the major families
in Triton Cove."

A storm of bad emotions gathers in her eyes, but Finn
doesn't linger to wait for her reply.

Inside the classroom, I spot Emily in her usual seat, and she
continues to pretend I don't exist. Her aloofness should bother
me, but I don't have enough emotional spoons left to care.

Out of Finn's friends, only Reid is here. He raises an
eyebrow and smirks, making me finally snap out of whatever
spell Finn put on me. I yank my hand from his grasp.

"What's wrong, babe?"

"I think you've made your point." I pull up a seat, trying to
avoid people's stares. But Eric's glower I don't miss.

Whatever. He's another jerk. I don't care about his opinion.

A couple minutes later, the teacher enters the room, and the
lecture starts. I force my attention to stay on Mr. Jonas and not
Finn, who picked the seat next to mine. He knows he's gotten
under my skin, and he's relishing tormenting me.

Halfway through class, a knock on the door interrupts Mr.
Jonas midsentence. Someone from administration enters,
looking a bit distraught.

"May I help you, Miss McGee?

"Yes, I need Miss Alexis Walker to come with me."

I tense on the spot. Knowing I can't account for what I did
last night, whatever is going on can't be anything good. *What the
hell did I do now?*

"Why?" The question leaves my mouth before I can stop myself.

Tiffany snickers. "Who did you screw now, *Lexi*?"

"Shut your mouth, Tiffany," Finn barks.

"Everyone, pipe down," Mr. Jonas interrupts.

"Sheriff Bennet is here to see you," Miss McGee replies.

My eyes widen, and then I make the mistake of looking at Finn, seeing concern in his blue eyes.

"Miss Walker, please follow Miss McGee," Mr. Jonas says.

I collect my things, regretting my stupid outburst. Before, everyone was thinking I was being called into the headmaster's office because of inappropriate behavior. Now who knows what stories will spread through the school's hallways. I'll take being called a whore rather than a delinquent any day.

Once in the hallway, I ask, "What's this all about?"

"I'm not at liberty to discuss it," she replies in a clipped tone.

Great. Another shrew with a stick up her ass.

The walk to the headmaster's office only gives me time to conjure up the worst possible reasons for the sheriff's visit. He found out that Finn lied, and he's here to arrest me. No, that can't be it; otherwise, Finn would have been called too. My warped imagination takes me on more sinister roads, and by the time we arrive at Mr. Cain's office, I'm certain the sheriff's visit has something to do with my midnight activities.

Miss McGee knocks on the headmaster's door first, then announces my presence. Sheriff Bennet stands and turns to me sporting a grim expression, which makes me even more certain he's here to arrest me. I focus on the headmaster, hoping the sheriff can't see the guilt shining in my eyes.

"Mr. Cain, you wanted to see me?"

"Yes. Please have a seat, Miss Walker." He points at the chair across his desk.

"Uh, what's the sheriff doing here?" I ask, not making a motion to accept his offer to sit down.

The sheriff clears his throat. "I'm afraid I come bearing bad news."

My stomach twists so savagely, it almost forces me to bend over like a pretzel. My hands are balled into fists already, and my nails are digging into my palms. The rising panic is mixed with my darkness, and I can't let them win, not in front of the sheriff and the headmaster. Bad things happen when I'm not in control.

"Go on, then," I manage to say through the lump in my throat.

"Your safe went missing from the evidence room."

It takes a moment for my brain to process that he didn't come to arrest me after all. But when his words finally sink in, I blurt out, "What? How is that possible?"

He shakes his head. "We don't know yet. We're investigating the matter."

Tears of frustration gather in my eyes. I want to scream at the sheriff for his incompetence, punch him in the face, but I might end up in jail if I attack him. The surge of violent intentions makes me shake.

"I can't believe this. Do you know who did it?"

"No, I'm afraid not."

That's total bullshit. He's lying. I know it. "How can that be? You must have security cameras in your precinct."

"Of course."

When he doesn't elaborate, it solidifies my suspicion that he's hiding something. "You have nothing, do you? No leads, unless it was an inside job."

He flinches. "Now, let's not jump to conclusions and start accusing my team."

"What other explanation is there?" I snap.

Mr. Cain stands and walks around his desk. "Please, Miss Walker. Let's not say anything we don't mean. I'm sure Sheriff Bennet is doing everything he can."

I ignore the headmaster in favor of glaring at the sheriff. "What about the man you have in custody? Did he say anything useful, or did you lose him too?"

He narrows his eyes, clenching his jaw. "I'm going to give you a pass only because you're distressed."

"Damn right I'm distressed. That safe is one of the few things I have left of my father."

Guilt shines in the man's eyes, but he quickly recovers, and his gaze turns hard again. "I understand the sentimental value, but most importantly, that safe was the weapon used to kill a man."

My heart seems to stop beating for a second. For a moment, I forgot about that grim detail.

"In self-defense," I remind him.

He nods. "Yes, of course." He turns to Mr. Cain. "Thanks for letting me use your office, Simon."

"Not a problem."

Wait, is that it?

"What's going to happen now?"

"I'll let you know when I have more information."

"What about Finn? Does that affect his situation?"

A vein in the sheriff's forehead throbs, and his cheeks hollow as he grinds his teeth. "I can't discuss his case with you, Miss Walker."

He's not going to spill the beans, and insisting on it will not work in my favor.

I let the sheriff walk out first because I'm still reeling from the news. My father's safe is gone, something he clearly didn't want to fall in the hands of someone or he wouldn't have buried it in a wall.

"Are you okay, Miss Walker?" Mr. Cain asks.

I turn to him in a daze. "What?"

"You look quite pale. Do you need to sit down for a minute?"

I shake my head. "No, I have to get back to class."

He nods. "Very well, then. Don't forget you have detention today."

Forcing a smile to my face, I say, "Thanks for reminding me."

Jackass.

43

FINN

I can't pay attention to Mr. Jonas's lesson to save my life. My legs keep bouncing up and down—Luke style—and I keep looking at the door every few minutes, waiting for Alexis to return. My plan to not care about her lasted less than an hour.

"Mr. Novak," Mr. Jonas calls.

I whip my face to him. "What?"

"May I know what you find so fascinating out in the hallway?"

Tiffany and Jackie snicker.

"Oh, he's trying to catch sight of his girlfriend being escorted out in handcuffs by Sheriff Bennet," Tiffany chimes in.

I open my mouth to reply, but Eric Danes beats me to the punch. "No chance of that happening. She's one of you now. She could get away with murder."

Chills run down my spine, and the hairs on the back of my neck stand on end. His statement hit too close to the truth to be a coincidence. I turn and look him dead in the eye. He matches my hard glare without flinching, but unfortunately for me, his face reveals nothing.

"That was not a helpful comment, Mr. Danes," Mr. Jonas retorts.

The bell rings, ending this torturous lesson. I'm torn between cornering Eric to ask what he knows and going after Alexis. In the end, I don't want to make him suspicious in case his hateful comment was nothing more than chance. Decision made, I grab my stuff as fast as I can and run out of the room.

The hallway fills up fast, making my progress slow. I shove people out of the way, but someone grabs the back of my jacket and pulls me backward.

"What the fu—" I start but then see it's Halsey. "You," I seethe.

She looks like shit, with dark circles under her eyes and a pale face, but that doesn't work in her favor.

"How is Cameron?" she asks.

"How dare you ask me about him after what you've done."

Her eyes grow larger. "I-I didn't do anything."

"Bullshit!"

Her lips quiver, and I know she's on the verge of crying her eyes out, but I don't care.

"Leave Halsey alone, meathead." Emily steps in.

I glare at her. "This doesn't concern you."

"I know, but it doesn't concern you either."

"It's okay, Emily. Finn is only looking out for his friend." Halsey hastily wipes a tear from the corner of her eye.

"Well, you shouldn't worry about that asshole either." Emily sneers in my direction.

I'm about to blow up on these two, but that wasn't my goal

to begin with. "I can't deal with this bullshit. The warning stands, Halsey. Stay the fuck away from Cameron."

I don't stick around to see the look on their faces. I need to find out what Sheriff Bennet wanted with Alexis. He wouldn't drag her out of class if it wasn't serious. It must have something to do with the incident on Saturday.

When I finally manage to get to the headmaster's office, both the sheriff and Alexis are gone, and Mr. Cain is on a conference call.

"Do you know where Alexis went?" I ask his assistant.

She gives me an exasperated look. "I hope to her next lecture."

Hell. That's Miss LeFleur's class. The last thing I want is to interact with that woman, but I can't just sit on my ass without knowing what happened. I pull my cell phone out and text her.

ME: Where are you?

I stare at my screen for far too long, praying for those damn three dots to appear. Nothing. Grinding my teeth, I shove my phone in my pocket and then make my way to the other side of the building. I'm pissed that I'm acting like a whipped motherfucker, worried sick about her.

Distracted, I end up colliding with someone. I'm ready to yell at the person when I see Sage carrying a piece of canvas half her size.

"Sorry, Finn. I didn't see you there," she says.

I recheck my attitude, reeling in my anger. "No worries. Are you going to art class?"

"Yeah. Can you tell?" She chuckles, and that's surprising. I haven't heard her laugh since the whole drama with Justice.

"I need a favor. Can you check if Alexis is in there?"

Her eyebrows arch, but understanding quickly shines in her eyes. "Oh, yeah. Give me a second."

I stay rooted to the spot and watch her walk toward Miss

LeFleur's studio. A moment later, Sage sticks her head out and shakes her head.

Fuck. Where the hell is she?

I retrace my steps, but I'm just pretty much walking aimlessly. It's possible Alexis left campus, and if that's the case, tough luck finding her if she didn't go home.

"Finn, wait up," Reid calls.

I pause, berating myself for not thinking of asking Reid if he knew why his father was here.

"Jesus, why did you zoom out of class like a bat from hell?"

I give him a droll look. "Why do you think? Tell me what you know about your father's visit."

His eyebrows almost reach his hairline. "Whoa. Since when am I your bitch, Finn?"

"This is serious, Reid. Quit playing the offended card."

He watches me through slitted eyes for a second but then shakes his head. "God, aren't you whipped?"

"I'm not whipped," I grit out.

"Are you sure? I mean, why else would you lie to my father and say you killed the bastard who tried to rob you?"

Fuck me. I should never have told him the truth when I called him. Then again, I wasn't planning on taking the blame. It just happened.

My phone vibrates in my pocket, cutting off my retort. I fish the device out too fast, almost dropping the damn thing.

"Aren't you eager to see who texted you?" Reid laughs.

I ignore his stupid remark and read Alexis's reply. She's home, which means that's where I'm headed.

Before I put the phone back in my pocket, another message pops up.

ALEXIS: I need you.

"Oh, booty call." Reid chuckles.

I shove him away from me. "Quit being such a fucking busybody."

He shakes his head. "Neveeerrrr. Go on, Finn. Duty calls."

The bastard is still laughing as he walks away. I, however, am not. For some reason, I don't think Alexis's text meant she's looking for cock fun.

44

ALEXIS

I know I'll get in a heap of trouble for skipping class and detention, but I couldn't stay, not after Sheriff Bennet's visit. When I pull into the garage, I'm relieved to find it empty. In my current state of mind, dealing with Grandma is the last thing I need. I head for the stairs, but before I can take two steps up, the new maid calls me.

"Miss Alexis?"

"Yes?"

She hands over a stack of letters. "These arrived for you earlier. Your grandmother asked me to give them to you at once."

There's a good chunk of them, which makes me curious. Who sends letters these days? A quick once-over clues me in to what they are—the RSVP responses to my birthday party that's happening this coming Saturday. Thanks to the charity event last weekend, I couldn't celebrate my birthday on the actual date.

"Thanks," I mumble absentmindedly.

"No problem, miss."

She starts to turn around, but I ask, "Do you know where Narissa is?"

Her eyebrows arch. "Narissa? I'm not sure who that is."

Damn, so she did leave.

"Never mind, then."

I run up the stairs and lock myself in my room. Then I toss all the envelopes on my bed, knowing if Grandma asked her new maid to give them to me, it's because she wants me to do something about them. But I'm choosing to ignore them for now. Dejected, I sit on the edge of the mattress and rest my head in my hands. What am I going to do about Dad's safe? I have to find it, but I don't even know where to start.

Uncle Damian knew about it, so maybe I should see if I can get more information from him. I grab my phone with the intention of texting him, but I see Finn's message first. He wants to know where I am. I stare at the screen for far too long without doing anything. I want to reply, but at the same time, I'm scared of the feelings I've developed for him.

"This is stupid." I throw the phone on top of the letters, and one of the envelopes falls to the floor.

It's light blue instead of the cream color of the others, which piques my interest. Maybe it's a belated birthday card, but who would think to send me one?

It doesn't have the sender's information though, which, considering how my life is going, makes me leery of opening it now. But I've already fucked up once by not reading the contents of Damian's letters to my mother; I'm not about to do it again. I rip the envelope open and pull out a birthday card. My heart is hammering even before I read the personalized note inside.

Don't worry about the safe. It's secured. So are the letters from Uncle Dearest you were too chicken to read.

Make sure you take care of that scratch on your cheek. The barbed wire was rusty. I'll be more careful next time.

By the way, your friend Carmen is up to no good. Her new friends are dangerous. Stay away from her.

If you haven't figured out who this is yet, let me give you a clue.

Happy belated birthday to us.

PS. I might be changing my mind about Finn. He was fun in bed.

I let the card fall from my fingers as tears gather in my eyes. It's not a cruel joke. This is my handwriting. My mind is spiraling out of control, and I'm afraid if I don't do something about it, I might fall into an abyss and never come back out.

I don't think any amount of self-harm will help me this time. I pick up my phone and finally text Finn back. He might interpret my message as a booty call, but it doesn't matter as long as he comes to save me from myself.

I lie down on my bed on top of all the RSVP cards—not caring one bit if they get wrinkled—and curl into a ball. I've always suspected there was someone else living inside my head, and now I have irrefutable proof that I was right. I know what I should do, but I'm afraid of that decision. For now, I'm content in closing my eyes and trying not to fall into complete despair.

My phone pings, announcing an incoming message. It's from Finn. He's on his way.

The tension in my body eases a bit. It's crazy how the fact that he's coming over is calming me down. If anyone had told me that a few weeks ago, I'd have laughed in their faces. I don't know when it happened, but somehow, Finn managed to carve out a place in my heart.

FINN

I TRY to sneak into Alexis's home like the many times I've done so in the past, but unfortunately, they have a new maid, and she wasn't interested in my bribe. A mix of watchdog and drill sergeant, she makes me wait in the entry foyer while she goes to check if Alexis wants to see me. It didn't matter that I told her I was Alexis's boyfriend. What a fucking pain in the ass. She either needs to become more amenable or she's out of here. With the way people like my folks and Alexis's grandparents change house staff as if they're disposable items, it'd be easy to get rid of her. It won't do to have a meddling maid blocking my access to Alexis.

I only wait until she disappears up the stairs before following her. I wouldn't put it past her calling the cops on me if I ignored her "orders." She glowers when she sees me walking toward her in the hallway.

"I asked you to wait downstairs."

"Yeah, yeah. Alexis is expecting me, so if you want to keep your job, I'd suggest you shut your fucking mouth already."

Alexis's door opens suddenly, and she steps out looking annoyed. "What's the matter?"

The maid's jaw drops an inch. "Uh, he claims to be your boyfriend."

Her eyebrows shoot up, but her surprise quickly wanes. "He *is* my boyfriend. I was expecting him."

I smirk. "Told ya. Just run along now, and don't even think about interrupting us."

I steer Alexis back into her room and kick the door shut, not bothering to see how the new maid took my dismissal. Maybe I should have tried to be nicer, but I didn't bring any diplomacy tokens with me today. I bet she's calling Alexis's grandmother right now to tell her I'm here. Oh well. I lock the door to avoid a possible bust.

"I'm sorry about the new maid," Alexis says.

I shrug as if it's no big deal. "Just a minor inconvenience."

She sits on the edge of her bed and won't look me in the eye.

"What did Sheriff Bennet want?" I ask after a moment.

"My dad's safe went missing from the precinct."

"What? How is that possible?"

"He wouldn't say, but it doesn't matter." She glances up, and I read all the anguish in her eyes. It hits me straight in the chest how much I want to erase that emotion in them.

"Why?" I walk over and drop into a crouch in front of her.

"Because I know who took the safe, Finn. It was me."

I wince, thrown back by her reply. "Are you serious?"

She nods and then hands over a birthday card. "Read it."

I scan through the note quickly, then read it again slower the second time around because it doesn't make any sense. I look at her. "What's this? Who sent you this?"

"I did. You must have suspected by now that things happen to me that can't be explained."

"Like you not remembering kicking me out of your room, or accusing me of stealing your letters when you knew I didn't take them?"

"Yeah. Now I know why. I think...." She bites her lower lip and glances down. "I think I suffer from multiple personality disorder."

I place my hands on her thighs, needing to touch her. She looks so broken, and I should revel in it, but it's been a while since I stopped wanting to hurt her.

"Why are you telling me this? I thought I was the enemy."

She swallows hard and meets my eyes again. "You *are* the enemy... I think." Sighing, she covers my hands with hers. "It's all so confusing, but I think the reason I'm telling you is because you're just as fucked up as I am."

I try not to flinch and fail. She got that right. I get up and walk away, giving my back to her. "You're not wrong. I wouldn't have started anything with you if I was sane."

"Ouch. Tell me how you really feel, why don't you?"

I look over my shoulder. "Don't sound so offended. It was the same for you, wasn't it?"

She stands up and walks over. I turn to her, unable to resist her pull.

"Yes, you were my new method of self-harm."

I frown, confused by her statement, until she pushes her sleeve up and shows me a bite mark that's just about healed. My stomach coils tightly. Only someone who's hurting terribly would resort to that coping mechanism. Impulsively, I bring her flush against my chest, crushing her body against mine into a bear hug. I've never hugged anyone like this before, as if I wanted to take their pain away. I thought the only way to feel better about myself was to nurture her hate for me, but maybe I want something else from her. Maybe I want… *more.*

Alexis melts into me, pressing her cheek against my chest. I can't help but think how perfectly she fits in my arms. My heart is thundering when I pull her back and claim her mouth, prying her lips open with my tongue. She didn't ask me to come over for sex, but she owes me seconds, and I'm taking it.

Possessively, I grab her ass and haul her up. She wraps her legs around my hips, pressing her pussy against my erection, making me groan like a caveman. My shoulder throbs. I keep forgetting about that damn bullet wound, but hell, it's worth it.

I carry her to the bed, and together we tumble over the mattress, scattering the pile of fancy envelopes that were lying there. Impatient and hungry for her, I shove her skirt up and once again rip her cotton panties in two.

She bites my lower lip in retaliation, then whispers against my lips, "That's the second pair you've destroyed, Finn."

"You need new ones anyway. Sexy, lacy, and black." I grind my hips against her naked pussy, mimicking what's to come.

Arching her back, she moans. "Oh, that feels good. Do it again."

"I will in a sec." I lean back just enough to unzip my slacks and get my dick out. Then I enter her with a single thrust, grinding my teeth when her tightness wraps around me.

"Finn," she gasps, closing her eyes.

I pull back almost all the way only to slam back inside her. Man, this is going to be a fast one if I'm not careful.

"What is it, babe?" I nudge the crook of her neck with my nose, then bite her earlobe.

"I need more of you. I need harder."

I kiss her again, roughly, not caring if I'm bruising or biting her lips, while I fulfill her request. I try not to think how good she feels, how deliciously tight and wet she is, but it's a vain effort. The more I try, the harder my cock gets and the tighter my balls become. Squeezing my butt cheeks together won't do the trick this time. I'm going to explode into her again very, very soon.

But not before she does.

It's that mission that keeps my orgasm at bay. I want Alexis to shatter first before I follow her into blissful oblivion.

"I'm so close, Finn. Please don't ever stop fucking me."

I chuckle. "I'll try."

If I could, I wouldn't stop ever. Who in their right mind would want to stop this amount of pleasure?

When she curses loudly, trembling underneath me, I lose the fight against my body and come hard, pumping my hips in and out so fast that the headboard bangs against the wall loudly. I keep fucking her even when I'm empty, stopping only when she begs me to.

I collapse half on top of her, leaving my left arm and leg draped around her body as I try to catch my breath. For a moment, neither of us speaks. I don't want to think about anything; I just want to bask in this moment when I realize I may have found my match.

"Thank you," she says, making me chortle.

"You're welcome."

She turns to me. "I don't mean the orgasm, but that was amazing too."

I'm still smiling when I meet her eyes. "What do you mean, then?"

"For not freaking out and bailing when I showed you how insane I am."

I reach for her face, rubbing my thumb over her lips. "It's okay that you're crazy."

She stares at me with her beautiful brown eyes without blinking for a couple seconds, then blurts out, "I think I love you."

It's my turn to freeze. I actually don't think I'm breathing, caught in the vortex her simple statement caused. "All because I don't care that you're a little psycho?"

A blush spreads through her cheeks. "Yes, because of that. Don't make a big deal out of it, okay? It doesn't mean anything."

Right. She was never able to lie to save her life. She loves me for real, but I won't call her on her bullshit today, not when my heart is beating a little faster, and I think I finally understand what butterflies in the stomach mean.

45

ALEXIS

I'm a moron. Not only did I tell Finn my darkest secret, but I also said the *L* word. I'm grateful he didn't make a big deal out of it when I backpedaled. I'm sure I was blushing all the way to kingdom come.

He left before Grandma got back home, and judging by how she didn't burst into my room, spewing fire from her nostrils, the new maid didn't rat me out.

That doesn't mean I'm not in the doghouse though. During dinner, the topic of my bailing class is brought up.

"I was distraught about the news, Grandpa," I reply. "That's why I had to leave."

"I don't appreciate Mr. Cain letting the sheriff disrupt you like that, but you should have asked for permission," he grumpily replies.

"You ought to have a word with him, Richard. Sheriff Bennet should have come to us with such news. We're Lexi's grandparents, for crying out loud."

He nods. "Don't worry, dear. I already made him aware of my displeasure regarding how the affair was handled."

As they continue to discuss the matter, I tune them out and replay Finn's earlier visit in my mind. It's not a smart move on my part, because just the memory is enough to turn me on.

"What are we going to do about that ghastly mark on your face, Lexi?" Grandma's voice breaks through my thoughts.

"Uh?"

"That scratch you have there." She looks pointedly at it. "I still don't understand how you managed to get that."

"Like I said, I tripped and fell into the bushes outside."

Her eyebrows arch. "But what were you doing near the bushes in the first place?"

"Eh... I thought I saw a bunny rabbit."

"Don't be silly, child. There aren't wild animals roaming around on our property."

I fight the urge to roll my eyes. Only Grandma would consider a bunny a wild animal.

The maid comes into the dining room to collect our plates, providing a much-needed interruption. Once she leaves, Grandma tells Grandpa, "We're having bread pudding for dessert tonight, darling."

"Oh, I'm not staying for dessert. I'm meeting Florian Novak at the club."

"I see." Her gaze narrows. "When did you make that appointment? It isn't on the calendar."

He wipes his mouth with the napkin. "I'm sorry. It was a last-minute arrangement. He's been hounding me since Alexis started dating Finn."

My face becomes hot in a split second, but I manage to rise through my embarrassment to ask, "Why?"

"What do you think, honey?" Grandma replies. "He

obviously wants to strengthen his relationship with us in case you and Finn turn into a serious affair."

Oh God. Are they already planning to marry me off to Finn?

"I wish that was the case, but I'm afraid Florian has ulterior motives for wanting some one-on-one time with me," Grandpa chimes in.

"What do you mean? What other motives could he possibly have?" she asks.

I lean forward in my seat, highly interested in Grandpa's answer.

He shakes his head and stands. "Don't worry about that, honey. I shall not be late."

I watch him leave the room, curious now about his statement. Florian Novak did not make a good impression on me, so if Grandpa believes he has ulterior motives, I'm sure he's right.

I don't have time to dwell too much on those thoughts, however, because Grandma quickly draws my attention.

"Well, since it's just the two of us, we can discuss your upcoming birthday party without irritating your grandfather."

I lean against my chair. "Must we?"

She widens her eyes. "Of course we must. Now, did Raquel give you all the RSVP letters that arrived today?"

"Yes."

"Good. I need a list of who's coming and who isn't."

"Why didn't you use an app to collect the RSVPs?"

She groans. "Not you too. The party organizer suggested it, but it's just not how one properly does these things."

There's no point in arguing with that logic. "All right. I'll make a spreadsheet for you after dinner."

She nods. "Good. Are you free tomorrow after school?"

"I have detention, but otherwise I'm free."

That is, if my alter ego doesn't decide to take over and wreak more havoc.

Grandma's face twists into a scowl. "Don't remind me of that aggravating fact. Mr. Cain better not extend your detention because of what happened today."

I want to say it won't make a damn difference to me, but I'd rather not contradict her.

"What do you need from me tomorrow?" I ask.

"I made an appointment for your dress fitting. And then the hairstylist and makeup artist will test out some hairdos and makeup. Oh, I do hope she can cover that hideous scar."

I cover the offending wound. "It's just a scratch, Grandma. You make it sound like I'm *The Phantom of the Opera* villain."

The new maid returns with dessert, and once again I'm grateful for her perfect timing. I practically inhale the treat because one, it's my favorite, and two, I can't wait to return to my room and not hear another word about the stupid party.

***

FINN

I DON'T PLAN on staying for dinner, and I'm on my way out of the house to check on Cameron, who's still at Luke's, but my father prevents me from leaving. Hell, I should have never come home after seeing Alexis.

"Finn, get in here. Now!" he bellows from his office.

"Yes, Father?" I say innocently enough.

"Where do you think you're going?"

"Why do you care?" I blurt out like a fucking idiot. I should have told him the truth meekly instead of provoking the bastard.

He glares and points at me. "Watch your fucking mouth,

punk. Your bruises are fading, but I'll be more than happy to freshen them up."

I work my jaw as the rage flows freely through my veins. What would happen if I struck him back when he doles out his punishment?

"I'm going to Luke's."

"I was made aware that you skipped class again. I'd threaten to pull you out of Maverick, but your rebellious act is only going to work in my favor."

"How so?"

"You can't be part of the Maverick Sharks if you're on academic probation."

I hate that he's right about that, but I won't give him the satisfaction of knowing he got to me.

"I expect you to smooth things over for me with Mr. Cain, considering I had to bail to further your agenda."

He watches me through slitted eyes. "You'd better expand on that. I don't have time to read between the lines."

"I went after Alexis. She received bad news today, and I had to play the devoted boyfriend. Isn't that what you want?"

The lie feels bitter on my tongue. I left because I wanted to be with her, not because I'm my father's bitch.

"Yes. You'd better pray you've done a good job gaining Richard's favor. I'm meeting him in an hour at the club."

"I've done all I could. But you're the business mastermind."

"Don't fool yourself into believing that. If you think you've done all you could, it means you could have done more."

I turn my hands into fists. "I charmed the man, and his granddaughter is eating from the palm of my hand. That was the bargain."

"We'll see." He drops his gaze to his laptop and waves me off. "You can go waste your time with your friends now."

"Gladly."

I spin around and march out of his office. This quick

meeting aggravated me so much, I forgot to check on Mom. But it's my luck that I see Grandpa outside the guesthouse. He waves me over, no doubt wanting to pressure me again about Saturday. He can sit and wait until he rots. I ignore him and get behind the Escalade's steering wheel, peeling out of the driveway a moment later. Perversely curious, I check the rearview mirror and catch the open glare he's sporting now. A satisfied grin unfurls on my lips. At least I could diss one asshole today.

46

ALEXIS

*T*he rest of the week went by mercifully stress-free. There weren't any more blackouts, no more revelations or attempts on my life. Also, Finn acted like the perfect boyfriend, making me believe that what's going on between us is the real deal. I'm too jaded to believe in the fairy tale though, expecting something awful to happen at a moment's notice.

"Oh, my dear." Grandma clasps her hands together. "You look lovely."

I don't recognize myself as I stare in the mirror. I do look pretty, but all the makeup and hairstyling turned me into a stranger. I love the dress though. The light chiffon fabric in lavender is ethereal, and it makes me look like a fairy.

"Stand up and turn around. I want to see you properly," she tells me.

The makeup artist steps out of the way so Grandma can

appraise me. She gives me a once-over and then focuses on my face. "Oh, I can hardly see that nasty scratch. Well done, Viola."

"Thank you, ma'am."

I touch my cheek, but Grandma almost bites my head off. "Don't. You'll ruin Viola's hard work."

"Sorry."

She waves me over. "Come on now. The photographer is downstairs waiting to take pictures."

I follow her out and try not to stress too much about the next few hours. Grandma is acting as if today is my wedding day. I can't imagine what she'll be like when I decide to tie the knot. Maybe I'll elope. *Oh, she would love that.* A chuckle bubbles up my throat, and I end up snorting.

She looks at me with a raised eyebrow. "Why are you laughing?"

"Nothing. It's just… well, this is a bit surreal to me. I feel more like a bride than a birthday girl."

Her eyes become soft and dreamy.

Hell, I shouldn't have said that.

"Oh, honey. When you do get married, it's going to be the event of the decade."

Yikes. So not looking forward to that. But maybe I'll never marry. Who wants to have a crazy wife?

I'm still musing about that when we make it down the stairs and Finn emerges with Grandpa from one of the rooms. My heart does a somersault in giddiness. Finn wearing a tux is nothing short of dreamy. The room suddenly feels unbearably hot.

"Ah, there she is. The lady of the hour." Grandpa beams. "You look lovely, Lexi."

My cheeks are warm, which means I'm blushing furiously. I hope the makeup hides my red face. "Thank you, Grandpa."

Finn doesn't speak a word, but his gaze says enough. He really needs to stop eating me with his eyes before I combust on the spot. He turns his attention to Grandma, giving me some reprieve from his smoldering stare.

"Good evening, Mrs. Montgomery. You also look lovely."

"Oh, thank you, Finn."

"Way to show me up, kid." Grandpa claps Finn's shoulder, making him wince. "Oh my goodness. I'm so sorry. I forgot about your injury. Are you all right?"

Still sporting a pinched face, he groans. "I'll live."

"Oh, I feel dreadful. Perhaps you should take a painkiller."

He shakes his head. "No, it's okay, Mr. Montgomery. I'm really fine."

"Nonsense, young man. It won't do to have you suffer for no reason. I'll go fetch the painkillers," Grandma replies resolutely before walking away.

Grandpa looks at his wristwatch. "Oh, darn it. Look at the time. I have an important phone call." He glances at me. "Shhh, don't tell your grandmother. She'll be very cross with me if she finds out I'm working tonight."

I laugh. "It's okay, Grandpa. Your secret is safe with me."

He marches away, and finally I can say a proper hello to Finn. He walks over, his lips twisted in a sexy, crooked smile, and I'm once again burning from the inside out.

"Wow," he says.

"Do you like it?"

"Do I like it? You look fucking stunning, babe."

He glances left and right in a cheeky manner before capturing my face between his hands and slanting his lips over mine. It's a slow and tender kiss but just as devastating as when he kisses me hard and fast. My toes curl inside my sandals, and my legs feel like they're disintegrating. I reach for his arms, needing the support.

He pulls back first and gazes at me with hooded eyes. "I think I'll have to kidnap you at some point during this party, because there's no way in hell I'll be able to keep my hands to myself until the end."

My heart speeds up as desire curls at the base of my spine. "If I don't kidnap you first."

His eyes widen just a fraction before a mischievous glint flashes in them. "Are you busy now?"

I open my mouth to reply, but Grandma puts the kibosh on our sexcapade plans for now.

"Finn, I'm not sure what type of painkillers you prefer, so I brought them all."

We jump apart before she can see that we were making out a second before.

"Oh, you didn't need to go through the trouble, Mrs. Montgomery. Any will do."

"Well, now you have your pick." She shows him the three options, and when Finn makes his selection, she turns to the waiter who was hovering nearby carrying a tray with a single glass of water.

Wow, Grandma. Could you be more extra?

I'm still smirking when she looks at me and gasps. "What in the world happened to your makeup, Alexis?"

Oh shit. Busted.

Finn chokes on his water, but I feel no sympathy. He was laughing. Jackass. Of course kissing him would smear my lipstick.

Grandma grabs my arm and steers me back up the stairs. "Come with me."

"Where are we going? I thought you wanted to take pictures."

"Not with you looking like that. I'm glad I asked Viola to stay."

I glance over my shoulder, expecting to see Finn still amused at my expense. But his eyes aren't dancing with glee. They're dark, swimming with yearning.

Hell, if he keeps this up, I might have to change my underwear.

FINN

I DON'T REGRET GETTING Alexis in trouble early on. It's been an hour, and I have yet to share another moment alone with her. Her grandparents make sure she meets every single one of their friends, and I'm annoyed as fuck. I'm watching her across the pool, and even with the distance, I can see her discomfort.

"What are you staring at?" Luke asks as he stops next to me.

"The usual bullshit parents'—or in this case, grandparents'—pull."

"Ah, they're still busy parading her like a prized horse, huh?"

I bring the glass of whiskey I was able to snatch earlier to my lips. Usually I'd have finished it by now, but getting drunk tonight is not an option.

"What are you waiting for? Go save the princess from the evil dragons."

"I've tried already."

He laughs. "Is that defeat I hear in your voice?"

"I'm not defeated, dumbass. I have to bide my time. Can't risk antagonizing the Montgomerys."

"Oh, because of the deal with your father?"

I give him the stink eye. "Don't remind me of that."

He shrugs. "Why do you care?"

"You may not have any aspirations for the future, but I don't want to depend on my family's money forever."

I stomp away, not willing to wait for another asinine remark from Luke. His comments usually don't bother me, but something about this party has set my teeth on edge.

I was fine when I got here. Happy even, which I haven't felt in a long time. Then I see Tiffany and Amber ahead, and my mood turns even more sour. *Fuck this shit.* I toss my drink back, swallowing what's left in a single gulp. When a waiter passes by, I trade my empty glass for a full one. This time it's champagne, which I also inhale.

By the time I see Alexis across the room, the alcohol is already starting to work. I'm far less edgy, though a lot hornier. It's time to fulfill my promise. When I reach her, her grandparents are already poised to drag her somewhere else.

"Hey, babe, I've been looking all over for you," I say.

I notice my endearment doesn't please her grandparents. Tough shit.

"Sorry, they've been introducing me to a lot of people."

"Yes, and I just spotted Mayor Wen and her husband. We really ought to greet them," her grandma says.

"I need to use the restroom," Alexis blurts out, saving me from a stupid move.

Mrs. Montgomery pinches her lips first, then replies, "Oh, all right, then. But don't take too long."

I can see that her grandma's about to suggest she tag along. I step in, curling my arm around Alexis's waist. "I'll escort her inside and make sure she doesn't get lost."

I don't wait for a reply before steering Alexis away from them.

"Thanks for the save," she says.

"Thanks for thinking of a good excuse. I was about to say something rude to them." I feel her gaze burn a hole through my face, so I turn and ask, "What is it?"

"Are you okay? You're acting a little strange."

I grin. "Yeah, I'm good now that I finally got you away from the dragons."

She chuckles. "Dragons?"

"Luke's word, not mine."

"Oh, I didn't see him yet."

"How could you when your grandparents have kept you busy meeting the geriatric portion of the party?"

"They're trying to make up for lost time."

"You're cute when you defend them."

We're finally inside the house, but it's still far too busy here. "So, where's a good spot to make out in this house without getting interrupted?"

"My bedroom is off-limits. The makeup artist is there in case I need retouching."

I give her a wolfish smile. "Oh, you're gonna need retouching for sure." I snap my fingers when the memory comes to me. "I know where we can go."

"Where?"

"Someplace where I can eat your pussy until I have my fill and then fuck you until you can't walk straight." I lace my fingers with hers and steer her to the wine cellar in the basement.

"Oh my God."

"That's exactly what you'll be saying in a moment, gorgeous."

47

ALEXIS

My heart is thundering as I let Finn steer me down to the basement. I'm ashamed to admit that I haven't explored my grandparents' house, and I have no idea where he's taking me. I keep quiet, afraid my voice will carry back up the stairs.

He stops in front of double glass-paneled doors and opens one with a flourish. "Ladies first."

My jaw drops as I enter the high-ceilinged wine cellar. I was clueless that it existed until now. "Wow. How did you know about this place?"

"Do you think the first time I stepped foot in your grandparents' house was after I met you?"

I turn to him. "I hardly believe my grandfather would have brought you here."

He takes my hand and pulls me flush against his body. I let out a little gasp. "You know I don't need permission to get anywhere I want." He kisses the corner of my mouth, making my toes curl.

I close my eyes for a second. "Finn."

"I love when you say my name like that." He runs his tongue down my neck, and I shiver in his arms.

"Like what?"

"Like you're about to come." He lifts me off the ground, seemingly forgetting that his shoulder is busted.

"What are you—"

He cuts me off with his mouth, and I taste whiskey and champagne on his tongue.

My back meets something hard, forcing me to open my eyes. He just set me on one of the rungs of the wooden ladder in front of one of the floor-to-ceiling wine racks.

I lean back to ask, "What are you doing?"

"I told you I was gonna eat your pussy, and I intend to keep that promise." He drops to his knees, already fumbling with the layers of chiffon on my skirt.

I help him with that task, because with the way he's looking at me, he might tear the whole thing to bits. He spreads my legs as far apart as they can go and brings his mouth to my throbbing clit over my underwear.

"Oh God." I reach for the ladder with my free hand so I won't slide off it completely.

"You taste fucking delicious, gorgeous." He pushes the fabric aside and really goes to town. He slides his tongue from my clit to my entrance, and then he literally fucks me with it.

And here I thought nothing would top his dick inside me, but it turns out his tongue is just as delicious and unmerciful. I can already feel the telltale sign of an orgasm approaching. This must not be normal. Either I'm a nympho who gets turned on easily, or Finn is a sex god.

He switches from plunging his tongue in me to flicking it

across my clit. I close my eyes, trying not to make too much noise, but everything he's doing feels so damn good.

"You like this, don't you, my filthy girl?" he asks, and his hot breath fanning over my sensitive parts is just as devastating.

"Yes," I hiss.

He stands from his lower position, already unzipping his pants. "I want to feel you fall apart when I'm buried deep inside you."

His mouth covers mine at the same time that he sheathes himself inside me with a powerful thrust. It makes the bottles stored behind me jostle.

"We're going to break something."

"The only thing that's going to break is you, darling."

He silences me once again with his mouth, and there's nothing tender about this kiss, or the way he's fucking me. He does want to destroy me, even now when he knows I'm putty in his hands, when he knows I've fallen for him. But I don't care, and that's the most fucked-up thing. I still need him to punish me for all the sins I can't remember.

"Tell me how much you love me, beautiful."

"I don't love you."

"You're such a filthy liar." He digs his fingers into my hips in a bruising way as he increases the tempo of his thrusts.

In this position, everything hurts. The hard wooden rung presses against the backs of my thighs, and I keep bumping my shoulder blades against the shelf behind me. But the pain works as an enhancer of the pleasure. The more he punishes me, the more I revel in it.

"I'm not lying," I murmur.

"Yes you are." He captures my lower lip and bites it—not hard enough to draw blood but enough to push me over the edge.

"Fuck!" I shout.

"That's it. Scream for me, babe. Louder."

"I hate you."

He kisses me again and then whispers against my lips, "Well, that's too bad."

He lifts me off the ladder, pulling out in the process. I don't understand what he's doing until I'm on my hands and knees and he's fucking me from behind, pulling my hair back so hard that I have to stretch my neck or risk losing a chunk of it. The hardwood floor hurts my knees terribly, but Finn doesn't go easy on me. He just keeps pumping in and out until he grunts loudly as he fills me with his seed.

It drips down my legs, probably getting on my skirt, but there's nothing I can do about it. After one final thrust, he pulls out and releases my hair. I let out a breath of relief but don't move from my position. I'm coming to terms with what we just did, to what *he* just did to me. This wasn't a sexcapade; this was Finn making sure everyone knows I'm a filthy girl. One look at me and people will know I got railed.

I push myself off the floor, purposely hiding my face from him. I don't want Finn to see I'm on the verge of crying.

What the fuck is wrong with me? I knew what I was getting into when I started this twisted game with him. If I allowed myself to believe the lie, I have no one to blame but me.

"Let's see you walk now." He laughs.

"What?" I ask through the choke in my throat. Shit, there's no way he won't notice that.

He walks around me and pinches my chin, lifting my face to his. "What's wrong?"

I jerk back, freeing myself from his hold. "Nothing."

His cheeks hollow as he grinds his teeth and stares at me as if trying to read my mind. "I see. We'd better get back to the party before your grandparents send out a search party for you."

I flinch and look away. "You go ahead. I need to freshen up."

"I can wait."

"It's fine. We'll draw less attention if we aren't together."

"Right. Well, see ya at the party, then."

He marches to the door and yanks it open so hard, I'm afraid he'll pull it off its hinges. I wince when it bangs shut again, but I don't linger. The longer I'm away from the party, the higher the chances Grandma will come looking for me. I can't let her see me like this.

FINN

Before I venture into the party, I find a restroom. I don't want to give Alexis's grandparents a heart attack when they see my post-sex look.

I can't help thinking I should be in a better mood. I just had one of the best fucks of my life, and I feel like shit. It was the look on Alexis's face that did that to me. I don't get it. I thought she was having as much fun as I was. She likes it rough, or at least I thought she did.

I wash my face and then fix my clothes. They aren't terribly wrinkled, but you can tell I was up to no good. The old me wouldn't give a rat's ass if people knew I was busy screwing someone, but I don't want Alexis's name on vicious, gossipy tongues. Yeah, that's also a first for me.

I run my fingers through my hair, trying to understand what the hell is going on with me. I cannot under any circumstances develop feelings for her. We're having fun, but our story has disaster written all over it. I don't need more problems in my life.

I'm still reeling from all the conflicting thoughts bouncing in my head when I bump into my father.

"Where the hell have you been?" he asks.

Every muscle in my body goes taut. He's in a foul mood, and he's about to take it out on me.

"Fucking the birthday girl. Why do you care?"

His nostrils flare a second before he grabs me by the lapels of my jacket and drags me to a corner. "You little piece of shit. I gave you an easy job, and even that you manage to screw up."

"Let go of me," I grit out, fighting the urge to shove him off me. The only reason I don't do it is because I don't want to cause a scene.

He clearly has no issues with that. He shoves me against the wall, and white-hot pain shoots from my bullet wound. "You're supposed to butter Richard up, make him easy to convince to invest in our company. Instead, you only thought about sticking your dick in his granddaughter."

"I did my part. If you fucked up on your end, it's not my problem."

"What?" Alexis's high-pitched voice interrupts us, and immediately my chest constricts.

Shit, she heard what I said.

My father finally releases me, stepping back and allowing me to see her betrayed expression.

"That's right, darling. My good-for-nothing son was only screwing you to gain favor with your grandfather. You didn't think a Novak would really care for someone like you, did you?"

She squints. "Someone like me?" Her voice is dangerously low now.

"Diner trash," he replies with a hateful smile.

"You son of a bitch," I snap, and before I can think about the consequences, my fist meets his odious face.

His head is thrown back, making him stagger. When he regains his balance, I see murder in his eyes. He's gonna put me in a wheelchair—or at least he'll try.

Fuck him, and fuck my family.

"What in the world is going on here?" Mrs. Montgomery asks.

Naturally, she and her husband had to show up when I looked bad. I ignore them to glance at Alexis. She's no longer looking hurt. Instead, she has that eerie, dead glint in her eyes. Chills run down my back. That's not her.

"Finn had too much to drink," my father replies after he wipes the blood from his busted lip. "Frankly, I'm appalled that you allow underage kids to consume alcohol at this party."

"We didn't!" Mrs. Montgomery retorts. "If he's drunk, he must have brought a flask."

A commotion at the entrance draws everyone's attention. I frown when I see a group of guys that most definitely don't belong here. They're all wearing leather jackets and ripped jeans, which makes them look like they're either in a rock band or a gang. I'm betting the latter.

"Who the hell are you? And how did you get in?" Mr. Montgomery asks.

"My name is Cristiano, and I'm Alexis's friend." He glances at her meaningfully.

I'm watching her with rapt attention now. Is she going to snap back to herself, or is she going to deal with the newcomers as her alter ego? She blinks a couple times, and then it's like a switch flips.

"Cris? What are you doing here?" she asks.

"I wouldn't have come if it wasn't important."

"Lexi, do you know these people?" her grandma asks.

"Yes, they're my friends from high school."

Dad snorts. "Why am I not surprised?"

It's an effort to ignore him, but Mr. Montgomery is observing him through slitted eyes. God, how I wish he'd kick the bastard out.

Alexis takes a step forward. "What's going on? Is Carmen here?"

317

The arrogance on the guy's face crumbles. "No, that's why I'm here. She's gone missing, and the sheriff's department is blowing us off."

Her face turns ashen. "How long has she been gone?"

"Two days."

"Two days?" she shrieks. "And you only thought of coming to me now?"

From my periphery, I catch a sign of discomfort from her grandparents, and I begin to suspect this is not news to them.

On cue, Cristiano cuts his eyes to them. "I tried to contact you, but apparently my message was never delivered."

"Couldn't you have called her cell?" I chime in, because his story doesn't add up.

He glowers at me. "She blocked me."

"No I didn't. You're the ones who pretty much canceled me."

"I fail to see how coming here uninvited is going to help your case," Mrs. Montgomery grumbles.

"And I'm sure Sheriff Bennet is doing all he can," her husband adds.

Not likely. Reid's dad is a self-serving bastard, and he only cares about making sure the wealthy side of Triton Cove is protected.

"Yes, I heard you the first time," Cristiano manages, grinding his teeth.

"What do you mean?" Alexis turns to her grandparents. "Did you know Carmen was missing?"

"Well, we thought he was exaggerating," Mr. Montgomery replies.

Once again, her face crumbles with disappointment and the hurt of betrayal. I hate that she also gave me that look before. I have to find a moment to explain to her that I wasn't with her only because of my father. But first, I need to be useful for once. I pull my cell phone out and dial the sheriff.

"Hello, Mr. Bennet," I say when he answers.

"Finn, why are you calling me? Aren't you supposed to be at your girlfriend's birthday party?"

"Yes, I am, in fact, at Alexis's party, and we just learned that her best friend has gone missing, and you aren't doing jack about it."

Alexis's eyes go rounder, and her jaw slackens. From the corner of my eye, I catch the sneer on my father's lips. He can rot in hell for all I care.

"Who do you think you're speaking to, son?" Sheriff Bennet retorts.

Mr. Montgomery waves at me, demanding the phone. I frown, not keen to hand it over.

"Let me speak to him," he says.

Not wanting to dig a bigger hole for myself, I let him take over the call.

"Hello, Sheriff. It's Richard Montgomery. I'd like to know what's being done about the disappearance of Carmen...." He glances at Alexis.

"Concepción," she replies. "Her name is Carmen Concepción."

Mr. Montgomery repeats the information to Sheriff Bennet —not that he already didn't know—and nods every few seconds as he listens to the reply.

"That's good to hear. The missing girl is a good friend of Alexis's, which means I have a vested interest in this investigation."

I'm fucking pissed that Mr. Montgomery is riding on my idea to get on Alexis's good side. I doubt that he cares at all about her friend. If he did, he would have put pressure on the sheriff already.

He ends the call and returns my phone.

"Done," he says. "I'm sure your friend will be found in no time, honey."

319

Cristiano scowls. "You make it sound like she disappeared of her own free will."

"Didn't she, though?" my father pipes up. I forgot he was still here.

"What are you insinuating?" His stance is aggressive.

"Nothing," I butt in. "And he's leaving."

Dad glares at me. "And so are you."

I laugh without humor. "I don't think so. I'm going to help Alexis find her friend."

"The hell you are! You're coming home with me right now, so help me God, Finn."

"Or you're going to do what? Give me another black eye? Or maybe you'll break my arm this time to end my swimming career for good."

Mrs. Montgomery gasps. Shit, I must have lost my mind to unload all that in front of everyone.

"I believe it's best if you leave, Florian." Mr. Montgomery steps between us, forming a shield in front of me.

I don't know how to feel about that. No one has ever protected me from anything in my entire life. It's always been me against the world. Jason tried to help, but he had his own issues to deal with. At least he found Isabelle.

My father stomps out of the house, and the air becomes obviously lighter.

I glance at Alexis. She's staring at my father's retreating figure with a look of pure loathing in her eyes. It makes me feel something that I can't quite put my finger on. Then she turns to me, and her gaze softens. Guilt and regret spread through my chest like an oily and dark entity, making me wish I'd met her before I became a monster. I no longer find myself needing her hate. I want the opposite of that. I want her to love me, because I think that's how I feel about her.

Someone's phone rings, and a moment later, Cristiano

answers it. His eyes widen, and his tanned face becomes paler after a moment.

"Okay, we'll be right there. Thanks for the tip, man."

"What happened? Any news from her?" Alexis asks.

"Yeah, someone finally talked. We may have a location of the last place Carmen was seen. We're all headed over there to search."

"I'm coming too."

"You aren't seriously considering leaving your own party, Lexi," her grandmother complains.

"I never wanted a big celebration anyway."

The woman opens her mouth to offer another retort, but Mr. Montgomery talks over her. "Let her go, Lillian. As far as I'm concerned, this party is over."

"I'll text the guys. Where are we going?" I ask Cristiano.

He raises an eyebrow. "You're coming too?"

"You don't have to keep pretending you care, Finn," Alexis chimes in.

I whip around to face her. "You got it all wrong. I was never pretending."

Her eyes widen, but I know it will take more than a simple statement to convince her I'm not a heartless bastard like my father.

48

ALEXIS

*W*e've been searching in the forest near La
Salamandra for over half an hour, and it's like
trying to find a needle in a haystack.

"Can someone tell me again why we're looking for this chick
in the middle of the night?" Reid asks.

"This chick has a name," I growl. "Besides, no one asked you
to come."

He hitches his thumb toward Finn. "He did."

"And you're going to keep looking without bitching about it,"
Finn retorts.

"What are you complaining about? This is like an adventure,"
Luke chimes in with a cheerful tone that makes me want to
punch him in the throat.

"Who gave the tip pointing to this location anyway?"
Cameron asks.

I glance at Cristiano, who's walking ahead with the rest of

my former crew. He didn't want to tell me, which shows how much I've messed up things with them. The message my alter ego left for me comes to the forefront of my mind, and the guilt swirling in my chest grows heavier. She told me I shouldn't trust Carmen any longer because she'd made dangerous friends, and I just let that slide. I should have gone after Carmen instead, tried to help her, but my rancor kept me from doing it.

A rogue tear rolls down my cheek, which I hastily wipe off. Finn moves closer to me and touches my arm. "Are you okay?"

"I'm fine." I pull away from him, glowering in the process.

If he thinks I'm going to simply forget the conversation I overheard between him and his father, he's mistaken. I'm putting my anger aside and letting him help because of Carmen alone. I want nothing to do with him anymore. He's an asshole and a liar—something I've always known, and yet I was still dumb enough to fall for him.

From the corner of my eye, I see he's about to reply, but Cristiano's light shines on us. "We should split up. We're gonna keep going ahead. You guys should veer left and right."

"Alexis and I will go left," Finn pipes up before I can.

"I don't want to go anywhere alone with you," I retort.

"Fine, if you insist, I'll join you and Finn, Lexi." Luke walks over, smiling from ear to ear like a deranged fuck.

"Whatever." I whirl around and begin to head in the new direction.

I know they're following me, but I try my best to ignore the duo as I scan the forest, shining my light left and right and yelling Carmen's name every so often.

We make the trek in silence for a while. Luke is quiet because his mouth is busy with a cigarette. Finn must have wised up and finally figured out I don't want to hear his half-baked excuses.

My foot gets caught on an exposed root, making me trip. I

would have fallen face-first if Finn didn't grab my arm and steady me.

"Are you all right?"

I hate that his touch makes me shiver in pleasure despite the fact that I'm furious with him. He's much too close, watching me intently. He can't possibly see that I'm blushing in the gloom, but it doesn't matter. I bet he can hear how fast my heart is beating now.

"I'm fine."

"Hey, I think I found something," Luke says.

Finn releases me, and we both turn to see what caught his attention. He bends over and picks up something from the ground. It's a denim jacket stained with something dark, something that looks like blood. But that isn't the reason I'm suddenly sick to my stomach and shaking from head to toe. I recognize the heart-shaped rhinestone appliqué on the back.

"That's Carmen's," I choke out.

"Shit," Finn mutters.

Still holding the jacket, Luke turns around and continues exploring ahead. I'm frozen, unable to take another step.

Finn places a hand on my lower back. "We don't need to keep searching."

I shake my head. "No, I have to."

"Okay, then."

Ahead of us, we hear Luke let out a string of curses.

"Hell, what now?" Finn says.

I force my legs to move, and before I know it, I'm running.

"Alexis, wait up."

I halt suddenly when Luke blocks my path, his eyes startled. "No, girl. You shouldn't look."

"Get out of the way." I shove him to the side and take a couple steps forward.

Then I understand why he didn't want me to continue. The first thing my flashlight beam hits is her feet. One shoe is missing. Unable to stop myself, I aim the flashlight higher and higher until it illuminates her dead face. The beam of light is unsteady as my body takes on the brunt of this gruesome discovery. I should look away, but I can't.

"Jesus," Finn blurts out. Then he pulls me into his arms, pressing my face against his chest. "Don't look, babe. Don't look."

I don't resist him this time. I let him comfort me as the tears gather in my eyes.

"They shaved her head," I mumble, then immediately berate myself for that comment. Who cares if they shaved her head? What good does having hair do for Carmen? She's dead.

"They also tried to destroy her neck tattoo," Luke chimes in.

"What?" I pull away from Finn and force my eyes to return to her corpse.

Luke's pointing his flashlight at the back of her neck. "Look. They slashed her skin, crisscrossing it."

"For fuck's sake, Luke. She doesn't need to see that."

I step closer, fighting the nausea that's turned my stomach into knots.

"Carmen was always against tats," I mumble to myself.

Finn stops next to me, then leans forward with his brows furrowed. "Does that look like a mask to you, Luke?"

Now both are crouching close to Carmen's body as if they're from the sheriff's department.

I sense the darkness trying to come to the surface. I drive my nails into the softness of my palms, hoping the little bit of pain will be enough to keep me in control for a little longer. I know I won't be able to keep my other side from showing up, but I'd rather it didn't happen here in front of Finn and Luke.

Why are you fighting her, Alexis? When she's around, there is no pain.

"It is a mask, like the ones from Venice," Luke says.

Finn stands straighter, his body much more tense. "I've seen that design before."

I remember then who has a Venetian mask tattoo on the back of her neck. "Piper Phillips has one. That's where you've seen it before, right?"

His eyes are troubled when he meets mine and says, "No."

There's a new heaviness in my chest, and dread licks my spine. I'm afraid of what his answer is going to be. "Where have you seen it before?"

"Finn! Luke!" Reid calls not far from us, but Finn doesn't answer.

"We're here!" Luke walks away from the body, but I'm still watching Finn closely.

He makes a motion to follow Luke and meet their friends before they can reach our spot, but I stop him. "Where have you seen that tattoo before, Finn?"

He runs his fingers through his hair, pulling it back. "I can't tell you right this second."

"Why the hell not?"

"Because telling you means confessing something else, and now is not the time."

I open my mouth to protest, but he cups my cheek and rubs his thumb across my lower lip, weakening my stance against him.

"Please, Lexi. I'll tell you. Promise."

Annoyed that he's managed once again to play me like a violin, I step away from him. "Your promises are worthless, Finn."

49

FINN

*I*t's past three in the morning by the time I pull into the driveway. I park the car but don't make a move to get out. The outside lights are on, but most of the ones inside my father's mansion are off, save for the one in his office. Hell. He must be waiting for me. I can't imagine what his punishment will be now that I defied him, but that's the least of my concerns.

I glance at the guesthouse. The lights inside are on as well. My stomach churns as I think about the ramifications of my discovery. A year ago, I wouldn't have made the connection. But knowing what kind of monster my grandfather is, I can't brush off the similarities between Carmen's new tattoo and the symbol I saw carved in his wooden box. And then Alexis mentioned Piper had a tattoo like that too. It can't be a coincidence that I saw the bastard cornering the poor girl.

After we called the sheriff, I didn't have a moment alone

with Alexis. She was distraught, but once her grandparents came for her, she no longer accepted my comfort. I need to make things right with her, but I can't do it without coming clean about everything. But first, I need to be certain of my suspicions.

Taking a deep breath, I get out of the car and stride toward the guesthouse. I don't knock, just turn the knob knowing it's not locked.

"Grandpa?" I call because I can't stomach catching him doing something horrible.

"So you finally decided to dignify me with a visit," he replies from his comfortable position in front of the fireplace, sloshing the whiskey in his glass.

"I needed to think. But I've made my decision now."

"About?" He brings the glass to his lips and takes a sip.

"Whether or not I could trust you."

He raises an eyebrow, then smirks. "I take it you figured out you *can* trust me?"

I nod, keeping my face locked in a cold mask. I'm glad I've had years of practice hiding behind a facade.

"Yes."

"Go on, then. Tell me what really happened last weekend."

"The criminals weren't after my car. They wanted Dennis Walker's safe that was in the back seat."

Grandpa's bushy eyebrows arch, almost meeting his hairline. I'd believe him to be truly surprised if I hadn't also caught the glint of interest in his blue eyes.

"Why did she have her father's safe with her?"

"She wanted to open it, and I was going to help her."

He leans back in his chair, relaxing his stance. "And then you used it as a self-defense weapon, which means it's now in police custody."

"*Was.* The safe has been stolen from the precinct."

He blinks fast, and his face grows a little paler. He was not expecting that, which means Sheriff Bennet didn't let the news of the theft leak. I wonder how in the world Alexis's alter ego managed to steal the safe from under his nose. That's a mystery I may never be able to solve.

"That's preposterous," Grandpa finally says, clearly agitated. "What kind of security does that man have in place?"

"I've been asking myself the same question. We suspect it was an inside job."

"*We?* Oh, you and that girl."

I don't like how he mentions Alexis as if she were an insignificant bug, but I don't let my emotions show.

"I heard your father blew the deal with Richard Montgomery," he continues.

"Yes, and he tried to blame me for it."

Grandpa takes another sip of his drink but keeps his shrewd gaze locked on my face.

"It doesn't surprise me. So, are you done with her?"

I clench my jaw, a knee-jerk reaction that I wish I didn't have. Now Grandpa knows the question bothers me.

"Not yet. My father hates her, so that's a major motivation for me to continue."

His lips curl into a disgusting smile. "Plus I bet the sex isn't bad, eh?"

I force my face to mimic his odious expression. If I'm to gain his trust, he needs to believe my mind is just as perverted as his.

"Not bad at all. Virgins are always more fun."

He nods. "You got that right, son."

Silence follows as he simply sits there and stares at me.

"It's been a long evening. Do you mind if I help myself to a drink?" I ask.

"Go ahead."

I head to the bar, hoping the box with the mask design is still in the same spot. My heart speeds up when I see it is. I force myself to remain calm as I fill my glass with whiskey, then drink it all in one go.

"Easy there, son. Those spirits are meant to be savored," he pipes up.

I set the glass down and refill it. "I know. I just needed a shot to take off the edge quickly."

Gingerly, I pick up the box. "What's this?"

Grandpa stands and walks over. He takes the box from my hand and opens it, revealing a skeleton key that also bears the same intricate mask design.

Holding it between his fingers, he says, "This is the key to Wonderland, and I think you might be ready to visit it."

I frown. "Do I need to take a potion and go down the rabbit hole?"

He chuckles, then places the key in my hand. "No. Just the key will suffice."

"And when am I going to Wonderland?"

"You'll receive a text tomorrow with instructions."

I bring the key to eye level and inspect it. "Is this a solo invitation, or can I bring a guest?"

He squints. "It depends. Are you referring to the Walker girl?"

I meet his stare and curl my lips into a cruel grin. "Yes."

His eyes shine with malice, making me shiver. "Oh yes. You can bring her. I can't promise you'll leave with her, though."

I chuckle, and it costs me everything to pretend I'm on the same wavelength as him. "I wasn't planning to."

50

ALEXIS

*T*here's a knock on my door, which I ignore. I can't even open my eyes properly because they're swollen shut. I have no idea what time it is; all I know is I cried myself to sleep after Grandma gave me a sleeping pill.

I can't believe Carmen is gone, but the ache in my chest tells me it's real. The image of her body comes to the forefront of my mind, but it doesn't make me want to cry again. It makes me angry as hell at myself for not being there for her. Regret is a serrated knife, carving my heart out of my chest.

"Lexi, dear. You have a visitor," Grandma says through the door.

"I don't want to see anyone," I croak.

"It's me. Finn."

The sound of his voice works like a shot of adrenaline in my veins. How dare he show up here after what happened last night?

Fury propels me into action. I jump out of bed and yank the door open, ready to tell him to go fuck himself. But the words get lodged in my throat when I see his pitiful expression. His eyes are bloodshot, and the dark circles under them remind me of bruises.

"Oh dear. You look dreadful," Grandma tells me.

"I look like I feel." I step out of the way, allowing Finn to enter.

"Leave the door open," she says.

"I don't think so." I shut the door in her face, locking it for good measure.

I expect her to let out a string of complaints, but she simply mutters something unintelligible. She's the least of my worries, though. I'm too busy staring at Finn and trying to read his mind.

"What do you want?" I cross my arms.

He releases a shaky breath, running his fingers through his curls. Even after a rough night, his hair looks as soft as ever. I must look like a banshee, but I'm too brokenhearted to care about my appearance.

"Where to start?"

"The beginning is always a good place."

"I'll get to that in a minute. I just want to tell you something first. I didn't get close to you because of my father."

I snort. "Yeah, right. I heard you last night."

"Yes, you heard me bullshitting him."

"Are you saying you came after me because you liked me?" I raise an eyebrow.

"No. I started those games with you because I hated you," he deadpans.

His admission should make me sad, or angrier. But I don't feel anything. Maybe I'm numb because I know I fell in love with Finn. I just can't get in touch with those emotions right now.

"Ditto. I had reasons to hate your guts, though. What was yours?"

He holds my stare, and for the first time, he allows me to see all the emotions swirling in his eyes. "I hated you because I wanted you in a visceral way I couldn't explain. And then I realized I needed your loathing, your insults because that was the punishment I never received for what happened last year."

I swallow the lump in my throat as the image of Peter Danes on that gurney comes to the forefront of my mind.

"So, you *do* feel guilty."

"Of course I feel guilty," he snaps. "I'm not a monster, Alexis."

"You sure tried your best to look like one."

He dips his chin, letting out a loud sigh. "I know."

There's a new pang in my chest, one that's removed from the ache of having lost Carmen. But I can't let that emotion gain strength. I can't fall for his charms again.

"That's your big confession? You came after me because you wanted to feel a bit of pain?"

He looks up. "No. That's not my confession. I wasn't drunk or high when I crashed into Mr. Danes's store. I was beside myself, that much is true, and I should have never gotten behind the steering wheel or driven like a maniac."

"Why did you, then?"

"I guess I was running away from the ugly truth I discovered earlier that day."

His face is pinched, and his eyes are so sad, it makes me want to shorten the distance between us and engulf him in a bear hug. I fight the urge. For all I know, Finn is an excellent actor.

"You're stalling."

He exhales loudly. "I discovered Florian Novak isn't my biological father. I'm the product of a rape."

Suddenly, I can't breathe, caught in the vortex of Finn's pain. "Do you know who—"

"My grandfather," he chokes out. "He raped my mother."

Giving his back to me, he walks toward the window. His shoulders are slumped forward, a posture of defeat I've never seen him display.

Before I know it, I'm hugging him from behind, resting my wet cheek against his wide back. "I'm sorry."

He covers my arms with his own. "It doesn't excuse my reckless behavior. But I wanted you to know I wasn't driving that fast seeking a thrill, or because I don't give a shit about the law."

I hug him tighter. "Thanks for telling me."

I should add to it, but I don't know what to say. Everything I can think of doesn't seem adequate.

He turns around and faces me. At once, I'm very much aware that I look like a troll with rancid breath, and I'm dying for Finn to kiss me. I step back, then run to my bathroom.

"Uh, what are you doing?" He follows me.

My cheeks become warmer. "I had just woken up when you came in."

I grab the toothbrush and smear some toothpaste on it.

He leans against the doorframe with arms crossed and smirks, "Oh, you thought I was about to kiss you. How very considerate of you to get rid of morning breath."

This banter is surreal. He just shared with me his darkest secret. I went to bed crying over the brutal murder of my best friend and hating Finn for his betrayal. Both things are still true, but it seems I'm in survival mode now. Or maybe I'm not a hundred-percent me.

The thought is scary, and it makes me tense on the spot.

"What's wrong?" he asks.

How can he pick up my mood changes so swiftly like that?

I rinse my mouth and wash my face before I answer him with a question. "You can tell when I'm not me, right?"

His expression matches my serious tone. "Yes. It's like your soul vacates your body."

Chills of dread run down my spine.

"Am I still me now?"

His brows furrow. "You can't tell?"

I chew on my bottom lip, lowering my chin. "I'm not sure anymore. My best friend was murdered, yet here I am, flirting with you. Who does that?"

He walks over and invades my space, forcing me to look into his eyes. "People grieve in different ways. Maybe you need to feel something other than pain and sadness."

"I was set on being angry with you."

"You should be angry with me. I've done terrible things to you."

I cock my head. "Be specific, because the lines between good and bad are blurred beyond recognition when it comes to us."

"Last night when I fucked you in the wine cellar, for example. I went too far."

My stomach clenches painfully, and my heart seems to shrivel. "The rough fuck wasn't the problem. It was the realization that you only did it to humiliate me that hurt."

He winces. "That was never the intention. I wasn't thinking straight. I got lost in the moment." He cups my cheek. "I got lost in *you*."

My traitorous muscle skips a beat, then gallops away in giddiness.

"What are you saying, Finn?"

He rubs his thumb over my lips, awakening every nerve in my body.

"I'm saying every time I look at you, I unravel. I'm saying you're on my mind all the damn time."

"Finn—"

He presses his finger against my lips. "Shh, let me finish. You drive me crazy, but I love every single thing about you, Lexi. Your hair...." He runs his fingers through a strand. "Your freckles…." He bops my nose with his finger. "Your unwavering loyalty to your father's memory."

That makes my eyes tear up, but I bite the inside of my cheek, not willing to start the waterworks and distract Finn from his declaration.

"Your lips." He kisses the corner of my mouth. "Your sharp tongue," he whispers against my lips.

"Do you also love the unhinged side of me?" I ask through the lump in my throat.

"Yes, babe. I love that part of you too."

I'm on the verge of bawling my eyes out, so I do what any sensible person would do. Rising on my tiptoes, I throw my arms around his neck and press my lips to his. I don't know if he's telling the truth or if this is a nightmare disguised as a fantasy. I don't care. He cracked the dam that was keeping all my emotions trapped, and now I want to let them flow freely. I want to feel everything. The taste of his tongue dancing with mine. The roughness of his unshaven face chafing my skin. The grip of his fingers as they dig into my hips.

Finn picks me up, spinning around at the same time, and then he sets me on the bathroom counter. Without breaking apart, he shimmies my pajama bottoms plus underwear off me, and then his fingers are between my legs, invasive and wonderful. But they aren't enough. I want everything from him. His love, his roughness, his heat. I want to be consumed by him, by the darkness that binds us together.

"No fingers. I want to be properly fucked," I tell him.

He pulls his hand away and captures my face with both. "God, I love you."

I'd say it back, but he silences me with his mouth. Fine. I'll show him, then. I free his cock from his jeans and guide it to my entrance. I'm more than ready for him; if I were any wetter, I'd probably slide right off the counter. He sheathes himself inside me in one smooth thrust, and for the first time since we started our twisted story, I feel whole.

"Finn...," I murmur against his lips. "Tell me this is real."

"It's real, babe. The only real thing in my life."

I close my eyes, surrendering to the sensations, to what's happening to us. I don't want to think about anything. I just want to soar above the world as light as a feather. We may have confessed our love for each other, but this is by no means lovemaking. It's hard, raw, and bruising. It's us.

A pinch of pain in the turbulence tears me apart. I taste blood on my tongue, and in the following second realize Finn bit me—whether by accident or not, it doesn't matter. It makes me come harder than ever before, and I black out for a moment. When I come back to myself, he's slowing down, and his breathing is out of control. His release is already trickling down my legs. I missed when he climaxed, which means for a couple seconds, she took control.

And now I'm jealous as hell.

51

ALEXIS

"You've been awfully quiet," Finn says as he runs lazy circles over my arm.

After we fucked in the bathroom, we made it back to bed for round two. Now what happened before is weighing heavily on my mind.

"Did you notice anything strange in the bathroom right before you climaxed?" I ask.

"No. Why? Should I?"

I turn on my side so I can look at him. "I think she took over for a moment."

His eyes widen. "Are you sure?"

I nod. "I blanked, and then you were finished."

His brows pinch together as he studies me. "I swear I didn't notice a thing, but I closed my eyes for a couple seconds."

"I'm not blaming you or anything."

"I know you aren't, but you're also not ecstatic about it, are you?"

"No. I don't want to share you with her. I know it sounds stupid, but—"

"It's not stupid. I don't want to be with her either. I love *you*. Whoever you become is a stranger to me."

A shiver runs down my spine. "I'm scared, Finn. What if she keeps coming back? What if she takes over for good?"

"We won't let that happen. We'll seek help if needed."

I drop my eyes to the hollow of his throat. "I'm afraid to tell anyone. I don't want to be locked into a psych ward."

He places his forefinger under my chin and lifts my head to face him. "You won't get locked up. I promise."

Seeing the determination in his gaze mollifies me a little.

"It seems like the problems keep piling up. In the letter, my alter ego said I shouldn't hang out with Carmen anymore because of her new friends. I fear those people are responsible for what happened to her."

Finn's gaze darkens. "That's the other thing I wanted to talk to you about. My grandfather is scum, and I suspect he might be involved with Carmen's fate and with Piper's weeklong disappearing act."

My entire body becomes as rigid as a board in an instant. "What do you know?"

"Carmen had a new tattoo on her neck that looked like a mask, and you said Piper had one too. Not long ago, I noticed a wooden box in my grandpa's things that also had an intricate mask design on it. It felt out of place among his things, but I didn't connect the dots until you mentioned Piper had a tattoo of a mask."

"That's a giant leap. You must have other reasons to suspect him besides the fact that he's rotten to the core."

"I saw him talking with Piper during the charity event at

school. She looked stressed out afterward. I can't peg it as coincidence."

My mind is whirling, coming up with the most horrible scenarios for why a rapist would be interested in teen girls—besides the obvious reason.

"I went to see him last night," Finn continues.

My stomach is twisting so savagely, I might throw up at any second. Not only because of what he discovered, but now that I know his secret, I also share his pain.

"I played a part, pretended I'm as sick as he is. I needed to convince him he could trust me."

"And did it work?"

He nods. "Yeah. I asked about the box with the mask design, and he finally told me what it was. Inside there was a key, which he said would lead me to Wonderland."

"What's that?"

"I don't know. He was all mysterious about it, but I suspect it's an exclusive club. He gave me the key, which will grant me entrance. I was sent the directions via text message from an unknown number earlier today."

My heart is hammering in my chest, and in the back of my mind, I can feel an oily presence. Shit, I wonder if my alter ego has lingered and is privy to this conversation.

"When are we going?"

"It could be dangerous, Lexi."

"I don't care. We need to find out who killed Carmen and why."

He caresses my cheek with the back of his hand. "I know. And that's why I asked if I could bring a plus-one. But I didn't like the glint of malice I saw in his eyes when I mentioned I might bring you. We have to stay sharp and not lose sight of each other."

"That goes without saying. What should I wear?"

"Something that looks expensive and... filthy." The corners

of his lips twitch upward, the first sign of levity since we started on this topic.

"You love using that word, don't you?"

"When it comes to you? Yes." He kisses the corner of my mouth, sending tingles of desire through my body. I fight the urge to come closer and explore his body again. We can't lose focus now.

"I don't know what dressing up filthy means. You don't mean like a whore, right?"

He laughs. "No. Something elegant but sexy as hell. I have a feeling Wonderland caters to depraved tastes. We need to dress the part and try not to stand out... too much."

"Too much? How about not at all?"

"I don't think that's a possibility. We're too high profile in this town—*especially* you."

"Why especially me?"

He chuckles. "You're the lost granddaughter of the Montgomerys."

I frown. "I wasn't lost."

"And there's the issue with your father's safe. We still don't know why people were after it."

"Do you think there's a link between that and everything else?"

He shakes his head. "Without knowing what's inside that safe, it's impossible to tell."

I nibble on my lower lip. "If only I could get access to the memories of my alter ego, that would be one problem solved. It aggravates me that the answers are all in my head but beyond my reach."

Finn squints, and I can almost hear the gears in his head working.

"What?" I ask.

"Maybe we don't need to see a doctor to try to unlock your memories."

"What do you mean?"

"Have you ever heard of hypnosis?"

I snort. "Yeah, but I can't say I believe in it. It sounds like hokum."

"It's not. Luke did it after…." He glances away.

"After what?"

He closes his eyes for a second and sighs. "I'm sorry, babe. I can't say. It's his secret."

Damn it. Now I'm gonna crawl out of my skin with curiosity, but I can't force Finn to betray his friend. "It's okay. But how would his experience help me?"

"He learned about the process. He even put Cameron under hypnosis once."

"Shut up. How do you know it wasn't a hoax?"

I shake my head. "There's no way Cameron would do what he did only for a practical joke."

"You're not going to tell me that story either, are you?"

"Nope." He smirks. "Sorry."

I hit his arm. "Then stop teasing me with secrets you can't reveal. That's mean."

"Okay, I'll stop now. But anyway, would you be willing to let Luke help you?"

Do I want a psychotic jerk to put me under his control? That's a tough one.

"I have to think about it." Reluctantly, I get out of bed and head to my walk-in closet. "Now I have to see if I have something that screams excess wealth and filthy at the same time."

"Do you want help?"

"Are we going to pretend we're in a movie where they do a fashion montage?"

"I'm not sure what that means."

I shake my head. "Never mind."

Finn doesn't follow me into the closet, but after a few

minutes of perusing my options, I can tell I have nothing that fits the bill.

When I return to my bedroom empty-handed, he's already fully clothed.

"Oh, are you leaving?"

Regret shines in his eyes. "Yeah. I have to deal with the consequences of my rebellion."

"Oh, Finn. You can't keep living under your father's roof if he's abusing you physically."

His gaze hardens, and his mouth becomes a thin line. "I don't think he'll dare lay a hand on me now."

"How do you know?"

He walks over and kisses me sweetly but too fast. His eyes remain as dark as a stormy sky when he replies, "Because I made a deal with the devil."

***

FINN

I LIED TO ALEXIS. I have no idea what awaits me at home. Yes, I've gained Grandpa's favor, but I've always been his favorite, and that never stopped my father from using me as a punching bag before. I'm sure the old bastard took some perverted pleasure seeing my bruises. I've always been able to justify my black eye or busted lip at school. To be honest, I don't think anyone in the faculty cares, not even my swim coach. As long as it doesn't interfere with winning, he's more than fine to look the other way. No one wants to piss off the Novaks.

It's past six when I pull into the driveway. My father never misses dinner if he's in town. He likes to be around to torment me, and since he couldn't take out his aggression last night, I'm sure my confrontation with him will be explosive.

When I walk in, the sound of polite conversation reaches my ears. Then I hear my mother's laughter, which surprises me. I can't remember the last time she was amused by anything. Not even when she's drunk does she laugh.

I follow the noise into the predinner room, and my shock turns me into a statue. Mom is sitting next to my sister, Tara, who I haven't seen since last Christmas. Even though she's the perfect, dutiful daughter, she tries to avoid coming home.

My father is standing on the opposite side of the room, facing the fireplace, but I can see his sulking profile.

"Finn, you're finally home!" Tara jumps from the couch, all joyous and shit. That's a first.

"Hey. What are you doing here?"

"Oh, everyone on campus got some type of virus, and most of the classes got canceled or are being held virtually, so I decided to come for a visit."

She hugs me tightly, but when she steps back, I can see the smile doesn't reach her eyes. Tara didn't come to Triton Cove because she was homesick. Something is going on with her, but I already have enough going on to figure out why she's here.

I flick my gaze in Dad's direction, expecting to find him glaring at me. But his expression is cold and his face emotionless. That's not his MO. He's either planning to kill me or getting really close to it.

"I don't even need to ask where you've been," he says with a sneer.

"Just because you fucked up your venture with Richard Montgomery doesn't mean the same happened to me."

"I see you're still determined to keep that diner trash around."

I curl my hands into fists. "Alexis isn't diner trash."

He raises an eyebrow. "Wow. Her pussy must be something magical for you to be defending her like that."

My nostrils flare. It's an effort to not make a move. I've done enough damage, showing him that I care about Alexis. He's going to use that to exact his revenge.

"Who's Alexis?" Tara asks.

"No one," I reply.

"Oh, that's Richard and Lillian's granddaughter. She's Finn's girlfriend." Mom is more than happy to supply the information, making me wonder how that detail penetrated her brain. She was intoxicated when she met Alexis at the charity event.

Tara's eyebrows shoot to the heavens. "You're dating someone? I can't believe it."

"Why is that so hard to believe?"

She shrugs. "I thought you only cared about swimming and spending time with your friends."

That statement is true enough. But I don't want to keep talking about Alexis.

"How about you, sis? Any prospects on the horizon?"

She twists her face into a grimace. "No. I just want to focus on my studies for now."

"That will change soon, honey," Dad tells her. "I'm coming to Boston next week, and the Carmichaels can't wait to host us."

Her face becomes paler. "What's that supposed to mean?"

The Carmichaels are an old and powerful family, and I'm sure our father would love to join our families through marriage.

I laugh in derision. "It means, dear sis, that Daddy Dearest found your future husband."

Tara whips her face to mine, glaring. But like the perfect daughter she is, she doesn't offer a retort. Pathetic.

"Someone has to put the family first," Dad pipes up.

This time, I don't fall for his trap and choose to ignore his barb. "When is dinner? I'm starving."

"We're waiting for Grandpa."

God, I forgot about him. My stomach becomes tight again. I doubt I'll be able to eat anything.

"Plenty of time for you to get rid of that sex dungeon stench, Finn," Dad says.

I work my jaw but don't reply to his goading. One thing I notice though is that he's restrained. That's not what I expected from the bastard after I humiliated him in front of the Montgomerys. But I take the excuse he provides and get the hell out of there before Grandpa arrives.

As I lock myself in my room, I have every intention of skipping dinner altogether. I doubt ditching them tonight will get me in bigger trouble.

52

FINN

As I expected, no one came knocking on my door to demand I make an appearance at dinner. I showered, got dressed, and then headed out, using the service stairs to avoid bumping into anyone. Inside the SUV I've been using, I find a black box with that damn mask printed on the lid in silver foil. It's bigger than the wooden box that contained the key. Grandpa must have left it here for me, guessing he wouldn't be seeing me before I went to Wonderland.

Inside, I find a pair of masks; one is simple and black, and the other is lacy and doesn't conceal much. Once again, I feel the acute pain in my stomach, and for a second, I consider leaving Alexis out of this. But if I do, Grandpa will know I'm only pretending.

We're not expected to be at Wonderland until much later, but I don't want to wait until then to see her. I text her to let her know I'm coming now.

Thinking about her helps ease some of my tension but not all of it. There's a stormy cloud of dread hanging above my head, and the certainty that whatever we discover tonight will change everything.

When I'm about five minutes from Alexis's place, Luke calls me.

"What's up?" I ask.

"What are you doing tonight?"

"I have plans with Alexis. Why?"

"Oh, so you made up with her, then?"

"Yeah, you could say that."

"How is she doing?"

Wow. Luke asking about the well-being of a girl he didn't seem to like very much is surprising.

"Not great. That's why I'm taking her out tonight. You know, to get her mind off things."

The lie feels bitter on my tongue, but I can't tell him what's going on.

"Look at you playing the devoted boyfriend and shit." He laughs.

"I'm not playing," I grit out.

"Ohhh, so you're pulling a Jason move?"

I roll my eyes. "Sure."

"Well, if you guys need to dispose of a body tonight, don't come to me."

I grumble. It's been months since he mentioned that incident. I choose to ignore his comment. "What are your plans?"

"Sage is driving me up the wall. I need to get out of this town."

I snort. "Do I even want to ask?"

"She's decided to act all rebellious and shit again."

Fuck. The last time that happened, Luke went nuclear. "Another boyfriend you don't approve of?"

"Something like that. But I won't bore you with the details."

Maybe if I was a better friend, I'd ask him about it. But I have too much on my plate, and if he's not on the verge of burning down the entire town, then it's not as bad as last time.

"Where are you going?" I ask.

"Probably Olympus Bay. Going to check out the infamous underground fights at Olympus U."

"That sounds fun. Are you taking Cam and Reid?"

"Bro, I cannot deal with Cameron right now, and I couldn't get a hold of Reid. So I'm going solo."

"Well, I hope you have fun... but not *too* much fun."

He chuckles. "Don't worry. That's the Godaires' territory. I'm crazy, not suicidal. Have fun with your *gurlfriend*."

"Bite me, asshole." I end the call before he can add another stupid comment.

Just in time anyway, because I'm right in front of the Montgomerys' gate. It opens without me needing to identify myself to the security camera, and I know the reason in the next moment. Alexis walks out the front door as I circle the fountain. She's wearing a black coat, which makes me think what she has underneath would freak out her grandparents. Despite where we're going later, the sight of her makes me fucking giddy.

I park and get out of the car so I can open the door for her. I'm sure her grandparents are watching from inside.

"I would have come in," I tell her.

"No, it's best if you don't." She rises on her tiptoes and kisses me on the cheek.

How demure. They're definitely spying on us.

"Am I persona non grata?"

She grimaces. "Sort of. I think they're only allowing me to go out tonight because they don't want to see me spiraling again." Her eyes grow sad. "My father's death was hard on me."

I pull her into a hug. "I can imagine. I'm sorry."

She presses her cheek against my chest, and now there's no hiding from her how fast my heart is beating.

"Me too." She leans back and asks, "Where are we going?"

"It's a surprise." I smirk, making her squint.

"It'd better be a good one. I'm done with nasty surprises."

I open the door of the car for her. "Get in before your grandparents decide they'd rather lock you up instead of allowing you to go anywhere with me."

She slides inside but keeps her glare locked on my face.

Shaking my head, I fight to keep my smirk from blossoming into a wide smile. I know she can be a little savage when she's mad, which is a huge turn-on for me, and I'd like to keep my mind out of the gutter until we drive off her grandparents' property.

"You're really not going to tell me where we're going?" she asks as soon as I'm behind the steering wheel.

"I'll tell you if you let me see your dress."

I flick my eyes to her while I wait for the gates to open. She's blushing furiously now, which makes me even more keen to see.

"Let's get where we're going first."

"Aw, babe. You're being mean now." I reach for her leg, trying to shove my hand under the front of her coat, but she bats it away.

"Finn. I'm serious. No peeking."

"Fine," I grumble.

I need a distraction now, so I turn on the music, and the first song on my playlist blasts through the speakers.

"What song is that?" she asks.

"'Surrender' by Angels and Airwaves."

"It's... different."

"Yeah, they're cool."

"It's not something I'd associate with you, though."

I look at her. "Why is that?"

She doesn't speak for a moment and appears to be in deep thought. "I don't know. Maybe because I like it?"

Her comment makes me laugh. "Oh, so you're the only one who's allowed to have good taste in music?"

"It's not that. I didn't expect to have anything else in common with you besides our fucked-up baggage."

Ouch.

"Is that a bad thing?"

"No. It's a good thing. It means this could actually be real."

I don't like the direction this conversation is going. I confessed what I feel for her, but what if it's all in my head and the emotions are fake, nothing more than a coping mechanism?

"Well, we have a couple hours before our mission. Let's make it count and get to know each other without bullshit or games."

The corner of her mouth turns up slightly. "I'd like that, although I'm afraid you'll find that without the crazy, I'm utterly boring."

"I didn't know you were nuts before and I didn't think you were boring. On the contrary. You were a rush of adrenaline— not were, *are*."

"You'd better pray I don't go Glenn Close on your ass."

I snort. "God, you really went back in time for that reference, huh?"

"I like the classics."

"If you're gonna talk about psycho blondes, we can't forget Sharon."

She scoffs. "Ugh! Of course you had to mention her."

"What? That movie was awesome."

"You just like the interrogation scene."

I laugh. "I swear that's not the *only* part I like." From my periphery, I catch her eye roll. I reach for her hand. "Aw, babe. Are you jealous?"

"Nope."

"You know, maybe we could role-play that scene one day."

"One day? What makes you think I'm not going commando right now?"

"What?" I whip my face to hers too fast and end up turning the steering wheel in the process. The car swerves sharply to the right.

"Watch the road, Finn!"

I regain control of the vehicle and force my eyes to stay ahead, but now I can't stop thinking about what she said. I decide it's best if I don't say anything at all until we reach our destination. The road up the mountain is dangerous with sharp curves, and I have to stay focused.

"Isn't this the way to Luke's house?"

"Yes, but we aren't going there."

I slow down when I see the sign for Trident Lookout Point, then take the exit to park. It's my luck that there aren't any tourists today.

"This is it?" She looks at me.

"Yeah. Have you ever been here before?"

"Once with my parents."

"It's one of my favorite spots. Come on or we'll miss the sunset."

I get out and walk around the car. When I reach her side, she's already out and looking at the horizon. I snake my arm around her waist and steer her closer to the edge.

"I've never watched the sunset from up here," she says.

"It's beautiful, but not as breathtaking as you."

She turns in my arms and looks at me intently. "When you came into the diner with your friends, I disliked you on the spot, and that was before I recognized you."

I smirk. "I noticed."

"But then we shared a moment. I can't remember what you said, but you let me see a glimpse of the real you, and I liked that."

"And then you kicked me out."

She drops her gaze. "Yeah."

"I used to go to the diner all the time my sophomore year. I can't believe I never bumped into you."

"My father didn't let me work too many hours when I was younger. He wanted me to have a normal high school life. This was the first summer I worked full-time."

"Do you think you'd have disliked me at first sight if we met a couple years ago?"

She shrugs. "Who knows? Were you an ass back then?"

I wrinkle my nose. "I want to say no, but I probably was."

She smirks, getting a twinkle in her eyes. "You have your answer."

Unable to keep my distance any longer, I capture her face between my hands and kiss her deeply, greeting her like I wanted to when I picked her up. Her lips are soft, and her tongue tastes like strawberries and dangerous promises.

She pulls back and lets out a shaky breath. "We're gonna miss the sunset if we keep making out."

"I'm okay with that. But also...." I run my fingers down the front of her coat, teasing her nipples through the thick fabric. "I want to see your dress."

I expect more resistance from her, but she steps back, creating a gap too big between us. I'd complain if she wasn't already fumbling with the sash of her coat. My entire body freezes save for my heart. It's hammering inside my chest, as if it's trying to run away.

"I guess I'd better show you now. Please don't laugh."

My eyebrows arch. "Why would I laugh?"

She parts her coat, and at first, all I glimpse is a plunging neckline. When her coat is finally off, I see her "dress" is nothing more than two pieces of shimmering fabric held together by thin silver chains that are wrapped around her middle. The long skirt has slits on the sides, and I bet when she moves you can see everything.

Why would she think I'd laugh? There's a high chance I'll burst into flames, though.

"What do you think?" she asks.

My tongue feels thick, stuck to the top of my mouth. "What do I think?" I groan.

"I had to go shopping in town, and this is all they had. I'm not sure if it fits the bill of expensive and filthy."

I swallow hard. "Are you seriously not wearing any underwear?"

She shakes her head. "You could see the panty line. It looked ridiculous. But now I'm afraid I went overboard."

Hell, I won't be able to keep my hands to myself until the evening is over.

I glance at the setting sun, then at the SUV.

Fuck it.

"Come here." I take a step forward and reach for her hand.

"Did I go too far?"

"No... and *yes*." My voice comes out like a growl as I lead her back to the car.

"Where are we going? We're missing the sunset."

"Fuck the sunset."

I open the back door and urge her inside, following and closing the door. Then I'm all over her like a hobo on a hot dog, kissing her as if I were a drowning man and she's the air I need to survive.

She scooches back, breaking the kiss. "Finn, what are you doing?"

"What does it look like?" I kiss the column of her neck, loving the throaty moan she lets out.

She threads her fingers through my hair, yanking at the strands. "In case you haven't noticed, this dress is very flimsy."

"I'll be careful." I continue my exploration south, running my tongue down the curve of her breasts.

With my fingers, I push the fabric aside and suck her nipple into my mouth. She arches her back, pulling my hair harder. I bite her in response while my right hand disappears underneath her dress. Holy fuck. She wasn't kidding. My fingers glide between her folds with ease—that's how wet she is already. God, I want another taste.

I release her nipple and go farther down, getting her skirt out of the way.

She leans on her elbows and looks at me. "Finn, what are you doing?"

My lips curl into a wolfish grin. "I haven't had dinner yet. Open wide for me, gorgeous."

I nudge her legs apart when she doesn't move and get right to it. Her taste is intoxicating and goes straight to my head. Or maybe it's the little sounds she makes that are quickly unraveling me. I flick my tongue across her clit fast, and she cries out. My balls are tight, and my cock is as hard as it could be. But I don't want to stop eating her pussy, even if it gives me pain and pleasure in equal measures.

Her breathing is already coming in bursts, and her body shakes increase. I dig my fingers in her hips, sucking her bundle of nerves hard into my mouth. Her lips buckle as she curses loudly. I can feel her orgasm on my tongue, how it makes her body tight at first and then soft in my hands. And yet I don't want to stop, so I keep going.

"Finn, please... I can't take it anymore."

"Yes you can," I groan.

"You're gonna make me come again."

I lean back and look at her. "So?"

Her hooded eyes become sharper as she squints. "I want your cock inside me when I do."

She closes her legs as she sits straighter, denying me access. But my mind has already switched to what's next. Eager, she doesn't wait until I can get my pants unzipped. She traps my face between her hands, then shoves her tongue down my throat and straddles me, grinding her pussy against my erection.

"Do you want me to jizz in my pants, babe?" I ask against her lips.

"No." She kisses my jaw, then continues peppering kisses on my neck until she bites my earlobe lightly. "But I can't resist you, Finn. You're like a drug to me."

"Let me get you high, then." I nudge her back so I have room to do what's needed.

Alexis takes over from there, wrapping her fingers around my length and guiding it to her entrance. She lowers her hips painfully slowly, making me grind my teeth. I want to impale her, so I take back the reins and bring her down on me fast.

She gasps, her eyes widening. "You're a bad boy, Finn. *I* was in charge."

"Not anymore." I claim her lips, kissing her as furiously as I'm moving her hips up and down my shaft.

She's so damn tight it won't take long for me to explode inside her heat. Her hand brushes against the bullet wound. It's still sore, but not as much as before, and the bit of pain heightens the pleasure.

Before I can stop it, I'm falling to pieces. In the rush, I forget about making her come first, but she follows me into oblivion, crying out my name as she comes undone once again.

53

ALEXIS

I'm still tingling after the romp in the back of Finn's car. We're lucky the fabric of my dress isn't the kind that wrinkles easily—we sure were careless about it. I'm glad I had the presence of mind to shove compact powder and lip gloss in my purse, because Finn destroyed my makeup.

He stopped by an In-N-Out after we left the lookout point, but I couldn't eat a thing. My stomach is now coiled tight as the jitters finally take over my body. Screwing Finn was a distraction—not that I didn't want to get down and dirty with him.

The directions he received lead us to the middle of nowhere, and the narrow gravel road we're currently on is spooky as hell with tall trees lining each side.

"I thought this place was an upscale club, but it looks like we're going to a slaughterhouse," I say.

Finn doesn't offer a comment, so I glance at his profile and find his jaw locked tight. If this is hard for me, it must be ten times worse for him. I can't believe he went an entire year carrying the burden of his secret and having to pretend his grandfather isn't a bastard who deserves to rot in prison.

Automatically, my fingers curl into fists, and I pinch my palms hard with my long nails. I didn't even sense the darkness trying to come to the surface this time, but my body did, and it reacted on its own. I feel it now, coiling around the edges of my mind like a snake. *Shit. Is she going to make an appearance tonight?* I can't let that happen, which means I have to remain calm. She usually comes when I'm under great stress.

Finally the trees become sparse, and we see a grand mansion ahead of us. It's an unusual style for this area with red bricks and white columns on the front. Most of the mansions in Triton Cove are modern or rustic. If it weren't for the black-suited security detail manning the entrance and guiding traffic, I'd think we were about to go to an innocent dinner party.

There's a line for valet, but Finn opts for parking the car himself. Smart. We don't want to get stuck here without the means to run away if the situation arises. When we're parked, he pulls a black box from the compartment between our seats.

"What's that?"

"A gift from my grandfather," he replies, opening the lid. Inside are two masks. Finn pulls out a lacy one and hands it over. "We're supposed to wear them."

He seems unhappy about it, but I'm not. The mask will add a layer of protection despite mine being so sheer that it won't conceal much.

"I suppose only the guys can be truly anonymous," I say, eyeing his sturdier mask.

"We don't need to do this. Say the word and we'll get out of here."

I shake my head. "No. I have to know who killed Carmen and bring them to justice."

"This might lead to nothing."

"I know, but not going means we'll never know." I put the mask on. "How do I look?"

His gaze softens. "You're gorgeous no matter what."

A blush spreads through my cheeks. "You don't need to shower me with compliments. You're already getting in my panties."

He leans forward, bumping his nose with mine. "I don't do it to get lucky. I'm only speaking the truth." He gives me a quick peck on the lips and retreats, already looking like he means business. "Are you ready?"

"As ready as I'll ever be."

Finn puts his mask on, and I can't help the smirk that blossoms on my lips.

"What?" he asks.

"You look like Zorro."

He snorts. "Maybe I should grow a 'stache, then."

"No! Oh God, please don't."

"Kidding. Come on." He opens the door and gets out.

I follow his lead, but I'm not prepared for my legs to lock tight and refuse to move.

Finn steps next to me, snaking his arm around my waist. "Are you okay?"

I take a couple of deep breaths, willing my heart to slow down. "Yeah."

"I won't leave your side. Promise."

"Okay."

He laces his fingers with mine, and we walk toward the front of the mansion together. Suddenly, I'm all too aware of how revealing my dress is, and the butterflies in my stomach change into radioactive bugs that are trying to crawl their way out with sharp claws and teeth.

Finn doesn't stop until he's facing a burly security guard who's also wearing a mask. He shows the guy his key, and he inspects it for a couple seconds, then flicks his gaze to me. My spine becomes even more rigid. Is he going to make an issue about my presence? He gives me a once-over and then nods, setting my teeth on edge. I guess I passed his inspection. *Asshole.* He steps aside and allows us entrance.

The exterior of the mansion may have given the illusion of a homely dwelling, but the inside is nothing like that. The walls are dark, but I can't tell their exact color because there's barely any illumination save for purple lights that are spread too far apart. There's a sweet scent in the air, and it's a little cloying. Finn squeezes my hand, but I don't glance at him. It'd be pointless before my eyes adjust to the gloom.

We walk down a wide hallway, going with the flow until it opens to an atrium that's a little more lit, but not by much. There's a huge chandelier hanging from the high ceiling, but the lamps are also purple. What's up with that?

I can see the checkered pattern on the marble floor, though, and all the waiters circulating are wearing long-eared black bunny masks. There isn't a single waitress in sight. The music playing in the background is sultry and a little hypnotizing. The small hairs on the back of my neck stand on end. What if that's their intention, to put us in a trance?

"All right. Keep your eyes peeled," Finn says.

"I'm not sure what I'm supposed to be looking for."

"You've never met Carmen's new friend?"

I open my mouth to say no but then remember it isn't true. "There was a guy hanging out with her at La Salamandra. But I'm not sure I'll be able to recognize him when everyone is wearing masks and it's so dark in here."

The music changes abruptly, turning even sultrier than before. I can't describe it, but it makes me want to do nasty things with Finn in front of everyone. People around us begin to dance provocatively, making me uneasy and oddly aroused.

Jesus, what's wrong with me?

A waiter approaches us. "Drinks?"

I shake my head, instinctively knowing I shouldn't consume anything in this place.

"No, thanks," Finn says.

The waiter begins to move away, but a tall and dark man stops him. He has the height and physique of a linebacker. "First time?" He looks at Finn.

"Why do you ask?" he replies.

The man smiles broadly, showing teeth. "I could tell." He grabs two glasses of what looks like champagne, but who knows when the purple light is messing up everything?

"Drink this. It'll make you enjoy the experience more."

Yeah, fat chance of that happening, buddy. I'm surprised when Finn accepts the offering and hands me one of the glasses. The stranger takes one for himself and says, "Cheers."

From my periphery, I see Finn bringing the glass to his lips. I follow his example, but I don't swallow it. I hope he did the same. It tastes like champagne, but there's another flavor in there too that I can't identify.

"Come find me in an hour or so. I'd love to get to know you better." He flicks his gaze to me for a second, and that's all it takes to make me feel hella dirty.

As soon as he walks away, I spit the drink back in the glass. Finn does the same, and I exhale in relief.

"What was that all about?" I ask.

"That was our welcome." He gives the room a cursory glance, then reaches for my hand again. "Come on. We have to blend in."

When another waiter comes near us, we get rid of our glasses, and then Finn pulls me flush against his body. We sway to the music, and I feel myself getting swept under its spell. The hunger I see in his eyes tells me he's feeling the same way. Without a word, he kisses my neck, running his hot tongue down to my collarbone. I throw my head back, granting him easier access. He's grinding his pelvis, pressing his arousal against my belly. I don't care that we're in a roomful of strangers, and when his mouth finds my nipple, I don't mind either.

What's going on with me—with us?

No. No. No. We have a mission. We can't get distracted.

I step back, fixing the top of my dress so my breast is no longer exposed.

"We need to keep moving," I tell him.

He's still looking at me through a lustful haze when he says, "Yeah, we should."

Now it's my turn to clasp his hand and steer us through the place. I have no idea where I'm going or what I'm looking for. I do spot couples and throuples engaged in different stages of sex along the way. I try not to ogle them. If we had any doubt about what kind of club this is before, definitely not anymore.

Finn stops suddenly, holding me back. "Wait."

I turn around and follow his eyes. "What?"

"It can't be."

"What are you looking at?" I squint, but it's hard to see now. We're back in the part of the club where it's super dark.

"Son of a bitch." He takes off, dragging me with him.

"Finn, wait up."

He doesn't listen, but a moment later, I understand what got into him. Piper is dancing on top of a table, half-naked, while men triple her age watch like horndogs. She's not even eighteen.

Finn lets go of my hand so he can drag her off the table. She opens her eyes and yelps.

"What do you think you're doing?" One of the creeps stands up.

"Back off, asshole," Finn retorts.

"Who the fuck do you think you are?" the second guy asks.

"They can't be members," the third of the party chimes in.

"Let go of me!" Piper pulls her arm free from Finn's grasp.

There isn't an ounce of recognition in her eyes as she glares at him.

"Piper, it's me, Alexis," I say, pulling my mask off.

Her eyes widen, and then her face contorts in horror.

"Is there a problem here?" a security guard asks, and then I feel the cold touch of a gun barrel press against my back.

Shit.

54

FINN

*A*lexis has gone as still as a statue, and even in the dark, I notice her frightened eyes.

"There isn't a problem," I say.

"They've broken the code," one of the pervs says.

Two other security guards box us in, severely diminishing our chances of getting out of here without creating a bigger commotion.

"You're coming with me," the guy behind Alexis orders.

"No, we aren't. We're leaving." I try to take her hand, but he moves ever so slightly, revealing the gun he's pointing against her back.

Son of a bitch.

"Like I said, you're coming with me." Piper takes a step back, trying to slink away, but the man holding the gun notices. "You too, sweetheart."

"We weren't done with her," one of the pervs complains.

"Gentlemen, look around. There are plenty of delectable things to feast on tonight. But the party is over for this trio."

The goon nearest me grabs my arm hard enough to leave bruises. I turn to glare at him and stop cold, recognizing him despite the mask. Eric Danes. God knows I spent way too much time staring at the guy and wishing I could undo the harm I've done.

His gaze connects with mine, and he must have noticed I recognized him because he shakes his head slightly.

I don't know what the hell is going on here, but the best course of action is to follow along and pretend I don't know him. My instincts are telling me Eric isn't in cahoots with the guy holding Alexis at gunpoint. I hope I'm not wrong.

We're escorted away from the main party and down a narrow hallway. With each step I take into the unknown, my heart rate increases. Adrenaline is coursing freely through my veins, but I try to think logically and not let nerves get in the way. If Eric isn't a criminal, then he could possibly be an ally.

The guy with Alexis takes us through a set of double doors into what looks like a private entertaining room. Every single piece of furniture here is a bold color, and from my periphery, I notice a leather lounge chair that I've seen advertised somewhere as "the sex chair."

The room isn't empty though. Two girls are on their knees, giving head to the same guy. His eyes are closed as he holds a chunk of hair from each of the girls in his fists. I can tell he's either already in the throes of an orgasm or about to come.

"Get out," the guy holding Alexis orders.

The man opens his eyes and glares, but his annoyance only lasts a second before he shoves the girls away and zips up his pants. His companions aren't as fast to scramble back to their feet. They look drugged. The asshole grabs them by their hair and "helps" them unfurl from their kneeling positions. I tense, but Eric holds me tighter and shakes his head.

When we're finally alone, the man holding Alexis tosses her onto the couch. She staggers forward and falls awkwardly, unable to prevent her skirt from revealing too much. My blood boils. The asshole holding Piper does the same to her, but Eric keeps his tight grip on my arm.

"Who are you?" Alexis asks.

The bastard tilts his head. "You don't remember me, sweetheart?"

She narrows her gaze and doesn't speak for a couple of beats, but I know the exact moment the memory comes to her. Her eyebrows arch. "You're the one who let us in La Salamandra."

"Ah, you *do* remember."

Her face is now twisted in rage. "You killed Carmen, didn't you?"

He shakes his head. "Tsk, tsk. That's some serious accusation."

"You can't keep us here," she seethes.

"Oh, honey, you're wrong about that. I can do whatever I want."

"Do you know who you're messing with?" I snap.

He turns to me and smirks. "I know very well who you are, Finn Novak. I was told you were coming."

I swallow hard. "How did you know? Did my grandfather tell you?"

"Why am I here?" Piper whines before he can reply. "I've done nothing wrong. I've been a good girl."

Eric reacts to her statement by flexing his fingers on my arm.

"You're here because I don't know if you are truly a good girl. You have to prove your loyalty."

"H-How?"

"I think I'm in the mood for some girl-on-girl action." He smiles slyly and looks at me. "What do you think, Finn?"

I try to get free from Eric's grasp, but he holds me tighter. The other guy makes a motion to restrain me as well, but Eric says, "I got him. He won't go anywhere."

Alexis whips her face to us, but she doesn't give any indication that she recognizes him.

"What do you want me to do?" Piper asks in a small voice.

"I want you to go down on your redheaded friend."

"You fucking asshole. Leave them alone!" I thrash against Eric's hold again, but it's only for show.

I could break free from him. I noticed he's not really holding me that hard. I'm not sure what he's waiting for though. I imagine he has a plan, though I realize I'm putting way too much faith in the hands of a dude I don't know. As far as I can tell, only the guy in charge is armed, but the other one might be packing as well.

"I-I've never been with a girl before," Piper replies.

Alexis glances at the guy holding the gun, and then she looks at me. At first, her eyes are round and frightened, but then her gaze changes. It becomes colder, harder. Deadly.

Fuck me. That's not her anymore.

She switches her attention to Piper and smiles. "It's okay. It's my first time too. Let's give them a show, shall we?"

Piper's eyes bug out. She flicks her gaze toward the asshole, unsure of herself.

He relaxes his stance, lowering the gun, and then nods. "Go on, sweetheart. Show me you're worth being part of my harem. Unless you want to have the same ending as your buddy."

Buddy? Is he referring to Carmen?

"No. I'm not like her. I'm loyal. I know my place."

Damn it. What have they done to her? It's like she's been brainwashed.

Alexis leans forward, framing Piper's face between her hands, and then kisses her deeply, not holding back. Rage runs freely through my veins. My Alexis would never do that, and I know she'll be mortified when she finds out what her alter ego did.

The third security guard takes a step forward, already clutching his junk. I want to bash his face in. His boss is also watching Alexis and Piper make out with great interest.

"Now," Eric whispers and then shoves me toward the third guy.

I collide with him, and we both fall to the floor. Piper screams, and then there's a loud crash, but I can't see what's happening, as I'm trying to not lose the upper hand in my own fight. My opponent is strong, and he has the advantage of not having a healing bullet wound. I know he'll overwhelm me in no time, so I have to fight dirty if I want to get out of here alive.

I press my thumbs into his eyes hard, making him howl in pain. Unfortunately, it's not enough. With a roar, he pushes me off him, and I bump my injured shoulder against a table. White-hot pain shoots down my arm, making me see stars.

He's reaching for the gun that was concealed underneath his jacket, but a kick to his face renders him unconscious. Eric appears in front of me and offers me his hand.

I'm already looking for Alexis before I'm back on my feet. I see the guy who was in charge sprawled on the floor, unconscious. There's a big gash on his forehead, and a pool of blood has formed a halo around his head. But Alexis and Piper are gone.

"Where the hell are they?" I ask.

"Piper took off, and Alexis went after her."

"Let's go, then." I rush to the door, not waiting for Eric.

In the darkness, it's impossible to see much of my surroundings. I push people out of my way, not caring if I'm drawing attention to myself. I have no idea where Alexis went, but if Piper is trying to escape this place, the safest bet is that they are headed to the main entrance.

I burst out of the house like the devil is after me in time to see Alexis jump behind the wheel of a random car and take off. The valet is clutching his bleeding nose. *Jesus.* More security guards appear out of nowhere, a few holding their earpieces and sporting frowns.

"Shit," Eric mutters. "We need to get out of here."

"Come on, my car isn't far." I get ready to run, but Eric grabs my arm.

"Don't. You'll look suspicious. Walk at a normal pace and look unbothered."

I grind my teeth, but I can't offer a retort. He's right.

We give the security guards a wide berth, but the moment we step into the dark, I jog the rest of the way, ripping the damn mask off my face. Eric barely has time to get inside before I put the car in Reverse.

When I hit the dirt road, there's no sign of Alexis's car, but she couldn't have gone far. The vehicle she stole is red, easy to spot. I hold on to that thought as I press the pedal to the metal.

A moment later, Eric asks, "What were you doing at Wonderland?"

"I could ask you the same thing."

He doesn't reply, but I can't risk taking my eyes off the road for a second to look at him. I'm going way too fast on an uneven road, and the last thing I need is to hit a tree or drive over a big hole and get a flat tire.

"I can't tell you why I was there," he answers, "but I can guess why you were."

"Is that so?"

"You were looking for answers about Carmen's fate."

I grip the steering wheel tighter. "Yes."

"You shouldn't have come. You don't know what kind of people you're messing with."

A humorless laugh bubbles up my throat. "That's rich coming from you."

He snorts. "I don't know why I'm trying to help you. You're the asshole who hurt my little brother."

"That's right. You shouldn't help me. I don't deserve it, but Alexis does. I'll do anything to help her find her best friend's killer."

"She doesn't look like someone who needs help. Besides, she already found him and dealt with the bastard accordingly."

We're finally back on the main road, so I risk a peek at him. "Did you see her kill him?"

"No. But I saw her holding the murder weapon."

I curse under my breath, knowing it wasn't Alexis.

"Good riddance."

Eric hits the door hard. "It wasn't good riddance, you jackass! That lowlife was the key to get—"

When he stops talking, I cut my eyes to him. "The key to what? What the fuck are you involved with, Eric?"

His cheeks hollow as he grinds his jaw and glances out the window. "I already said I can't tell you. You know too much as it is."

His response sets my teeth on edge. I'd press for answers if I didn't catch sight of a red car zigzagging through traffic.

"That must be Alexis," I say.

"Where the fuck is she going?"

"I don't know."

She cuts in front of a car, forcing it to brake suddenly to avoid a crash, then takes the next exit. I almost don't have time to stop when the road becomes completely blocked.

"Fuck!" I jam the heel of my hand on the horn. I can't lose her now.

"You're clear on my side. Go, go!" Eric urges.

The tires burn rubber when I accelerate too fast, and I almost collide with an idiot on a motorcycle who had the same idea as me.

"Jesus! You said it was clear."

"That guy came out of nowhere," he grumbles.

I open my mouth to retort, but sirens cut my reply short. I look at the rearview mirror and curse loudly. Cops are behind us.

"Shit," Eric mutters.

"I don't have time for this," I say as I maintain my speed.

"What are you doing? You have to stop."

"I'll lose Alexis."

"With the way she's driving like a maniac, she must have cops on her tail as well."

He's right, but knowing she isn't in the driver's seat makes me less keen to let the cops catch up with her. However, when another police car joins the chase, I realize I'll be fucked if I don't stop.

I pull over, hoping I can use the Novak card one more time to get out of this mess.

55

ALEXIS

*T*he sharp pain of a seat belt digging into my skin is as jarring as it is alarming. My heart is beating fast and hard, almost painfully. Confusion hits me as I take in my surroundings. I'm inside a sports car parked just behind a silver sedan on Juno Bridge, which means she must have taken over for a good chunk of time. The last thing I remember was being held at gunpoint in Wonderland.

I glance at my hands, which are covered in blood, and immediately begin to spiral. *No, not again.*

I would have continued to freak out if a movement ahead didn't catch my attention. Hell, it's Piper Phillips still wearing almost nothing. The wind is blowing her long hair in all directions, but that doesn't stop her from climbing over the bridge's railing.

Shit. Is she planning to jump?

I get out of the car in a flash. "Piper, please don't."

She looks over her shoulder. "Don't come any closer."

I take a small step forward. "Please. You don't need to do this."

Her face crumbles. "You don't understand. My life is already over."

"No, it isn't. Whatever happened to you, you can get past it. I swear to you that things will get better."

She shakes her head. "No one leaves the society. Your friend tried, and they killed her."

I swallow the huge lump in my throat. "Don't let them get away with it. You can testify. You can send them all to prison."

"And then what? Everyone will know what I did, how I debased myself to filthy men. I can't live with the shame."

I dare to move closer. "Fuck everyone. You don't owe the people in this town any explanation."

Her eyes widen. "I wish I was as strong as you are. It's not only my life they'll destroy if I come forward. They'll ruin my parents' lives too. Ending my life is best for everyone. Trust me."

"No, it isn't. I bet your parents would rather have their lives ruined than lose you forever."

She closes her eyes for a moment. "I wrote everything in my diary. It's hidden in a loose board by the window in my room."

"That's good. We can use that as evidence."

The sound of approaching sirens makes her open her eyes again. She looks over her shoulder fleetingly, then back at me.

"No, *you* can use that as evidence. Tell my parents I love them and that I'm sorry."

She looks away, dipping her chin. Her body is poised to jump.

"Piper, no!" I run toward her, but she leaps before I can reach her, getting swallowed by the darkness. "No!"

I clutch the railing while hot tears drench my face. Ugly sobs make my entire body shake. I see nothing but utter darkness. She's gone. I failed her.

"Alexis!" Finn yells.

I turn, surprised to hear his voice. He pulls me into a bear hug, pressing my face against his chest. I wrap my arms around his waist and try to meld myself to him.

"I couldn't save her, Finn," I choke out.

He runs his fingers through my hair. "Everything will be okay, babe. I promise."

"What's going on here?" a man asks.

I ease out of Finn's embrace to see who's talking. It's Sheriff Bennet, who's presently glowering at me.

"Piper Phillips jumped from the bridge. I tried to stop her, but…." I close my eyes again, unable to continue because the guilt is like a vise around my neck, squeezing it so tight I can't breathe.

Amazingly, he doesn't ask more questions. Instead, he proceeds to issue orders, and then I tune him out.

"Let's get out of here," Finn tells me.

"Can we? I mean, won't the sheriff need a statement from me?"

"He can get that later."

I let Finn steer me toward his car, and there comes the second surprise of the evening. Eric Danes is standing next to it, looking hella grim.

"What are you doing here?" I ask.

"He came with me," Finn explains.

My eyes widen. "But he hates your guts."

"That's true. However, you and your boyfriend meddled in my affairs. I had no choice," Eric replies.

"Your affairs?" My voice rises to a shrill.

"I can see you're already gearing up to fire a thousand questions at me. Let me save you the trouble and say I won't answer any of them."

"Piper Philips just committed suicide because of what those motherfuckers at Wonderland did to her," I seethe. "How dare you stand there like a fucking heartless asshole and say you won't share what you know. Unless you're one of them. If that's the case, I should hand you over to Sheriff Bennet right now."

Eric's face twists into a scowl. "I'm not one of them. I was trying to bring them down when you and Finn got in the way."

"Bring them down how?"

He passes a hand over his face, cursing under his breath. "I can't tell you."

Finn presses his hand on my lower back. "We should leave before the sheriff decides he needs your official statement now."

"Listen to your boyfriend, Walker." Eric opens the back door and gets in Finn's car.

Jackass.

"He's coming with us?" I ask.

"Apparently so."

I look at Finn and struggle to get my next question out. "Did I...? How did I escape Wonderland?"

He cups my cheek. "You did what you had to do, love. Don't stress about it now. Let's get out of here first."

His answer doesn't give me comfort, but speaking about what happened at the club while surrounded by cops is not the smartest idea.

Finn walks me to the passenger side and opens the door for me. The moment he closes the door, the magnitude of what happened tonight drops on my shoulders like a heavy burden. I look out the window as a great heaviness settles on my chest, caving it in. Ignoring Eric in the back seat is easy when I have this enormous guilt swirling within me. I didn't think the feeling could get any worse after I discovered Carmen's fate, but I was wrong. It seems there's no limit to it. For the first time ever, I wish she'd take over so I don't have to feel the pain.

Finn gets behind the wheel and takes off before our way is

blocked. No one speaks during the drive. It's not until we're on the highway and getting close to the exit toward downtown that Eric breaks the silence.

"You can drop me off at my grandfather's store. You remember where that is, right, Finn?"

"Yes, I remember."

Eric's jab jars me from the bottomless pit of despair, fueling the anger the guilt was smothering a second ago. I want to yell at him for reminding Finn of the biggest regret of his life. It's crazy that I want to protect him from the pain I was keen to inflict on him not too long ago. But everything I've been through since joining Maverick Prep has taught me I don't have the moral high ground. I'm not a saint, and I'd bet an arm and a leg that Eric isn't either.

"If you're not working for the people behind that hateful club, who *are* you working for?" I ask.

"I already sai—"

"I don't give a fuck about what you said! Whether you like it or not, we're involved. We're all part of this twisted game, and it's in our best interest to join forces."

He laughs without humor. "Join forces. That's rich."

"She's not joking," Finn butts in. "We know more than you're aware. I bet we have information you don't."

"Oh yeah? Like what?"

"Nice try, buddy. We aren't telling you jack until you come clean about why you were in that disgusting club," I say.

"If you came in tonight as patrons, you must have had a key. I'm guessing you got one from your grandfather, Finn."

"What do you know about my grandfather's involvement in this?" Finn asks.

I turn in my seat so I can see Eric's reaction.

"He's one of the founders."

Shit. That doesn't surprise me. The Novaks built this town,

so it makes sense for that horrible man to have started the disgusting club.

I glance at Finn, trying to gauge how Eric's statement affected him, but his face reveals nothing. His expression is locked into a cold mask.

"I guessed as much," he replies.

"And how did you get involved in all this?" I ask Eric.

"I was... recruited. And that's all I can say. You have to trust that I'm one of the good guys."

I squint. "Rumor says you went to military school before coming to Maverick. Is that true?"

"Yes."

"Is enrolling at Maverick part of your assignment?" Finn asks.

It's Eric's turn to narrow his eyes. He doesn't answer right away, but the clench of his jaw tells me he's done answering questions.

"Does it matter?" he finally replies.

"I guess it doesn't."

"We know Bad Grandpa is one of the founders, but who else is part of the scheme?" I mutter.

"That was what I was trying to find out," Eric says. "The list of other founders isn't something shared widely."

"How come you knew about my grandfather, then?" Finn asks.

Eric laughs. "He's a cocky son of a bitch with a god complex. He believes he's untouchable."

"Piper told me she wrote everything in her diary," I say.

"I doubt she knew anything about the ones on top."

"My grandfather approached her at school," Finn pipes up.

"And you seriously believe he did anything to incriminate himself?"

"If he fucked her, then he's guilty of statutory rape," Finn replies angrily.

"She's gone. Even if she wrote in her diary what happened, there's no evidence besides the ramblings of a teenage girl. He'll never get a conviction. We need more than that."

"What we need is to get our hands on that diary," I say.

"Did she say where she kept it?" Finn asks.

"Yeah. In her bedroom."

"Her father is your counselor, isn't he?" Eric asks Finn.

"Yeah. I suppose I could pay him a visit to offer my condolences, but it feels fucking wrong to do it only to snoop around in his daughter's belongings."

"Really? That's where you draw the line?" Eric retorts.

"I don't think it's right to see the man so soon after he's lost his daughter," I say. "Her diary is hidden. We can wait until the wake. It'd be easier to snoop around when the house is full of guests. No one will notice if I disappear for a moment."

Finn passes a hand over his face. "Jesus. I can't believe she's gone."

My heart clenches painfully when the guilt returns with a vengeance. I should have done more to prevent her from jumping.

A heavy silence falls inside the car, and it's only broken when Finn parks in front of Mr. Danes's convenience store.

"What's the game plan?" he asks Eric.

"We keep acting as if nothing has changed. That means we give each other a wide berth at school."

"Sounds good," Finn grumbles.

He doesn't drive off right away after Eric exits the car, just keeps staring ahead.

"What's wrong?" I ask softly.

He turns to me. "She took over again tonight, didn't she?"

I avoid his gaze. "Yeah."

He reaches for my hand. "You know that doesn't change a damn thing about how I feel about you."

"Thanks for saying that. It doesn't matter though. She's inside me, doing things I can't control, and I'm done with it."

"What are you saying?"

I look at him again. "I want to see Luke about the hypnosis. I'm ready to know what she's done."

56

FINN

*I*t isn't until I make it back home that I begin to worry about my grandfather. I showed my hand in the club. The pervs who were hounding Piper didn't recognize me, but the asshole who took Alexis at gunpoint did.

I go straight to my room because there's nothing I can do but wait for the hammer to fall—or not.

I should try to get some sleep, but I'm too wired to rest. I grab my cell phone with every intention to text Luke, but it's Jason's contact that I pull up.

ME: Hey, how's it going?

I don't expect a reply right away, so when the three dots appear, it feels like the universe is trying to tell me something. I've been keeping my best friends in the dark, telling myself they don't need to learn the sordid truth about my family. But in reality, carrying the burden alone is taking a toll on me. I'm on the verge of snapping again, and I can't allow that to happen. It's not only my life on the line now. I have to protect Alexis at all costs.

JASON: Not much. We're taking a break from traveling. Currently chilling at Nicola's parents'. How about you?

ME: Honestly, things aren't great.

A second later, Jason calls me.

"What's wrong?" he asks.

I pinch the bridge of my nose, letting my shoulders sag forward. "I don't know where to start."

"The beginning is always a good place."

Hesitation grips me. Jason sounds happy. Do I really want to pull him back into our fucked-up family drama?

"Never mind. I'll deal with it."

"Finn, I swear to God, if you don't tell me right this second what's wrong, I'll hop on a plane and come to Triton Cove to kick your ass."

"You got out. I don't want to drag you back into the filth of this family."

"The reason I was able to get out is you. You've always had my back, and I have yours. Now stop pussyfooting around and spill."

I release a shaky breath and then a bunch of word vomit. Once I start talking, I can't stop. It's like an avalanche of problems, and I'm dumping it all on Jason. He only interrupts me to ask a question here and there. Half an hour later, he knows almost everything—Alexis's condition isn't my secret to tell—but I told him about the ugly truth of my conception. Hell, there's no point in hiding that from him. I'd like to say I feel better confessing, but my chest is still as heavy as a sack filled with rocks.

"I'm so sorry, Finn. If I'd known...."

"I didn't want anyone to know."

"I've always been aware that Grandpa was an asshole, but that's pure evil."

"It makes my father look like an angel in comparison."

Jason snorts. "I wouldn't go as far as that."

"You're right. There's a high chance he's involved with that disgusting club as well."

"Maybe. I'm glad you told me though. I'll be on the first flight to Triton Cove."

"Jason, you don't need—"

"I'm not going to let you keep fighting those demons alone. I'll be there for you as you were there for me. It's a done deal. Just try to stay out of trouble until I arrive."

"I'll do my best."

Although we both know that means nothing.

AT SOME POINT in the night, I ended up falling asleep. The kink in my neck tells me I passed out in an awkward position. I'm still wearing the same clothes as yesterday save for my jacket.

I glance quickly at my phone to check the time and see I have a message from Luke. He's back from Olympus Bay and can meet later, past noon preferably.

I don't remember, but it seems I did text him last night. Looking at the message I sent, I kept it vague. I didn't even mention I was bringing Alexis.

As if I summoned her with my thoughts, a text from her pops on my screen.

ALEXIS: Hey, are you up?

ME: Yeah, just.

ALEXIS: My grandparents know about Piper. Sheriff called half an hour ago asking me to go to the precinct. I'm freaking out.

Shit. We knew this was coming, but we failed to prepare for it. I call her instead of texting back.

"Hey," I say. "When do you need to go to the precinct?"

"As soon as possible."

"I can come over in ten."

"No, it's best if you don't come. My grandparents think this is all your fault."

I run my fingers through my hair. Of course they'd think that, and I can't blame them. It *is* my fault. I shouldn't have taken Alexis to Wonderland. I told Sheriff Bennet I had a fight with her and was driving like an idiot in the hopes of catching up with her. It was hard to tell if he bought my story or not, but he did allow me to follow his cruiser until we came up the bridge.

"I hate this. What are you going to tell the sheriff?"

"The same thing I told my grandparents. I was on my way home when I spotted Piper hanging from the bridge's railing."

"And the car you stole?"

"That's the part that's freaking me out. The owner covered for me, told the sheriff I borrowed it."

That doesn't bode well.

"Did he say who the owner was?"

"Nope, and mercifully, my grandparents were too distraught to even think to ask that question. But I'm sure once the shock wears off, they'll hound me for an answer."

"I don't want you to worry about that. It's possible the owner didn't want to draw attention to himself."

She sighs. "Yeah, maybe. How about you? Is everything okay at home?"

"I haven't seen anyone since I got back."

"Do you think your grandfather knows the havoc we wreaked at his club?"

"I hope he doesn't, but I have to be prepared to deal if he does."

Alexis releases a shaky breath. "Things keep getting worse the deeper we dig."

I wish I could say they'll get better soon, but that'd be a lie. "Luke can see us this afternoon," I say to change the subject. There's a pause, and I fear she's spiraling. "Babe? Are you okay?"

"I'm fine."

I don't believe that for a second.

"Please call me as soon as you're done with the sheriff."

"I will. Thanks for having my back."

"Babe, I love you. There's nothing I wouldn't do for you."

There's another pause, which is making me reconsider not going to see her in person.

"Aww, aren't you sweet?"

My entire body goes rigid. That's not Alexis.

"You," I seethe. "Get the fuck out of my girlfriend's head."

"I wish I could, but you see, Alexis can't take the shitstorm that's coming. Hence why I'm here."

"You're wrong. She's stronger than you think."

"Is she? Do you think kindhearted Alexis would have been able to kill two men to save your ass? Now, Finn, where's the fucking gratitude?"

"You think you're helping her, but you're only making things worse."

"Maybe. But until Alexis grows a backbone, I'll stick around. You know she made me, right?"

"What?"

She laughs, but it's without warmth. It makes my blood turn cold. "I was born the day her uncle murdered someone in cold blood."

Fuck. Talk about a head-spin-inducing comment.

"He was convicted of manslaughter," I grit out.

"And you believe that?"

I begin to pace, questioning everything I've learned so far. "I have no reason to trust you."

"Suit yourself. Gotta run."

She ends the call before I can get another word in. It's clear she plans to stick around through the interview at the precinct, and there's not a damn thing I can do about it.

57

ALEXIS

She took over again. I don't remember a damn thing I told Sheriff Bennet, but whatever it was, it was enough to get him off my case. Unfortunately, I'm still in the doghouse where my grandparents are concerned. They sulked the entire drive back home and blamed Finn for every terrible thing that's happened to me.

"You're not to see that boy again, Alexis," Grandma tells me before I can run to my room.

If I was having a normal day, I'd have rebelled against her order. Right now, I don't have it in me to pick a fight.

"I'm tired," I say instead.

Her expression softens. "Oh, darling. I can imagine. You don't want to eat first?"

I shake my head. "I'm not hungry."

"Go take a nap, then. I'll have Raquel bring you a light supper later."

"Okay."

I trudge up the stairs. It's not a ruse. I'm exhausted, only I have no intention of lying down. No rest for the wicked and all that. I'm sneaking out to meet Finn. More than ever, I have to unlock my mind. My alter ego is making too many appearances and I have to find a way to stop it from happening permanently.

I text Finn the moment I'm alone in my room.

ME: I'm home. When can you pick me up?

FINN: Give me ten minutes. How did it go?

I bite my lower lip. I was talking to Finn when the blank space in my memory happened, which means he might have talked to her.

ME: I don't know.

FINN: It's gonna be okay, babe. I promise.

ME: I know. God, I can't wait to see you.

His reply is a string of cute emojis. Not something I'd ever expect from him, but his sweetness does the trick and makes my heart less heavy.

Damn it. I love this boy.

ME: Park outside and text me once you're there. I have to sneak out.

FINN: Got it.

Knowing he'll be here soon, I hurry to change clothes and look like I give a damn. The urge to shower again is great— knowing she was in control makes me feel dirty—but I don't have the time. I look at my reflection in the mirror and almost don't recognize myself. I've lost weight, and the stress is showing as dark circles under my eyes.

A text draws me back to my room. My heart beats a little faster, believing it's a message from Finn, but it's Julie asking if I'm okay. The news must have already spread like wildfire. Great. I can't wait to deal with that on Monday.

I reply to her because I'm not an asshole. It's sad that she's the only one who reached out. I didn't expect Emily to do so, but my uncle's radio silence is a surprise.

Is it though? On the few occasions we interacted, it didn't sound like he wanted a lot of contact. Maybe he left Triton Cove. No, he couldn't, thanks to his parole. It's better this way. It's clear he's involved with people I should stay away from. I have enough problems as it is; I don't need the extra complication.

When Finn's text finally comes, my heart doesn't take off like before. There's a new burden weighing it down. But there's no time for feeling sorry for myself. I shove the morose emotion to a dark corner of my mind and head out. On soft feet, I make my way downstairs. I hear Grandma's voice coming from the den. She's on the phone with someone, and the topic isn't something that concerns me. I manage to slip out the front door without getting caught, and the moment I'm outside, I sprint toward the gate.

Finn gets out of the car when I hit the curb, and I run straight into his arms. He hugs me tight, kissing the top of my head. His heart is beating faster than normal, just like mine. I don't move, allowing myself a few precious seconds to breathe him in. My eyes prickle, and a lump lodges in my throat.

No. I can't let the waterworks flow freely. I have to fight the wave of sadness.

Leaning back, I look straight into his beautiful eyes. "She took over again."

"I know. I had the pleasure of exchanging a few words with her."

Jealousy spears my chest. I haven't forgotten that she made an appearance when we were in the middle of sexy times.

"What did she say?"

He clenches his jaw as his gaze darkens. "Let's get going. I'll tell you on the way to Luke's."

Shit. Now I'm afraid of what that psycho said to him. Whatever she told him is clearly bothering him.

"What do you know about your uncle's conviction?" he asks once we're on the move.

That was not what I expected him to say.

"Not much. Only that he was convicted of manslaughter. I couldn't bring myself to read all the details."

Because I'm a fucking coward.

"I looked into it. He killed a lowlife during a bar fight."

"Why are you bringing up my uncle's rap sheet?" I watch his profile closely, and when he swallows hard, it's audible.

"She said you created her on the evening your uncle committed murder." He glances at me briefly.

"I don't understand."

"According to her, he killed a man in cold blood."

My stomach clenches painfully, making me sick. "No, that's not possible. He would have been convicted of murder, not manslaughter."

"I know."

"And how is his crime related to her presence in my head?"

"Multiple personality disorder is usually triggered by trauma. Something happened to you when you were young, and if what she said is true, it's related to what your uncle did."

To fight the nausea, I curl my hands into fists, digging my nails into my palms. "Do you think... he hurt me?"

"I don't know what to think. Hopefully, Luke will be able to unlock her memories."

I look out the window as I process this new information. "If my uncle tried to hurt me, my mother wouldn't keep in touch with him. Maybe he killed that man to protect me."

"Wait. Your mother kept in touch with him while he was in prison?"

"Yeah. I found a stack of their letters in my dad's garage. I only read one of them before they disappeared from my room—before *she* hid them."

Finn covers my hand with his. "We could go talk to your uncle before going to Luke's."

"No. I'd rather find out what she knows first."

"Okay."

"Did you hear from Eric?" I ask to change the subject.

"Nope," he replies curtly.

"Was there any word about the man I—*she* killed at Wonderland?"

"No, but I don't think we would hear anything about it. That would draw attention to the club. My bet is they got rid of his body."

I look out the window again as sudden jitters take over my body. If the session with Luke works out, I'll remember everything she did, including her two kills. Am I ready for it?

I'VE ONLY BEEN to Luke's mega mansion once, and I can't say I have good memories of the place. I glance at the spot where Tiffany and Jackie cornered me, and chills run down my spine. At the time, I could still prevent *her* from taking control. I wonder what would have happened if I'd let the darkness free that night. Maybe those two bitches would be buried in a shallow grave now. The thought makes me happy, and I can't find an ounce of remorse for thinking about their demises and enjoying the daydream. Am I turning into my alter ego, or have I always been bad and she's just a projection of my true self?

Grim musings, Alexis.

In the daylight, Luke's place is bigger than I remember. To my surprise, he's waiting outside the front door, looking like the devil may care with his messy blond hair, faded jeans that hang low on his hips, and nothing else. He's not as big as Finn, but he's corded with muscles. He's the type that's deceptively thin.

The moment I step out of the car, I know he wasn't aware I was coming. His sharp eyes narrow as he takes a drag of his cigarette.

"Hey, Luke," Finn greets his friend.

"When you said you needed a favor, I didn't realize it involved her."

"I have a name," I grit out.

His eyebrows arch, and a second later, his lips curl into a smirk. "I'm sorry, I didn't realize you were bringing diner princess."

It's still not my name, but it's an upgrade from rat and trash.

I glance at Finn. "You didn't tell him what this was about?"

He rubs the back of his neck. "No. I figured it was safer to not disclose the details over text."

Luke's spine goes taut. "All right. My interest is piqued. I'm not even annoyed anymore that I got ambushed with visitors I wasn't expecting."

I roll my eyes. "Dramatic much?"

His smirk turns into a deranged smile full of teeth. "Drama is my middle name, darling."

"Can we go in, or are you gonna make us grovel for it?" Finn asks, clearly annoyed.

Luke flicks the butt of his cigarette and then opens the door for us with a flourish. "By all means. Welcome to my humble abode."

There's a difference between luxurious living and a grotesque display of wealth. I wonder if Luke's parents have an unhealthy obsession with royals and wanted to live in a palace. Every single detail in the grand foyer screams money, but for all the cash spent here, the place looks like a haunted museum. I'd go insane if I had to live in this house.

I snort in my head. *You're already insane, Alexis.*

"Are we alone?" Finn asks, and his voice echoes.

"Yeah. Sage is out, and I haven't seen any staff in hours. But if you want privacy, we can head to the pool."

"Yes, let's go to the pool area," I reply quickly.

This place is giving me the heebie-jeebies. Hopefully, I won't feel like I'm being spied on by the very walls once we're outside.

It takes a good minute to walk out of the house, and once I do, I can breathe better.

Luke plops onto a chaise lounge and brings another cigarette to his mouth. "So, what's the big secret?"

I trade a look with Finn, getting nervous all over again. I'm sure he can read the anxiety in my eyes because he's the one who replies, "Who said anything about secrets?"

He shrugs. "You're acting übersus."

There's no point beating around the bush. Might as well get to the point. "I need you to hypnotize me."

His blue eyes go round. "Come again?"

"I told Alexis you learned a thing or two about hypnosis therapy," Finn says.

"Oh? And why do you want me to work on your girlfriend?"

"I'm the one who wants it because... well...." *Here goes nothing.* "I may suffer from multiple personality disorder, and I'm missing big chunks of my memories."

Luke becomes as still as a statue.

Shit. Is he going to kick us out? Or maybe make fun of me?

His shrewd gaze is more alert than ever as he stares at me. "I see. I'd love to help, but there's one minor issue."

"What is it?" I ask, already wriggling my fingers.

"For it to work, you have to trust me completely. Can you do that, Alexis?"

I hold his stare as I try to control my heartbeat. "No" is on the tip of my tongue. I trust him as far as I can throw him. But what choice do I have?

"Yes," I lie.

58

FINN

*I*t's been over thirty minutes, and Luke hasn't been able to hypnotize Alexis. I can tell he's getting frustrated by the tone of his voice.

"You're resisting," he tells her for the umpteenth time.

"I don't mean to."

He jerks to his feet. "I need a drink."

"Sit down," I growl. "You'll get a break after you finish the task."

He glowers. "In case you forgot, I'm doing you a favor. It's not my fault your girlfriend lied when she said she could trust me."

Alexis sits up. "It's not me. It's her."

Luke frowns. "Are you saying your alter ego is preventing you from reaching a hypnosis state?"

She nods. "Maybe I need something to relax. Pot?"

He shakes his head. "No. The whole point of hypnosis is

heightening the ability of all five senses, and marijuana does the opposite. It muddies them. If the goal is to retrieve your memories, pot won't help."

Her shoulders sag forward. "Then I don't know what else to do."

I crouch in front of her and take her hands. "You can do this, babe. Don't let her win. You're a Walker."

Her eyes widen, and then her spine goes taut. "You're right. I *am* a Walker."

"And I need a Johnnie Walker," Luke mumbles. I whip my face to him, but he's quick to add, "I'm joking."

Alexis lies down again, linking her hands together over her belly. "I'm ready. Let's do this."

Luke remains standing and recites the prompts to help her relax. After a few minutes, I can see the difference in her body. Her facial expression softens, and her breathing deepens. We told Luke about the events when her alter ego took over so he could steer her in the right direction.

"How are you, Alexis? Are you comfortable?" he asks.

"Yes."

"Do you remember going to the precinct earlier today?"

Her eyebrows furrow, and it takes a moment for her to reply. "Yes. Sheriff Bennet seemed frustrated."

"Why?"

"He knew I was lying about the car and how I came to be at the bridge when Piper jumped."

I notice she doesn't flinch or hesitate to speak about Piper's suicide, which makes me wonder if it's Alexis narrating or her alter ego.

"Do you think he suspects foul play on your part?"

What the hell? Is he insinuating Alexis pushed Piper off the edge? I throw him a look in warning, which he ignores.

"I didn't kill Piper," she replies in a flat tone. It's like she's been stripped of all emotions. "I tried to save her, but she was past listening to reason. They broke her spirit."

"What did you tell the sheriff?"

"I told him I got into a fight with Finn and borrowed a car to get home. Then I spotted Piper on the bridge."

I wince. No wonder her grandparents think I'm persona non grata.

"Where did you hide your uncle's letters?" I butt in, knowing that's what Alexis wants to know the most, and Luke is taking forever to get there.

He switches his attention to me, sporting a "What the fuck?" look.

She groans, drawing my gaze back to her. Her face is contorted as if she's in pain.

"What's happening?" I ask Luke.

"I don't fucking know."

"Alexis?"

She begins to thrash as if she's caught in a nightmare.

"Do something!" I yell at Luke.

He moves closer and touches her arm. "Alexis, can you hear me?"

"Please, don't hurt her," she whines in a childlike voice.

I trade a worried glance with Luke. "Why does she sound like a kid?"

"I think she went way too far down memory lane."

"Goddamn it, Luke! Bring her back."

"Leave me alone. Mommy!" Her cry is desperate; it feels like a dagger piercing my chest. She's trapped in a horrible memory, and I can't do anything to help her.

I grab her by the shoulders, ready to shake her awake, but Luke pushes me back. "What the hell are you doing? You can't jolt her back to us like that. It needs to be a gradual process."

Pulling my hair back, I retort, "You can't expect me to just sit here and do nothing."

"Mommy!" she wails again, then bursts into tears.

ALEXIS

I've never been more scared in my life. I retrieved the memories of my alter ego—Rebecca—and discovered where she hid the letters from my uncle, as well as my father's safe that she stole from the precinct. She did have inside help to get the safe out, and how she attained that help makes me sick to my stomach.

I didn't want to stay in that particular memory, but I didn't expect to jump back to the very beginning when she came to be. And now I'm trapped. I'm watching things unfold as if I were a spectator, but the fear in my chest is real, and it's making my heart feel like it's going to explode.

My mother and I were kidnapped when I was young, maybe four, and the criminals took us to the woods not far from Luke's mansion. They raped her while I watched, and they would have done the same to me if my father and uncle didn't find us. They killed those men, and then Rebecca was born.

I want to get out of here. I can't stand to relive the pain all over again.

No. You wanted to know. Here's your chance.

I push through the ache and the trauma and let the memories flood my brain. And then everything makes sense. My uncle's letters to Mom. His love for her wasn't unrequited. She was with him too. Dad shared Mom with his brother. My stomach twists painfully when the realization that I may not be my father's daughter hits me.

My eyes fly open, and I see the blue sky instead of that dark wood. Then I turn around and empty the contents of my stomach.

"I'M SORRY ABOUT THE MESS," I tell Luke.

"Nah, don't stress. Finn has done worse." He offers me a glass of chilled water.

"Thanks." I glance at Finn, but he doesn't seem bothered by his friend's remark. He's watching me intensely, sporting a deep V between his brows. "I'm okay."

"You scared the shit out of me."

"I'm sorry."

Luke plops on the chair in front of mine with a cigarette already between his lips. "So, what was that all about?"

"Dude, are you for real?" Finn snaps.

I touch his arm. "It's okay, Finn. I can talk about it now."

He keeps staring at me like he doesn't believe me. As traumatizing as recovering my earlier memories was, it pales in comparison to what she did to steal the safe from the precinct. Even though it wasn't my fault, Rebecca used my body to accomplish her goal, and the guilt swirling in my chest is real. So I'd rather talk about the gruesome evening that created her than any other more recent memories.

I don't even care that Luke is here as I dump everything on them, not stopping until they know everything I do about that horrible evening. I feel lighter than I have in years, and the ever-present darkness in my chest is gone. Maybe that means Rebecca won't return as well.

One can hope.

A long silence follows. Finn's blue eyes are brighter. He must be thinking about what happened to his mother. What a terrible thing to have such a dreadful event in common. I can't hold his heartfelt stare because it's going to make me cry. I turn to Luke, who's a little paler than before.

"Jesus." He runs his hand over his face. "I'm sorry that happened to you and your mom, Alexis."

"I am too."

"Are you sure about your mom and your uncle?" Finn asks, and it doesn't escape my notice why he veered the topic to that detail.

I nod. "Yeah. Now his love letters make sense. But he lied to me. He swore there had never been anything between him and Mom."

"Did you really expect him to confess that he was railing your mother?" Luke pipes up.

"I would have appreciated an honest answer," I retort.

"Do you know where Rebecca hid the letters and the safe?" Finn chimes in.

My nostrils flare. Only a deranged fuck would pick the location she did. "Yeah. The exact spot where she was born."

Finn's eyebrows shoot up. "Wait. She hid them in the forest where you were attacked?"

"What a character. Is she gone for good?" Luke asks. "I'd love to meet her."

"You're an idiot, then," I say. "She's a cold-blooded murderer."

"But do you think she's gone?" Finn asks.

"I hope so. Only way to tell is the next time my life is in danger."

Finn throws his arm over my shoulder and pulls me flush against his body. "I'm gonna make sure that doesn't happen ever again."

Luke snorts. "Keep dreaming, buddy. This is Triton Cove. Its very soil is drenched in blood. Make sure you watch your backs."

"This won't be over until we put away those responsible for Carmen's and Piper's deaths," I say.

Finn lets out a heavy sigh. "I know. We should follow Eric's advice and lie low until we can get our hands on Piper's diary."

"Wait. Are you talking about Eric Danes?" Luke chimes in.

"You didn't tell him about Eric?" I ask Finn, but it's rhetorical. It's obvious he didn't.

"I didn't have the chance."

Luke sits across from us and leans forward. "You'd better tell me everything. I can't help if you keep me in the dark."

Finn shakes his head. "I don't want to involve you. It's bad enough that Jason decided to fly over—"

"Jason is coming?" His eyes go rounder. "Then you bet your ass I'm getting involved. We made a pact, Finn. Remember?"

Dread runs down my back. I have no idea what kind of pact he's talking about, but knowing these boys, it must be bound by blood.

"Fine, but I don't like this."

Luke jumps from the chair, bouncing around like he's the Energizer bunny. "What are we waiting for? Let's get Alexis's safe."

59

ALEXIS

*E*ven though the forest isn't as terrifying during daylight, I can't help the shakes that run through my body as I trek to where Rebecca hid the safe along with Damian's love letters. The hardest part is keeping my nervousness from Finn. I've burdened him enough already with my baggage; I don't want him worrying about me when he has his own shit to deal with.

"Are you sure we're going in the right direction?" Luke asks me, swatting at a branch that's in his way.

"Yes."

"One thing is certain: this is the perfect spot to hide something. No one would think to venture into this part of the woods," he replies.

"How much farther?" Finn asks, breaking a long silence on his part.

"After that big, crooked tree." I point in the distance.

He grows quiet again, and since I can't think of anything to say, I do too. Even Luke is keeping his cakehole shut. I know why I'm not in a chatty mood, but I can't guess why Finn and his friend are quiet. Are they feeling sorry for me and don't know how to behave around me? I hope that's not the case. I can't have Finn treating me like I'm breakable.

"That's it." I rush toward a piece of rock Rebecca used to mark the spot, but my heart sinks when I see it's been moved, and behind it, there's an empty hole where the safe should be. "No!"

"What's the matter?" Finn stops next to me, then sees the problem. "Shit. I thought no one else knew about this place."

"Do you think Rebecca moved the safe again?" Luke asks.

I shake my head. "No. I was able to unlock all her memories."

He furrows his brows. "How can you be sure?"

"I just know, okay?" I snap. It's not his fault I'm on edge, but I can't rein in my annoyance.

"All right, all right."

Finn moves closer to the hole and drops into a crouch as if looking for something. A moment later, he pulls from the dirt a silver bracelet that has a small plaque with the letter *W* carved on it.

My stomach bottoms out. I know that bracelet.

"It seems the thief dropped something," Finn says.

"I know who took the safe," I reply.

"You recognize this?" He unfurls from his crouch.

"Yep. My father had a bracelet just like that one. Since he was buried with it, I can only assume Damian had one too."

I don't tell them Mom also had a matching bracelet. I still can't wrap my mind around her sleeping with my dad and his brother.

Finn's gaze is dark when he says, "I think it's high time we pay Uncle Dearest a visit."

I TRIED to get rid of Luke. Arriving at Saul's Garage with an entourage wasn't my choice. But the pest insisted on tagging along, which is something I should have known he'd do since he loves drama and chaos. He might have helped me recover my memories, but I haven't warmed up to him just yet. His brand of crazy is volatile and not compatible with mine.

Finn convinced me not to call my uncle beforehand. He wants the surprise element in case Damian decides to disappear.

At this time of day, the parking lot is full—probably cars waiting to be fixed. The same creepy-looking guys are at the front of the garage, pretending to be busy. The only people working are farther back. The advantage of having Finn and Luke with me is that none of those pervs will dare to look at me funny.

"Can I help you?" one of them asks.

"Yes, we're looking for Damian Walker," Finn replies before I can.

"You're out of luck, kid. He ain't here today. We haven't seen him all week."

"Where did he go?" I ask.

The guy squints at me. "Hey, I remember you. You came looking for him a few weeks ago."

"That's right. Do you know where Damian is?"

He shakes his head "No, sugar."

Finn takes a step forward, body coiled tight with tension. "Her name is not sugar."

The creep's eyes widen. "Relax, kid. I meant no offense."

"Who owns this joint?" Luke chimes in.

The creep gives him a droll look. "Uh, what does the sign say?"

He shrugs. "Is he here?"

"Yeah, in his office in the back."

We head that way and find him on the phone yelling at someone.

Great. He already looks pissed. Let's see if he's going to cooperate with us.

He sees us standing there and ends the call.

"What do you want?" he barks.

"Do you remember me? I'm Alexis—"

"Yes, yes. I remember. You're Damian's niece. He ain't here, kid."

"We've been told. I was wondering if you could tell me where he's staying. I can't get a hold of him over the phone."

He leans back in his chair, narrowing his eyes. "Maybe he doesn't want to be bothered. Ever thought of that?"

"This is important. I need to talk to him," I grit out.

"I can't disclose personal information, not even to family."

Finn steps forward, holding a crisp hundred-dollar bill between his fingers. "Perhaps this will help."

Saul's eyes shine with interest as he sits straighter in his chair. "If you triple that, we can make a deal."

What a greedy son of a bitch.

"Or I could just drop my lighter in a can of gasoline." Luke demonstrates the flame from his wicked-looking *Game of Thrones*-inspired lighter.

"That's arson."

"Good luck proving that to the cops." I shrug. "You know folks like you can't win against the elite of this town."

"So what's it going to be, pal?" Finn pipes up. "Hundred bucks in your hands or your business going up in flames."

Saul's decision is quick. He goes for the money and then scribbles something on a piece of paper. "Here, that's your uncle's address. I'm not sure you'll find him there though. He asked for unpaid time off a week ago."

I read the address and get raving mad. I bite my tongue though and stride out of his office with quick steps.

"You're welcome!" the jerkface yells.

I don't stop moving until I'm back in the car. As soon as Finn is behind the wheel, he asks, "What's wrong?"

"The address Damian gave Saul is my old address. Meaning we're back to square one."

"Maybe he's squatting at your old place," Luke replies.

"The house was supposed to be on the market."

"That doesn't stop someone from living there if they have access to it," Finn points out. "It's worth checking."

"It's the only lead we have, so might as well," Luke agrees.

I'm angry as hell, but trying to explain why to Finn and Luke is hard. The idea of Damian staying at my parents' house feels like a violation. It hurts now that I know about their arrangement.

Maybe I'm being judgmental. There are plenty of people who are in similar situations, but they aren't my folks. I wonder if that's why my mother and her parents didn't get along. There's no chance they would have approved of her lifestyle.

Luke's phone rings, but he doesn't answer it. It rings twice and stops.

"Who was that?" Finn asks.

One, two, three seconds pass, and no reply comes forth. I turn in my seat to see what's going on and find him staring at his phone.

"Luke?"

He looks up and says, "Can you please drop me off at the next light?"

"Why? What's going—?" Finn looks at the rearview mirror.

"There's someplace I have to be."

I won't deny that I'm curious as hell about what's going on, but he's not my friend, and I won't pry. Finn doesn't press him either before he lets him out of the car.

"Who do you think called Luke?" I ask as soon as the door closes.

"No idea."

He doesn't elaborate, and another long stretch of silence follows. I know something is eating at him, and I wonder if his troublesome thoughts are the same as mine. When I can no longer keep my mouth shut, I ask, "What's going on with you? You've been awfully quiet since the forest."

"I have a lot on my mind."

"I figured as much. Care to unload?"

He looks at me then, sporting a pitiful smile. "It's okay, babe. Let's focus on one problem at a time."

I can't help but feel disappointed by his answer. I thought we were past keeping secrets from each other. Maybe he doesn't want to add more to my plate, or maybe he simply doesn't trust me completely. My insecurity comes back with a vengeance, and I don't have any more positive thoughts to spare to counterattack that.

When we arrive at my childhood home, I'm hit with a wave of sadness so great that it robs me of air. I would have cried if the sight of my dad's old truck—now Damian's—parked in the driveway didn't make me see red. I fuel the anger, I let it run freely through my veins. It's way better than moping in misery.

"Son of a bitch. He *is* staying here," I say before getting out of the car.

Finn follows me, but I don't stop marching to the house until I'm standing in front of the door. I notice the porch is clear of dried-out leaves and dust. I don't know why it never occurred to me that Damian might be staying here. He managed to get inside the garage to retrieve the truck, after all.

The lack of a For Sale sign in front of the yard is telling. Either Damian took it down or my grandparents didn't get around to listing the property yet. I'm more inclined to believe the former. But surely if the house was on the market, there would be activity. People would be coming by to see the house. Ugh. I don't know what to think anymore.

Since I don't make a move to open the door, Finn takes the initiative. It's unlocked, which does surprise me. Damian has been nothing but secretive and suspicious since he got out of prison. He wouldn't leave the door unlocked unless he was ready to leave.

"Damian Baker?" Finn calls.

Smart. The old hardwood floors are noisy, and I wouldn't put it past my uncle to shoot first and ask questions later. Although, he's the one trespassing, not us.

"Who wants to kn—" He stops short when he sees us, his eyes wide. "Alexis? What are you doing here?"

"I could ask you the same thing, but I won't waste my breath with silly questions. Where the hell is my father's safe?"

60

FINN

I'm tense, ready to beat the truth out of Alexis's uncle if necessary. He doesn't speak for a couple seconds, but his expression reveals plenty. A neon sign flashing the word "guilty" would have been less obvious.

"How did you know?" he asks finally.

"You left something behind." I toss the bracelet I found at him.

It hits him in the chest, but his reflexes are fast, and he manages to catch it before it falls to the floor.

"How did you find out where the safe was buried?" Alexis asks in a voice that's cold and tight.

For a second, I think Rebecca is back, but when I look at Alexis—at her eyes—they aren't lacking emotion. On the contrary, they're swimming with it, yet it doesn't give me comfort. Her sadness rolls off her in waves, crashing against me and amplifying my own. I knew we had a dark connection from

407

the very beginning, but I couldn't have imagined how deep it went.

Damian's eyes become gloomy. "I followed you. I didn't know you still remembered that place. I wish you didn't."

"I didn't until recently. You know what else I remembered? That you and my mother were lovers."

His eyes widen, and then his expression falls. He looks away, rubbing his chin. "I'm sorry I lied to you when you asked."

"Why did you, then?"

He whips his face to her. "Because I didn't want you to look at me like that. It also didn't seem important to tell you when Dennis and Evelyn were already gone."

"Is there any chance that you could be my biological father?"

"No." His voice is gruff. "I had leukemia when I was young. I can't have children."

Alexis hastily wipes tears from her face, turning up my protection mode to eleven. Staying on this topic will cause nothing but more pain.

"Why did you want the safe? What does it contain that would send criminals after us with guns blazing?" I ask to change the subject.

Damian's gaze hardens as he narrows his eyes. "Information that's too dangerous, and you two should stay far away from it."

Alexis takes a step forward, hands balled into fists at her sides. "Bullshit! That's my father's safe. I deserve to know what's in it. What was he trying to hide?"

"Alexis…."

I step next to her, throwing my arm over her shoulders in support. Damn it. She's shaking. "If you don't tell us what's in that safe, I'll call Sheriff Bennet. He's still looking for the culprit who stole it from the precinct. What would that mean to your parole if they find it in your possession?"

A vein on his forehead throbs. "Are you blackmailing me, boy?"

"We aren't children," Alexis snaps.

He looks from me to her and then sighs. "Dennis had been collecting dirt on the powerful families of this town since we were in high school."

"Why?" I ask.

"To protect himself from the assholes who attended Maverick Prep."

"I don't understand," Alexis chimes in.

"My brother got a full ride at that school thanks to football. That's where he met Evelyn."

"You said in your letter to her that you saw her first."

He nods. "That's true. I worked at the marina, and your mom loved to sail."

Shit. We're getting off track again. "What type of dirt did Dennis find that would almost get us killed?"

He laughs without humor. "Information that could end an empire—yours included."

My pulse skyrockets. "If there's any information about my family, I demand to know."

"Demand?" He raises an eyebrow.

"If Dad had information against the Novaks, why didn't he ever expose them?" Alexis pipes up.

"He used what he had to keep me from spending my entire life in prison. He made a deal with Florian Novak—his silence in exchange for a lighter sentence for me."

My stomach drops through the earth. "I don't believe this."

"I'm not lying. How else would a poor son of a bitch like me get sentenced to manslaughter when everyone knew I killed that man in cold blood?"

"Why *did* you kill that man?" she asks in a small voice.

He levels her with a hard stare. "Because he ordered your abduction. But there was no way to prove it."

Jesus Christ. It doesn't matter what side of town you're from. The rot is everywhere.

"Do you know the nature of the secret that was so valuable that would drive my father to make a deal with Dennis Walker?"

"I didn't until today. I'm not sure you can stomach it."

"Does it have anything to do with a certain exclusive club called Wonderland?" Alexis asks.

Damian's eyes widen. "How do you know about that club?"

She and I exchange a glance, and then she replies, "My best friend was sucked into that disgusting club and was killed when she tried to leave. Another girl from Maverick also got involved and committed suicide thanks to those pervs. We want those responsible for their deaths to pay."

"They'll pay when the time is right."

"That's not good enough!" she shouts. "They have to pay now."

"Things are not that simple, sweetheart. That nefarious organization goes beyond the Novaks. The feds want to nail them all, not just one powerful family."

"The feds?" I ask. "They know about this?"

"Yes. I've been working with them since I was in prison. I received parole on the condition that I'd give them all the information Dennis had collected."

"And have you?" Alexis whispers.

He looks guilty when he replies, "Yes."

"What does that mean?" I ask, letting frustration seep into my voice. "Will my grandfather stay free and continue to cause harm?"

Damian seems surprised by my question. "Are you telling me you're on board with the destruction of your family?"

I lift my chin. "I want them to burn in hell, especially my grandfather."

He stares at me for a couple of beats before he admits, "I don't know what's going to happen. It's out of my hands."

"That's not fair!" Alexis cries. "Carmen and Piper deserve

justice. This could take years. Meanwhile, more innocent people will be preyed upon."

"I'm so sorry, Alexis. I did what I had to do."

She wipes her tears with a jerky movement. "Not sorrier than I am."

I place my hand on her lower back. "Come on, babe. We're done here."

She lets me steer her out of the house, but before she gets into the car, she turns to me. "We can't wait, Finn. We have to put a stop to what's going on in that club."

"I know. We *will*."

"Do you think Eric is working for the feds too?"

That's something I didn't consider until now.

"If he is, it's in our best interest to act quickly. He already knows about Piper's diary, which could have more incriminating evidence. We need to get to it first."

Her eyes grow troubled as they round. "Does that mean we won't wait for her funeral?"

"I'm afraid we can't risk it. We have to get the diary tonight."

Her phone rings, and she quickly fishes it out of her purse. "Shit! It's my grandmother. I was hoping she wouldn't notice I snuck out. It's going to be a pain to slip out again later."

"You don't need to come with me. In fact, I'd prefer if you didn't."

Her brows furrow as she sends a death glare my way. "There's not a chance in hell you're doing this alone."

Her sassiness is like a shot of libido in my veins, but I can't let my thoughts wander to how much I want to fuck her in the back seat of my car.

"Who says I'm going alone?" I reply.

She puts her hands on her hips while her face turns beet red. "That's right. You aren't, because I'm coming."

To hell with restraint. I pull her flush against my body and slant my mouth over hers. She resists, which means she's truly mad. But her fight only makes the furnace inside me burn hotter. I'm already melting from the inside out. I turn with her in my arms, trapping her between the car and my body. My tongue finally pierces between her lips, but even then this isn't a kiss—it's a battle of wills.

Oh, it's on, babe.

I run my hand down her side and then shove it underneath her skirt. She tries to keep her legs closed, but I force them open with my thigh, making it easier for my fingers to find the target. She moans against my lips when I flick my fingertips over her clit.

"People can see us," she murmurs against my mouth. "My uncle can see us."

"So? You shouldn't have provoked me, babe. Now you have to pay." I insert two fingers inside her, and they glide in easily.

She grabs my arms, digging her nails into them. "I hate you."

I chuckle. "No, you don't. If you want me to stop, just say so."

Her eyes lock with mine while hot air whooshes out of her partially open lips. I keep fucking her with my fingers while teasing her clit with my thumb.

"Oh fuck it." She grabs a handful of my hair, yanking the strands hard, and crushes her lips to mine.

The fact that we're doing this in broad daylight in front of her childhood home where we could get caught at any moment makes it almost impossible to keep me from exploding in my pants. I'm torn between continuing what I'm doing and replacing my fingers with my cock. But the decision is made for me when Alexis's entire body convulses, and her internal walls squeeze my fingers. I swallow her cries of ecstasy but keep moving my hand until she melts into me.

She releases my arm only to curl her fingers around my T-shirt. "You're the worst."

I kiss the tip of her nose. "No, you are."

"How am I the bad guy here?"

I brush my thumb over her swollen lips. "You've always been the bad guy, sweetheart. And that's why I love you."

"If that's the case, then you need me tonight."

I sigh, resigned. "I teed that one up, didn't I?"

Her lips curl into a wicked grin. "You sure did."

61

FINN

Five minutes after I drop Alexis at her grandparents', Jason calls me. "Hey, bro. What's up?" I answer.

"Hey, wanna pick me up?"

"Wait. Are you in Triton Cove already?"

"Yep. Perks of private flying."

"Yeah, I can be there in ten minutes. Did Nicola come with you?"

"No. I decided to leave her out of our shenanigans for once."

I release a breath of relief. The poor girl has been through enough in life already. She should stay far away from the disease that's our family.

"Smart."

"So, anything happened since we talked earlier?"

"If you're asking if I stayed out of trouble, you'll be please to know that I did. But there's been developments. It's best if I tell you in person."

"Agreed. See you soon."

He ends the call, which is no surprise. He was never one to waste time with inane chat. I'm glad he got here fast, but I can't help the thorn of guilt that pierces my side. I'm once again roping him into our family drama, and it's only going to get worse.

In the end, I make it to the private airport in less than ten minutes. My foot was heavy on the pedal, something I didn't even notice.

I haven't seen Jason in a year, and I almost don't recognize him when he walks to the car with his duffel bag slung over his shoulder.

"Holy shit. Is that really you?" I ask through a smirk.

"What?"

"I was expecting Edward and I get Jacob. Since when do you have a tan?"

"Fuck off." He tosses his bag in the back seat of the car. "Try to stay out of the sun while in Costa Rica."

"You lived your whole life in Cali and you managed."

"The concerning detail in this conversation is not the color of my skin but the fact that you're referencing fucking *Twilight*."

I roll my eyes. "Don't tell me you were unaware that all the girls at Maverick called you Edward."

He gives me an annoyed glance. "Don't make me regret coming to this godforsaken town."

A chuckle bubbles up my throat. In some ways, Jason hasn't changed one bit.

I stop teasing him for the time being. There are more serious matters to focus on. I give him a hug. "It's good to see you."

"Ditto."

We break apart, and he immediately gets in the car. He's more relaxed since he started dating Nicola and less likely to bite my head off, but some traits are impossible to reprogram, like his impatience.

I walk around the car and get behind the wheel as fast as I can. The sound system turns on at maximum volume, but before he can complain about my choices, I decrease the noise to background music.

"How are things with Auntie?" I ask.

"After she lost the fight to get her hands on my money, she disappeared. I'm sure she's now busy sucking blood from the young motherfuckers who cross her path."

I shake my head. "And you get mad when people call you a vampire."

"I don't want to talk about Bitchtoria," he grumbles.

"Fair. How is Nicola, then?"

I chance a glimpse at his profile and catch his lazy smile. "She's good."

"You're still whipped, huh?"

He turns to me, but instead of a glower, his eyes are amused. "You're one to talk. I can't wait to meet the girl who has you confessing to crimes you didn't commit."

"Touché." The drawback of spilling the beans to Jason is that he has an infinite arsenal of teasing possibilities now.

"All right, enough with the pleasantries. Fill me in on what I missed."

And just like that, we're in business mode. I tell him about Alexis's uncle, the deal he made with the feds, and the nuclear bomb that's about to obliterate the Novak name. When I finish, he's grinning broadly.

"I didn't expect that reaction from you," I say.

"I can't believe you aren't smiling from ear to ear. Grandpa and your asshole father will finally get what they deserve."

"Not according to Damian. Weren't you listening when I said the feds want to nail everyone in the operation, not just one powerful player?"

"Yes, but we're about to retrieve a key piece of the puzzle

tonight. It's my experience that girls who have diaries pour every little secret in them."

"Your experience?" I raise an eyebrow, peeling my eyes off the road for a split second.

His lips break into a sly grin. "I've read my fair share of diaries."

Shaking my head, I laugh. "Yeah, it fits your MO."

"Well, it used to. If Nicola had a diary, I wouldn't dare touch it."

"She'd rip your nut sac off, wouldn't she?"

"You betcha."

"Be glad that, in your case, it's only figuratively."

I feel Jason's stare burn a hole through my face. "I thought you said your girlfriend's alter ego was gone."

"Alexis believes she is, but who knows? Only time will tell."

"You must really love her to put up with the crazy."

"The crazy is one of the reasons I do."

He snorts. "Hell. Nothing but complex women for us, huh?"

"You got that right."

ALEXIS

I'VE BEEN QUIETLY LISTENING to my grandparents take turns chastising me. They never raise their voices, but that doesn't mean they can't get their message across.

"I cannot believe you deliberately disobeyed our orders to meet with that boy," Grandpa says with contempt.

"You've covered that part already," I say, breaking my silence. "You're going in circles."

A vein on his forehead throbs. "And I'll keep repeating

myself until it gets through your thick head. Oh, it's Evelyn all over again." He throws his hands in the air.

At the mention of my mother's name, I bristle. "At least I'm only sleeping with one guy."

Both freeze and widen their eyes.

"What did you say?" Grandma asks in a feeble whisper.

Oh shit. I shouldn't have said that. But the cat's out of the bag now. Maybe talking about my mother's dirty secret will take the heat off me.

"I know she was in a relationship with Dad *and* Uncle Damian."

"That's... that's absurd," Grandpa replies, flustered.

"Oh, please. Don't tell me you didn't know. It's why you were estranged, wasn't it?"

Grandpa turns beet red, and, pointing a trembling finger at me, he finally yells, "Don't ever repeat that sordid story, do you understand?"

Man, I've hit a nerve.

"I don't intend to as long as you stop comparing my life choices to Mom's. Trust me. Finn is not the bad guy here."

"He's a Novak. They're all rotten. One day, all their sins will be exposed to the world. I'd hate to see you get caught in the mudslide."

Grandpa has no idea how close his wishes are to becoming a reality. Or maybe he does. Perhaps he knows more about what's going on in this town than I do.

"Is that just a desire to see them fall, or do you actually know something I don't?"

His spine goes taut, and his expression morphs from anger to a steely calmness. "I've been around for much longer than you, sweetheart. Just listen to me and stay away from Finn Novak. It's for your own good."

Nice evasion, Grandpa.

It's pointless to keep arguing. They won't change their

418

minds. Maybe the only way Finn can salvage his reputation with them is when he has a hand in his grandfather's downfall. Even then, there's no guarantee my grandfolks will ever trust him again.

"I'm tired. I'm going to my room," I say finally.

"And you're going to stay there for the foreseeable future," Grandma replies.

"What? Am I a prisoner now?"

"Don't be so dramatic. You're grounded. That's all."

"Are you kidding me?"

"It's clear we've been too lax with you. You need boundaries. You're only allowed out of this house to attend school," Grandpa says.

Nothing will change their minds, so I don't even try to argue my way out of it. I have to put on a show though, or they'd suspect something is going on.

"You suck!" I yell and then storm up the stairs. Then I bang my door shut for good measure, and call Finn.

"Hey, babe. How did it go with the grandparents?"

"They were pissed I snuck out. I'm grounded."

"For real? I'm sorry."

"You don't really sound sorry. If you think I'm going to accept my fate and not go with you tonight, you're sorely mistaken."

He sighs. "I can't hide anything from you, can I?"

"Nope. What time are you coming to bust me out?"

"Not late, after dinner."

"Wait. We aren't going to do it in the middle of the night when everyone's asleep?"

"Too risky. I'm going to pay Mr. Phillips a visit while you sneak in through the back. I'll keep him and his wife distracted."

My stomach twists painfully. I've never done anything illegal in my life—besides when Rebecca was in control. Breaking into someone's home hardly compares to killing people, but I can't help the nervousness from spreading. If Finn suspects how I'm feeling, he'll try to convince me to stay behind.

"Sounds good."

"Are you able to slip out again without your grandparents finding out?"

"I'll manage."

My voice is steady, filled with confidence I don't have. But I owe it to Carmen and Piper to see this through. I'll find a way to get out.

62

FINN

*A*lexis shows up fifteen minutes after I texted her, looking a bit rough around the edges.

"What the hell happened to your girlfriend?" Jason asks from the passenger seat.

"Shit. I don't know." I get out of the car to check if she's all right.

"Are you okay?" I give her an overall glance, noticing a smear on her jeans and a tear in her sweater.

"Yeah, I'm fine," she replies in a clipped tone.

She's on the defensive, and I don't like it. I reach for her face and wipe at the dark smudge she has on her cheek. "You know you don't need to wear camouflage, right?"

"Ha ha. If you must know, I had a fight with nature and lost."

I frown. "Not following."

She lets out an exasperated sigh. "My grandparents put their new maid on watchdog mode. I couldn't get out of the house using the front or back doors, so I climbed down the vines next to my window, but they broke when I was halfway down, and I ended up falling in the bushes."

I know I shouldn't find the scenario amusing, but I can't keep the snort from escaping my mouth.

"Don't laugh. I could have broken something," she complains.

"Sorry, babe."

A car door opens—Jason. I forgot about him. Alexis's eyes widen, and then her face turns beet red.

"So you're the famous Alexis Walker," he says. "I'm Jason, Finn's cousin."

"Hi." She nervously tries to wipe the dirt from her jeans. Her reaction to Jason almost makes me laugh again, but I manage to control myself this time. He has that effect on every single female he meets.

He tilts his head to the side. "I can see why Finn lost his mind over you."

I elbow his arm. "Dude! Shut up."

"He didn't at first." She looks pointedly at me.

Jason shrugs. "Well, a hate fuck is so much better anyway. We should get going before a nosy neighbor calls the cops."

He veers for the back door, leaving shotgun for Alexis.

"Damn it. This is so not how I wanted to meet your cousin," she says.

"Why?"

"Look at me. I'm a walking disaster."

I throw my arm over her shoulder and kiss her cheek. "Nah, you're just a klutz, that's all."

"I'm not clumsy, okay? Do you know how many plates I can carry on one arm?"

"No, but you'll have to demonstrate one day to convince me."

I walk around the car and pretend I don't see she's sticking her tongue out at me. I'm smiling like an idiot when I drive off.

Strangely enough, I'm in good spirits. I don't know if it's the interaction between Jason and Alexis that's put me in a good mood, but I'm not feeling like the world is about to end. And when Jason decides to shower Alexis with questions, getting her flustered, my amusement grows.

But as soon as we reach our destination, the gloominess takes hold of me again.

"Does Mr. Phillips know you're coming?" Alexis asks.

"Yeah, I called. It didn't seem right to show up out of the blue," I reply.

"How did he sound on the phone?"

"Broken. I think he only agreed to see me because of my link to you."

She looks at the house in a nervous motion. "Do you think he blames me for what happened?"

"I seriously doubt it," Jason chimes in. "He probably hasn't processed what happened yet."

"Finn?" she asks me.

"I agree with Jason. I wouldn't be surprised if he asks to talk to you another day."

"Then maybe we should all go in instead of my sneaking in like a thief."

"No, we can't risk it. He and his wife might monopolize your time, and then you won't be able to look for the diary," Jason replies.

"I could always ask to use the restroom," she argues.

"That'd be fine if you find the diary fast, but what if it's not where Piper said it was?"

Her shoulders sag forward. "What's the plan, then?"

"Finn and I will go in, and then one of us will unlock the back door for you. Gives us five to ten minutes."

"Do they have any pets?"

"I don't think so," I reply.

The deep *V* between her eyebrows tells me she's

overthinking things. I lean across the space between us and kiss her cheek. "It'll be okay, babe."

"Yeah, I know. Don't worry about me." She forces a smile to her lips.

Not worrying about her is an impossibility. I can't voice my thoughts out loud though. She might think I don't have any confidence in her.

"Let's get this show started," Jason says before getting out of the car.

My heart is beating a staccato rhythm. I have no idea what I'll find inside that house, but whatever it is, I must keep my game face on.

ALEXIS

I WAIT five minutes in the car, then sneak around the house to wait in the back. Wearing a black hoodie was a smart choice; my hair is too noticeable even in the dark. I try to ignore how fast my heart is beating and the ache in my stomach. Rebecca made breaking the law look so easy. Her lack of fear probably had to do with the fact that she wouldn't have to pay for the crime if she got caught. That burden would fall on me.

The neighbor's dog starts to bark through the fence. I hide behind the bushes framing the back of the house, hoping the ruckus won't draw its owner's attention. No such luck. I hear a back door open, and then a guy starts talking to the dog. Mercifully, he's not nosy and doesn't investigate what got his dog's attention, simply brings his pet inside and shuts the door. I release the breath I was holding.

A moment later, Mr. Phillips's back door opens, stopping my heart.

"Psst. Alexis, where are you?" Jason whispers.

I come out of my hiding spot, scratching my hand on a prickly branch. *God, I hate fucking nature.*

"I'm here."

"What were you doing in the bushes?"

"Hiding from the neighbor's dog. Didn't you hear it?"

"Nope. They must have double-glass windows here. Come on. We don't have much time."

"Why? What's going on?"

"Stop asking questions. Hurry up."

He practically drags me inside the house and shuts the door softly. Then he presses his forefinger against his lips and signals for me to follow him. Like I would open my mouth now that I'm in Mr. Phillips's kitchen and risk being overheard.

Jason sticks his head out, and a second later, he waves me over. I slip by him and, on soft feet, head up the stairs. I'm glad the steps are carpeted and the boards beneath them don't creak. The house isn't big, and I find only three closed doors to check. The first one leads to a bathroom, but the second I try is definitely a teen's room.

I close the door behind me and then go check the spot where Piper told me I'd find her diary. The floorboard under the window is loose, and in the hole is the diary. A gale of relief whooshes out of my body as I clutch it against my chest.

I'm in the process of unfurling from my crouch when a shadow lands in front of me and a black cat that shouldn't be here hisses at me. I let out a yelp and jerk backward, falling on my ass. *Fuck. Was I too loud?* The cat keeps making menacing sounds at me, and I'm afraid it's going to attack at any second.

I scramble back to my feet and head for the door but stop short when I hear a woman's voice.

Shit! That must be Piper's mom.

"I didn't know Piper had a cat, Mrs. Phillips," Finn says close enough that I can hear him clearly.

Oh my God. What am I going to do? I can't hide anywhere in the room because the damn cat will give me away.

I eye the window. It's my only chance of escaping. I can't believe I'm considering that route again.

But the damn cat is in my way, giving me the stink eye. Its back is arched, which I don't take as a good sign. I use the diary to make a shooing motion, but the pest won't budge.

Fuck. Piper's mom might come in at any second.

I reach for a pillow on the bed and throw it at the cat. It finally jumps out of the way, only to bang against a hat stand, toppling it over. I try to reach it in time to prevent it from crashing against the desk, but too late.

"What's Morpheus doing?" I hear Mrs. Phillips ask.

I reach for the window's latch, saying a silent prayer that it's easy to open. I peer down and don't see any way I can climb to the ground.

The door behind me creaks as it opens.

Hell. There's nothing for it. I jump, landing in the bushes. They don't do much to soften my fall, and judging by the white-hot pain that shoots up my arm, I'm guessing I broke it. Biting my lower lip, I get back on my feet and run back to the car.

Tears gather in my eyes as I try to move my arm. Yep. Definitely broken. At least I got the diary.

I text Finn with my left hand, resulting in a message that's barely legible with all the typos.

FINN: Did you fucking jump out of the window?
ME: Yep.
FINN: Are you okay?
ME: No.
FINN: We're coming.

I toss the phone to the side and try not to think about how

much my arm is killing me. Black dots appear in my vision, and the fear that Rebecca is trying to take over again is real.

No. I won't let you come back. This is my life, not yours. Back off, bitch.

Thankfully, I don't pass out, and then Finn appears with Jason in tow. He gets in the back seat with me while Jason climbs behind the wheel.

"Are you injured?" he asks.

I wince. "I think I broke my right arm. I can't move it."

"All right, the ER it is." Jason puts the car in gear.

"I'm sorry, Finn. That cat from hell came out of nowhere."

He shakes his head. "No, I'm the one who should be apologizing. I should have come up with an excuse to prevent Mrs. Phillips from going upstairs."

"Did you get the diary?" Jason asks me.

"Yeah. At least the mission wasn't a total bust."

"The diary is the least of my priorities right now," Finn cuts in. "I can't believe you jumped. You could have broken your neck."

"I panicked."

"That's interesting. You were yourself the entire time?" Jason chimes in again.

"Yeah. There are no blank spots in my memory. For a second, I thought I was going to faint. I didn't though."

"It doesn't mean she was trying to take over. Your body could have been shutting down because of the pain," Finn argues.

"The important thing is I didn't. But hell, my grandparents are going to lose their minds when they see my arm in a cast."

"We don't know if your arm is broken yet. It could just be a sprain."

"She'd still have to wear a brace. No way to hide it. Can't you stay at a friend's house tonight?" Jason asks.

I throw my head back, resting it against the seat. "I don't have any friends anymore."

"Maybe not from your old school, but how about Julie?" Finn asks.

"I only spoke to her a few times." My shoulders sag forward. "It's no help. I'll have to face the music. Just pray they don't decide to ship me to a boarding school in Switzerland."

Finn looks into my eyes, and the intensity in his gaze sends a shiver of pleasure down my spine. I even forget the pain for a second.

"If they do, I'll follow you."

63

FINN

*A*lexis's grandparents aren't kidding around. They called the sheriff soon after they realized she'd left the house, which led the hospital staff to notify his department that she'd been admitted to the ER. They arrive like two banshees from hell while she's having her arm x-rayed, and I swear to God, I think I'm about to have my ass kicked by an old man.

"You!" Mr. Montgomery points at me, his face red and contorted in rage. "What have you done to our granddaughter?"

I brace for the impact—I'm sure his hand curled into a fist is meant for my face—but Jason steps in front of me. "You'd better calm down, sir."

"Who the hell are you?"

"That's the other Novak boy," his wife replies. "The violinist."

He scoffs. "Another good-for-nothing prick, then."

Jason scowls. "Hey, I may be a prick, but I take offense at the good-for-nothing part. I'm excellent at pissing off older people."

429

Jesus, that's going to calm the man down. I walk around Jason, not afraid to deal with Mr. Montgomery. He has the right to be furious. Alexis did get hurt on my watch.

"I understand you're upset, sir, but you can't lock Alexis in a gilded cage."

"I can, and I will! She's my granddaughter, and I'll be damned if I'm going to let an entitled punk destroy her life."

"I'm not destroying her life," I grit out.

"You task me, boy. You'd better get out of here before I have you arrested for kidnapping."

Jason pulls me away from him. "Come on, cuz. Let's go home."

I shake him off. "I'm not leaving until I can talk to Alexis."

"Oh, you are leaving." Mr. Montgomery takes a menacing step forward.

Jason gets in front of me and stares me down. "You're digging yourself a bigger hole by staying. Alexis's life is not in danger."

He's right, but I hesitate on leaving. From my periphery, I see Mrs. Montgomery returning to the scene with a security guard by her side. I didn't notice when she walked away.

Damn it.

I let Jason steer me to the ER's exit, and as soon as I'm in the car, I text Alexis.

"She'll be fine," he tells me.

"You don't know that. What if her alter ego decides to come back?"

"You can't let that fear control your actions. You can't be at your girlfriend's side twenty-four seven."

I keep staring at my phone, waiting for her reply. Nothing. She must still be in the X-ray room.

"We should focus on finding out what was in Piper's diary," he continues.

"Yeah." I twist around to grab the diary from the back seat, but I find nothing. "Fuck! Alexis must have put it in her purse."

"There goes my idea out the window. Let's get back to my hotel, then. We can catch up."

I sink against the seat and look out the window. "Yeah, whatever."

"Jesus. When did you turn into such an emo boy?"

"I'm not emo. I just have a lot going on in my life."

"I hear ya. I know it sounds corny as fuck, but it *will* get better. Trust me."

A snort escapes my lips. "Do you have another expensive violin I can sell?"

"No, but you don't need millions of dollars in your bank account to break free from your father's clutches. What about your swimming career?"

"Thanks to my injury, I've been out of commission."

"You can return soon, right? Don't tell me you haven't received scholarship offers?"

"Yeah, I have." I sigh. "Don't mind me. I'm just not in the mood to see the brighter side of things."

"Fine. Let's get some cheese to pair with that *whine*, then."

I laugh despite my dark mood. "I'd rather upgrade the whine to tequila."

"Now we're talking."

JASON GOT TRASHED. I didn't in case Alexis needed me. She texted me back with updates from the hospital. Yeah, her arm is definitely broken, and her grandparents are now talking about suing me.

It's past one in the morning when I leave Jason's hotel suite. I could stay, but the prospect of dealing with his hangover tomorrow isn't appealing.

I'm replying to a text from Luke when I sense I'm not alone in the parking lot. I look up and find Miss LaFleur standing next to my car.

"Hello, Finn."

"What are you doing here?"

She takes a step forward. "Waiting for you."

The small hairs on the back of my neck stand on end as leeriness drips down my spine. "Why?"

"We need to talk."

I walk around her. "We have nothing to talk about."

She reaches for my arm, digging her long nails into my skin. "Don't be like that, Finn. We had good times. Surely you haven't forgotten about them."

I pull my arm free from her grasp. "Oh, I have. You were nothing but a blip in my life."

Her face twists into an angry scowl. "I'm sorry you feel that way."

Something pricks my neck, and almost immediately, the area becomes numb. I reach up and find a dart sticking out. "What the hell?"

Dizziness hits me next, and then my legs give out from under me. I fall to my knees and barely have the strength to look up. "What have you done to me?"

She bends over and grabs my chin roughly. "Your girlfriend has something I want, and you, my dear Finn, are the insurance that she'll deliver it to me."

My body is giving up on me, but my mind is spiraling out of control. The only thing Alexis has is Piper's diary. Why would this bitch want it?

She shoves me back, and I fall on my side. I can't move, and I can't speak. From my limited vision, I see a pair of male boots approach. Miss LaFleur's culprit.

"How long will the effects of the tranquilizer last?" she asks him.

"No idea. It knocks out big cats for a couple hours."

Shit. They shot me with an animal tranquilizer? That can't be good for humans.

"He might not wake up," the man continues.

My vision is already dimming despite my attempt to remain conscious.

"Don't care," she replies right before I pass out.

64

ALEXIS

I'm not being shipped to a boarding school out of the country just yet, but my grandparents did confiscate my phone. I was only able to give Finn one update last night, so this morning, I'm on pins and needles, dying to see him. Piper's diary is in my backpack, and it feels like I'm carrying the *Darkhold*. I'm terrified to read her story. The ER doctor gave me painkillers that knocked me out, hence why I didn't even crack it open. I'd rather not be alone when I dig into its secrets anyway.

I arrive early at school on purpose and go straight to the swimming pool, Finn's domain. His teammates are in the water, but I don't see him in the stands, watching the early morning training session. I retrace my steps and wait for him in front of the school.

The influx of students coming in increases, but no sign of him or his friends. People stare, probably because I was the last person to see Piper Phillips alive. I ignore them. I spot Halsey in the crowd, and no surprise, she makes a beeline in my direction. I haven't talked to her in ages, but she's suddenly interested in me now.

I raise my shields, but when she's near enough, I notice she looks awful, like she's been through hell. My irritation fades into the background. You never know what kind of demons people are fighting. Maybe there's a valid reason she ignored me, and to be fair, I never really tried to be a better friend.

"Hey, what happened to you?" She eyes the cast.

"I'm a klutz." I figure being vague is the best way to go.

"That sucks. But besides the arm, are you okay?"

"I've been better." I tilt my head. "How about you?"

"Same." She glances at the incoming traffic of people as if looking for someone. "Can I ask you a question?"

"Sure."

She turns to me. "Did Finn ever mention anything about Cameron to you?"

Her question takes me by surprise. "No. Why are you asking? I thought you hated his guts."

"Believe it or not, we used to be best friends."

My heart constricts painfully inside my chest, making it a little harder to breathe. I know too well what it feels like to lose a best friend. The guilt returns with a vengeance, sinking its claws in my already torn muscle. I could have saved Carmen if I wasn't so wrapped up in my own problems.

"What happened?"

Halsey shakes her head and glances into the distance. "I was a coward. And now I'm afraid I've only made things worse."

I touch her arm. "Hey, if you want him back in your life, fight for him. The only problem that can't be fixed is death."

"You're right." She smiles weakly. "We'd better get inside or we'll be late for class."

"I'll be there in a minute. I'm waiting for Finn."

"Why don't you text him to ask if he's running late?"

"I can't. My grandparents confiscated my phone."

"Oh my God. What did you do?"

I let out a loud exhale. "It's a long story."

She looks away and frowns. "Ugh. I'd better go. Luke is coming, and none of Cam's friends like me very much right now."

"All right, see you later," I reply, already in motion to meet him halfway. Maybe he knows what's going on.

"Hey, have you heard from Finn?" I ask as soon as I reach him.

His brows pinch. "I haven't heard from him since yesterday. He's not answering my texts. What happened to you?"

I ignore his question. Worry is gnawing at my insides, and the last thing I want is to waste time telling Luke how I broke my arm. Finn wouldn't ignore him without reason.

"It's not important. My grandparents have my phone, so I don't know if he texted me or not."

His phone rings at that precise moment, making me hold my breath. Maybe it's Finn calling him back.

"Hey, Jason. Long time."

Hopelessness floods through me. Why is he calling Luke? I get more concerned by the second. He locks his gaze with mine, and I don't like the shadow I see in his eyes.

"We'll meet you in ten," he tells Jason before he ends the call.

"What's going on?" I ask.

"What's going on is that things just got real."

I ball my hands into fists as my annoyance quickly turns into rage. "For fuck's sake, give me a direct answer, damn it!"

"Finn has been taken, and the kidnapper wants Piper's diary in exchange for him."

My stomach drops through the earth, and my legs become weak. "Oh my God. When did they contact Jason?"

"Just now. They tried you first, but since you didn't reply, they had to find someone else to deliver their message."

I cover my mouth with my hands as tears of anger and frustration cloud my vision. They could have held Finn for hours and I didn't know.

"Come on," Luke says. "We're meeting Jason at his hotel. Do you have the diary?"

"Y-Yes." I follow him in a daze. He has his phone glued to his ear, so I ask, "Are you calling the cops?"

"No, someone better," he says, then speaks into the phone. "Hey, Reid. We have another DEFCON 1 situation. It's all hands on deck."

How is the sheriff's son better? I don't voice my question out loud, though. I'm way out of my depth, and also consumed by guilt and worry. I can't think straight. I don't know how anyone could have known we stole Piper's diary last night. The only person who knew of its existence was Eric. But he wouldn't kidnap Finn, would he? Unless he lied and he *was* working for the owners of Wonderland this entire time.

Luke speed walked and is already next to his car. I increase my stride to catch up with him. He's calling someone else. I'm guessing Cameron, but when he says the name Eric, my blood freezes.

"If you get this in time, we're meeting at Triton Beach Resort in ten minutes. It's urgent."

"You shouldn't have done that," I say.

He frowns. "Why not?"

I'm about to reply when his eyes flick to a point over my head. His gaze softens, and then the strangest thing happens—his face becomes red. I look over my shoulder to see who triggered that reaction, and holy shit, it's Emily Frost, looking like a veritable ice queen.

"This is not what you think it is," Luke tells her.

"You can't presume to know what I'm thinking." She turns around and marches toward the school building.

Luke watches her go with a pitiful expression on his face.

"What was that all about?" I ask.

He shakes his head, and when his eyes meet mine, they're sharp and cold. "Nothing. Get in. We don't have much time."

"No kidding," I say when we're both in the car. "You just left Eric a message."

"And why would contacting Eric be a bad thing? I thought he helped you escape Wonderland."

"He was the only person outside our circle who knew about Piper's diary."

"You don't know if Piper told someone else about her diary. Let's face it, the girl wasn't the smartest tool in the shed."

"That's a mean thing to say. She's dead, Luke."

He glances at me. "So? Death doesn't erase a person's shortcomings."

I narrow my eyes. "Why are you defending Eric? I thought you all hated him."

"Look, I don't like the guy, okay? He's a cocky asshole, but he's not behind Finn's abduction. Trust me."

"What do you know that you aren't telling me?"

He laughs. "I probably know as much as you do. Eric isn't dumb or desperate enough to pull a stupid move like that. Whoever took Finn is."

"If they acted that fast, they must have been following us."

"Yep. They must have figured out that since you ended up in the ER last night, you didn't have a chance to read the diary."

"Finn had better be okay," I mutter.

"Or what? Are you thinking about doing some more killings?"

I can't tell if he's joking or not, but I'm dead serious when I reply, "If they hurt him, you bet your ass I am."

65

FINN

My head is pounding when I finally wake up. I'm in a chair, and my arms and legs are bound. Every single muscle in my body aches, but my shoulder burns the most.

It takes a moment for my eyes to adjust to the gloom. I'm in a shack as far as I can tell, and it's pretty bare. There are only a few rays of sunlight coming through the cracks between the boards.

I try to break free, but that bitch and her accomplice used plastic zip ties. There's no cutting through these without something sharp.

The door creaks loudly as it opens, making me tense in an instant. Miss LaFleur enters, sashaying my direction with a smile.

"Good morning, Finn," she purrs.

I can't believe she's still pulling that crap with me. It must be a kink of hers, to flirt with someone who's at her mercy. I was like that when I fell for her seduction trap last year. Lost in my grief and guilt, I was easy prey for her. I've never really dealt with what happened, with how she took advantage of me. I simply chose to ignore her and forget about it. But now all the anger I buried comes back to the surface.

"Fuck you!"

She shakes her head. "Been there, done that, bought the T-shirt."

Despite knowing it's futile, I fight against my restraints. "Why do you want Piper's diary so badly? Who's paying you to do this?"

"My, my. Aren't you all fired up this morning? I remember when you used to be like that in my bed too."

Her reminder brings bile to my mouth. I swallow the bitterness, trying to shove those disgusting memories into a dark corner of my mind.

"You're in Piper's diary, aren't you? Are you behind getting her into that despicable club?"

She laughs. "Wouldn't you like to know?"

"Whatever it is, you'll never get away with it. And adding kidnapping to your repertoire?" I whistle. "We're talking decades in prison."

"Oh, my dear boy. You think I'm going to wait around to get arrested? As soon as that little redhead bitch brings me the diary, I'm out of here. You'll never see me again." She comes closer and runs her nails over my cheek. "It's a pity. I'll miss your pretty face."

I jerk back from her touch. My pulse is going at a hundred miles an hour. I don't want Alexis getting near this psycho. I don't believe for a second that she's gonna let us go after she gets what she wants.

"I hate to burst your bubble, but Alexis isn't coming. She hates me."

She raises an eyebrow. "You really think your pathetic lies are going to work on me?"

"If I'm lying, then why hasn't she come yet? I bet you called her as soon as you kidnapped me."

I see a crack of doubt in her expression, meaning my assessment was correct. I hope she believes my bluff. If Alexis hasn't come yet, it's because she didn't get the message.

"I had a backup plan. One way or another, I'm getting that diary."

Fuck. Is she going to take Alexis too? My heart feels like it's going to explode out of my chest, beating even faster than before.

"Alexis won't be as easy to take as I was," I grit out.

Her evil smile broadens. "We'll see."

ALEXIS

Why must villains always take their victims to the middle of a creepy forest?

The location for the exchange is just outside Triton Cove. They demanded that I come alone, which Jason, Luke, Reid, and Eric unanimously agreed was a terrible idea. Cameron was a no-show, but I bet if he were here, he'd agree with his friends.

I still don't trust Eric, despite Luke's argument that someone else must have known about the diary. I'm riding in the back of the car and keep eyeballing him, trying to read his facial expression.

He catches me staring for the third time and finally asks, "What?"

"I was against you tagging along."

He puckers his lips. "Gee, thanks for letting me know."

"She thinks you're behind Finn's abduction," Luke pipes up from the driver's seat.

Eric pinches the bridge of his nose. "If I were working for the bad guys, I wouldn't have waited to steal Piper's diary."

"Fine, but what's your stake in all this?" Reid asks.

Being late to the party, we had to fill him in quickly on the details. I'm not his biggest fan, but at least we're on the same page when it comes to Eric.

"I can't tell you."

The shaggy blond narrows his eyes. "You're working for the feds, aren't you?"

"Believe whatever you want," Eric replies as if he's dealing with children and he's tired of it.

"Can you stop bickering back there?" Jason retorts. "We're getting close to the exchange location."

Anxiety replaces my annoyance, wrapping its thorny vines around my heart. I'm reaching high levels of stress, and yet I don't sense the familiar darkness trying to take control. Rebecca must be truly gone, but a part of me wishes she was still around. It's a crazy thought, but for Finn, I'd do anything, even allow a psycho bitch to take over my body.

Luke parks the car at a rest area and says, "This is the closest I dare go with our entourage. If they're smart, they have scouts surrounding the rendezvous area. We'll continue on foot."

We all get out of the car, and then the guys proceed to get their backpacks from the trunk. For all intents and purposes, they look like they're going on a hike.

Eric walks over. "Are you clear on the plan?"

I nod. "I'll continue to drive until the next rest area, and then I follow the trail there."

"Are you sure you can drive?" Reid eyes my cast.

"Yes," I grit out. "I can use the wheel controls to change gears, and I only need one hand to steer the car."

"Anyway," Jason continues, "there will be a red scarf tied to a tree to let you know when you need to veer off the path."

"Got it."

It's the third time he's told me that, but I decide biting his head off for not trusting me to memorize such an important detail is futile. He must be as nervous as I am.

I check my backpack to make sure the diary is there. I'm usually not this paranoid, but Finn's life is on the line here. I frown when I notice something strange. I fish the diary out and, to my horror, realize it's a different one.

"What the hell?" I drop my backpack so I can flip through the pages. "This isn't Piper's diary."

"What do you mean? You said you had it." Luke comes closer.

"She did. I swapped it for a fake one," Jason replies calmly.

"You did what?" I shriek.

"We can't let them have the diary. It's too important. I copied the contents from the first pages to the fake one."

"You don't think they'll check the whole thing?" Eric glowers at Jason.

"Probably, but not before we eliminate the threat." He pulls a gun from his backpack and cocks it in a demonstration.

"Fuck. Are you all packing?" Eric glances around.

"Yeah," Luke and Reid answer in unison.

"Great." Eric throws his hands up in the air. "Whatever you do, don't do it in front of me."

"Why is that?" Luke asks.

"Plausible deniability."

"Can we please get back to the fact that Jason gave me a fake diary and didn't bother to ask me if I was okay with it? In case you forgot, I'm not carrying a gun, and now my only bargaining chip is worthless."

"I have a gun for you." Jason offers me a small weapon.

"I don't want a fucking gun!"

He widens his eyes and steps back. "I'm sorry, okay? You weren't supposed to know the diary in your backpack was fake."

I gesture wildly with my good hand. "Oh, that makes me feel so much better."

"I'm coming with you," Eric announces.

I whip around to face him. "What?"

"You're right. Jason shouldn't have replaced the diary without telling you. It was already dangerous for you to go alone before. Now it's simply reckless."

"You can't come with me. If they spot you—"

"They won't see me. Trust me." He gives me a meaningful glance.

I had my misgivings before, but that loaded stare says a million truths without revealing anything. I can't explain what I see in his eyes that changes my mind about trusting him.

"If you don't want the gun, take this." Luke hands me a switchblade.

I accept the offering without complaining about it. At least I know how to use this weapon without accidentally hurting myself. Plus, it could be useful for other things, like cutting Finn out of any bindings.

Pocketing the knife, I say, "Let's go."

66

ALEXIS

I'm still riding on my anger toward Jason when I reach the next rest area. Eric is in the car. He plans to slip out after I get on the trail, figuring if there are scouts, they're going to follow me. I hope he's right.

It takes me ten minutes or so to finally reach the tree with the red scarf tied to it. I need to bear right onto a path that's barely visible. If Eric is already following me, he's doing a great job at staying off my radar. The loudest noise around me is the sound of my pulse drumming in my ears. I'm trying my hardest to keep a cool head, but the stress and worry seem to be getting the better of me. My stomach is coiled so tight it's making me sick.

My pace is much slower during this part of the trek, thanks to the thick vegetation and uneven ground. Thin, spiderly branches scratch my face and hands. I'd say a prayer that I didn't have to walk through this in the dark if I knew Finn was okay, but my lack of response to the kidnapper's demand might have cost him dearly.

No, I can't focus on bad scenarios. I need to believe he's unharmed.

I lose track of time; only the sweat dots that formed on my forehead and dripped down my back tell me I've been walking for a while. Eventually the vegetation thins out, and I can see an old hunter's cabin not far from where I stand.

Finn. That's where they must be keeping him.

My impulse is to run at breakneck speed, but something holds me back. My survival skills kick in. I could be running into a trap.

I strain all my senses, trying to see or hear anything amiss as I walk forward at a slow pace. Suddenly, something tight wraps around my ankles, and I'm swept off my feet. I cry out when the cord squeezes them tightly. It was a trap, and I failed to see it. Now I'm dangling upside down from a tree while my heart feels like it's going to explode out of my chest from terror.

My backpack slides off my shoulders, but I catch it before it falls to the ground. I need to break free before my captor arrives.

Where the hell is Eric? I could use his help.

After I readjust the straps and make sure they won't slide down again, I reach for the knife in my pocket, glad I stuffed it in there. Crunching up so I can reach the cord around my ankles is another story. I don't have enough muscle strength to fold myself in half. I need momentum.

Jerking my body back and forth, I begin to swing, but the movement only makes the cord dig deeper into my skin. Plus, my broken arm is throbbing. This is hell.

"I wouldn't bother, girlie. You ain't getting out of there anytime soon," a male voice tells me.

I twist my body so I can see the newcomer better. He's bald, tall, and muscular, sporting a deadly cold gleam in his eyes that tells me has no issues with killing me. I'm beginning to think I'm not supposed to get out of here alive. Does that mean Finn is already gone? The very idea brings a sharp pain to my chest, and suddenly I'm more afraid of that scenario than of my possible death.

"I thought this was an exchange meeting." I force the words out through the panic that's quickly rising in my chest. "Where's Finn?"

"You'll see him when you hand over the diary."

"Hell to the fucking no. I'm not giving you anything until I see proof of life."

His lips split into a malicious grin as he points a gun in my direction. "I was hoping you'd say that. I can simply shoot you in the head and take it from you."

Fuck. I'm totally screwed. Think fast, Alexis.

"You could, but I never said I have the diary on me."

He glowers. "You're bluffing."

"Am I? What is your boss going to say when they end up with a corpse and no prize?"

"It doesn't need to be a quick death, sweetheart. I can bleed you like a pig and—"

Like a ninja, Eric appears out of nowhere and puts the man in a choke hold, squeezing his neck with his thick forearm. The guy struggles, and in the commotion, his gun fires, the bullet zipping dangerously close to my ear. Eric bends the guy's wrist until he drops the weapon, and then in a move I've only seen in fiction, he twists the man's head, breaking his neck with a loud snap.

He then releases the man's body as if it were garbage and walks toward me. "Are you okay?"

"Besides the brush with death, I'm peachy. Can you help me down?"

Eric raises his hand, signaling me to keep quiet as his body tenses. Hell, there must be more goons nearby.

No sooner does the thought enter my head than Eric takes off and disappears into the forest.

Son of a bitch. It seems I have to save myself.

FINN

I WINCE when I hear a gunshot outside. *Alexis.*

On reflex and filled with adrenaline, I try to unbolt the chair from the floor. I almost succeed, and I know if I keep trying, I'll manage it, but the cold barrel of a gun pressed against my temple forces me to stop.

"Settle down, boy," Miss LaFleur's partner orders.

The bitch smiles before she looks out the window. "Oh, our guest of honor has arrived."

"What have you done to her?"

She glances at me, sporting a phony, innocent look. "Nothing, my dear. Well, that's not exactly true. I just made sure she couldn't try anything stupid. It's for her own protection."

"You're full of shit," I snap.

The pressure of the barrel against my temple increases. "Watch your mouth, punk. The only reason you're not dead yet is because of Jessica."

Jessica. I was in her bed for months, and she never allowed me to call her by her first name. It was always Miss LaFleur. If seducing a student wasn't already a red flag, that should have been my clue that the woman is a psycho.

I make sure I'm holding her stare when I say, "If you're still hoping I'll fuck you again, you're delusional."

"Oh, honey. But we had such good times."

A derisive laugh escapes my mouth. "Good times? Bile rises

up my throat every time an unbidden memory of your naked body pops in my head."

Her entire face changes as rage twists her features. She's always been a vain woman, and I hit her where it hurts.

"Your dick didn't think so," she retorts, but I catch the hint of insecurity in her tone.

I reward her with the classic Novak smirk, perfected to communicate how little I think of her. "Don't flatter yourself. Do you seriously believe your saggy boobs and flabby skin did anything for me? I was picturing someone hot and younger when I fucked you."

Her eyes bug out. "You're lying!"

I expect her partner to strike me, or come to her defense, but he doesn't utter a word. He probably doesn't give a fuck about her drama.

"Am I? Let me ask you one thing. Have you succeeded in finding a replacement?"

I'm totally bluffing here. Maybe she *is* fucking another student. I overexaggerated her flaws, playing on her complexes.

She strides toward me, and I brace for the slap to the face. Instead, she grabs the gun from her partner and heads for the door.

Fuck! What is she planning to do with that?

"Where are you going?" I ask.

The deranged look she gives me chills my blood. "You hurt me, Finn. Now I'm going to hurt you back."

She disappears through the door before I can get another word out.

Alexis. She's going to kill her, and it's all my damn fault.

The guy next to me laughs. "Now you've done it. Your girlfriend is toast."

Fear for Alexis's life ignites something deep in my core. Adrenaline shoots through my veins, and when I try to unbolt the chair from the floor, it comes off. My wrists are still bound behind my back, but I have the element of surprise. Using the momentum of my jump, I pivot and hit the asshole with the back of my chair. We crash to the floor, but now that the chair isn't attached to it, I can break free. But there's nothing I can do about my bound wrists for now, and that's my disadvantage.

I manage to jump back onto my feet first, but the goon is already getting back up, and he has a spare gun on him. Fuck.

He points the barrel at me. "Your cougar bitch isn't here to protect you now, pup."

On reflex, I close my eyes, knowing I can't run faster than a bullet. My ears ring when the loud pop of a gunshot comes, but my brains don't explode. My eyes fly open in time to see my wannabe killer drop dead on the floor without part of his head. I turn around and see Eric Danes lowering his gun. His eyes are dark and deadly, and his jaw is locked tight. It seems to me that's not the first time he's shot someone in the head.

"Nice shot," I say and then immediately make my way to him. "Is Alexis okay?"

His brows furrow. "The last time I saw her, she was hanging upside down from a tree. I had to deal with scouts who were in the area. When I went back, I saw the cord had been cut, so I'm assuming she's escaped."

My stomach twists tightly. "What about Miss LaFleur?"

He widens his eyes. "She was behind this?"

Fuck. If he's asking, that means he didn't see her either.

"She went after Alexis."

67

ALEXIS

*A*fter several attempts, I finally manage to reach the rope around my ankles to cut it. It's a slow process because I can't hold the cord still while I hack at it. That also means that when I finally finish the task, I fall at an awkward angle. At least there were dried leaves underneath me that softened the landing—somewhat, anyway.

Every single muscle in my body protests when I rise back to my feet, but the worst pain comes from my broken arm. I didn't take the painkillers, fearing they'd make me sleepy. I needed to be sharp for this mission.

I can't believe no one has come to investigate the gunshot yet. To make sure I'm not caught in the open, I hide in the forest and approach the cabin using the thick vegetation as cover.

When I'm only a few feet from it, the door opens. I drop into a crouch, hoping I'm completely hidden. It's a miracle I don't let out a gasp of surprise when Miss LaFleur walks out.

The shock of discovery only lasts a moment. Then the anger comes back with a vengeance. I already knew she was a worthless piece of shit. A teacher who uses her classroom as hunting grounds wouldn't hesitate to recruit young girls for that disgusting sex club.

I curl my fingers tighter around the knife's handle as the certainty that I'll end that bitch solidifies in my head. I hate her for what she did to Finn. I hate her for even the possibility that she roped Piper into that horrible club. The thirst for blood is foreign and familiar at the same time. Maybe it's Rebecca pulling the strings, or maybe it's me, the real me.

She heads straight for the spot where I was hanging but quickly sees the man Eric killed. She turns around, and I notice the gun in her hand. Fuck. I almost regret not accepting Jason's offering. Almost. Killing her from a distance would do the job, but it wouldn't give me any satisfaction. I want her to see my face when I plunge the knife deep in her throat.

Such violent thoughts should give me pause or make me scared. I don't know what's going on with me. Why doesn't the idea of murder make me queasy or guilty? Was Rebecca truly an entity apart from me, or was she a manifestation of something I repressed? Perhaps I wasn't ready to accept that I'm a psycho, but now I am.

I can't come out of hiding and confront her yet. I need to lure her into a thicker part of the forest so I can have the element of surprise.

She's still busy investigating the area near the body, probably trying to find track marks. Searching the ground, I look for a rock. Under the cover of dried, crunched leaves, I find one the size of a large apple. Perfect. When she has her back to me, I throw it as hard as I can in the direction I want her to veer. It crashes loudly against a tree, drawing the bitch's attention.

She falls for my bait and goes after the noise. Now it's my turn to follow her silently. I'm light on my feet, and to my surprise, I can move easily and with the grace of a jungle cat. I've never been this dexterous before, but I won't question why I'm able to move like I was born to stalk prey.

I quickly shorten the distance between us, and when I can get a proper visual, she's facing the other way. I pull my arm back and prepare to strike, keenly aware that I only have one chance to deliver a killing, or at least a crippling, blow. Considering my broken arm, if I miss, I'm pretty much fucked.

It's now or never.

I jump, but someone grabs my shirt while I'm in motion and yanks me back. On reflex, I whirl around using the momentum of the pull and stab whoever tried to stop me. The knife hits the man in his neck, going all the way in. His eyes bug out as blood starts to spew from his lips. I'm lucky it wasn't one of Finn's friends, but the commotion costs me.

"There you are, you little bitch," Miss LaFleur says, pointing her gun at me.

Now I'm exposed and weaponless, so my only hope is to stall and pray my companions find me before she puts a bullet in my head.

"I'd like to say I'm surprised to see you here, but knowing your reputation, I'm not."

She quirks an eyebrow. "My reputation? Oh, do you mean how I rocked Finn's world last year?"

I laugh even though her comment makes my blood boil. "You're not only the scum of the earth, you're also delusional."

Her eyes narrow. "And you're either stupid or hoping for someone to come to your rescue. My guess is you didn't comply with my instructions and brought a friend. You'd better tell them to come out of hiding or else I'll start shooting in places that won't kill you immediately."

It's an effort to keep my body from shaking. Sweat drips down my spine, but I can't let her see that I'm afraid. Even if she kills me, I won't give her the satisfaction. I'm sure she'd take great pleasure in torturing me.

I raise an eyebrow. "Aren't you full of assumptions? I killed one of your goons." I point at the dead guy next to me. "What makes you think I didn't kill the other?"

Her eyes become even more deranged. "If you're hoping for a quick death, think again. I quite like the idea of making you scream. But we're too far from the cabin. I want to make sure Finn can hear you." She waves the gun. "Move."

The last thing I want to do is give my back to her, but what choice do I have? With regret, I glance at the switchblade now embedded in the dead guy's neck. I wish I hadn't struck him so hard.

"How did you know about Piper's diary?" I ask, hoping if she keeps talking, it'll distract her from her nefarious plans for me.

She laughs. "That idiot told me. Desperate girls trust so easily."

"How did you convince her to join that despicable club?"

"I shouldn't tell you, because I can hear in your voice that you desperately want to know. But the details are too good to keep to myself. Piper was obsessed with Finn, and she was willing to do anything to get his attention."

My stomach feels queasy as I begin to see how Miss LaFleur lured Piper to Wonderland.

"I told her a guy like Finn wouldn't give the time of day to someone inexperienced like her." She chuckles. "Oh, how easy it was to convince that dimwit that she needed to be taught by older men. And do you want to know who had the honor of being her first?"

I can guess, and I want to puke.

"Finn's grandfather," she continues with amusement in her tone. "Isn't that poetic?"

Tears fill my eyes. Piper didn't deserve that fate. Killing Miss

LaFleur isn't enough. I want her to suffer through the end of times.

"You're a monster," I say past the lump in my throat.

"I'm not a monster," she replies in a voice that's dangerously cold. "I'm a person with peculiar tastes who's tired of being judged for them. We're close enough to the cabin. Turn around."

I do as she says, but fear is no longer the dominant emotion coursing through my veins. It's undiluted hate. My hands are balled into fists as I stare not at her face but at the barrel of the gun. I'm not dying today.

"Hmm, where should I start?" She aims at my legs. "I hear kneecaps are excellent."

My muscles tense as I prepare to leap to the side. I know I won't be fast enough to avoid getting shot, but staying put isn't an option either.

"No!" Finn screams as he runs toward her.

No! What the hell is he doing?

In a knee-jerk reaction, she changes her aim and points the gun at him. To my horror, she pulls the trigger, hitting him in his abdomen.

A ragged shriek rips from my throat. I charge the bitch, not caring about my safety. She doesn't have time to aim at me before I punch her in the face and knock her down. I fall on top of her and pry the gun from her hand, throwing it far away from us. I don't want the easy kill; I want to pulverize her with my own hand.

My broken arm hurts as I press the cast against her throat. She struggles and tries to scratch my face with her long nails. It's hard to maintain my position straddling her. The next time she bucks, I slide to the side. No longer pinned to the ground, she presses her advantage and rolls on top of me. Her hands immediately curl around my neck, cutting off my air supply. But my vision is still tinted red, and adrenaline gives me the stamina to not give up. I stretch my arm and try to find something solid to use as a weapon. My palm brushes against the hard surface of a rock as black dots start dancing in my vision. I put all my strength into crushing the side of her head with it. The crack of bone breaking is as satisfying as the ability to breathe again.

I shove her off me, but when I realize she's still breathing, I hit her with the rock again and again, until her hateful face becomes nothing but a red blob.

"Alexis...," Finn moans, breaking through my berserker mode.

Shaking, I drop the blood-soaked rock and crawl toward him. "Finn, I'm so sorry."

His face is contorted in pain, but his eyes are sharp and focused on me. "Are you okay?"

"I'm fine." I inspect his wound. Blood has already left a big stain on his shirt. "We need to keep pressure on it." I cover his hand with mine.

"I'll be okay. I think she missed all the vital organs."

"What the hell!" Jason shouts as he rushes into the scene, followed by Reid, Luke, and Eric.

My vision is blurry as I look up. "She shot him. We need to get him to a hospital."

Eric is the first to pull a cell phone out and dial 911. Luke and Reid, who I notice are looking a bit rough, simply stare wide eyed at Finn.

Jason drops to his knees next to him and touches his forehead. "You fucking idiot."

"Stop looking at me like I'm dying," Finn complains.

"You're not dying," I retort, but as the words leave my mouth, I know them to be false. There's just too much blood.

Way too much.

68

FINN

At first, I don't know where I am. My mouth is dry though, and when I try to move, pain flares up from the side of my torso.

"Finn. You're up." Alexis's worried face appears before me. Her eyes are red, her cheeks wet.

"You've been crying, babe?"

She nods and then wipes the corner of her eyes. "Of course, you fool. I was worried sick about you."

My last memories before I passed out flood my brain. Miss LaFleur shot me, and Alexis killed her. Pride fills my chest. I didn't think I could love my girl more. I was wrong.

I crack a smile. "I told you I wasn't gonna die."

"You almost did. You lost so much blood and... hell, apparently you have the rarest blood type in the world."

"Ah, yeah. The Golden Blood. I have them draw my blood periodically though. The hospital should have plenty."

She shakes her head. "Not enough. If it weren't for Eric…."

I frown. "What did he do?"

"He has the same blood type as you."

"What? Are you sure?"

"Of course I'm sure. He donated blood to save your life."

Shock takes my ability to speak. Golden Blood is so rare, only fifty cases have been reported. My father forbade the hospital to disclose that information, fearing I'd be used as a guinea pig. I'm sure he had to pay a lot of money for that to be kept a secret. What are the odds that Eric of all people would have the same blood type? Suspicion takes hold of me.

"Are you okay?" Alexis asks.

"Yeah. Why?"

"You got even paler than before."

"I…. Was Eric surprised we shared the same blood type?"

"I was freaking out, so I'm not sure. Do you think he could be related to you somehow?"

My cheeks hollow as I work my jaw. I wish that wasn't the case, but I can't ignore that possibility. "The thought crossed my mind."

Alexis's eyes become rounder. "No…. Do you think your grandfather got to Eric's mother too?"

"Yes. I need to speak to Eric. Is he still around?"

A shadow crosses her gaze. "Yes. Everyone is. Eric's sitting apart from the rest though. He seemed down, and now I understand why."

"If he didn't know, now he suspects something. I have to tell him."

"Yeah, he deserves to know. The sheriff has Piper's diary now. I read some of it, and it was worse than I thought. Your grandfather…." She pauses and looks down.

"I heard Miss LaFleur," I say. "He's going to pay for what he did."

"He will. It's only a matter of time before his arrest warrant is issued. At least that's what Reid said, and Eric confirmed it."

She makes a motion to walk away from the bed, but I reach for her hand. "Wait. Where are you going?"

"To get Eric."

I pull her toward me. "That can wait a bit. I need to greet my badass girlfriend properly. Come here."

The moment she leans closer, I reach for her face and press my lips to hers. I just meant it to be a quick peck, but her tongue pries my mouth open, and then it's impossible to control the fire that spreads through my veins. We're explosive together, and we always will be. I deepen the kiss while my hand dives for her hair, curling around a strand.

The machine monitoring my heartbeat beeps louder, forcing Alexis to end the kiss too soon. She presses her forehead against mine. "I love you so damn much."

"Not more than I love you."

A knock on the door catches our attention. She takes a step back and turns. "Hey, Jason."

"I heard the noise and had to check if Finn was all right." He smirks.

"I'm fine," I grumble, fixing my blanket so he can't see the tent forming beneath it.

"I had to call Uncle Florian," Jason says, regret obvious in his tone. "He yelled at me for ten minutes straight."

"Did he come to see me?"

"Yeah. Aunt Marissa and Tara came too. They left an hour ago."

Alexis grimaces. "He tried to pull the yelling crap on me, but Grandpa put him in his place."

"Ah shit. Your grandparents came too?"

She nods. "Of course."

"Are you grounded for life now? Do we need to run away?"

She laughs, erasing her previous grim expression. "No, I'm

not grounded for life. And they don't hate you anymore after I told them why I was sneaking out."

"I can't imagine they were happy about it."

"They weren't, but I guess you almost dying to save my life worked in your favor."

"Nothing beats the hero's sacrifice," Jason jokes, but then he grows serious. "Although, I still maintain you were a fucking moron for doing it."

I raise a brow. "Did you expect me to simply watch the love of my life get shot?"

Alexis's face becomes beet red, and that makes me wish we were alone again.

Jason pinches his lips together. "No. I'd have done the same thing for Nicola."

"When are you going back to Costa?"

"Not until the whole mess with Grandpa is resolved. Nicola is coming in a few days. But anyway, I'd better let the guys know they can go home. I'm pretty sure you want to resume what I interrupted." He gives Alexis a sideway glance, smiling like a fiend.

"Actually, I'd like a word with Eric. Could you send him in?"

"Sure thing."

"I'll come with you. I need a drink." Alexis follows him.

I wasn't planning to ask her to leave the room, but it's better if I have this conversation with Eric alone. She already knows my secret, but I'm not sure Eric wants a witness to the convo.

A minute later, he comes in.

"Hey, how are you feeling?" he asks.

"Much better, thanks to you."

He shoves his hands in his pockets and shrugs. "I'm sure you would have done the same for me."

"I would. One hundred percent."

Silence follows. I don't know how to start on the topic. One simply doesn't ask, *"Hey, was your mother raped by my grandfather?"*

"You must be wondering why we both have the rarest blood type in the world," he says.

"Yes. Aren't you?"

He crosses his arms, and for the first time since meeting him, I sense vulnerability. "I can only think of one explanation—my mother had an affair with your dad."

It makes sense that that's the conclusion he would come to. "That would have been a better scenario than the actual truth."

He furrows his brows. "What do you mean?"

I let out a shaky breath. "On the day I crashed into your grandfather's store, I had just discovered something terrible about my family. I was distressed, out of my mind. It's not an excuse for what happened, and I'll carry the regret for the rest of my life. I'm just telling you because the secret I unveiled then may relate to our unusual situation."

I pause, letting my words sink in. Eric rubs his chin and then says, "Go on."

"I'm the product of a rape."

His eyes go round, but before he can say anything, I continue. "My grandfather raped my mom."

He doesn't say a word; I don't think he's breathing. But he's grinding his teeth pretty hard, making his cheeks hollow.

Then his nostrils flare, and his eyes spark with fury. "I'm going to kill him."

"No!" I blurt out. "Dying isn't punishment enough. I want him to rot in prison."

"Don't you get it, Finn? People like you don't go to prison."

"I'm nothing like my grandfather, or my father," I grit out.

He shakes his head. "Maybe you're different. It doesn't change the fact that powerful people never pay for their crimes."

"It's high time we change that. Please don't mess things up

now. If you kill him in cold blood, you're the one who's going to jail. That's a waste. Don't let that bastard win."

"Why do you care what happens to me?"

"For starters, you saved my life. And there's also the fact that I don't want to lose my brother."

"You don't know if we're related," he retorts, but it doesn't have the same intensity.

"We can easily find out."

"I'm not sure I want to know."

Disappointment rushes through me, though I don't know why. I have a sister, and Jason is like a brother to me, so it isn't like I'm lacking in the sibling department.

"Don't give me that look," he continues. "I'm not afraid to learn the truth."

"Then why are you hesitant?"

"Because it'll be fucking impossible to hate my half brother, but I can't forget that you put Peter in a wheelchair."

His words are like a punch to the chest. It makes me tear up, and that hasn't happened in a while.

"It's okay if you keep hating me," I say. "I won't reciprocate the feeling though."

We stare at each for several beats without speaking. It's Eric who looks away first. "I'll do the test."

"And if it proves our suspicions?"

He looks at me. "We'll cross that bridge then."

"Just please think about what I said. Don't do anything stupid."

"I won't... for now."

69

FINN

I dig my fingers into her hips, forcing her to stay still because she keeps wiggling her pussy out of reach.

"Babe, why are you running away from my mouth?"

She releases my cock with a loud pop and looks over her shoulder. "I can't concentrate on what I'm doing otherwise."

"Can't you multitask?" I grin right before I swipe my tongue from her clit to her entrance.

She moans loudly, resting her forehead against my thigh, but she keeps her fingers wrapped around my shaft. I'd keep teasing if tasting her wasn't a better option. I don't care that she can't blow me while I feast on her.

It's been too long since I could savor my girl. My stay at the hospital lasted three long days, and if it weren't for Alexis's company, I'd have lost my mind. I was released earlier today, and she was the one who picked me up and drove me home.

Only my mother and Tara were around to welcome me, but as soon as I could, I dragged Alexis to my room, and here we are. I can't move too much or my stitches will open, so a sixty-nine was the logical decision. I can't complain. It's one of my favorite positions.

She licks my cock's head while she works my length, pumping her hand up and down in an awkward way. Even though she's having a hard time concentrating on her task, my balls are tight, ready to explode. As for me, I've never tasted anything sweeter, and if I could, I'd never stop eating her pussy. I drink her juices, alternating between lazy and long strokes and flicking her clit with my tongue. I sense she's ready to come by the soft kitten sounds she's making and the way her body begins to shake.

I press my fingers harder into her hips and suck her clit into my mouth. She stops working me to let out a cry.

"Yes, Finn, yes!"

I'd give anything to be able to flip her around and rail her. As if reading my mind, she wraps her luscious lips around me, swallowing my entire length. It almost feels like her pussy. Spurred on by her orgasm, I explode into her mouth, shattering as she drinks every last drop of my release.

It seems our combined climaxes go on forever, but eventually our tremors stop, and her legs give out. She doesn't collapse on top of me though, mindful of my injury. She drops next to me, breathing hard against my leg. I don't move a muscle save for running my fingers through her hair as I try to catch my breath. My stitches pull as I draw air into my lungs. It's painful, but fucking Alexis with my tongue was totally worth it.

She leans on her elbow and asks, "Are you okay?"

"I couldn't be better," I reply, a lazy smile tugging the corners of my lips.

I have to stop getting shot though. At this rate, I'll end up looking like a spaghetti strainer. I don't voice my thoughts out loud, fearing she's already suffering from guilt.

"Well, you could." She pouts, making her swollen lips look fucking irresistible.

"Come here." I wait until she changes position and I can look into her eyes. "I don't want you to think for one second that you're to blame for what happened."

"I was supposed to kill that bitch before she could hurt anyone else."

"I was the moron who screamed and announced my presence. I don't regret it though. I'd take a bullet for you anytime."

Her brows furrow. "I don't want you to do that. You're not dying before me."

My eyebrows shoot up to the heavens. "Oh, so you want *me* to be left alone and grieving your loss?"

"Yes, of course." She kisses the corner of my mouth.

"Hmm, you're cruel, darling." I capture her lips, thrusting my tongue into her mouth for a slow and delicious kiss. Even though I just climaxed, my dick is already getting hard again. This girl puts my libido on steroids. I ease back before I make a hasty decision and say to hell with the doctor's orders.

"Don't you know I'd die of a broken heart if you left me?" I ask.

Her pretty eyes widen. "Do you really mean that?"

I tuck a loose strand of her hair behind her ear. "You're the love of my life, the perfect match for me in every way. Yes, I fucking mean it."

She smirks. "Crazy loves crazy."

"It's not only that. I can't explain it. I was drawn to you before I knew how much we had in common, or how nuts you were."

She hits me playfully on the arm. "Hey! I got the craziness under control. I haven't felt Rebecca's presence since the hypnosis session with Luke, and because of that, I haven't felt the urge to hurt myself."

The reminder that she used to self-harm puts a damper on my amusement. "I'm glad, babe, but you have to promise me that if you feel the desire again, you'll tell me. I don't want you to go through that alone."

Her brown eyes become brighter. "When my father died, I was lost… forlorn. I was never close to my grandparents, and I don't think I ever will be."

I cup her cheek. "I'm sorry."

She leans into my caress, covering my hand with hers. "It was like a piece of my heart went missing. But you came along and slowly rebuilt the part that had been torn. I'm not saying it's complete again—I'll always miss my dad—but I don't feel as hollow as before."

"My situation isn't the same as yours, but I'd been dead inside for a very long time. Honestly, I was just going through the motions. You, my fiery vixen, reanimated my heart, and now it beats as strong as ever for you, only you."

A rogue tear escapes the corner of her eye, rolling down until it reaches my hand. "I'll love you forever, Finn."

"I'll love you forever and a day." I smile.

I can tell she's about to call me on my corniness when there's a knock on my bedroom door.

"Finn? Are you still… *busy?*" Tara asks.

"Yeah. What do you want?"

"Dad is home and looking for you. He doesn't look happy. Something to do with Grandpa."

Ah hell.

Alexis and I trade a meaningful glance. I read in her eyes the same worry that's swirling in my chest. Has Grandpa finally been arrested? I never told my father what was in the diary or about Grandpa's involvement with that club. I wasn't sure if he was involved, for starters. And even if he wasn't, he could try to interfere and prevent the police from doing their job so the Novak name wouldn't be dragged through the mud.

"We'll be right down," I reply.

ALEXIS

I WAS HOPING I didn't have to meet Finn's father again after my last encounter with the man. It was wishful thinking on my part. I'm with Finn for the long haul, so dealing with the man is inevitable.

Piper's diary didn't mention him, and according to Eric, Florian Novak wasn't a person of interest. I'm still not sure how Eric knows certain things or what exactly he does, but he isn't a mere high school student, that much is clear.

We find Finn's father pacing in one of the living rooms with his hair disheveled as if he'd been running his fingers through it. His mother and sister are sitting on the couch together, looking at the man with apprehension.

"I'm here. What's going on with Grandpa?" Finn asks.

His father stops and turns around. His eyes are bloodshot, and the lines on his face seem more pronounced. He looks like shit, so the news can't be good, at least not for him.

"He's been arrested."

A wave of relief washes over me. Finally, they caught the bastard. Finn maintains his cold mask, revealing nothing. I marvel at his ability to keep his emotions hidden like that.

"What did he do?"

Florian's face contorts in rage. "Don't you dare pretend you don't know what this is about. I know it was you and your girlfriend who handed over Piper Phillips's diary to the police."

Well, at least he didn't call me diner trash, but the hatred aimed at me can't be denied.

Right back at you, asshole.

"Piper Phillips?" Tara asks, confused. "Isn't that the girl who jumped off the bridge?"

Finn's mother looks pained and sad. She drops her gaze to her lap while curling her fingers around her skirt.

"Yes. That brat wrote in her diary that my father raped her. I've never heard of a more preposterous thing. If he fucked her, she was probably on board."

Finn's mother whips her head up. "She was only fifteen!"

"Oh, Marissa, give me a break. Girls are spreading their legs much younger than that."

I watch Finn closely and finally see his armor crack. His body is coiled with tension, and his hands are balled into fists. I step closer to him, curling my arm around his. I don't want him to lose his head and punch his father. He's injured, and I have no doubt the asshole would strike back.

Marissa stands up, her body now shaking. I've only met her once, but she seemed to be pretty passive then, the complete opposite of her expression now.

"If Piper wrote that that son of a bitch raped her, then he did."

Florian eyes his wife as if she's gone mad. "How can you make such an accusation? Is it because you were fucking her dad?"

Whoa. What?

She straightens her spine. "No, asshole. I can say that with absolute certainty because your father raped *me!*"

Tara gasps, covering her mouth with her hands. Finn's only reaction is to look at his mother with tears in his eyes. I can't imagine what he must be feeling to witness his mother finally reveal that awful secret.

"You lie," Florian grits out.

"She isn't lying." Finn steps forward, positioning himself as a shield for his mom. "I heard the confession from his own mouth."

"Oh, Finn, you heard that conversation, didn't you?" his mother asks.

He nods. "Yes, Mom. I know everything."

Her face falls, and a ragged sob escapes her lips. She drops onto the couch, trying to hide the tears that are now freely falling down her cheeks. My own eyes burn as my heart bleeds for her and Finn.

"What's 'everything'?" Florian chokes out.

Finn turns to him. "Can't you guess? I'm not your son."

His eyes widen, and the blood seems to drain from his face. He staggers back and needs to lean against the wall to remain standing. A heavy silence fills the room save for Marissa's crying.

"Come on, Mom. Let's get you back to your room," Tara says, then helps her mother get up from the couch.

Finn keeps glaring at his father—no, not father, half brother. Only now has the coin dropped.

"I wouldn't try to get *our* father out of this mess if I were you," he says.

Florian shakes his head. "It's over. We're ruined. You finally got what you wished for."

"I never wished for the family ruin. I just wanted justice for Mom, and for all his other victims."

The man stares at Finn without a lick of love or compassion. "You'd better pray you're as good in the pool as you thought you were. From now on, you aren't getting a dime from me. You aren't my flesh and blood after all."

God, I want to punch that son of a bitch.

Finn laughs without humor. "And do you think I'm heartbroken about that? And good on Mom for cheating on your sorry ass, if that's even true."

I expect Florian to drop another hateful remark, but he simply leaves the room and disappears down the corridor.

I'd say it's too bad that he wasn't part of the Wonderland scheme, but the man who walked out isn't the same as the one who treated his family horribly. He's broken, and I hope he stays like that for the rest of his life.

70

FINN

A WEEK LATER

*N*o money was spared in the grand reopening of Dennis's Diner. It's clear from miles away that the Montgomerys had their hands all over it. The place looks awesome, even if it lost part of its original charm.

Alexis doesn't seem to mind the changes though. She's radiant the whole time, doling out smiles and hugs to everyone who approaches her. It's hard for me to hang back and let her do her thing, but this is her moment, and I'm not going to hog her time. Even her grandparents reined in their controlling ways.

I stay in a booth in the corner with Luke, Reid, Jason, and Nicola. Cameron was supposed to come, but he canceled on us last minute. Halsey is also MIA, so it doesn't take much to conclude she's the reason Cam didn't come. I hope to God we don't get a repeat of last time. He's been a mess since she returned to Triton Cove.

"I can't believe your grandfather is still in jail," Nicola pipes up when the subject veers to the Novak scandal.

"Me neither," Jason replies. "It makes me think that maybe there's still hope for humanity."

"We'll see," I say, not sharing his optimism.

"Have you guys heard from Eric?" Reid asks.

"Nope," I reply.

"Unfortunately, I have," Luke grumbles, tossing a fry back onto his plate.

We all look at him and wait for him to elaborate, but Alexis stops by our booth, and I completely lose interest in what he has to say.

"Hey, babe." I smile from ear to ear at her. I have it bad for her and don't care who sees it.

She leans down and kisses me on the lips, but it's too quick for my liking. I wish I could properly claim her mouth, but she straightens her spine and moves out of my reach.

"How is everyone?"

"Pretty good." Nicola beams. "I'm glad we decided to extend our stay in Triton Cove. The diner looks amazing, Alexis."

She blushes. "It does, doesn't it? And the food is still the best in town."

"Who's going to manage it now?" Reid asks.

"Someone my grandfather hired with my stamp of approval. Kevin is still around, and he'll report to me as well."

"Are you going to keep working here?" Jason pipes up.

A shadow crosses her eyes. "No. My grandparents want me to focus on my studies for now. It's part of the deal I made with them."

I snake my arm around her waist. "The diner will be here when you're ready to take over, babe."

"I know. Anyway, I just came by to let you know we'll be closing soon."

"I'll be damned. She's kicking you out again, Finn." Luke smiles like a fiend.

"I'm not kicking you out," she retorts. "Where's Cameron, anyway?"

"We don't know. He bailed on us," Reid replies.

"Well, if this party is over, let's continue at my place," Luke chimes in. "I've got some wicked fireworks."

In unison, everyone says, "Of course you do."

ALEXIS

AFTER A TERRIBLE MONTH, I can finally start to believe the worst is over. The reopening of my father's diner went off without a hitch, and even my grandparents were on their best behaviors. We've been hanging out in the wooded area near Luke's place for a few hours. He set off his damn fireworks, and now we're chilling around a bonfire. We've consumed a few bottles of wine, and I have a nice buzz going. But the best part is leaning against Finn's chest with his arms around me.

It's crazy to think how our relationship started and how it is now. I glance around the fire and see Jason and Nicola in a similar position. That brings a smile to my lips. Then my attention switches to Luke and Reid, and it's impossible not to wonder if they'll find what we did. I'm not sure if Reid and Julie are still hooking up, but if they are, I hope he wises up and sees beyond the family feud.

I pull my cell phone out to check if Halsey texted me back. I had invited her to the reopening, and she said she'd come. I know she has issues at home, but the fact that Cameron was a no-show as well makes me think her absence is related to him.

A loud crash nearby breaks the peaceful silence. Finn tenses behind me while Reid jumps to his feet as quick as a ninja.

"Who's there?" he asks.

There's no answer, just the sound of rustling leaves and branches rubbing against one another. A moment later, Cameron staggers forward, carrying someone in his arms. Alarm bells sound in my head, and I prepare to stand. When the glow from the fire reaches him, a gasp escapes my lips. He's covered in blood, and it's Halsey he's carrying, unconscious.

Luke gets up. "For fuck's sake. What happened?"

His eyes are wide and not focused on anyone when he says, "I killed her. I killed Halsey."

TO BE CONTINUED...

This is the end of Alexis and Finn's story. The Filthy Gods series continues in *DANCING WITH CHAOS*, Halsey and Cameron's story.

ONE-CLICK NOW!

FREE NOVELLA

CATCH YOU

Want to read another enemies-to-lovers sports romance? Then **scan the QR code** to get your free copy of *Catch You*.

Pride and Prejudice meets Veronica Mars in this enemy-to-lovers romance.

Kimberly

I had always thought Owen Whitfield fit the mold of the

brainless jock perfectly. Group of idiot friends? Check. Vapid girlfriend? Check. Ego bigger than the moon? Check. As long as he stayed out of my way, coexisting with his kind was doable. Until one day our worlds collided, changing everything. He pissed me off so badly that I had no choice but to give him a taste of his own medicine. Little did I know that my act of revenge would come back to bite me in the ass. How was I supposed to know Owen would turn out to be the best partner in crime I could hope for?

Owen

I never paid much attention to Kimberly Dawson, but I knew who she was. Ice Queen was what we called her. She was gorgeous, no one could deny that. But she was also a condescending bitch, which was enough reason for me to stay the hell away from her. She thought I was a dumb jock, and that was okay until she came crashing into my life. Against my better judgment, I let her embroil me in her shenanigans, forcing us to spend too much time together. It was my doom. She got under my skin. She was all I could think about. I never thought I would be the knight in shining armor to anyone, not until she came along.

Scan the QR code to get your FREE copy!

ABOUT THE AUTHOR

USA Today Bestselling Author Michelle Hercules always knew creative arts were her calling but not in a million years did she think she would become an author. With a background in fashion design she thought she would follow that path. But one day, out of the blue, she had an idea for a book. One page turned into ten pages, ten pages turned into a hundred, and before she knew it, her first novel, The Prophecy of Arcadia, was born.

Michelle Hercules resides in Florida with her husband and daughter. She is currently working on the *Blueblood Vampires* series and the *Filthy Gods* series.

Sign-up for Michelle Hercules' Newsletter:

Join Michelle Hercules' Readers Group:
https://www.facebook.com/groups/mhsoars

Connect with Michelle Hercules:
www.michellehercules.com
books@mhsoars.com

facebook.com/michelleherculesauthor
instagram.com/michelleherculesauthor
amazon.com/Michelle-Hercules/e/B075652M8M
bookbub.com/authors/michelle-hercules
tiktok.com/@michelleherculesauthor?
patreon.com/michellehercules

Made in United States
Orlando, FL
12 February 2023

29889879R00288